CELESTIAL ACADEMY

THE COMPLETE SERIES

SARAH BIGLOW

MOLLY ZENK

LUCIFER'S EMBLEM

 Created with Vellum

1

ZURI

Whoever said the road to Hell is paved with good intentions has never actually *been* to Hell. For one thing, it doesn't even have roads. Besides even if they did, they sure wouldn't be paved with anything. Trust me. I've lived in Hell my entire life and as my dad likes to remind me, I'll rule it all one day.

That's what being the daughter of Lucifer gets me. Yes, that Lucifer—rebel angel and leader of the Fallen. He gets a bad rep thanks to the Archangels spreading bullshit about him. Maybe I'm biased, but I like to think he's a decent guy who fought to better the lives of people who couldn't fight for themselves. Still history is always written by the winner and they obviously think their shit doesn't stink.

At the moment, I was lounging in dad's chair in the board room. He likes to keep things modern. His throne had been a cushy office chair with the family crest—falling stars—for as long I could remember. He was probably off checking on all the other people who lived here. He's good like that. The door to the office squeaked open on its hinges and a familiar face appeared.

Damien, my best friend and partner in mischief since we were in diapers.

"Thought I'd find you in here," he said and slid into the seat next to me.

"Were we supposed to hang today? My head's been a little off lately," I said, not meeting his gaze.

"Nah, we didn't have plans, Z. I know you've been stuck in that big brain of yours. Your mom again?"

I sighed. I'd never met my mother since she'd died in childbirth. She'd been human and by all accounts, the love of my father's life. I could count the number of half siblings I had on one hand, spread out through millennia. Their portraits hung on the walls in our house. Many of them had lived short lives. Dad was a one-woman guy and it took him a really long time to get over losing someone. "Are you absolutely sure you can't just peek behind the veil just this once?"

Damien's father is the Angel of Death. It's not as grim or creepy as it sounds. If I were into guys, I'm told his dad is pretty hot actually. But inheriting his dad's powers meant Damien could reach across the veil past death and pull a soul back to Hell. It would cause too much shift if he tried to do it on the earthly plane, but Hell was off the radar enough it could work.

"Even if I was strong enough, it's against the rules. Some rules you just don't break, Zuri," he answered, leaning forward enough to reveal the starting swirls of the tattoos that circled his forearms.

"What about your dad? Can't you convince him it's a birthday present for your best friend?" I pressed.

Damien shook his head. "He loves you like a daughter, but he can't risk pissing off the cosmos or whatever. Have you thought about asking your dad?"

I leaned back against the leather. "It's too painful for him. I think if he saw her again, he'd lose his shit like for real. Anyways I'm not ready for all of this," I replied, gesturing to the room around us. I was only eighteen.

"Sorry, Z. I know you really want this, but I don't think it's gonna happen," he said, patting my hand.

"Whatever. It's fine." I waved my hand in the air to emphasize the need for a change in topic. "What about you? Things work out with that cute barista?"

He snorted and rolled his eyes. "No. She got a little too interested in my family for my comfort anyways. Is that a mortal girl thing? Wanting to know everything about you on the first date?"

I laughed. "Fuck if I know. I can't remember the last time I went on a date. Mortal just isn't my speed and no one around here wants to take the risk of pissing off daddy."

"Seriously, that happened once, Z." The accompanying eye roll told me he thought I was being stupid and making excuses.

Maybe he was right, but I had my whole—very long—life ahead of me to find the right girl. I didn't need to rush into things. Damien was the one who wasn't truly happy unless he was bitching about his latest failed romance. He wasn't picky though. He'd already dated his way through most of Hell, even some of the demons. Boy had balls; I'd give him that much.

"Come on, let's get out of this boring ass office and do something fun," Damien said, leaping from his chair and taking two long strides to the door.

"Why not?" I answered and pushed myself out of the chair. As I eased the door shut behind us, the tiny hairs on the back of my neck tingled. I opened the door a crack, but there was nothing out of the ordinary.

***

LIKE A LOT of days when we were bored, we ended up in what passed for Hell's history museum. Most of the Fallen who had fought by dad's side during the Heavenly War kept away from it. Something about bad memories or maybe PTSD. If humanity had learned one thing in the span of all existence, it was that therapy could be a good thing. Most of the angels I'd known growing up could have really used time on a couch breaking down their feelings. The museum was more a gathering spot for the younger generations.

Given it was almost eight o'clock at night—according to my phone—it was completely deserted which suited us just fine. The place was locked up at night. I pulled a blank ID badge from my pocket and studied the lock on the employees only door. The card rippled between my fingers, configuring itself to fit the lock and any matching scanner inside the building.

"I really wish I could do that," Damien sighed as I slid the transformed key card into the lock. A tiny beep signaled we were in.

I just rolled my eyes at him. He had plenty of cool angelic powers of his own. With mine I could do what amounted to parlor tricks with my forgery skills. Granted, it had gotten me out of some serious shit in school growing up. Dad had sent me to public school in New York in the hopes of socializing me with mortals. I'd lost count of the number of times I'd been told to "go to Hell" over the years. But hey, at least I knew what a Starbucks was and had a healthy Instagram obsession just like any teenage girl my age.

"Where are we going?" He whispered as I walked down the hallway to the lobby.

"You know where," I answered without looking to see if he was keeping up. The sense of being watched was back, but I ignored it. No one would be dumb enough to jump us.

"Is that a good idea?" He continued to talk in hushed tones.

"Like I care? It's technically my property, too." We wound our way through the west hall through ancient, but well-maintained suits of armor. Continued past the hall of paintings reminding the denizens of Hell what they'd fought for. Canvases that portrayed images of humanity in bondage and landscapes with the sky on fire. I wasn't so sure it wasn't some twisted way to punish the Fallen for losing the war and getting banished here.

We stopped just outside a room marked 'Restricted Access.' A black velvet rope presented the first barrier which we easily stepped over without issue. The lock on the door wasn't a key card this time. It was a fingerprint scanner. I pressed my thumb to it and it beeped twice. The lock hissed as it released and I shoved the door open. Inside sat the few items from the war that were deemed too dangerous for public viewing like Dad's emblem. It was a seven-foot-tall standard with the family crest. He'd told me bedtime stories as a child of how he used it to lead his troops into battle against his brothers—Michael, Gabriel, and Uriel—and it had kept him safe. I didn't entirely understand its power. Still I knew every time I was near it, I felt it calling to me like a magnet pulling at something deep inside me. Today of all days I could feel it calling to me even from a distance.

"This place creeps me out," Damien said.

"Pussy," I snorted and stepped up to the emblem.

"We've seen it. Can we please go now?" He whined.

"Fuck, dude. Stop being such a wuss," I snapped as my fingers pressed onto the glass case around the banner.

Maybe I put too much pressure on the case —sometimes I don't know my own strength— but the glass shattered beneath my fingertips. Tiny shards embed in my fingertips as I skidded back. The feeling that had drawn me here sang out to me like a siren lures sailors to their doom. My hands trembled as I reached forward only to find myself flat on my back, Damien straddling me. It's not as sexual as it sounds, though.

"Get off me," I said, shoving against his considerable weight.

Before he could answer or move, a flash of movement caught my eye. Someone had been following us after all. A tall figure in what had to be a school uniform darted past us, snapping up the emblem in their grasp before running away.

"Move," I said, my wings unfurling against the ground, pushing me upward.

Damien staggered off me and I took off sprinting. I didn't recognize the uniform, but only someone with angelic or demon blood could get in here. I was pretty sure that demons weren't into the whole uniform thing so that left angel. Once outside I kicked off the ground, letting my wings buoy me into the air as I scanned the surrounding area for the thief.

"There!" Damien shouted, gesturing off to the right.

I raced after the figure. Even on the ground, they seemed faster than me. Then, wings sprouted from their shoulders as they slung the pole of the emblem across their back. Short wavy black hair rippled in the wind as they made a break for one of the portals back to the earthly plane.

"Zuri, what are you doing?" Damien yelled, coming up on my left.

"That asshole stole something that belongs to my family. I'm getting it back."

He shook his head, but kept pace with me as we neared the portal. Our thief darted through and we followed. Traveling through to Earth isn't like what most people assume. Time doesn't exist, but neither do things like gravity or air. You may be in there for only thirty seconds, but that feels like an eternity as your lungs and brain crave oxygen.

We both tumbled out of the portal onto soft grass. I coughed as my body reacclimated to gravity and air. My body felt heavy for far longer than it should have as I struggled to my hands and knees. I had to focus on retracting my wings. They weighed me down until finally they disappeared from sight.

"Where are we?" Damien wheezed.

Getting to my feet, I looked around. I could see a dark ocean sparkling in the moonlight. Tall gates rose up in front of us and I squinted to make out the words crafted in metal at the top, Celestial Academy.

"Well fuck," I swore.

"Oh ... Oh that's really bad," Damien added.

"We need to find a way in there. If some Archangel asshole stole Dad's Emblem, who knows what sort of shitstorm they could cause."

Damien grabbed my arm. "You are seriously suicidal today, Z. You can't go in there. Like literally, you cannot enter the grounds."

I was about to test that theory. Besides, Fallen only assumed we couldn't set foot on campus grounds. We had no proof it was actually hallowed or sacred. I pressed my hands to the bars of the gate. No shocks or anything remotely like turning me to ash happened. I dug the toe of my boots in and scaled the gate, landing softly on the other side.

"I am not going in there," Damien said with a nervous shake of his head.

"Don't worry. I'll be in and out before you know it." Now I just had to figure out a way to sneak in without getting caught.

2

MIRYAM

Sometimes I wished my life was like a musical full of flash mobs, choreographed singing, and dancing where everybody knows all the dance moves even though they've never practiced. It would make my usually boring day totally amazing if—instead of just walking down the halls at school—everyone sang and danced with some hidden orchestra accompanying us. I would be the star of my own life musical and all attention would be on me. That's the problem, see, I needed attention. I needed someone to sing about how amazing I was so I could feel amazing about myself. I wasn't exactly proud of it, but it is what it is. The sky's blue and the grass green.

Miryam bat-Michael needed attention to feel worthy.

Notice me. Notice me. Notice me. That would be the refrain in the musical in my mind. You'd think it would be easy to be noticed when your dad was an actual Archangel, but I guess not. People never paid me any real attention, anyway, except maybe Chris. Everyone else just sucked up. I never thought when Mom told me I was Archangel Michael's kid that I would end up being so lonely.

"Hey, Miry, I love your hair," one of the newbie kids said as I walked by her, my black Mary Jane uniform shoes clicking on the hallway's marble floor. The start of a new school year and new semester always brought in a crop of eager angelic and saints' kids looking to be my friends. Dad locked himself away in his office so much, the fastest way to impress him was to impress me. I didn't tell them that they were sucking up to the wrong person. An endorsement from me meant absolutely nothing to Dad. Just like I meant nothing to Dad.

Mom told me who my dad was all the time when I was growing up. It was practically a religious experience for her with all her candles, shrines, and alters. "You're special, Miry. You're special. Don't let anyone else tell you otherwise. You are meant for great things. If you weren't, your father wouldn't have chosen me to bring you to life." Mom was never great at telling the truth. It sounded super crazy, so it must be super crazy. My Celestial Academy acceptance letter changed all that though. I had thought I could escape Mom and her particular brand of crazy. All Celestial Academy got me instead was a daddy complex.

I shook my head to banish the memories. Mom was proud of me and I should be proud of myself.

"Miry, can I get a selfie with you?" One of the newbs called.

"Miry, what do you think about my new haircut?" Another one said.

"Miry, can I ask your advice later?"

Blah, blah, blah. It's all so *meaningless.* The one good thing about your dad being the actual Archangel Michael and not some crazy dude that told your mom he was Archangel Michael meant I was kind of like Angel royalty.

Notice me. Notice me. Notice me. I hummed to myself, making up the tune as I went. I wasn't as good as Cecelia—or CeCe as she liked to be called—but no one was. It's only nine a.m., but

I've been wandering the halls to avoid a summons from Dad. He called me for a meeting two hours ago and I hadn't shown up yet. I knew that wouldn't win me any good-daughter points, but I'd rather stay away than have him look at me with those accusing eyes. Making me feel as if all he could see was some dirty half-human instead of someone who truly deserved the wings on my back.

"Hey, CeCe, do you have that music theory homework you promised me?" I stopped short when I saw her in the hall. She doesn't get out of her duties just cause my head was in the clouds instead of on the ground.

CeCe dug around in her backpack before pulling out a typed double-spaced report on Gregorian chants that was due today. "Here you go, Miry. I have your next topic in mind, too. I call it 'Harping on Harps: Angelic Music or Stereotype.'" She looked at me with bright puppy dog eyes as if my happiness was her happiness. "What do you think?"

"I guess it will do." I flipped through the report, but didn't bother to read it. "Just make sure you get some things wrong next time so it doesn't look like I know too much about music."

CeCe nodded until it looked like her head was

about to fall off. "Of course, Miry. Anything you say, Miry. Is there anything else I can do for you, Miry?"

I waved my hand dismissively and she scurried away like a cockroach. We don't have cockroaches here, but if we did, they would scurry exactly like CeCe just did.

Dad would be more disappointed in me than he already was if he ever found out about my network. The thing is, if I cared about school, I would do my own homework instead of getting everyone else to do it for me. I had built a whole network of homework helpers over the last six years. That also meant I had a whole network of favors and secrets to call in whenever I felt like it. Sometimes I do, sometimes I don't. I liked to keep my network guessing.

"Attention students," the daily kidnapper update piped all over the Academy. "Today's count for total number of missing students has risen to fifty-four. Remember to use the buddy system and always report suspicious activity. That is all."

Suspicious activity, my ass. Someone's kidnapping kids and the board (including Dad) act like it's some videogame where the higher the body count, the better the score. I wasn't worried, though. The kidnapper would have to be epically stupid to kidnap me. Dad would bring down all of Heaven and Earth, and maybe even Hell to find me, too. At least I thought he would. I didn't plan to get kidnapped to find out.

"Hey, Ant!" I called when he ducked behind one of the soaring pillars to try to get away from me. He couldn't hide that easily, after all he had my math homework. "Don't you have something that's mine?"

Ant stepped out from behind the pillar. He adjusted his glasses as if he wasn't being all sketchy. *Nice try, dude.* "Hey, Miry. How's Chris?" He attempted to distract me. It was a good tactic as far as tactics go, but I had math in thirty minutes. I needed my homework.

"I haven't seen Chris today," I said. "Maybe he got kidnapped." I crossed my arms over my chest. "Stop playing dumb. You know why I'm talking to you. Did you forget to give me something yesterday?"

Ant fidgeted—he adjusted his glasses, put his hands in his pockets, and bounced on his heels. Pretty much doing anything to stall. "Chapter 26 Calculus, right? I got it right here." He rummaged in his backpack and pulled out some crumpled-up sheets of paper. "You should copy it into your own handwriting. It's not like I can type your math homework for you. Everything you need is right here. Easy A."

"I guess this will do." I tapped my foot, making sure I looked disappointed in his efforts and the fact that I had expected Chapter 26 last night—not this morning. "But just remember the dirt I have on you, Ant. You wouldn't want my dad to learn about your secrets, now would you?"

Ant's pale face managed to go even whiter. "If you don't tell your dad, I'll take your Calc test for you too. All you have to do is keep quiet, see, and we're all good."

I made a big show out of thinking it over, but really it was a pretty sweet deal for me. No homework to do. No test to take. Why would I say no? "Just don't let it happen again," I said. "This is cutting it way too close."

Ant adjusted his glasses again. *Jesus*. If he kept doing that, I would break them myself. "Got it, Miry. Say hey to Chris for me, okay?"

"Sure. Whatever you say."

"Attention students," the kidnapper announcement rang through the halls again. "The current total number of kidnapped students has now risen to fifty-five. Remember to always use the buddy system and report any suspicious activity. That is all."

Buddy system, my ass I thought again. I ignored the warning like I always did. Instead, I headed for the little alcove by the school knave where I liked to hang out when I didn't want anyone to bother me. It was the perfect place to copy my homework. I needed to make sure I got some of the answers wrong. Ant was way too good at Math and I wasn't.

I almost made it to the alcove. I say almost, because as I passed by the janitor's closet, someone grabbed me and pulled me inside.

3

ZURI

The damn campus was deceptively big for being situated on a tiny island. I'd wasted most of the night wandering the grounds trying to find a way—any way—into the buildings. I'd finally had to just sit and wait for someone to come outside so I could slip past them inside.

Damien had blown up my phone all night with dire texts like 'you're going to die' and 'if they don't kill you, your dad will.' I'd turned my phone off around midnight. He was being an alarmist. At least with the part about my dad killing me. I could start World War Three and he'd still defend me. Although Damien wasn't wrong about what would happen if I got caught by an Archangel.

As morning light filtered through the windows, I huddled in an alcove, fighting off the urge to sleep. Giving in to exhaustion was a good way to get caught. Besides, this building was huge and the thief could be hiding anywhere. As I sat there with my knees pressed to my chest, I wondered why someone who was supposedly on the "good" side would want Dad's Emblem. Besides, I didn't think they could set foot in Hell. Just like we can't step back into Heaven. Dad had told me it was a way to keep the sides at a stalemate. Everyone seemed to agree that Earth was neutral territory. Don't want to terrify the humans. Still the Emblem had some kind of power. It wouldn't have protected Dad during the war if it didn't. I had to get it back.

Blowing out a breath, I stood up and marched down the hall like I was supposed to be there. My wandering led me to the entrance hall, currently decked out in silver and gold streamers with balloons. A giant banner overhead proclaimed 'Welcome New Students.' An idea formed in my head. It was foolish and dangerous as shit, but it was still a plan. I needed to blend in long enough to track down the thief and get the emblem back. I couldn't do that walking around as Zuri bat-Lucifer.

Luckily, I'd studied religious history on my own time. Sometimes humans could be beautifully useful. In the Jewish tradition, when someone wanted to avoid an encounter with Azrael, they changed their last name to Hayyim. That way, he would be looking for someone with a different name. It seemed like a stupid trick. Azrael was no idiot, but he insisted if the name didn't match, he couldn't take the soul.

So, I had a name. I could be Zuri Hayyim. Still this was a school and a preppy one from the looks of it. My clothes weren't going to cut it. I studied the photos hanging on the wall of the hall and saw prepubescent kids all the way up to older teens. Which meant young kids came here and probably for years too. I needed an explanation for why I was just showing up now. I could say I only just found out about my angelic parentage. It was a weak excuse. I caught a tiny gold name plate below one of the pictures: graduating class of Middle Eastern campus with Archangel Gabriel.

Gabriel stood at the back of the pack and even in the photo he looked distracted. "Perfect".

"Hi," a young voice said from behind me.

I whirled to find a boy no older than twelve standing there in a school uniform that looked remarkably like what the thief had worn. He clutched a piece of paper in his hand.

"Hi," I replied. *Could he be the thief?* "What's your name?"

"Max. What's yours?"

"Zuri. You new here, too?"

Max nodded and brandished the paper. "Got my letter. Mom wasn't sure if I had to bring it with me."

"Can I see?"

He handed it over without question. Damn, he was trusting. I unfolded the single page and skimmed the text. Pretty standard stuff about congratulating him on being accepted to the school. It provided a list of supplies he'd need—things I could probably bribe my way into—and it told him to bring the letter so they could verify his parentage. I turned my back to Max and hastily grabbed a brochure, making a copy of his letter with a reference to my transfer from the Middle East campus. Forging Gabriel's signature was a crapshoot. Having never seen his handwriting, I winged it.

"You must be excited," I commented, handing the letter back to the kid.

"Is it your first day, too?" He pressed.

"Yeah. Well, here. I just transferred from the

Middle Eastern campus." I held up my forged letter.

His brow wrinkled. "I don't want to sound rude, but you don't sound like you're from there."

I gave him a disarming smile. "I'm not. My mother is in the military and she was stationed there. She got special permission to bring me along when we got the acceptance letter," I lied effortlessly.

"Is it as cool as it sounds? All the classes and meeting the Archangels?"

"I think every campus is different. They're run by different angels. We didn't see a lot of Gabriel," I continued, hoping he believed my words and that there was some truth to them. Lies always went down easier if they contained a little fact.

Max pointed to my clothes. "Where's your uniform?"

"They lost our luggage when we were coming back. I'm sure they have some spares I can use."

"Oh."

The front doors opened again and a massive wave of uniform-clad students poured in. Some headed in other directions while some gathered in small clusters in the hall. Max moved to chat with kids his own age. I needed to find a way to snag a uniform. A large winding staircase rose up to the second floor and I spotted a man standing there, lording over the whole thing. He looked tired, almost like this was all such a bore for him. His gaze fell on me and everything changed. His demeanor sharpened and the dullness in his eyes vanished. He rounded the banister to the top of the stairs and strode down. I caught the hint of a limp, but he walked without aid. I stayed put.

"I don't recognize you and as head of this campus, I make it a point to know all of my students," he said in a clipped tone.

I held out my forged letter. "I'm a transfer from the Middle East campus."

He took the letter, unfolded it and skimmed it. "I see." He tucked it under his arm and scanned my outfit. "You know you aren't permitted to be out of uniform during the week."

I glanced down at my boots, hoping he took the gesture as embarrassment. "I know. My mother and I just returned from her tour of duty. Our luggage hasn't arrived yet. I was hoping you had some spares?"

A speaker crackled and an announcement echoed in the space. "Attention students, the current total number of kidnapped students has now risen to fifty-five. Remember to always use the buddy system and report any suspicious activity. That is all."

"We can do that. Follow me," he said, as if the announcement about kidnapped students hadn't just blared through the whole damn building.

I turned back and caught Max's wide-eyed look before following the man down the hall and into a large office. A massive sword hung behind the desk and the nameplate read Headmaster Michael. *The Michael.*

My stomach churned and my blood turned cold as the being responsible for my father's expulsion from Heaven sat down behind the desk and rifled through papers. I wanted to punch him in the face, take that sword, and chop off his pompous, self-righteous head. Instead, I sat on the edge of the chair opposite him and said nothing.

"I'm sure Headmaster Gabriel will be able to confirm your transfer. You're about eighteen, yes?"

"Yes."

"And your father …?"

"Never met him," I lied.

"Are you aware of who your father is? We have specific courses for our secondary level students based on parentage."

"I know he was an Archangel." There was no way I was going to be able to hide my wings so I didn't even try.

"I see."

"All I know is he's not one of the ones everyone knows," I added.

Michael nodded. "Fine." He passed me a paper with a schedule blocked out. "Here are your classes. You'll be rooming with my daughter, Miryam."

"I don't need a roommate, sir," I said.

"School policy, I'm afraid," he answered. He waved me off with a dismissive gesture. "I have a meeting with my daughter." He checked his watch. "She should be arriving shortly. Until then, please remain here."

I remained seated, irritation making my neck warm. I needed to be out looking for the thief not sitting here waiting to meet the daughter of my father's greatest enemy. Michael busied himself with looking over papers and I pulled out my phone, turning it back on. A single new text from Damien waited.

'If you're being tortured, I'm not saving your ass.' It read.

I typed back. 'That's up for debate. But I've got an in. I'll be out of here in no time, D. I promise. Just keep things quiet back home, okay?'

After a few tense seconds, the tiny trio of dots materialized on the screen, indicating he was writing back. 'Zuri, what exactly are you doing?' I didn't need to hear his voice to know the words carried a mixture of annoyance and curiosity.

'What I do best,' I typed back and stowed the phone in my pocket. I'd suffer through meeting this asshole's daughter. Then it was time to fool all these suckers and get what was mine.

4

MIRYAM

A strong hand clamped over my mouth as an equally strong arm wrapped around my chest. Was this it? Was I being kidnapped by some asshole with my dad only a flight of stairs away? I struggled; my screams muffled by his hands. He pulled me closer to him. *OMG, dude was getting off on this.* I bit down on what I could reach of the dude's hand closest to my mouth. He yelped and let me go, shoving me toward the door.

"Christ, Miry, settle down. It's just me."

I pushed my hair out of my face and turned back around toward the sound of my boyfriend's voice. "Chris? What the hell is wrong with you? Didn't you hear the announcement? I thought you were the kidnapper."

He waved his wounded hand before sticking his index finger in his mouth. "Would it be so bad if I were?"

I crossed my arms over my chest, determined to make him work for my forgiveness. "Seriously, don't joke about something like that. Fifty-five missing kids isn't a prank."

"Guess we'll just have to be better about using the buddy system." Chris blew on his hand. "Do I need to get a tetanus shot for this?"

I held out my hand, palm up. "Get over here."

He placed his injured hand in mine. I put my other hand over the top of it and hummed. It was a song older than time. Uncle Raphael taught it to me to see if I had any of his healing abilities. Turned out I did too. I couldn't bring people back from the dead or anything that extreme, but I could heal small wounds. The space between my hands glowed gold as I hummed. When I lifted my top hand, Chris was healed. He waved his hand again, as if testing out my skills. I'd been at Celestial Academy since I was twelve. I easily knew how to heal a bite wound by now.

"Thanks."

I crossed my arms over my chest again. "What are you doing pulling me into a coat closet right after the kidnapper announcement anyway?"

He hopped up onto a dusty folding table. "It's not a coat closet, it's a janitor's closet."

"Same difference," I sighed. "What do you want, Chris?"

"Do I need an excuse to want to hang with my girlfriend? I missed you, Miry. Is that such a crime?"

"It is when I've already kept my dad waiting for three hours when he summoned me for a meeting."

Chris hopped off the table and walked slowly toward me. He smiled, which he knew was like a flashy fishing lure to me. Cast the smile, lure me in. Between the smile and his classic boy next door—blonde hair, blue eyes—good looks, he appeared more angelic than most of the actual angel kids here. My feet moved on their own accord. *Lure me in.* I ended up meeting him halfway across the empty classroom being used as a janitor's junk closet.

"Fine," I said. "What do you think you can do in thirty minutes?"

His smile widened to a grin. "Oh, you know what I can do in thirty minutes."

I tip-toed to kiss him. *Lure me in.*

"You're late," Dad barked when I finally appeared in his office. "Hours, in fact."

I adjusted my skirt, school uniform tie, and double checked that all my shirt buttons were buttoned correctly before answering. "Sorry. I lost track of time."

Dad stood. He was wearing what I called his 'regular clothes' today instead of the Greco-Roman red toga and armor he liked wearing to look more like the religious paintings of himself. It impressed new students to see the expected Archangel Michael look. I thought his suit and tie were more intimidating than any armor he could ever throw on though.

"How many times do I have to tell you, when I call, you come?" Dad moved from behind his desk. He limped slightly. It was an old War in Heaven injury that seemed to plague him as much as I did. "You don't ignore a summons, Miryam ... Ever."

"I said I was sorry." I scuffed my toe on the Venetian tile floor. "I was doing homework."

Dad's nostrils flared which was never a good sign. I closed my eyes, waiting to be torn into for what I knew he saw as my lack of potential leadership ability and, really, just inability to follow his rules.

"We have a new student," Dad said. "She is your responsibility now."

I cracked an eye open. Wait, what? A new student? That wasn't what I had expected him to say. "Define responsibility?"

"You will learn the full meaning of 'the buddy system.'" Dad paced the room, his hands laced behind his back. "Starting now. That includes sharing a room with our new student."

"Share my room?" I shake my head as if being upset about something would change Dad's mind about it. "But what's the point of having you as my dad if I can't get some perks like a single dorm room? Chris says—" I clamped my hands over my mouth. Holy Hell, I almost brought all manners of angelic wrath down on Chris and I both by outing our sleeping arrangements.

Dad narrowed his eyes. "I'm well aware where Christopher sleeps at night. He is lucky I've looked the other way for this long. Your new roommate is Zuri Hayyim." He motioned toward the shadows of his ginormous office. A girl stepped into the light. She wore all black—black shirt, black pants, black combat boots. She was either goth or from Hell. I'd say "or both," but I know there's no way anyone from Hell could get into Celestial Academy. We have wards for keeping out the riff-raff.

"Hey." The new girl sounded just as enthusiastic about our arrangement as I was, which meant not at all.

I rolled my eyes. "Hey. Let's get this over with. I'll take you back to the room and loan you a uniform. I've got plenty. You can keep your boots." That was just the sort of rebellious act that would drive Dad nuts.

The new girl followed me out of Dad's office and down the big winding staircase to the main lobby area of campus. I walked fast to my dorm room, not bothering to check if she kept up with me or not. Buddy system, my ass.

5

ZURI

I resisted the urge to ditch Michael's daughter the moment we were out of his line of sight. It was clear that neither of us wanted to be in this situation, but maybe getting close to her wasn't such a bad thing. After all, she was bound to know all kinds of secrets.

"So, where'd you say you were from again?" She asked, traipsing onward down a hallway I hadn't noticed before.

"The Middle East campus," I said. I was repeating the lie so many times, I was starting to believe it myself.

"Uncle Gabriel wasn't around much. He and Uncle Uriel are supposed to run the other campuses, but they are here a lot," she said.

"Yeah," I muttered. Did she really see the other Archangels as family? Would she feel that way about my father?

I glanced down at the class schedule Michael had foisted on me before his cherubic daughter showed up. Celestial History, Archangel training, and something called a service project. *Fuck that.*

"You don't talk much, huh?" Miry said.

"It's been a long day. Getting used to this time zone is throwing me," I replied. It was probably the first entirely truthful statement I'd made since leaving Hell.

We finally stopped walking and she unlocked a door leading into a spacious dorm room with two beds. One side of the room was clearly lived in, if irritatingly neat. The other was a blank canvas. One I would fill until I got what I'd come for. Being around so many Archangels made me nervous. If her words were true, Gabriel and Uriel were both on campus giving me more suspects to investigate. Miryam crossed the space to a dresser and pulled out a skirt, blouse, and tie. She passed over a pair of socks next.

"I'll let you get changed," she said and started for the door.

I rolled my eyes. "What, like you've never seen

tits and ass before?" I quipped before I realized the words had spilled from my mouth.

Her cheeks burned bright pink at my words and she turned her back to me. "I'm just not used to having a roommate."

"Not a female one, anyway," I muttered under my breath. I pulled my shirt over my head, glancing over my shoulder. She turned back around, a fresh wave of blush creeping over her face at the fact she'd been caught looking.

"You really don't seem like the other kids who come here," she said.

"I'm going to try and not take that as the fact that I'm black," I commented.

She gave an audible gasp. "Oh, no. I swear I didn't mean anything like that. It's just … well you seem kind of edgy. Not like the other angel kids. That's all. I really didn't mean to offend you," she rambled.

"Good to know. And aren't we all works in progress?" I answered.

"I guess we are."

The borrowed blouse and skirt ended up being a little tight on me. Not that I'm averse to tight clothes, but the whole Catholic school uniform look wasn't really a turn on for me. I flopped onto the neatly-made bed and studied

Miryam. She really did have the rosy, chubby cheeks of those stupid little statuettes humans loved so much. She had a decent cup size in proportion to the rest of her. If she wasn't the daughter of my father's sworn enemy, I might have thought she was cute.

I could hear Damien's commentary in my head. *"Leave it to you to fall for the one person you literally can't be with."*

"So, Miryam, what's the deal with the kidnapping announcement? Is that like some scare tactics for the new kids or something?"

She flipped her strawberry blonde hair over one shoulder. "You can call me Miry. And no, it isn't a prank. Every year, kids go missing. We don't know why, but the announcement is to remind everyone to be vigilant."

"Yeah? And how's that working out? You can be vigilant all you want. Still if you don't know what you're supposed to be looking for, how can you expect to stop it?"

She sighed and flung herself down on her own bed. She propped her chin on the heel of her palm. "Dad says it's important. Personally, I don't understand it either. Don't they like have the same thing at the other campuses?"

She's testing me. "Nope," I said confidently. "Maybe it's just an American thing."

Miry's gaze narrowed, but she seemed to buy my answer. "We don't get a lot of transfer kids, especially not ones in the secondary program. You must have been really special."

"I'm not, really. Just the daughter of an angel who probably forgot I even existed."

Understanding washed over her face. I'd seen the way Michael spoke to her. She may be his daughter, but he wasn't happy about that fact. He probably wished she didn't exist. "However, you don't know what that's like. I mean, look at your dad," I said, luring her in.

"Being his daughter isn't all it's cracked up to be. Don't get me wrong, I love it here. But sometimes I feel like he doesn't see me. Not the real me anyway. Mom was her own brand of crazy, but sometimes I almost miss it … just being the two of us. At least then I didn't have a person to physically disappoint. Now, I can count on his disapproving looks like clockwork. You can't tell anyone I said that, okay? Everyone else thinks we have this amazing relation-ship. Ugh … I don't know why I even told you that."

She was needy and desperate for attention. I could definitely work with that. "I won't say a word." I mimed zipping my lips. "Since you are the Headmaster's daughter, I bet you know everything there is to know at this school."

She tilted her head to one side, drumming her fingertips against her lips. "What do you mean?"

"Well, I bet you're well connected. Come on, every school has their Queen Bee. Don't tell me that's not you."

Her lips quirked into a smile and she bounced into a seated position. "Well, I mean … everyone knows me and likes me, if that's what you mean."

"So, maybe you can help me. See, when I got here, I saw something bad. Something I'm sure your father would want to know about."

Her eyes widened and she leaned forward. "What?"

I crossed the room and put a hand on her shoulder. I couldn't influence people like mind control, but I did find that having a physical link with someone helped when I wanted them to believe what I had to say. "There's a thief who stole something really important to angelic history and I think they're hiding here. Can you help me find them and bring them to justice?"

Miry's eyes widened to the size of silver dollars and her mouth hung open. It was almost cute. Almost. "We'd never harbor someone like that."

"Of course not, but I know for a fact they are hiding out here. We can't let them get away with it. Let's bring them to justice."

6

MIRYAM

"Saving angelic history and bringing a creep to justice will be like the best service project ever!" I hopped off my bed and did a little squee dance that involved a lot of clapping and bouncing. Zuri looked at me like I'd lost my ever-loving mind.

"Uh, sure, like totally," she said.

She was probably mocking how I talked, but I didn't care. Saving angelic history would prove to Dad once and for all that I wasn't some screw up. I could be noble and worthy of his name all at the same time. Either that, or he would still count all of my wrongs against me and not even look at any of the rights. Dad was tricky that way. I hadn't found a way to impress him yet, but that didn't mean I would stop trying.

"Let's buddy up on the project." I stopped squeeing long enough to get words out. "It's better than anything I could come up with on my own and Dad will love it. Saving angelic history and all," I added in a stage whisper. "This is going to be amazing!"

"So, you'll help me?" Zuri looked confused, though, duh, I had just told her it would be a group project. Wasn't she listening at all?

"Let's go see if Chris and Ant want to help! First though, I should probably bring Chris back his stuff." I crouched down and pulled a cardboard box out from under my bed. Some people gave their significant other a drawer in their dresser, I gave mine a cardboard box under my bed. I stood with the box in my arms. "Unless … how do you feel about, like, inter-dorm visitation and noise canceling headphones? I could go either way, but would totally continue my—umm—nocturnal activities if you're down with it. It's your room too now so thought I'd ask."

Zuri's eyes glazed over somewhere around 'like' and 'totally.' She blinked, frowning. I'd call it a smirk, but that was too close to a smile and I doubted she could smile. "What is wrong with you? You chatter away like a wind-up doll that someone wound up too tight. Slow down, alright? I'll take those noise canceling headphones right now just to cancel you out."

I bit my bottom lip. "That's not funny. I'm just trying to be nice."

"Well, you're being annoying so stop."

I set the box on my bed. I'll decide what to do with it later. "C'mon. I'll show you around campus a bit more and introduce you to Chris and Ant."

She begrudgingly followed me out the door. Her combat boots paired with the knee-high socks I loaned her looked totally badass. I couldn't get away with something that edgy. The edgiest I got was wearing colored socks instead of the white.

———

"This is the vestibule." I motioned at the gold-gilt walls and high ceiling. "It's where all the campus wide meetings are held. It's the only place big enough to fit the whole student body."

Zuri jerked a thumb at the maroon draped wooden benches that lined the room in two long rows. They faced a dais with a podium set up front and center. "It looks—"

"Churchy?" I guessed. "Yeah. Dad did that on purpose. He says the more gold, the easier it is to glow. Hey, do you have your wings yet?"

Zuri pursed her lips. She looked like one of those duck face videos on YouTube. "That's kind of a personal question."

I gave a little squeal and jumped back. "Oh, sorry. Did I offend you again? I'm just curious. I didn't mean any harm in it. I got mine this year. Wanna see?"

"I'm not into playing 'I'll show you mine if you show me yours,'" Zuri said. "Especially with someone like you. I haven't had enough booze to make that even the least bit appealing."

I couldn't tell if she was teasing or making fun of me again. I decided to laugh it off either way. "Oh … ha ha. You're funny. Do you mean to be funny?"

"No." She crossed her arms over her chest, the buttons on her loaned shirt straining to hold in her assets. One wrong move and those thingies would pop off and everything would come spilling out.

I looked around for a distraction. I spied Chris and Ant talking in the corner of the vestibule. "Hey, guys! Over here!" I bounced up on my toes and waved. Chris noticed me first. He smiled and waved back. I blew him a kiss. "That's my boyfriend Chris," I said to Zuri just in case she didn't have eyes and couldn't figure it out herself. "That's Ant with him. They're saint kids. Did you know a lot of saint kids at the Australia campus?"

"I, uh, didn't hang with saint kids all that much," Zuri gave another one of her less than detailed answers.

I cocked my head to the side, my hair falling over my right shoulder. "Seriously? Why not? I mean, angelic powers are awesome, but like, saint kids are where it's at. Their specialized abilities are so amazing. It's totally useful for all sorts of situations."

"Hey, Miry." Chris leaned in to non-tongue kiss me once he and Ant reached our spot near the last pew. He's totally respectful considering how much the vestibule looked like a church. "Who is your new friend?"

"New roommate if you can believe it," I explained. "Dad went totally bananas about me not following the buddy system rules and … ta da! … this is the result."

"I thought I was your buddy in the buddy system scenario," Chris said. Zuri grimaced, looking like she might lose her breakfast or lunch or whatever she last ate all over her kickass combat boots.

"Chris, you know I'm not into role play." I giggled and leaned into him, tucking myself against his side. His left hand slid to the waistband of my skirt. Now I was positive Zuri was going to lose it all over her boots. "And, to answer your question, this is Zuri from Australia."

"Australia, huh?" Ant extended a hand to shake, which Zuri ignored. "G'day mate. Time to put another shrimp on the barbie."

"It was the Middle East campus, actually. And you know people from Australia don't really talk like that, right?" Zuri's mouth twitched into the closest thing to a smile I'd seen from her since Dad sprung her on me in his office. I think it was because she was internally laughing at us, but hey, you take what you can get.

Ant pulled his hand back and ran it through his red hair as if that had been his plan all along. "Oh. Sorry. Hey, are you a saint or angel kid?"

"Angel."

"Zuri loves one-word answers and not giving as much detail as she should." I grinned. "Oh! Tell her your heritage and abilities! She didn't hang with many saint kids in the Middle East."

Chris straightened a little as if reciting something ultra-important in Celestial History class. "Saint Christopher. Patron saint of travelers. I can provide safe passage to anywhere. I haven't tried it much outside of school so don't really know the implications and ramifications in a real-world setting, yet."

"Oh, you should totally do that as your service project." I patted his chest. I don't take my hand away when I'm done. "Dad would love it."

Ant was up next. He gave Zuri a flourishing mock bow. "Saint Anthony. Patron saint of lost things. I can find anything that's lost. Unlike my boy Chris here, I *have* tested my abilities in the real world and they rock."

"Lost things, huh?" Zuri sounded actually interested in Ant's abilities. "Can you find something for me?" She grabbed a 'Welcome to Celestial Academy: Your Heavenly Home Away from Home' orientation brochure from the pew closest to us, produced a pen from seemingly nowhere and scribbled a picture on the back of the brochure. She held it out for us to see. Some banner looking thing with falling stars on it. "Can you find this?"

"I'll try." Ant took the drawing from Zuri. He closed his eyes and mouthed the words of the

Prayer to Saint Anthony. The ink of the drawing turned from black to gold. Ant swiveled in a semi-circle toward the entrance to the bell tower, his arm raised as if on its own accord to point in the same direction. "There. What is lost is there."

We all looked in the direction he indicated. A slim person with white shoulder length hair wearing a Celestial Academy uniform stood in the shadows. The weird part to the whole thing wasn't that I'd never seen that student in my whole life. The weird part was that their eyes glowed red in the darkness.

"Beelzebub," Zuri muttered. "You're not going to get away with this!" She glared up at the weirdo student before they vanished.

7

ZURI

I stared after Beelzebub as they vanished from sight. This didn't make sense. Why would they have stolen dad's relic?

"Come on. They're getting away," I huffed and started to follow.

"Sorry, but like who is Beelzebub?" Miry asked.

I looked to her friends, but they, too, lacked recognition. "Former Ruler of Hell, Leader of Demons," I answered. *What are they teaching at this place?*

Miry shook her head so vigorously her hair bounced against her cheeks. "That isn't possible. No one who is from Hell can come here."

Stupid, naive girl. "Well … I'm telling you that

is Beelzebub. They are a shapeshifter." Which made sense with how they could have gotten in. I'd been able to scale the gates and not turn in to a pile of ash probably, because despite being Fallen, my father has angel blood. I didn't know the extent of Beelzebub's power, but if they could change their appearance then why not their blood?

"Sorry," the kid with glasses interrupted. "Why do you keep calling him they?"

Maybe it was just a trick or my imagination, but I could swear I heard a frustrated wail in the distance. I grabbed the front of his shirt and pulled him close. His Adam's Apple bobbed in his throat. "You know what the worst thing you can do is?"

He shook his head, his glasses sliding down his nose. "Misgender the fucking Leader of Demons," I bossed.

"Let him go," Miry's boyfriend said, laying a hand on my arm.

I released my grip and the kid stumbled backward. "We are wasting time."

I marched off in the direction Beelzebub had gone, not looking back to see if my unwanted roommate and her friends were following me.

"How do you know all of that stuff?" Miry asked, falling into step with me.

"How come you don't?"

"I ... I don't know. I mean we learn all the important stuff or at least that's what Dad says. We start training our abilities early on, but we don't get to Angelic History until this term."

"Let me guess, they don't want to scare the little kids."

"Don't tell anyone, but it kind of scares me, too. Like thinking about all the evil that happened. It's just really awful you know?"

More than you know. "Got it, you're a wuss."

"No, I'm not! You know, we need to work on your sense of humor. It's not that funny."

"I don't mean to interrupt, but the ... um person we are looking for went that way," Glasses said and pointed off to our left.

He looked at me for approval. I'm not sure Beelzebub ever considered them self a person, but it was still better than 'he.' I strode onward, suddenly missing my own clothes instead of being forced to wear this ridiculous school uniform. The stupid skirt was so constricting. Clothing issues aside, I should have known Beelzebub would have ducked into a populated area where they could hide in plain sight. Our search led us right into a giant gaggle of preteens. I skimmed the faces, but nothing demon-like caught my eye.

"Did you lose them?" Miry's boyfriend said to Glasses.

"I'm trying. It's like they can tell I'm looking and are hiding from me," he answered.

"Smart demon," I said under my breath.

"What do we do now?" Miry's lower lip protruded in a pout and damn it, if it wasn't the tiniest bit adorable.

Anger washed over me in a wave and I had to fight every instinct in my body telling me to sprout wings and take flight. I was foolish to think these do-gooders could be of any real use. They couldn't understand the real danger of the Emblem falling into the wrong hands.

I shoved Glasses forward. "Look harder."

"You need to stop pushing my friend around," Miry's boyfriend snapped, putting himself between us.

"I'm all for like preserving angel history and everything, but you didn't really explain what it is we're looking for," Miry added.

I grit my teeth to keep from biting her head

off. I'd managed to convince them I belonged here so far. Still if I slipped and said the wrong thing, I'd tip my hand and they'd know I was an imposter. "It's one of the original relics from the War in Heaven. From what I know, they are insanely powerful and incredibly dangerous in the wrong hands. Like Beelzebub."

"Oh. Right. Yeah. We should tell Dad what we know," Miry suggested.

"Or, we keep looking. They can't hide forever. Eventually, they'll make a mistake and we'll catch them. Though we'll need to be careful since they can change form," I said.

"They could be anyone," Miry gasped, her gaze flitted over her friends.

"Guess we'll just have to keep a very close eye on each other," her boyfriend said, sliding a possessive hand over her ass.

"We should get to class. If we don't want to panic everyone, we need to make it look like everything's fine," Glasses said. "That way it's a bigger win for us when we actually take them down."

I EXPECTED class to be some trite torture about being a good person or whatever the service project garbage was, but we ended up in what the others described as Self-Defense. They led me into a large room with padded walls and mats on the floor. At the far end of the room, a man—at least I thought it was a man—sat in a meditative pose.

"Good morning students. I hope you're ready for the day," the man said and stood up in one languid motion, rotating to face us. He wore a flowing kimono and no shoes. His gaze met mine and I was almost reminded of my father.

"That's Uncle Uriel," Miry whispered helpfully in my ear.

The ends of his shirtsleeves were singed with ash. Dad had insisted I know about the other Archangels so I could protect myself. Uriel may look unassuming, but he had a penchant for lighting shit on fire. He shed the kimono, eliciting a few gasps from other students. He wore tight camouflage pants and a tank top underneath.

"We're going to be studying swordplay today. Can I get some volunteers?" His high-pitched voice took a hint of glee.

Everyone around me shuffled back. Either no one felt comfortable with swords or this was some elaborate hazing ritual for the new girl. Either way, I didn't care. I'd show all of them. With my chin jutting out at a confident angle, I marched forward and held my hand out for a weapon.

"Let's do this," I said and accepted the hilt of the blade.

"Anyone else?" Uriel called, his gaze drifting over the assembled students. He pointed the blade of the second sword at Miry's boyfriend. "Christopher. Lovely, thank you for volunteering."

"I didn't," he mumbled, but stepped forward anyway.

"Hope you don't mind being humiliated in front of your girl, Saint Boy," I taunted, getting into a fighter's stance.

"Do you even know how to use that thing?" He hissed.

I gave it a swirl, finding the center of balance. "Guess you'll have to find out."

"Enough flirting. It's time to test your skills. Now, there are no failing grades in this course, but it pays to be the victor," Uriel said and clapped his hands, ushering the rest of the class back.

Miry's boyfriend took a step back and leveled

his blade straight at my chest. Boy was he in for a surprise. He charged—complete with a less-than-intimidating yell—and I sidestepped him, slapping the end of the pommel into his shoulders. A rasp passed his lips as air fled his lungs.

"You can do better than that," I goaded.

"I was just giving you a chance to look good before I wipe the floor with you," he answered and spun to face me.

The tips of our swords touched and he advanced with a much more professional approach. He didn't have bad form, but it was clear he hadn't been trained to my level. We thrust and parried around the room before I landed a solid kick to his solar plexus. He crumbled to the ground, wheezing. I stood over him, blade pressed to the sensitive flesh above his carotid artery.

"Guess I don't really need a lesson in self-defense," I said, eyeing the Archangel watching from across the room.

"It would appear not. Maybe you'd like to share your expertise with the rest of the class." Uriel gave me a smirk and a wink. I felt my skin crawl in response.

I already didn't know how I was going to sleep here. I didn't need the added nightmares of someone that humans might consider related to me hitting on me. Even if with a quick glance he looked very feminine.

"Everyone pair up. Our new star pupil is going to teach us all," Uriel said before shoving Miry at me.

8

MIRYAM

I held the sword with the pointy end down. If I had to use two words to describe my views on sword fighting, they were "ew" and "gross." I don't mind watching. It was exciting to watch. But fight? No thank you.

"What are you waiting for, Miryam?" Uncle Uriel taunted. "Have at her. The floor is yours. Show us what you got." A fire ball flashed in his palm. He threw it at me, forcing me to dodge. It hit the padded wall behind us, leaving a smoking, black singe mark.

"Uncle Uriel, you know I don't do my own sword fighting," I reminded him. "That's what Chris is for."

"Christopher can't always save you." Uncle

Uriel circled the room, his palm glowing with yet another fire ball. "What will you do when there's no one around to protect you, but yourself?"

"Um, probably die?"

"Wrong answer!"

He threw a fire ball and another and another. Right when I dodged left, another would come at me from the right.

"Just pick up the damn sword and fight already," Zuri snapped. "It's what he wants. Parry and thrust. That's all you need to remember. Parry and thrust. Parry and thrust."

"I ... Can't." I sat on the floor. If there was a class for freaking out and crying, I'd ace it. "You don't understand. Swords and me—"

"There's no excuses and no crying in my self-defense class," Uncle Uriel barked. "Now, get up and show me what you got, or die trying."

I shook my head. "I can't. Please don't make me, Uncle Uriel."

His eyes glowed red to go along with the fire ball resting in his palm. "Don't say I didn't warn you."

"What is your problem?" Zuri stepped in front of me, sword raised in a fighting stance. "Do you get off on scaring little girls? She may not want to fight you, but I do."

Uncle Uriel grinned. "Insubordination on your first day. I like it."

All Hell broke loose. Instead of just targeting me, Uncle Uriel lobbed fire balls at anyone and anything in the room. Zuri deflected them with her sword—hitting them as if she was hitting a homerun at a baseball game—but most everyone else just screamed as they ducked and covered. I yelped when a fire ball nicked me on the thigh.

"Miry!" Chris slid on his knees out to the center of the classroom. He recited the Prayer to Saint Christopher so fast I wasn't sure that's what he was even saying until a force field rose from his outstretched palm, protecting the kids from Uncle Uriel's rampage. "Anyone who wants safe passage out of class has it. Go now!"

He didn't need to ask twice. Everyone ran screaming into the hallway. Chris wrapped one arm around me, helping me stand, while maintaining his force field with the other. Zuri glanced our direction, looking annoyed or—as I liked to think of it already as—her normal expression.

"I had it covered, Saint Boy," she lashed out at him. "I didn't need your safety prayer or whatever the fuck you just did."

"I didn't do it for you. I did it for Miry." Chris

checked the burn wound on my thigh, having to lift my skirt to get a good look at it. "We need to get you to first aid."

"Zuri can take me," I said. "She needs to know where first aid is anyway. We'll meet you in history class."

Chris doesn't look entirely convinced with this change in plans. His force field wavered slightly with the lack of concentration, allowing Uncle Uriel to land a fire ball at our feet. "Are you sure?"

I nodded. "Just get us safely out of here and I can take it from there."

Chris, Zuri, and I inched toward the door. Uncle Uriel's fire balls bounced harmlessly off of the force field. I let out the breath I didn't realize I was holding when we all three stumbled into the hallway.

"Good class today!" Uncle Uriel called. "Shut the door on your way out!"

"Sadist," Zuri muttered under her breath.

"UNCLE RAPHAEL?" I called after limping my way to the first aid room. Zuri wasn't much help. She refused to put her arm around my waist to help me walk, even though I said it was okay. Chris wouldn't mind, especially if it was because she was helping me. "Uncle Raphael? It's Miry. Can I get some help out here?"

"Ah, Miry, how are you—" Uncle Raphael's expression went from kind to worried when he saw the scorch mark on my thigh. "Self-defense class again?"

"Sword fighting," I confirmed. "Uncle Uriel always gets, like… so strung out when it's sword fighting day."

Uncle Raphael pulled white doctor-like gloves on. "He has his reasons. Now let me get a better look at that wound."

I hopped up onto the examination table. "This is Zuri," I said by way of introductions. "She transferred from Uncle Gabriel's campus. It's totally her first day."

"First day on this campus," she corrected. "It's not my first day at any school."

"Pleased to meet you," Uncle Raphael said as he worked his angelic healing magic on my fire ball burn. "There. It's not healed completely, but it's better than before. There's only so much one angelic ability can do to counteract another. I expect you to rest for at least a half hour." He glanced at Zuri. "Can you stay with her?"

"Uh, I'm supposed to get to history class." Zuri looked at the door and then back at me. I flicked my skirt down to cover the wound in case seeing that was making her uncomfortable. "But I guess I can stay."

Uncle Raphael smiled. "Perfect." He leveled a long, thin finger at me. "Remember, young lady. Rest for thirty minutes."

"Thirty minutes," I repeated. "Got it. I can totally do that. Maybe we'll miss that pop quiz Uncle Gabriel likes to give at the beginning of class. Well, that is if he remembers to even give it."

Zuri and I watched Uncle Raphael disappear to his closet-sized medical research room. I patted the exam table next to me as an invite, but Zuri ignored it. "Thanks for staying with me," I said. "You were, like, totally awesome at self-defense too."

"Why aren't you?" She asked.

I scrunched up my face. "Why aren't I what?"

"Why aren't you good at self-defense?" Zuri sat in one of the hard-back plastic chairs across the small room. "Your dad is Archangel Michael. Using a sword should be second nature to you."

I cocked my head to the side, my hair falling

over my shoulder. "You sure know a lot about my dad."

Zuri crossed and uncrossed her arms and legs as if the implied question made her nervous. "I've heard some things around home."

"Where's home?"

"Not here."

I laughed. "That's all the answer I'm going to get out of you on that, right?" I stretched my arms over my head. Zuri looked at her boots. "Don't worry. I'll let you keep your secrets if you let me keep mine."

We're silent. It's not uncomfortable, just silence. Zuri ran a hand through her hair.

"Seriously, though, what's up with you and sword fighting?" She asked. "You should be able to handle yourself, not cower and cry like some helpless newb."

"I wasn't crying, thank you very much." I flashed a grin to show no hard feelings. "I was screaming too much to cry."

"That still doesn't answer my question." Zuri crossed her arms over her chest again. If she kept giving those uniform shirt buttons a work out, fire balls wouldn't be the only thing flying around a room today. "Why let your boy handle swords? He's not even that good at it."

"Handle swords," I snickered at my own joke. "Chris is top in the class. He's, like, golden. I can't compete with that, so why bother?"

"Answer the question, Miry." Zuri tapped—more like stomped—her foot on the ground.

I huffed an exaggerated sigh. "Fine, but no telling, okay?" I waited for her to nod yes before I continued. "Dad has this special sword that's like a really big deal ... Huge. He used it during the War in Heaven to smite the wicked and all that stuff. He cast Lucifer down to Hell with his magic, special sword. As his kid, I'm supposed to be able to manifest it or call it to me or something like that. I'm not sure what to call it, because honestly, I've never been able to *do* it. Every time I think of the sword and try to call it to me, I start to panic and nothing happens. I don't want to fight. I want to be a healer like Uncle Raphael." I pointed at my rapidly healing wound. "I can do a little bit of minor healing, but not anything against angelic powers. That's why I don't like sword fighting. I don't want to fight."

Zuri seemed to be thinking over what I said. I held my breath, waiting for her to call me a loser, to laugh or whatever else not cool she could think of (and I bet that was a lot). She didn't laugh, though. Instead, she just pursed her lips and nodded.

"For the record, your boy isn't the only one who will step up for you in self-defense class," she said. "The next time your crazy Uncle Uriel starts hurling fire balls at you, I'll be first in line to kick his ass."

I laughed and ruffled a hand through my hair. "Thanks. I needed that."

9

———

ZURI

I didn't know why I agreed to stay with Miry while she rested her leg. I had far better things to do like track down Beelzebub and kick their sorry ass. I still couldn't figure out their motive. Dad had always been nice and even let them have full control over the demons in Hell. Why would they come here? The Fallen were looked down on by the Archangels, sure. However, demons were considered even lower in their eyes. The likes of Michael would never stoop to team up with Beelzebub, would he?

"Uh, like did you hear what I said?" Miry's voice cut through my thoughts.

"Not a word," I replied.

She huffed and gave another pout. "Well, I

said I won't tell if you skip history. Lots of kids here owe me and I'm sure I could convince one of them to help with your homework too."

A snort escaped before I knew what was happening. Michael's precious daughter actually had a bit of a bad side. Sure, it was kind of pathetic as schemes went. Still behind that little cherub face was a secret rebel. "You're seriously telling me you make other kids do your homework for you? And they don't rat you out?"

She beamed. "They all want to be my friends, so of course they don't."

"I think we have very different definitions of friendship," I muttered, standing up from the plastic chair. "For your information I'm perfectly capable of doing my own homework."

Miry looked down at her hands. "I was just trying to be nice."

So, she kept saying. Girl wouldn't last five seconds in New York public school let alone Hell. *How had a child of the most powerful archangel turned out to be such a whiny bitch?* Glancing at the clock I turned for the door. "Get up. We are going to class."

"Wait … Uncle Raphael said we had to rest for a half hour," Miry protested.

I didn't give her a chance to say more. I just

grabbed her wrist, hauled her off the exam table and marched out of the room. I stopped about ten paces beyond the door, realizing I had no idea where I was going. I stopped walking, but Miry stumbled forward and let out an unhappy whine. "Why'd you stop?"

I resisted the urge to roll my eyes. "I realized I don't know where the fuck I'm going," I answered, glowering at her.

"Oh, right of course you don't! I guess you need me to show you."

The smirk on her face made me want to punch her in the mouth. The sooner I learned the layout, the better off I'd be. For now, I had no choice except to let her lead me to our destination.

"Can I ask you something?" I posed as we rounded what felt like the millionth turn in about ten minutes.

"Sure. Like anything."

I ground my teeth to keep from pointing out her overuse of the word "like" and that it was going to result in serious bodily harm if she wasn't careful. "Do your Uncle Uriel's eyes always glow red when he's flinging fire balls at people?"

"What?" Miry stopped walking. This time I didn't stop in time and slammed into her back.

"What are you saying?" Her tone was accusatory and maybe she had a right to be.

"All I'm saying is that it looked a little shady. He's an Archangel. Isn't he supposed to be a good guy?'

"Of course, he's a good guy!" Miry shouted, moving to stand in my way. "Why would you say that? You don't know him!"

"You're right, I don't know him. Still I've only ever seen one person whose eyes glow red."

Confusion clouded her face and I let out an exasperated sigh. "Beelzebub. The asshat we were chasing who stole shit they shouldn't have."

"You think he impersonated Uncle Uriel?" Miry scoffed.

I bristled. "They. Fuck, are you so thick you can't get a being's pronouns right?"

"I'm sorry, it's not something I'm used to dealing with. We don't have that many people ... like that around here."

"That's obvious. I mean, didn't you go to school with normal kids before you came here?"

"I've been here since I was twelve. Before that ... well Mom was kind of crazy about me interacting with other people. She was kind of paranoid. So, she homeschooled me."

"You seriously need to get out of here and

meet people. Like real people who aren't like you."

"Would you show me around sometime?" It came out timid, not at all like the tone she'd been using when I'd insinuated that her precious bat-shit crazy uncle was a shapeshifting thief.

I opened my mouth to tell her to go screw herself, that I didn't have time to babysit her and open up her horizons. Instead, I patted her arm and said, "Sure. But why don't we get to that class? I don't want to be late on my first day here. First impressions are important after all."

"Right. It's just down that hall," Miry said and smoothed her uniform. "Oh, and you know … I've never really noticed if that happened before with his eyes. Usually, I'm just trying not to die."

That didn't bode well. If Beelzebub could im-personate the highest angels in existence—com-plete with their powers—we were in a shit ton of trouble.

I followed Miry into the third room on the left and sat in the back of the class. She went up to join her boyfriend. Apparently, Glasses wasn't in this class or at least not in this time block. Her boyfriend slung his arm around her shoulders and leaned in close, whispering in her ear. I caught his hand sliding up her thigh. She winced. He stopped immediately and kissed her cheek.

I turned, ready to complain about the obvious display of affection to Damien when I remembered he wasn't here with me. I'd left him standing on the outside of the gates and he'd gone home to keep shit from getting stirred up. In that moment I realized how much I missed my best friend and how much more fun this would be if he were around.

The door opened and I looked to see a man in shabby clothes shuffle in, muttering to himself. Miry turned to look at me and mouthed 'Uncle Gabriel.' He wasn't at all what I had expected from one of the most powerful beings in the universe. He looked more like an absent-minded professor and one who hadn't seen a shower in ages. He bumped into his desk and a few students laughed. He looked up at the sound, blinked twice, and smiled.

"Ah, yes, hello everyone. How are we doing today?"

"Fine," a chorus of voices answered.

"Good, good. You'll have to forgive me. Jet lag is a bit overwhelming sometimes. Someone remind me where we left off?"

Miry's hand flew into the air. "We were just starting to learn about the War in Heaven."

Gabriel's face fell. "Ah, yes. I suppose it's time we deal with that topic, isn't it? You're all old enough to understand the ramifications of that battle."

I leaned back in my chair and propped my feet up on the empty seat in front of me. This was going to be good. I knew how it had really gone down. These pompous dickwads were probably going to get it all wrong.

"As most of you know, after God created humanity, the time came when division struck the Heavenly Host. There were those who wished to corrupt humanity and rule their basest desires. While there were those who understood that sometimes sacrifices should be made and sometimes bad behavior needed to have consequences."

"So, they cast out the evil angels?" A girl with mousy brown hair in the third row asked.

"They weren't evil," I said before I realized the words were out of my mouth.

The girl turned to look at me. "What are you talking about? Of course, they were."

"So, you were there when this went down, then?" I snapped.

"Well, obviously not, but Professor Gabriel was. That's what happened right? The evil angels got kicked out of Heaven like they were supposed to."

This bitch is about to get cut. "You do know that history is always written by the winners and they give it the spin they want. Of course, they're going to say they were casting evil out. Still did you ever stop to think about what those other angels were fighting for?"

"They wanted to tempt humans," the girl said, her voice less sure than before.

"Why? Because he said so?" I spat and gestured to Gabriel.

"Yes."

"They were defending humanity. God and the other Archangels wanted to destroy humans, because they were flawed by free will. Lucifer and the angels who fought with him were trying to protect them, not lure them into sin or whatever."

Gabriel cleared his throat in an obvious gesture to make me shut up. "And you are?"

"Zuri," I answered.

He narrowed his gaze at me. I could feel all eyes on me as the rest of the class waited for him to swat me down for heresy or some shit. "Yes, well, you do have a point, Zuri. There are always two sides to every story and perhaps we shouldn't only consider the one who we think is right." He shuffled through some papers on his desk before turning back to the door he'd come through. "I'm afraid I forgot I was needed elsewhere just now. Class dismissed."

The class erupted as everyone started talking over one another. I didn't have time to deal with this shit. I had a shapeshifter to find and I needed a boost from my best friend. I walked out of class, ignoring Miry and her boyfriend. I'd probably given them both heart palpitations with what I'd said.

As soon as I was out of earshot, I hit Speed Dial Number 2 on my phone. It rang once before Damien answered. "Please tell me you're on your way home right now."

"No such luck. I know who the thief is though."

"Really?"

"Beelzebub." I waited for a minute as my words sunk in. "You still there, D?"

"Yeah, I'm here. But why would they steal your dad's Emblem? Aren't they on the same side?'

"I thought so. Look, I need a little more time.

They can change shape and become anyone. They might even be able to mimic angelic powers."

"Shit. You aren't safe there, Z."

"I appreciate your concern, but I'm a big girl and I can take care of myself. I just ... I needed to hear a familiar voice. I about lost my shit in their stupid history class. Going on about how the evil angels were expelled from Heaven."

"Wait, you're in classes?"

"Duh. You didn't really think I was going to be able to sneak around unnoticed if I didn't have a good cover story. They think I'm a transfer student."

"You're playing with fire, Zuri. Your dad is already asking questions that I can't answer. You have no idea how terrifying it is to lie to the Lord of Hell."

"Trust me, D. I know exactly how you feel. Although I really appreciate it. Knowing you have my back makes me feel like I can get through this crazy shit."

"Be safe. If you're my first reaping I'm going to kill you myself. You hear me?"

"I hear you. Later."

I ended the call and the tiny hairs on the nape of my neck shivered. I spun around to find Uriel lurking in one of the alcoves. "Fuck, don't do that," I yelped.

He grinned, his eyes normal and not at all indicative that he might be a shapeshifter. "You were very impressive in class today."

I shrugged. "Yeah, I guess. No offense, but you kind of went ape shit in there. I get that Miry can be a whiny brat, but trying to burn the boss' daughter alive is going a step too far, don't you think?"

He waved his hand dismissively. "Oh, she was never in danger."

"You injured her. She had to go to the first aid room and everything," I pointed out.

"It was an accident. Besides I want to know more about how you got those skills." He stepped closer and slid his hand down my arm. "Maybe I can give you a few tips during a private tutoring session."

My stomach lurched and I swallowed back bile. "I think I'll just stick to normal class."

I pulled my arm free, tracing the hallways back to the room I was sharing with Miry. Maybe a little alone time would allow me to center things and get my head back in the game.

10

MIRYAM

"Your friend is weird," Chris said as we watched Zuri muscle her way through the crowd of students and into the hallway after history class.

"She's not my friend, she's just my roommate." I tilted my head to the side. "I do like her boots, though. They're pretty rad, huh?"

Chris slung an arm around my shoulders and led me out of class. "I like your shoes just fine. Don't try to be something you're not, Miry. It's exhausting."

I leaned against him, slipping my arm around his waist. "And what do you know about being something you're not? We don't have secrets, do we, Chris?"

"No, of course not. Just keep being you, that's all."

"I'll try."

We had study hall after history, but never did any studying … at least not books or homework assignments. I expected Chris to lead the way to the janitor's closet or maybe his room. Instead, he turned toward the grotto.

The grotto was what I liked to think Dad created when he got bored or maybe when he wanted us to get a little sunshine and fresh air for once instead of staying cooped up in school. There was a hedge maze with a giant fountain in the middle, benches scattered around—some hidden for extra privacy—and sculptures. It was full of tons and tons of sculptures of Dad. Dad standing in full armor with his sword raised. Dad stepping on Lucifer's head as he cast him down to Hell. Dad with his hands clasped in prayer. I had never seen Dad pray even once in the six years I'd been at Celestial Academy. I knew he had a rep to maintain, but seriously, it was false advertising.

"Dad and his swords, I swear." I motioned at the gold statue at the center of the fountain. "It's, like, totally phallic."

"I think it's more congratulatory." Chris sat on the edge of the fountain. I found a spot next to him. "Think about it. He's got to remind himself what he's known for. If you forget, history has a chance to repeat itself."

"There's no way there can be a second war in Heaven." I shook my head so hard my headband slid down my forehead and my hair hit me in the face. "Besides, if Lucifer and the Fallen were going to be all uppity or whatever, wouldn't they have done it by now?"

"I don't think time really has much meaning in Hell." Chris dipped his hand into the fountain water, watching the ripples it created across our reflection. Ripples on the water that could be a metaphor or something.

"You look tired," I commented. "Did using your safe passage ability for that long wear you out?"

Chris smiled, but just barely. "Yeah, something like that."

I knotted my hands in my lap. There was something not right, but I couldn't quite figure out what. Chris didn't seem all that interested in telling me either. "Did I do something? Should I have stood up to my dad when he went all buddy-system on me and stuck Zuri in my room? Joke's on him cause she just walked out of class without any buddying or systeming. Do you want me to get him to put her somewhere else? I can do that, you know. Just say the word and—"

"Miry!" Chris pinched the bridge of his nose with his thumb and pointer finger. "Just *stop talking,* okay? Trust yourself a little. You don't always have to do what everyone else wants you to, or what you think they'd want you to do. Stand up to your dad, don't stand up to your dad. I don't care, as long as it is *your* decision … not mine."

My hands fluttered to his arm before I pulled back just in case he didn't want me to touch him. But that was the problem right there, wasn't it? I deferred to everyone else when what I should do is listen to myself. Still I don't trust myself. I trusted Chris. He was the only person I felt really cared about me for me and not using me for a way to get on Dad's good side at this school.

"I'll try," I said. "But it's not, like, normal for me to do that, okay?"

Chris sighed. "I know, and I'm sorry if I upset you. You're right. I'm tired. I shouldn't take that out on you."

"Is there anything I can do to help?"

"There is, but it's kind of weird to ask." He watched me as if trying to decide if he wanted to say more or not. He picked not. "Forget it. Maybe some other time."

"No, tell me," I said. "I want to help."

"Some other time. I promise."

Chris leaned in for a kiss. I wrapped my arms around his neck and pulled him closer. His lips were feather light against mine, not exactly teasing, but definitely not into the potential make out session either.

"What else is wrong?" I pulled back, my arms still hanging loosely around his neck. "Tell me the truth, Chris. No secrets, remember?"

"I … When I was home for summer term, I found some letters and cards my mom had sent me over the years that Dad hid from me," he admitted. "Every birthday. Every holiday. There was a card addressed to me that Dad had just stuffed in some shoebox in his closet. He kept her from me. She was reaching out to me, Miry. She wanted me and Dad just threw that away."

"Oh, Chris … I thought your mom was dead."

"Dad never actually said she was dead. He always just said she was gone." Chris shrugged. "She didn't want to be blocked from my life. Dad made that decision for the both of us. It's like text book parental alienation. I don't know if I can forgive him for that."

"Was there a return address on the cards?" I

asked. "You know, so you can track her down if you want."

He shook his head. "No. Just a PO Box, but it's local. I hung out there this summer just in case."

"If she's sending you cards on birthdays and holidays, we'll wait for one of those to roll around and then see what happens."

His lips quirked into a half smile. "We?"

"You didn't think I'd let you do this alone, did you?" I perked up at the idea of having a project. "What are girlfriends for?"

"You're the best. Seriously." He kissed me a little more forcefully this time. "How much time do we have until our next class starts?"

I checked the time on my phone. "Thirty minutes."

Chris laughed. "We can do a lot in thirty minutes."

"Yes, we can." I pointed at the statue of Dad looking down at us. "Although not with him watching. Let's go back to my room."

11

ZURI

I paced between the two beds in the room I was now sharing with Miry. It wasn't nearly enough room to let me stretch my legs and vent my frustration. I also needed something to distract me from the utter creep fest that was my last interaction with Uriel. I needed to find a way to see if it was actually the Archangel or really Beelzebub in disguise. Maybe another call to Damien was in order. I pulled out my phone to make the call when Dad's face flashed on my screen with an incoming call. *Shit.* "Hey, Dad," I said as calmly as possible.

"Zuri, where are you?"

Fuck. I should have checked with Damien to get our stories straight. "I got bored and decided to head into the city. Just to do some window shopping."

"You're with people you trust?"

"I'm not with anyone. What's wrong?"

I heard him exhale over the line and I could just imagine him pinching the bridge of his nose. "There was a break-in at the museum last night."

"What? Was anything taken?" I feigned ignorance. A task made infinitely easier by the fact he couldn't see my face right now.

"Yes. My Emblem."

"That's not good." I couldn't hide the nervousness in my voice. It was the whole reason I was standing in the middle of enemy territory right now.

"No, it is not. It is extremely dangerous in the wrong hands. Zuri, I want you to be safe."

"I know it's dangerous. You told me every chance you got. It's why you'd never let me even touch it, remember? I can take care of myself," I replied.

"You need to promise me that you're safe."

"Fuck, Dad. I'm fine." I heard muffled voices in the hall outside growing louder. Any privacy I had was about to evaporate. "I need to go. Some asshole is glaring at me for holding up the line.

You know New Yorkers and their coffee. Love you, bye."

I ended the call just as the door opened. Miry and her boyfriend spilled into the room, hands already under each other's shirts. He noticed me first, retracting his hands and taking a step back. Miry looked at him with confusion before she turned and her mouth hung open in surprise.

"What are you doing in here?" She asked.

I pointed to the bed that I'd claimed. "My room, too. Look I'm all for sexual exploration or whatever, but I do not need to see his dick waving in the wind."

Her boyfriend—I should remember his name, but I just didn't care—glared at me. He looked paler than he had when I left history class. Maybe using his ability had taken a toll on him. After all, he'd said he hadn't really tested it extensively. Maybe I shouldn't have taken his head off for the assist.

"You know what, I'm going to wander. Get to know the campus so I don't have to be attached at the hip to Miss Priss here." I side stepped them and reached for the door knob.

"You know, you were pretty brave back there taking on an Archangel by yourself," he said.

"He was being a bully. I don't deal well with

people trying to push me around. Also, I know he's your uncle or whatever, but dude tried to hit on me and get me alone in a room. Gave off real rape-y vibes. Just giving you fair warning, if he tries it again, he may come away with fewer appendages than when he started."

"He's just … different," Miry offered unconvincingly.

"There's different and then there's a sexual predator. You sure you really know him that well?"

Miry's cheeks burned bright red at the insinuation. "He'd never do anything like that."

"Then you don't have a problem with me filing a formal complaint with your father about it."

Miry reached out her hand and clamped down on my wrist hard enough to leave a bruise. "Don't tell my dad, please. He's got a lot going on."

I wrenched my arm free of her grasp. "You think I care how much he's got going on? If one of his fellow Headmasters is making passes at students, he damn well is gonna know about it."

"You said you thought it wasn't even Uncle Uriel. You said it could be Beelzebub," she blurted.

Her boyfriend eyed us both. "Seriously?"

I shrugged one shoulder. "I've only seen Beelzebub's eyes glow red. Uriel's did the same in class. It's a reasonable assumption. If you say he's acting differently than normal, that would make sense, too."

He shook his head. "But we've seen Uriel use his powers like that before."

"So, he can throw fire balls. That's not like it's a big surprise or a hard power to duplicate. The bigger issue is not knowing if Beelzebub can actually replicate abilities."

"How would we figure out if it's really Uncle Uriel or not?"

"I might have a way, but I need to make a call. In private. Give me five minutes and I'll come find you. We'll see which of us is right."

I WAITED for Miry and her boyfriend to give me some privacy before making my call. Twice in one day. Damien would think I missed him. I'd never let him know that I really did. I had my tough girl image to uphold, after all.

"Seriously, Z, do I need to mount a rescue?" He said without preamble or greeting.

"Two things. What did you tell my dad about where I was?" I settled on the edge of the bed and scuffed the toe of my boot against the floor.

"I didn't really give specifics. He called to check up on you, didn't he?"

"He did. It's fine. Look, I need you to do me another favor."

I sensed the whine in his voice before he spoke. "Is it going to get me in trouble with someone who can do serious damage to my face?"

I smiled even though he couldn't see me. "Probably. Though you love me so suck it up. I need you to go into the Archives and get me anything you can find on the Archangel Uriel."

"The Archives. As in the place only two people have the key to. The same place where even you've never been allowed, because the information is too important … dangerous and world-ending?" After a pause, he added. "What are you into, Zuri?"

"I need to know something about Uriel that can't be gathered from a quick observation. Something only he would know."

"If I do this, you owe me even more than you already do. Seriously, you hook me up with the prettiest girl there."

"I'll let you know if she even exists. So, you'll do it?"

"I'll try."

"Great. I need the info like ... now."

"You're joking right?"

"Nope. I told you Beelzebub stole dad's Emblem. I think they might be impersonating people in authority."

"Why can't you just come back? Couldn't you just forge a key to get in?"

The idea of going home was appealing. I didn't feel comfortable here. Besides I missed the familiar passageways and faces. Not to mention it would put Dad's mind at ease if I put in an appearance. Although I really didn't have a way to slip off to Hell without Miry and her friends finding out who I really am.

"D, I wish I could," I started, but stopped speaking. A little trip back home couldn't hurt. I suspected if Miry really didn't want me to involve her father, she'd let me do whatever I wanted to get proof about her precious Uncle Uriel. "Fine. I'll come home, but you get that I have to come back here, right?"

"I don't like you being there. I understand you've got this whole family honor thing to uphold, but these people are dangerous."

You don't have to remind me. "Meet me at the New York portal entrance in ten minutes."

"That's not where we went through."

"It's where I told Dad I was."

"It's scary sometimes how easy it is for you to keep a lie going."

I ended the call and stepped into the hallway. Miry and her boyfriend shield were nowhere to be seen. I started back toward the center of the school when someone let out a low whistle. I turned to see Glasses leaning against the wall.

"You my stalker now?" I asked.

"No. I was looking for Chris to make sure he was okay after self-defense class."

"Right. Look, can you tell them I'll be back in like ten minutes. I need to make a quick off campus trip."

His eyes brightened behind the frames of his glasses. "Off campus? Where?"

"Nosy much? I need to check something at my house. It might prove useful. Just tell them I'll be back and not to do anything rash until then."

He crossed his arms over his chest in what I'm sure he thought was a challenging gesture, but it just made him look like a pouty nerd. "Fine."

It took more time than I wanted to find a door

that took me outside to the gates where I'd come in. Unlike last night, they stood open and I waltzed right through. Finding a portal to Hell was second nature to a Fallen and one opened up right in front of me as soon as my boots left sacred ground. It swirled in front of me, beckoning me home.

Jumping through from the mortal plane side isn't nearly as disorienting as going the other direction. No one's been able to figure out the reason why. Still I ended up right where I needed to be. Damien raced toward me and threw his arms around me.

"You're not dead," he said.

"Dude, you just talked to me like two seconds ago. Stop being so clingy." I shoved him off. "Besides, I'm here for a reason, remember?"

"I still think you're nuts."

We walked side by side to Dad's office. The Archives sat behind a locked door hidden in a bookshelf. He thought I didn't know about it. I'd learned most of his hiding spots by the time I was seven. Although I let him think he still had a few things that were his. I grabbed a jumble of paperclips from the desk and started to fashion them into a key. I bent to study the keyhole and pressed my mash of metal into the lock. It glowed bright in my hand as it formed to fit the lock and the bookshelf swung inward.

"You can stand guard if it makes you feel better," I told Damien with a pat on his shoulder.

He flipped me off, but turned his attention to the only door into the office. I slipped through the passage into the Archives and stopped for a minute to just take it in. I had always imagined it was filled with ancient scrolls tossed onto shelves haphazardly and disordered. For one thing, there were no scrolls whatsoever. Dad had gone digital at some point and there was a single computer terminal at the center of the room. Cracking my knuckles for dramatic effect I approached the terminal and typed in Uriel.

A bar appeared on the screen as it searched the available records before populating a single page with an image of the being I'd met earlier in the day. Most of the information was tactical about his powers—fireballs obviously—with a mention of something called a lariat. I scrolled down until I found a single note that read 'Burning Starlight.' I hit the 'Back' button and entered the phrase.

"You need to hurry your ass up," Damien hissed.

"Give me a minute," I answered as the system loaded.

A page with the heading 'Burning Starlight' appeared. As I skimmed the information, my mouth went dry. They were letters from Uriel to Dad. The kind of graphic letters you'd expect to find in bad erotica. There didn't appear to be any responses from Dad. I wasn't sure that Beelzebub didn't have this information. Still given I was almost certain no one except Dad and Azrael had been in here in millennia, they didn't know this little tidbit either. Now I just had to get back to put this theory to the test.

12

MIRYAM

"You said she'd be gone for ten minutes, but it's been, like, thirteen." I looked at Ant to confirm that my not cheating and looking at my phone time telling abilities was accurate. "What can we possibility do that's 'rash' in thirteen minutes?"

"I don't know. That's what she said. I'm just the messenger." Ant ordered three chocolate mocha frappes from the on-campus coffee cart. Dad didn't care how much caffeine a bunch of teenagers ingested as long as we got to class on time. "It seemed important, though."

"More important than figuring out if Uncle Uriel is some demon or not?" I pouted.

"Hey, why don't you say that loud enough for

the kids in back to hear." Chris sunk into a chair. "I'm not sure how much help I'll be in this Scooby Doo mission, Mir. Sorry." He closed his eyes, breath coming in jagged rasps.

I leaned over the back of his chair, wrapping my arms around his chest from behind. "Tell me what I can do to help you, Chris."

"Not now," he said. "I told you it was weird."

"I don't mind weird."

"Uh, that's a little TMI for my taste, thanks guys." Ant passed out the frappes. "Try some caffeine, buddy. That might pep you up."

Chris sucked the frappe through a straw, his eyes still closed, but it didn't do anything to make him peppy or up. Why won't he let me help him?

"If you're wiped from self-defense class, you're a liability." Zuri appeared from out of nowhere. She had a black backpack slung over her shoulder and some sort of flash drive clutched in her fist. She hid the flash drive in the small front zippered pocket of her backpack when she caught me looking. "Sleep it off or whatever you do, wuss. Though you're not coming with us if you can't contribute."

"Are all kids from the Middle East campus this hard core or just you?" I asked, hugging Chris tighter to show I had his back.

"Just me. I'm special." Zuri dug through her backpack, muttering to herself. "Fuck, D, I asked you to put one thing in and you can't even get that right. Do I have to do everything myself?" She mashed some buttons on her phone before sticking it in her back pocket.

I perked up at the mention of this mysterious D. Cutesy nicknames? There had to be some good dirt there. "Who's D?"

Zuri scowled. "None of your business."

"Ah! That reaction means it's totally my business!" I let go of Chris long enough to clap my hands and do a I-got-gossip dance. "Zuri has a boyfriend! Zuri has a boyfriend!"

"You wish," she snorted. "I don't need your cheerleader bullshit. Are we going to check out our Uriel issue or what?"

"He already went all fire in the hole in class today," Ant said. "I'm not really game for round two."

"Suit yourself." Zuri shrugged. "We don't need you anyway. The only one that I really need is Miry."

I scrunched my nose up. "Me? Why me?"

"Because he trusts you," she said. "He's your Uncle Uriel. I'll let you do all the talking. The only thing you need to do is make sure you mention 'Burning Starlight.' That's it. Then we wait for his reaction."

"Burning Starlight?" I chewed my bottom lip. "What's so important about Burning Starlight?"

"Don't worry about it," Zuri said. "It's, like, a safe word. Just use it. Uriel's reaction is the key here. Nothing else."

"Safe word," Chris roused himself from whatever was going on health wise to snicker at Zuri's word choice. "What do you know about safe words?"

Zuri crossed her arms over her chest. "I know enough to know, if you even have one, it's probably something completely lame like 'fluffy bunny slippers.'"

Chris pushed himself out of his chair. "Say that again, new girl?"

I stepped between them. I didn't want to break up a fight, but I would if I needed to. "Enough. Let's find Uncle Uriel and get this over with." I looked over my shoulder at the boys. "You guys stay here. It will be less obvious we're digging for dirt if it's just Zuri and I." I skipped over to kiss Chris good bye. "Hey, our safe word is still Pillsbury Dough Boy, right?"

Ant took a hit off his asthma inhaler. "TMI, guys. TMI."

"For once I agree with you, Glasses." Zuri held in her vomit just barely. "Can we get this over with, already? We can't save angelic history without recovering what Beelzebub stole."

I bounced up and down clapping. "Oooh, project!"

Zuri grabbed my arm and yanked me away. She didn't say a single word until we were out of range of the boys. "Let's get this over with. The less time I spend with your creepy uncle as himself or a shapeshifting demon the better."

"He's not really my uncle, I just call him that," I said as I lead the way to Uncle Uriel's office. "None of the archangels are really blood brothers or anything. They were created at the same time so sort of grew up together if that's the right word. They're like a family. Sometimes that's more important than blood relations, right?"

"I wouldn't know," Zuri opened up a teensy tiny bit. "My dad is kind of the black sheep of the family. I don't have any uncles—fake or otherwise."

"I thought you said you didn't know who your dad was, just that he was a low-level archangel."

Her pretty mocha complexion paled slightly. "I know enough to be positive there's no angelic uncles around. My mom's parents died before I was born and she didn't have any siblings so I didn't have any family from her side either."

"I wish my mom died when I was born," I said. "That way I wouldn't have had to live with her for twelve years."

"You don't know what you're talking about."

I frowned. I had said the wrong thing and offended her … again. "You're right. That was insensitive of me, I'm sorry."

"Let's just get this over with," she muttered. "The faster I get the relic back, the faster I can get out of here."

"You can't leave mid-semester," I informed her. "That's, like, not allowed. Dad's rules."

"I don't, like, care what your dad's rules are."

I jutted my lip out into a pout. "Are you making fun of me?" When Zuri doesn't answer, I plowed on. Listening to myself talk was sometimes easier than dealing with the places my mind sometimes went. Being perky was easy. Being introspective was not. "Here's a pro tip from me to you about Uncle Uriel. Never sit on his lap and never take any candy from him. He hides those firecracker popper things in caramels and then laughs his head off when kids bite down on them. The bigger the boom, the better. The off-campus dentist loves him, though."

"You said he had issues," Zuri circled back to our earlier discussion. "What are they?"

"I don't think I'm allowed to say." I turned one last corner down a hallway that would lead us straight to Uncle Uriel's office. "The War in Heaven messed him up. It messed all of them up. They all just have different ways of dealing with it." I knocked once on Uncle Uriel's office door before pushing it open. "Uncle Uriel! Check it out! My leg is totally healed thanks to Uncle Raphael."

"And no thanks to me." Uncle Uriel looked up. He had some sort of map spread out on his desk with little plastic soldiers marching across it. "I already apologized to your father, Miry. I shouldn't have targeted you again."

I shrugged. An apology was an apology even if he didn't actually come out and say 'sorry.' Apologizing to Dad was almost as good as apologizing straight to me. "It's cool. No lasting harm done. Except maybe to, like, my psyche."

Uncle Uriel stood and paced his small office. He rearranged his toy soldiers, talking mostly to himself as if we weren't even there. "Good soldiers need to be prepared. Good soldiers need to be ready for anything. Even the Fall ... No ... No, especially the Fall."

I glanced over my shoulder at Zuri, mouthing 'what do I do now?' She pointed at Uncle Uriel and mouthed back 'Ask Burning Starlight. Now.' Although I'm still not sure what that code word or safe word or whatever means. Still if it proved Uncle Uriel was actually Uncle Uriel and not that crazy shapeshifting demon, I'd say it.

"Hey, Uncle Uriel, I totally figured out what I'm gonna do for my service project this year," I said. "It's going to be all about preserving angelic history for the future generations. I call it 'Burning Starlight.' What do you think?"

Uncle Uriel's wings popped out of his back which he only does when he can't control his reactions. "What did you say?"

"Burning Starlight," I repeated. "Catchy, huh?"

"Never use those words in my presence again!" Uncle Uriel shouted. He scattered his toy soldiers with one angry swipe of his hand. "Get out! Get out now!" He held out his hand, palm up. His eyes flashed red briefly before a fire ball formed in his open palm. "Get out!"

Zuri and I booked it out of there before Uncle Uriel had time to throw the fire ball at either of us. Once we were a safe distance away from any potential pyrotechnics, I stopped and turned to Zuri.

"Okay. You saw his reaction. Was that good or bad?"

"Good and bad," Zuri commented. "Good in that I'm positive that was the real Uriel. Bad in we still don't know where Beelzebub is."

ZURI

My head spun as I stared at Miry. As creeped out as I'd been, I'd hoped it wasn't the real Uriel putting moves on me. If it had been Beelzebub, I could have trailed them to wherever they were hiding the emblem, steal it back and go home. I also didn't know how to feel about finding Uriel's love letters to Dad. I wasn't going to call Uriel out on being closeted—I knew how hard that was for some people to admit their truth—but I knew Dad was into women. So that begged the question: *did Uriel join Michael out of spite? Was it a way to hurt Dad for the rejection?*

"You got all quiet," Miry said, twisting a strand of hair around one finger.

"I'm just thinking," I answered and slid the

other strap of the backpack Damien had given me onto my shoulder.

"Are you going to tell me what Burning Starlight means?" The whine was evident in her tone.

"It doesn't matter. It did what it was supposed to do." I started back to the dorms. Maybe I could convince Miry to go cling to her boyfriend for a while so I could have some space to think.

Miry skirted around me until she blocked my way forward. "We both saw how Uncle Uriel reacted when I said it. He got super mad. Don't I deserve to know why? It was personal enough to make him want to burn us both alive."

She wasn't going to let this go until I gave her an answer. I opened my mouth to answer when my phone buzzed in my pocket. I pulled it out and stared at the message on the screen. Damien was outside the gates with what I'd asked him to bring. *Saved by the Reaper.* "Look. I'll explain, but I need to go take care of something first."

I shoved past her and headed toward the front of the grounds. I passed through the entrance hall where I'd forged my way into this place and stopped to take in the photos on the wall. Knowing what I did about Uriel, I studied the photo of him more closely. I thought I caught a forlorn look in his eyes, but it could have been my imagination playing tricks on me.

Pulling myself away, I slipped out into the afternoon air and wound my way to the gate. Damien stood on the other side looking decidedly unhappy that he was here. I smiled at him.

"Hey, thanks for coming."

"Didn't give me much choice, did you?"

"Well, if you'd packed everything like I had told you to, we wouldn't be having this conversation." I reached my hand through the bars so he wouldn't have to risk total annihilation or whatever from being on sacred ground. Damien passed a thin cord of red string over. I pulled it over my wrist and tightened it down.

"Is that her?" He whispered, his chin jutting in Miry's direction.

I couldn't help, but roll my eyes. "That obvious?"

"She's kinda cute," he snickered.

"Oh, shut up," I snapped.

"Aren't you going to introduce me?" Miry called and bounced her way over to the gate.

Damien took a step back. I couldn't tell if it was out of fear that she might somehow smite him or because her obnoxiously bubbly personality was vomit-inducing. I watched Miry's eyes widen when she noticed the ink that crept up the right side of Damien's neck.

"Miry, this is Damien. D, this is Miry. She's … my roommate."

Damien gave a little nod. "Hey."

"So, this is the mysterious D you wouldn't tell me anything about. How'd you two meet?"

Getting kicked out of the school for assaulting the head honcho's daughter wouldn't help me in my quest to retrieve dad's relic, but it sure would make me feel a lot better. "We grew up together."

"Did you go to the Middle East campus, too?"

I caught the panic flash over Damien's face. The way his lips pressed into a thin line told me he was done coming up with lies for me. At least for the time being, anyways. "Yeah. Our parents got transferred back together," I lied.

"Oh. So, why didn't you transfer here like Zuri?" Miry pressed.

Damien let out a series of coughs. "I'm sick … Like super contagious. So, yeah you should probably stay away." He turned to look at me. "Z, I'll catch you later."

"Later."

I watched him walk away, silently running my fingers over the bracelet now adorning my left wrist. It had been a gift from my father to my mother when he learned she was pregnant with me. He'd given it to me as a birthday present when I was ten.

"I'm sorry your boyfriend is sick," Miry said.

"He's not my boyfriend."

"So, he's just a boy who happens to be a friend?" She prodded.

"Yep."

"Who grew up with you."

"End of story."

Miry let out a giggle. "Oh, come on. There's way more to the story than that. He gave you jewelry." She pointed to the bracelet. "He's your boyfriend."

"Definitely not my boyfriend," I repeated through gritted teeth.

"You don't have to be embarrassed that you got transferred and he didn't. You know, I'm kind of surprised he got accepted to any campus in the first place."

I bit down hard enough on my tongue to taste blood. "And why's that?"

"Well I mean … like, you saw all those tattoos."

Damn, this girl is clueless. "Do you ever actually listen to the words that come out of your mouth? Or do you just love the sound of your own voice and don't actually pay attention?"

"What did I say?" She asked with that trademark pout. She must have thought it was endearing.

"You assume what, because he's Latino and has tats that he couldn't possibly go here? Not everyone is a pretty White girl, Miry. The rest of us have to fight for what we deserve. It's not just handed to us."

"I'm sorry I insulted your boyfriend's tattoos."

I grabbed her by the shoulders and shook her. "He's *not* my boyfriend. I don't like guys."

She blinked as confusion overtook her expression. "Huh?"

"I'm gay," I said in an exaggerated, drawn-out tone.

She took a step back and moved her torso enough to shake loose of my grasp. "You're just making that up, because I commented about his tattoos."

I balled my hands into fists to keep my temper in check. "If you had actual social skills, you'd know that people don't just pretend to be gay. You've lived some sheltered ass life … I actually feel sorry for you, because there's so much out there in the world that's beautiful and amazing. You're just stuck in your little hetero bubble hidden from all of it."

I saw tears welling in her eyes as my words sunk in. She'd never been confronted like that before. From what I'd seen and she'd told me, people just treated her like the golden child who could do no wrong. They didn't question when she didn't know something or how to react to a situation.

"So, you like girls," she finally said.

"Yes. I like girls. And yes, I checked you out when we met. Don't worry though, you're not my type."

"What is your type?"

"Bad girl."

She smiled. "I could be a bad girl. We've known each other for less than a day."

"Careful, angel. Don't want to tarnish that halo. Might risk those pretty wings of yours if you're not careful."

The smile vanished. "What is Burning Starlight? You said you'd explain."

"Uriel may not have entirely been against Lucifer. He had an affinity for Lucifer before the Fall."

"You don't have to be delicate. I can take whatever it is."

"Fine. Before the War in Heaven Uriel sent some seriously erotic love letters to Lucifer. I'm guessing it went unrequited and that's maybe why Uriel joined up with Team Michael to smite the so-called rebel angels."

"You think Uncle Uriel is gay?" Miry asked. "But I've seen him hit on plenty of female students. You even said he hit on you!"

"Maybe he's bisexual," I said. "I mean, sometimes he looks awfully feminine. If Beelzebub can change shape and is gender fluid, why can't an angel?"

Miry nodded her head and started walking back to the front of the school. "You know a lot about demons. I'm pretty sure they didn't teach that at the Middle East campus."

"Different school, different philosophy," I said.

"Dad has a standard curriculum. He's big on uniformity. It's why you'll hardly ever see kids out of uniform, even on weekends. He's real strict about that. So, if they taught anything about demons at the other campuses, we'd have learned about it, too. And we haven't."

"Don't you find that weird?" I prompted.

"Why?"

"If I'd fought in an epic war and come out the victor, I'd be teaching everyone I knew exactly what the enemy could do to ensure it didn't happen again. So that people would know what to look for."

"I guess." She spun around and walked backwards, arms swinging loosely at her sides. "How'd you even know this relic was stolen anyway?"

"I watched it happen," I admitted before I could stop myself.

"Where?"

"Why is that important? What matters is that we have to get it back."

"I've never seen any relic like the one you drew for Ant."

"Seen a lot of angelic relics in your time, have you?" I taunted.

"No, but I did visit the other campuses over the summer and I didn't see anything like that at either of them. Besides I know every inch of this school. So, where'd it come from?"

She was phishing and I knew it. I was confident in my lies, but they only went so far. I'd opened up to her by coming out and maybe now she sensed a vulnerability—a way in.

"Look, everyone has things they don't want to let people in on," I said. "Can we just keep it at that?"

"I don't like being lied to. Tell me what's really going on."

"Or what? You'll complain to Daddy? Somehow I don't think he'd give two shits about whatever you had to say."

"Everyone thinks I can't handle things. They think just because I'm pretty and I'm Michael's daughter I have to be protected. And sure, I don't like fighting, but that doesn't mean I won't if I absolutely have to."

"Oh, no. You can't take me in a fight," I commented.

"That is your problem, Zuri. You're cocky. You have this attitude like no one can touch you because you're a badass, but you're hiding things. I'm going to find out. I'm not going to share my room with someone I don't trust."

"I didn't ask to be your roommate," I reminded her.

Without warning, she took a swing at me. I dodged the blow easily and side-stepped. "You're just going to end up back in the first aid room with more bruises."

"You're afraid I'll learn something about you that you can't keep guarded. Secrets only weight you down. Don't you want to let people in?" She said, her eyes shining with what I thought might be excitement.

"I will hurt you," I said as she took another wild swing.

This time I grabbed her arm between her elbow and wrist, then twisted. She cried out in pain as I pulled her close. I felt the weight of her body against mine and damn if it didn't turn me on a little. I gave her arm an extra squeeze to make my point. "Your boyfriend isn't here to save you, Miry. Besides, I was trained by the best."

"Yeah? And who's that?" She grunted.

"Lucifer, Ruler of Hell." The words were out of my mouth before I realized I'd spoken them.

14

MIRYAM

"**Y**ou are such a liar!" I ducked down and yanked my arm free all in one fluid motion. Zuri didn't even resist me getting free from her Me-Strong-You-Weak game. "You expect me to believe Lucifer, Prince of Darkness, has time to train you to fight when your random Archangel Dad doesn't? And when exactly did this training sesh, like, happen? Everyone gets their letters when they're twelve and if you were at the Middle East campus you were nowhere near the Gates to Hell. I hear they're in, like Jersey by the way."

"Not everything is in Jersey." Zuri rubbed her arm as if it were her and not me that had just escaped from an arm lock. "Except this time, you're correct. The main Gate is on the New Jersey side of the George Washington Bridge."

I bounced on my toes and struggled to not laugh in her face. Since that would be mean. I may be a lot of things, but I'm not mean. "Prove it."

Zuri's eyes widened. "Prove the Gate to Hell is in Jersey? You wouldn't be able to cross into Hell any more than a Fallen or Demon could go to Heaven. You should know that." She crossed her arms over her chest. "Or were you slacking off when that was covered in Angelic History?"

I balled my hands into fists at my sides. "I'm not a slacker."

"Prove it."

I smiled. "I see what you did there. You turned my own words against me. Trying to get me to forget to call you out on your lies." I twisted my hair around my index finger, thinking. "You know what? I don't care. You can play your little Lucifer is my BFF game all you want. Being satanic is not going to get Dad to change your room assignment."

"Lucifer and Satan are two separate beings," she said as if it should be automatic knowledge. "Satan and the Devil are the same."

"Do you know him too?"

"*Them.* Get your gender pronouns right. You wouldn't last five seconds in Hell." Zuri stalked toward our dorm room. She at least seemed to have figured out where that was in the school. I followed.

"Maybe I can just ask Lucifer for a sword fighting lesson."

Zuri whirled to face me, her expression practically murderous. She grabbed my neck and pushed me back up against the wall. "Look, little girl, I'm done with your bullshit. Believe me or don't believe me. I don't care. Just remember when you're insulting the Ruler of Hell, he's an archangel, too—just like your precious daddy. Show some respect."

"Lucifer is Fallen," I croaked, not able to stop myself from laughing. It was a wheezy, weird laugh, but still a laugh. "He lost any and all rights to call himself an archangel after he started the War in Heaven."

I laughed again. This wasn't even funny. Zuri could probably snap my neck like a twig, but at the same time, she was the only one who had ever stood up to me. This was new and, okay, maybe a little bit exciting.

Zuri released my neck. "I'm going back to our room. Don't try to follow me."

I slid to the ground. I patted my neck, hoping it wouldn't bruise. I looked horrible in neckscarves. "Fine. Don't draw pentagrams or whatever on the floor. That's, like, totally destruction of property and will get you expelled."

"Thanks for the tip." Zuri stalked away without a single backwards glance.

"What a weirdo," I muttered. I climbed to my feet just as the kidnapper announcement declared "Attention Students, today's count for total number of missing students has risen to fifty-six. Remember to use the buddy system and always report suspicious activity. That is all." More kidnappings? I better check on Chris. He'd be an easy target in his weakened state. I pushed all thoughts of Zuri's BS Prince of Darkness story from my mind before swiveling in the direction of Chris' room. If I were especially lucky—which I usually was—Ant wouldn't be hanging around their room either.

"HEY, CHRIS, YOU IN?" I knocked on his door and waited, hoping Ant didn't answer. He was cool and all, but not the person I wanted to see right now. "Chris?" I pushed on the door. It swung open to reveal … no one there. "Chris? It's Miry. Just checking to make sure you weren't kidnapped."

I kicked off my shoes and sat on his bed to wait. For a second, I debated whether to check the communal shower or not, before deciding not. Communal showers had their fun uses, but that shiz had to be planned. I didn't need or want to see half the guys on the floor's ding dongs. Thanks, but no thanks.

"Miry?" Chris entered the room still wrapped in a towel. *Bonus!* "What are you doing here?" He glanced at his dresser. "Do I need to get dressed or stay in the towel? What kind of visit is this?"

I swung my feet back and forth. "Hmm … Towel. No wait, dressed. No wait." I cocked my head to the side, my hair falling over my shoulder. "You decide."

Chris shut the door and crossed the room to the dresser. "Dressed. It's more fun to get *un*dressed." He pulled khaki pants, a white button-down shirt, a plaid uniform vest, and tie out of drawers.

"Zuri was totally mean to me just now," I announced as I watched him dress. "She actually thinks Lucifer taught her to sword fight. Isn't that bananas?"

"Bananas," Chris repeated, though he didn't sound convinced. "How did she say it? Threatening? Joking?"

"Seriously, joking?" I scoffed. "Like, I know she just transferred, but have we ever seen her joke?"

"You're right," Chris agreed. "Do I need to challenge her to a duel to defend your honor?"

"Ooh, old school." I grabbed his school tie and pulled him over to me for a kiss. "I like it. But how are you feeling?"

He shrugged. "Better. I just needed to rest."

"You look better," I commented, running my fingers down his arm. "Not so pale anymore. I was worried you might, like, get picked off by the kidnapper or something."

"No such luck." Chris winked. "You're stuck with me."

I grinned. "I wouldn't have it any other way."

15

———————

ZURI

I was lucky to find my way back to the stupid dorm unaided. Anger always made me a little touchy and that usually led to distraction. Still, I slammed the door behind me with a concussive 'thump' that dulled the edges of my irritation. Miry was such a brainless idiot with her stupid perky smile, bouncy personality, and perfect tits. *Why am I thinking about her tits?*

"Fuck her," I screamed, slamming my fist into the wall.

I felt bone crack and skin tear as I connected with the plaster and brick underneath. My hand came away throbbing and bloody, but I didn't even care. *Why am I thinking about her breasts? She's not my type!* I really wanted to call Damien and vent, but I'd already asked too much of him. I'm fairly certain he needed a break from me. I could be overwhelming sometimes and I knew it. I needed to respect his boundaries if I was going to keep him as a friend.

The wall now stained with blood made me realize how close I'd come to blowing my cover. I didn't fit in here. Been here one day and I was already losing my shit and punching things. I would have taken Miry's head off if she'd pushed me much further. I may be able to set foot on their so-called sacred ground, but that didn't mean I was meant for this place.

I tried to flex my hand, but jolts of pain shot up to my elbow, making my eyes water with the pain. I'd probably broken a few bones. I wasn't a healer by any means. Besides if I ran into Miry and her stupid sycophants while covered in blood, she'd have even more reason to call me out. She didn't understand what it was like to hear everywhere you went that your father was evil and a villain by virtue of the fact that he lost the fight.

"Screw all of you assholes," I grumbled to the empty room before scooping up one of Miry's shirts and wrapping it around my wounded hand.

It took me a couple tries, but I found my way

back to the first aid room. I was thinking of just cleaning and wrapping the wound before sneaking away to let my angelic healing do its thing. Only Raphael stood in the middle of the room, gauze pads and peroxide in hand just like he'd been expecting me.

"Mind if I take a look?"

I unwrapped the fabric from my hand and winced as I looked at the damage done. I sat on the same exam bed Miry had occupied earlier in the day. He donned gloves and prodded the broken flesh.

"Do I need to inspect whoever did this to you?" He was soft spoken as he continued to probe the wound.

"Not unless you're in the construction business," I answered. "Also, you're a freaking angel with healing powers. So, what's with the medical gloves? I saw you heal Miry earlier remember."

"You're new here and I don't have any medical records from the other campus. Besides, I always wear gloves. One can never be too careful."

"Must be slow coming over," I answered.

"I suppose it does take time to cross barriers to this plane."

"What's that supposed to mean?" I asked as he

swabbed the injuries with peroxide-soaked cotton balls. Dirt and grime bubbled to the surface, burning my nerve endings. "Shit that hurts."

"Perhaps you should avoid punching walls then."

"You didn't answer my question," I said, taking short controlled breaths to keep the pain in check.

"No, I didn't."

"I think we've established I'm good at hitting things," I said.

He smiled as he arched a brow at me. "Is that a threat, Ms. Bat-Lucifer?"

My entire body went cold. Dread crawled up my skin like millions of tiny bugs scampering for cover. "What did you call me?"

"Ah, yes, I believe the name you gave was Hayyim. Clever girl."

I pulled my hand free of his grasp and scooted to the very edge of the bed. "You aren't Raphael."

"And why wouldn't I be?" He replied calmly.

"Because there's a shapeshifting demon on the loose."

"Is that so?"

"Damn right it is. And only they would know the truth."

"I don't suppose you'd believe me if I said I have remained on friendly terms with your friend Damien's father, Azrael?"

"Throwing out names of people I know isn't making you look less guilty, you know."

"I could heal your hand."

"They can impersonate abilities."

"They who?"

"Beelzebub," I snapped.

"I did always appreciate you getting that right," Raphael answered with a wicked grin and red glowing eyes.

"I'm going to fucking kill you," I howled and launched myself at the imposter.

"Now, now, that's not very polite. Remember you do have an image to uphold dear daughter of my enemy." Raphael transformed before my eyes, taking on the androgynous pale skinned form I'd grown up knowing as Beelzebub.

"My father has been nothing, but kind to you," I spat.

"Your father took what was mine and I shall do the same," they hissed before darting out of the room.

I sat there staring after Beelzebub, frozen in place. I'd had them in my grasp and they were gone. Again. How could I be so stupid or unprepared? My father had always made sure I knew how to hold my own in a fight. I'd never let him down until now.

"Oh, I'm sorry, I didn't realize anyone was in here," Raphael said from the doorway.

I tensed and scooted back from him as he entered the small room. He was wearing different clothes, but I was almost certain Beelzebub could change clothing if they wanted to.

"How do I know it's really you?" I said.

"Who else would I be?"

"Forget it. I'm out of here," I muttered and leapt off the table.

"I'd like to help. You were kind enough to look after Miry earlier. I know she's not really my blood, but I'm fond of her, even if not everyone else would agree."

"Do you know Azrael?" I asked.

"The Angel of Death? Once upon a time, eons ago, yes. Before the Fall, we were all like brothers. We bickered of course, but we were kin. Not in a way that mortals would understand, but we were bonded."

"So, you don't keep in touch?"

"I could no more enter the realm of Hell than

he could enter the gates of Heaven. I suppose if we happened to cross paths here on Earth, it would be nice to see him again. Although I don't leave the grounds much. I've got plenty of work to keep me busy. Why do you ask?" After a moment he nodded. "Ah, I suppose you've had a brush with him. Given your last name."

"Yeah. So, you're really *the* Raphael then?"

"I am. Would you mind if I took a look at your hand? I'm guessing it hurts."

"It's sure as shit doesn't tickle."

He gently took my hand between his own, probed the flesh and bone carefully as his hands warmed against mine. "Try not to move."

I sat ramrod still as he worked. The pain subsided and I watched in awe as the bones, tendons and skin knit back together. When he was done, you couldn't even tell I'd had a run-in with a wall.

"How does that feel?" He asked and took a step back.

I flexed the fingers on my hand. "It feels better than new."

"I do aim to please. You don't have to tell me, but did someone do that to you?" He looked so concerned. The slight furrow of his brow tugged at my heart. He really just wanted to help people.

"No one. I got mad and took it out on a wall," I admitted.

"Unlucky for the wall."

"Better for Miry's face."

Raphael laughed. It was soft much like the way he spoke. "Having trouble adjusting?"

"She's just so ignorant … on so many things. Honestly, I wonder how she gets through her day."

"What has she done to make you think that?"

"Called me a liar for one thing. Well okay, maybe I deserved it, but when I tried to tell her the truth, she stuck her head in the sand and pretended it wasn't real."

"Did it challenge things she believed to be true?"

"Obviously, her and everyone else at this school."

"If you need someone to talk to, I've been told I'm quite the good listener."

"Can I ask you something?" I leaned back against the wall behind the bed and studied him.

"Why not?"

"Why'd you choose this side of the fight? All those eons ago, you could have joined up with Lucifer, but you didn't. Why?"

"To be completely honest, I didn't think either side was truly in the right. Yes, they both had their valid points. However, I didn't fully agree with either side. I stayed out of the fight."

"But you still ended up here," I said. "Working for the winners."

"I suppose my neutrality was worth something to Michael and the others. Enough, at least, not to be cast out. So, I treat their children and I keep quiet."

"You could just leave."

"And where might I go, dear? I cannot imagine I'm welcome in Lucifer's domain."

"You aren't his enemy. If you didn't fight against him, he has no reason to distrust you."

"You seem to know quite a bit about his motives and his mind. How might that be?"

"I don't know what you mean," I said, my palms growing sweaty.

"I heard about your outburst in Gabriel's class. That combined with your skills in Uriel's self-defense class lead me to wonder about your true origins. You say your father was one of the lesser known archangels, but I happen to know none of the others have had children in the last century."

"Why would you know that?"

"They ask me to tend to any births to ensure

both mother and child survive. So, I'd know." He crossed his arms over his chest and his expression turned stony. "Now, why don't we be honest with one another, young lady. You clearly have archangel blood. That's impossible to fake."

"How do I know I can trust you?"

"I work at a school with teenagers," he said gesturing to me. "Some of whom make less than wise decisions. If I can keep their confidences, I think I can keep yours."

I swallowed the lump in my throat. "I know Lucifer personally."

"You're rather young to be a confidante of his."

"I'm his daughter."

"Ah. I see. Well, that explains a great many things. Although it does not explain why you are here, running about with Michael's daughter and her friends."

"Believe me, I'd rather not be here any longer than necessary. I've got a job to do though."

"What could Lucifer possibly gain by sending his child behind enemy lines?" Raphael asked. "That's not the angel I remember."

"He doesn't know I'm here," I said. "I came on my own. Something very precious to him was stolen and the thief is hiding here on the grounds."

"Why do I get the feeling this thief possesses the ability to change shape?"

My mouth hung open in surprise at his words. I pressed myself against the wall even more. He unfolded his arms and held his hands up palms out.

"You asked how you knew it was really me when I walked in. I remember Beelzebub and their particular abilities."

"You can't tell Michael any of this. My dad really has no clue what I'm doing here. Even Michael is paranoid and wouldn't believe me. He'd think another war was on the horizon and I refuse to let him hurt my father more than he already has."

"You are very brave to take on such a formidable adversary on your own, Zuri. But I can see that you care deeply for your father and his legacy. May I ask what was taken? Answer me that truthfully and I give you my word I will not speak of this to Michael, for now. I will give you until mid-term. If the issue is not resolved by then, I will have to inform him for the safety of the other students."

"My father's emblem."

"Oh. That's really not good."

"Why is that?"

Raphael rubbed his face with both hands. "Lucifer's Emblem can be used to counteract certain other angelic relics. Although it can also be used to unleash the End of Days."

Well, shit.

16

MIRYAM

"I don't want to go back to my room. Can't I just stay here forever?" I cuddled closer to Chris, burying my face in the junction of his neck and shoulder. We had holed up all day talking and making out. Even eating nachos and soda all because I didn't want to go down to the dining hall. I might run into Zuri if I did and I wasn't ready to see her.

Chris pointed at the dark sky beyond the dorm room window. "You can't. It's almost curfew. Your dad might look away for certain things, but everyone being in their own rooms at 6:30 is not one of them." He sat up, working on detangling me from him. It wasn't easy. "Maybe we can work out something later."

"Maybe?" I pouted. "Try to sound a little more enthusiastic, will ya?"

"Sorry." He leaned over to kiss me. "You know I'd spend all my time with you if I could, Miry, but we both have our own things to do."

"Like what?"

"Homework for one." Chris pulled his backpack out from under his bed before moving to sit at his desk. "You remember homework, right? The stuff you make Ant do for you?"

"Don't forget CeCe. She's the reason I have an A in Music Theory." I bounced off his bed and went to wrap my arms around his chest from behind. Chris pressed his palm against the back of my hand where it rested near his heart, but still seemed way distracted. "What's wrong?" I asked. "You never tell me when stuff is going on. I want to help you. Why don't you let me?"

"I'm good, Mir."

"Yeah, but are *we* good, Chris?"

Chris took my hand and led me around until I was standing to the right side of his desk chair instead of behind it. "We are. There is something you can do for me, though."

"Name it."

"Apologize to Zuri."

I scrunched up my face. "Please … Anything but that."

He pulled me onto his lap. "Just think about it, Miry. Do you want to be in some sort of turf war or whatever with her? Just be the bigger person, apologize, and start getting back to normal. Like it or not, your dad stuck her in your room for a reason. This year will be so much easier if you attempt to get along."

"I guess so," I said slowly. I glanced at the school books he had already spread across his desk. "Are you *sure* you want to do homework right now?"

Chris patted my thigh. "I don't want to, but I have to. Kinda like you apologizing to Zuri."

"Fine." I stood, making sure my uniform was on straight. "But if she kills me or whatever, it's totally your fault."

"Hey, Zuri, I got you this." I stuck out my arm to show off the prize. "Surprise! It's licorice. The twisty kind that you peel apart. It reminded me of you. There's layers, you know?" She doesn't bother to look up from reading my Angelic History textbook. "Sorry it's not a full pack. I ate half of it on the walk over."

"Why would you think I'd want used licorice?"

"It's not used," I said. "I didn't lick it or anything, I just ate some." I waggled the pack in front of her face again. "Want some? It's good."

"Weren't you the one who just told me to not accept candy earlier?"

"That's only if it's from Uncle Uriel. I'm good." I sat on my bed. "At least, I try to be." I took a big bite of candy. "Hey, I'm sorry about earlier. It's just I don't like being lied to and that was one ca-crazy story you told me. The whole throwing a punch thing was because I was bored. I'm not responsible for all my questionable decisions when bored. Seriously, if I had to cop to all of those, I'd be apologizing to the entire school and at least half the staff."

Zuri cracked a smile. "You're not such a good little angel, after all, are you?"

I swung my feet back and forth. "Not even close. It's easy to pretend, though, especially when you know how to look all cute and innocent." I fluttered my eyelashes. "Pretty good, huh?"

Zuri set the book down. She watched me silently for a good two minutes before giving me a hard stare. "I guess I should apologize too. Sorry for trying to kill you earlier. Next time I'll make sure I succeed."

I crinkled my nose. "Oh, ha ha. I'm being serious here and you're all like 'whelp, next time I'll make sure to kill you.' I don't mind morbid humor, but you kinda take it to the next level, you know? Can't you be real with me? Just once? Is it really that hard?"

"I was real with you and you called me a liar."

I tilted my head to the side. "Are you still on that whole 'Satan taught me to sword fight' train? Come on, Zuri. You can't really believe that, right?"

She sat up straighter. "It's Lucifer not Satan, and I can prove it."

I widened my eyes. *This ought to be good.* "Seriously? Good luck with that delusion. If you ask me, there's been something off about you since the second you got here, Zuri. You know way too much about demons. You fight like some thug Fallen. And your last name? Seriously, it's obviously a fake … Like fakeity-fake. It's almost embarrassing that you expect anyone to believe Hayyim is your real last name."

Zuri balled her fists at her side, but to her credit, didn't try to deck me. Her voice was mostly even when she said: "Why do you say that?"

"Oh, come off it," I scoffed. "Anyone who has studied any languages at all knows that Hayyim is Hebrew for 'life.' People used it during the plague to hide from the Angel of Death. What are you hiding from, Zuri? Who are you really?"

Zuri's answer was to take out her phone. She punched in her passcode and held it screen up in her palm, the drone of a dial tone let me know she'd turned on speaker phone. "I said Lucifer taught me to fight and I can prove it."

Oh, this was going to be epic. "Yeah?" I raised both eyebrows. "Prove it."

She scrolled through her contacts, stopping somewhere in the middle around D. She pushed a button. It rung and rung until someone finally answered.

"Hello?" a man's voice said. "Zuri?"

Zuri made eye contact with me. "Hey, Dad, it's me."

ZURI

"Two calls in one day from my teenage daughter. Am I the luckiest father ever?" He replied.

I kept my gaze trained on Miry. "So, I was out shopping and I ran into this girl who says she doesn't believe me when I told her who you were. She's the daughter of some angel named Michael."

"Zuri, are you safe right now?" Dad's concern made his voice jump an octave.

"I can take care of myself. Hang on," I said and flipped the phone to FaceTime, waiting for the connection.

Dad's face popped up on the screen. "Where are you right now?"

"Dad, I'm fine. This girl just bet me I couldn't prove you are who I said you were."

Miry's eyes went wide as the upside-down image of Dad furrowing his brow filled the phone screen. I smirked at her, knowing he could be impressive and a little scary when he wanted to be.

"How do I know you're really Lucifer?" Miry asked, her voice steadier than I would have expected.

"Well I'm afraid I don't have any horns or a tail to show you. My daughter says you are a child of Michael's? Does he still keep that damn sword of his on display like a trophy?"

I watched as Miry tried to form words. I'd seen the sword in his office on the one occasion I'd been there. I honestly hadn't been expecting Dad to go along with this whole charade. I needed to find a way to let him know I knew about the stolen Emblem. "So, you convinced?" I asked, eying Miry.

"You could have just had someone ready, pretending to be your dad."

"Young lady, I don't have a particularly high opinion of Michael, given our history, but I happen to think a great deal of my daughter. So, if she tells you she is the daughter of the Ruler of Hell, believe her," Dad said.

Miry's lips started to form a pout. "Did you really train her in sword fighting?"

"I did."

"She's into fencing or something," I said, trying to cover for the fact he didn't know where I was and so far, my cover story of shopping in New York hadn't been blown. "Look, Dad, thanks for settling this. She owes me some high-end shoes. I'll see you later, bye."

I ended the call before Miry could prod him more and blow my cover. "Happy now?" I tossed the phone on my bed and flopped down next to it.

"He doesn't know you're here, does he?" She sat on her own bed; knees drawn to her chest. The half-eaten package of licorice sat within reach. She tugged a strand loose from the plastic.

"It's better to keep it that way, too. He knows the Emblem's missing, but he doesn't know I know or that I'm trailing the thief. If he did, he'd show up in person to protect me and that would just be more trouble than I want to deal with right now."

"He couldn't come here," Miry said.

I raised an eyebrow. "I'm as Fallen as he is and I'm just fine. Seriously bored though and you all are a bunch of ignorant bitches, but I'm not bursting into flames or shit."

"Dad would like lose his mind if Lucifer showed up."

"No shit. Which is why I'm going to finish what I started and get out of here before World War Three descends on our collective asses."

"How much of what you told us about who you are was even true?" She asked, sucking on the candy.

"Well, my first name was real. And clearly, I'm the daughter of an Archangel, whether you acknowledge him or not."

"But Damien isn't your boyfriend?"

I bit my tongue and mentally counted to five before answering. "Nope. Definitely not my boyfriend."

"So, what's the truth then? Like about your family and stuff?"

I didn't like giving her the details of my life. It felt intrusive and I still didn't think I could trust her to keep her mouth shut when it mattered. She was too eager to be noticed and have praise heaped upon her to believe she was going to stay silent. "I never met my mother. She died when I was born. Broke Dad's heart."

Miry's eyebrows disappeared into her hairline. I bit back a growl of annoyance. "Yes, Lucifer is capable of love. In fact, he's kind of a romantic. I don't have that many half siblings, because when he loses someone he loves, it takes him a long time to get over it."

"I'm sorry you never met your mom. I feel bad saying that I wished mine was dead, now."

I involuntarily touched the bracelet on my wrist. "This was a gift my dad gave to my mom when she found out she was pregnant. I usually don't go anywhere without it. That's why I insisted D come give it to me. Stupid I know."

She shook her head. "That's not stupid. That's like so romantic."

"Whatever," I muttered. "I don't really do mushy stuff."

"You don't have to act tough all the time. It's okay to have feelings."

I snorted. "Oh, I have feelings. I just don't wear them on my sleeve in bright neon colors like you do."

Miry turned her attention to the licorice piece in her hand, nibbling it down to a nub. I could sense she had something else to say, but she wasn't going to come out and say it unless I pushed.

"Look, for the next five minutes you can ask whatever you want I swear to answer truthfully."

"Anything?" Her eyes twinkled with a mischievous glint.

"Excluding anything about sex. Some things should remain private."

"Fine. Um … what's Hell like? Is it really all fire and brimstone?"

I laughed. "Fuck no. I mean, sure there's some brickwork around, but it looks basically like any city you'd find here. Oh, and the only fire is in fireplaces during winter. And before you ask, yes, we get seasons. That whole expression about Hell freezing over is real. It happens every couple of years and it is really annoying. Have you ever tried to scrape ice two feet thick off a window? Even with angelic strength it's a giant pain in the ass."

Miry giggled and slid off the edge of her bed. She crossed the room to sit on my bed, uninvited. "Have you met other demons besides Beelzebub?"

"Yeah. Damien's dated a few. They're okay, not grotesque or anything. Most of them are at least half human anyway so you aren't going to see horns unless you run across an old-school demon. Usually that's just because they're bored."

"How'd you get here?"

"Portal. They don't just go to Jersey."

"If you can be here without exploding, maybe I can actually go to Hell. You said you'd show me the world."

The way she put emphasis on the last sentence sent flashes of warmth into the pit of my stomach. She said it like she wanted to spend time alone together. Not in a roommate sort of way though. "Like I told you before, you wouldn't survive five minutes in Hell."

"But if I had you to show me around, I'd be fine."

"You wouldn't survive the trip. Trust me, I've been traveling via portal for years and it still messes me up."

Miry gave an audible gasp and feigned shock. "The great and powerful Zuri has a weakness?"

"Shut up." I nudged her shoulder playfully, immediately regretting it. She was the daughter of my father's enemy. I still couldn't trust her. I glanced at the clock on my phone. "Two more minutes."

"You convinced everyone that you came from the Middle East campus. How'd you do that?"

"Forgery."

"What?"

"I forged a letter. It's kind of a special skill I've

got. I can forge basically anything. Keys, ID cards, letters."

"Homework?" She said hopefully.

"What is with you and not wanting to do homework? Seriously, I'm questioning your ability to even read."

"I resent that. I can read just fine, thank you. I just don't like doing homework," Miry said, not meeting my gaze.

"You don't like learning new things," I quipped.

"If I did my own homework, I wouldn't get the same grades. I'm not stupid like at all. Sometimes the information just doesn't stick in my brain."

"That's kind of the whole point of homework, Miry. It's to help you figure it out."

"My brain just doesn't work that way."

I knew I was going to regret it the minute the words left my lips, but I said, "I can help you while I'm here."

"How?"

"We'll figure out what makes something stick in your head. People learn in different ways. Maybe you just haven't found the right way for you, yet."

Miry flung herself against the pillows. "Just

another reason for Dad to be disappointed in me. I'm, like, defective."

"Okay, if I'm going to do this, we're going to have to get a few things straight. The first thing is stop whining. It makes me want to punch you. You aren't defective. If your dad makes you feel that way, that's his drama, not yours."

"No one's ever said that to me before," she blinked up at me from her pose on the bed.

"Probably because you don't let anyone get close to you. I guess that's something we have in common. We're both good at putting up a front for other people, letting them see what we want them to see and nothing else."

"Do you think we can start now?"

"I've had a long day, Miry. I just want to crash. Besides, I've got more pressing things to worry about."

Miry cocked her head to one side, her blond hair falling over her face. She blew the strands free of her mouth. "Like what exactly?"

I opened my mouth to tell her about what Raphael had shared, but stopped. Did I want her to know that I had a confidante on campus, one who was supposed to be on her father's side? I didn't have a chance to answer her question before she asked a new one.

"Why's the wall pink?"

I craned my neck to look at the patch job I'd done on the wall. I'd managed to get most of the blood out of the paint and Raphael had been nice enough to get me some plaster. "It was better than punching you in the face."

"You destroyed school property?"

"I fixed it ... Mostly."

"Your angelic healing must be way better than mine." She pointed to her leg and then to my hand. "You can still see a little redness if you look really close, but your hand looks like nothing happened."

"Wrong hand, princess. Besides you aren't the only one who can pay a visit to the first aid room. Raphael actually isn't a half bad healer. When it's actually him."

Miry shot up into a seated position. "You saw Beelzebub? Where? What happened? Are you okay?"

I hung my head. "They were waiting for me in the first aid room. Kinda like they knew I'd be there. I had them and they just took off. I was frozen, like I couldn't move. It won't happen again. Raphael patched me up afterward."

"What aren't you saying? Please, I won't tell

anyone. If we're going to be friends, we have to learn to trust each other."

"Fine. The Emblem that Beelzebub stole, it isn't just a family heirloom. For one thing it can counter other angelic relics like your dad's sword. However, the bigger issue is it can also unleash the End of Days. I have no idea why, but Beelzebub wants to unleash Armageddon."

18

MIRYAM

"I kept quiet for three whole days," I announced to Zuri as we got ready for class, except I was brushing my teeth so it came out more like 'I kep qui fer tee ho daz.' She gave me her patented 'you're high' look which I've come to know and expect whenever I open my mouth to say anything. I spat out my mouthful of toothpaste and turned back to her. "No, really. I haven't told anyone your super-secret amazingly awesome news for three whole days. You should be proud. That's like a record for me."

"What do you want me to do? Give you a cookie?" Zuri jammed her books into her black backpack. "Besides being the kid of the figure head of Fallen Angels while in a school for the asshats who cast him out of Heaven is not amazing or awesome," she added. "It would be like you going to school in Hell."

I tipped my head to the side. "*Is* there an Academy in Hell? What's it called?"

"None of your business."

I crossed my arms over my chest and bounced on my heels a bit. "None Of Your Business Academy has a nice ring to it. I'm kinda partial to Celestial Academy, though. It's where I belong."

"But not where I belong." Zuri slung her backpack over her shoulder and clomped out of the room. I grabbed my pink glittery bag that I had bedazzled myself and followed her.

"You're fitting in pretty okay so far," I said as we walked. "You're way cool at self-defense and better at remembering all the class stuff than me. The only place I have you beat is I remember my way around campus."

"As soon as I get my bearings, we won't have to walk everywhere together." Zuri looked straight ahead instead of at me. "You're way too peppy so early in the morning. It hurts my head to even think about how much sugar or caffeine you had to ingest to get that way."

"Red Bull Gives You Wings. Heh. I never realized how funny that was before. I already got wings, thanks, energy drink." I bounced on my heels again. "Ooh Pixie Stix are amazing if you need like a little legal pick me up. I like the pink ones."

Zuri stopped dead in her tracks and whirled to face me. "Legal? You mean you've done illegal stuff?"

I rolled my eyes. "Duh. You can't put a bunch of teenagers in a boarding school without any parents in sight—except mine, I guess—and expect them not to get up to a little something non parent approved. The normal stuff like fake IDs, keggers in the woods … and even S-E-X."

Zuri snorted. "Did you honestly just spell out sex? Miry, if you're big enough to do it, you're big enough to say it."

"What makes you think Chris and I are having sex?"

She gave me her 'you're high' look again. "So, you just let anyone park their hand on your ass? Not that I care. You do you, but if that boy isn't getting any, he's more of a saint than I thought." She grimaced. "Not that I think of him. Or you. Together. Never mind. Like I said, you do you. I don't care."

I meant to nudge her shoulder in a totally cool conspiratorial way, but she's way taller than me. I ended up leaning my shoulder into her upper arm. I didn't pull away after. "You're right. Chris and I are totally having sex." I did some quick math on my fingers. "Three years, though Dad had this lame 'you can't date until you're sixteen' rule. I showed him, huh? I snuck around. So, does that prove I'm a bad girl?"

"All it proves is you and Saint Boy are horny." Zuri stepped to the left so her arm and my shoulder weren't touching anymore. "You'll have to try harder than that, Miry. The kegger thing sounded mildly interesting, though."

I smiled. "I can totally plan one. It doesn't take long at all. You can invite your friend Damien."

She pursed her lips, staring straight ahead. "No."

"Why not?" I asked. "It will be fun for everyone."

"D is not some sideshow for you and your friends to giggle over."

"I don't giggle … much," I pouted. "Come on, Z! It will be totally awesome. A fun way to let loose and get to know everyone with, uh, booze involved." I mimed drinking. "That always loosens lips, right? I bet you're like a laugh riot when your guard is down."

"If that's what you think, you're going to be awfully disappointed," she said.

"I don't care." I pulled the door to the history classroom open and bounced inside. "I'm going to plan a party. Anyway, you *and* Damien are coming or else—"

Zuri shot me some side eye. "Or else what?"

"Or else I'll never speak to you again."

She laughed. "That would be a dream come true, Miry, not a punishment."

"Oh, ha ha." I flounced over to where Chris was waiting for me at our regular seats. "Just you wait! I'm going to plan it and-and-and make flyers too!"

"What was that all about?" Chris whispered once I sat down. His hand slid up my thigh to rest under my skirt.

"Just Zuri being Zuri and trying to knock a party I want to plan." I leaned over to give him a peck on the cheek. We don't do on the lips in class. "You'll help get it going, won't you, Chris?"

He smiled. "I'd do anything for you, Miry."

I grinned back. "Awesome. Kegger party next weekend. Spread the word."

Uncle Gabriel walked in before Chris could confirm or deny being on board with the party planning. He never had the best timing. "Good morning, ladies and gentlemen. Today's topic may be a little off putting to some of you, but it's essential that you learn it. Demons." A twitter of excited murmuring ran through the class. Finally! We got to the good stuff! "Demons, though we don't talk about them much in the hallowed halls of Celestial Academy, have existed nearly as long as angels have. Just like angels, saints, and archangels, demons can produce offspring. Just like most of you are Nephilim or half angel, half-demon offspring are known as Cambion. Can anyone name common demonic abilities?"

Zuri's hand shot up. At least she was waiting for Uncle Gabriel to call on her instead of just blurting out the answer. He nodded toward her. "Demonic abilities are usually tied to the elements. Weather manipulation. Water manipulation. Shape shifting."

"Ooh, like Beelzebub!" I said without waiting my turn. I clamped my hands over my mouth. "Sorry, Uncle Gabriel."

"That's quite alright, Miryam," Uncle Gabriel's eyes flashed red just for a second before they were back to their usual bright blue. "What do you know about Beelzebub?"

"They hang out in Hell and can shapeshift." I

shrugged. "They can be anyone, anywhere. Kinda freaky, huh?"

"Only to some," Uncle Gabriel murmured. "What our history books won't tell you is Beelzebub was the very first inhabitant of Hell. They were cast down long before the War in Heaven. However, did the Fallen give them any credit for successfully ruling Hell before they got there? No. The Fallen acted, much like angels do, as if everything is theirs. No prior claim mattered." Uncle Gabriel balled his hand into a fist. For just a second, I saw a streak of blonde sprout in his dark brown hair before it was gone.

"I have a question about Lilith!" Chris raised his hand. "I was doing some, uh, independent research over the summer, Archangel Gabriel, and had some questions about Lilith. How, uh, evil is she? Or perceived to be?"

"Evil is a subjective word and concept, young man," Uncle Gabriel said. "Lilith, like all creatures, just wants to be loved. Yes, she is known for kidnapping children and, at times, killing them. Still it is only because she can't have a child of her own. Grief makes us do terrible things sometimes."

Kidnaps kids? "Could Lilith be the one kidnapping all the Celestial Academy kids?" I asked.

"Don't be ridiculous," Zuri cut in. "No one with demon blood can get on campus unless they forge their way in or shapeshift. If Lilith is kidnapping kids, she has an accomplice on the inside."

"She's a demon," I insisted. "Is it so hard to believe she can figure out how to go about her evil plan without help?"

"Why must she be evil?" Chris asked. "Why must any of them be evil?"

"As scintillating as this discussion is," Uncle Gabriel interrupted. "We must remember—"

The door opened and Uncle Gabriel walked in. "Forgive my delay, class, but—" He stopped, his mouth falling open when he saw the second Gabriel standing at the front of the class. The second Gabriel's eyes flashed red again before his features melted away and turned into Beelzebub.

19

ZURI

Shrieks went up from the other students in the class as Beelzebub bared their teeth in Gabriel's direction. The Archangel stood there in the doorway looking confused. I launched myself out of my seat, shoving desks and kids out of my way in my bid to get to the demon.

"I'm going to fucking end you!" I howled, feeling my wings sprout from my shoulder blades.

More gasps went up from the kids around me. Maybe they'd never seen a kid with wings before. Or maybe they were just scared shitless by the demon standing in the front of the room. I reached the demon and almost had my hands around their neck when they shifted in front of me. Their mass redistributed, turning them squat, plump, and four-footed. The term scared-y cat came to mind, but it was a little too much on the nose given that the Leader of Demons was now a striped black and grey Maine Coon cat.

"Wait, they can do that?" Miry yelped.

I looked over my shoulder to glare at her. "What part of shapeshifter was unclear to you?"

"I thought you said just people," she answered.

"The cat's getting away," Miry's boyfriend remarked with a lazy gesture toward the door.

I turned in time to see Beelzebub as a cat dart between Gabriel's legs, leaving the Archangel to shriek like a child. *What a fucking pansy.* I shouldered past the angel and into the hallway. I caught the flick of a bushy tail off to my left and kicked off the ground, suddenly grateful Michael had decided vaulted ceilings were a must have in this place. It gave me room to glide.

Maybe the demon would get sloppy and lead me right to the Emblem. There was no way I'd let Beelzebub start the apocalypse. Their little tirade in class gave me some perspective on their motivation. From their perspective, Dad and the other Fallen had come in and taken control of Hell without a second thought. It still didn't explain their beef with humanity. The End of Days was meant to wipe the earth of humans, the nuclear option. What had humans done to them? They hadn't even existed when Beelzebub was created.

News of our imposter angel hadn't yet spread as I banked right and caught up to Beelzebub. I reached down to scoop them up when they shifted again, going even smaller into a tiny white mouse, scurrying into a crack in the wall.

"Damn it." I landed and fought the urge to punch yet another wall. I didn't need a repeat of a few days earlier. Although, a consultation with Raphael wasn't necessarily a bad idea.

***

"You really need to stop picking fights with inanimate objects," Raphael said when I walked in clutching a bruised hand.

"I didn't break any bones this time," I replied and sat down on the medical exam bed.

"That just means you're learning to be more strategic in your self-harm. That's not exactly a good thing."

"I needed an excuse to see you," I admitted as he placed both of his hands around mine.

The healing warmth of his power washed over me and took with it not only the ache in my hand, but some of the anxiety lingering over the potential Armageddon.

"And why would you need to see me?"

"I had another run-in with Beelzebub. They were impersonating Archangel Gabriel. I almost had them before they shifted into something I couldn't catch. I feel like they are toying with me. They have to realize I know what their endgame is."

"You are only one person, Zuri. Despite what you may believe, this is not your burden to bear alone," Raphael said. "As much as I would not wish to see what would happen were Michael and Lucifer to come face to face, perhaps you should allow your father to deal with this. After all, it is his relic. Not yours."

"It will be mine one day," I said. "And I need to prove that I can keep it safe."

Raphael shook his head. "I will never understand why they put so much pressure on their children. It's entirely unfair."

"Is there anything else you know about how the Emblem unlocks the End of Days?"

"I'm afraid that's all I know. Your father may have more answers. However, if you're determined to complete this insane task on your own,

I suspect you don't want him to provide the information."

"Nope. Although I might have an idea of where to look now that I think about it. Thanks for the chat and the healing touch."

"If you come in here again having lost a battle with another wall, I'm going to have to report your behavior to Michael. Don't make me do that."

I wanted to laugh off his threat, but the look on his face told me he was dead serious. "Got it."

I left his office and walked back toward the classroom. I doubted anyone would still be in class, but I needed to get my bag. Halfway there, my phone rang in my pocket. "Shit," I muttered as I realized I hadn't set it to vibrate.

"Hello?" I didn't check the caller ID before I answered.

"Have you looked outside lately?" Damien asked.

"No. Why?"

"You might want to. Also, you should change your password on your phone."

"Why?"

"I just got a text from someone claiming to be your roommate inviting me to some party this weekend."

"Fucking Miry. I'm going to punch that little shit in the face for touching my stuff." I moved to a window and peered outside. "It's a little rainy out, but nothing unusu—oh damn." The rain had rapidly given way to large snowflakes. What the … in September … in Georgia.

"It's like that everywhere. Weather going kind of weird."

"I need to call you back. I need to check something. Also, come or don't come. I don't care."

"Oh, I'm coming. She assured me it won't be on school grounds. Yeah and there's booze."

"Great. Guess I'll see you this weekend."

I made it back to the classroom to find Miry sitting there without her boy toy entourage. "What are you doing just sitting here?"

"I told them I wanted to wait for you to come back. And don't worry, I didn't say anything to them about you know … your secret identity."

"How do I know it's you?" I said, stopping short of the desk.

"I told you I'm throwing a kegger this weekend," she said with a pout.

"You said that when Beelzebub was in the room. Try again."

"You promised to help me with homework. Oh, and you even acted like I couldn't possibly have done anything bad, because I'm Michael's daughter. Also, Pixie Stix are delicious especially pink ones."

"Fine, you're who you say you are. Let's get out of here."

"Dad heard about Beelzebub and cancelled classes for the rest of the day. He's like searching or whatever. I thought you could maybe train me on sword fighting. I know I said I don't want to do my own fighting, but maybe you're right and I should know how to do it."

"I guess. But not here. I need somewhere with a computer connection first."

"You can borrow my computer," Miry said cheerily.

I didn't want to think about what nerdy porn lived on her computer, but I retrieved my bag and followed her back to the dorm. She passed over her sparkly pink laptop—did everything this girl own have to be bright pink? Then she sat back and watched as I stuck the flash drive I'd brought back from Hell into one of the ports.

"That's not going to give my computer a virus is it?"

"Not unless you've been to sketchy porn sites recently," I muttered and unzipped the computer files. I brought up the main database and skimmed it for references to the Emblem and End of Days.

"What are you looking for anyway?" Miry peered over my shoulder.

"We know the Emblem somehow brings about the End of Days. If you haven't noticed it's been snowing which is some weird weather shit especially for Georgia. We can't exactly stop Beelzebub if we don't know what we're up against."

"Oh, right. Where'd you get all this information anyway?"

"Dad has an archive. I may have copied the database back when I popped home to pick up a few things."

"Ooh, so that has like everything in it about what happened after the War in Heaven?"

"Yes, their personal accounts of what went down plus information they don't want getting out. Now shut up and let me focus."

I tried my best to block Miry out as I searched the database for information on the Emblem. Finally, at the very end of the search results was an entry listed under the heading Armageddon. *Helpful.* I skimmed it and my blood went cold.

"Uh, am I reading that right. It says Lucifer's blood unlocks it?"

"Not just his blood. His bloodline. Which means anyone who shares his lineage."

"Meaning you," Miry offered.

"Fuck me ... they've already got some of my blood."

"How?"

"My little incident with the wall over there."

"Yeah, but that wasn't like a lot or anything."

"It's not like it's a recipe, Miry. We don't know how much blood it takes to unlock things. Besides if the weather is already going all wonky, we could already be too late."

"I think we'd notice if like the Riders of the Apocalypse showed up. Aren't they supposed to be all scary and riding on big horses?"

"I ... I don't know. It's possible. Look, can we talk about something else. Anything else?" I wasn't in the mood to contemplate my own mortality. I had never believed I'd live forever, but I was pretty certain I'd make it beyond eighteen. And there was no way Dad would ever be tricked into bleeding openly.

"Like what?"

I glanced around the room. "Self-defense training. You wanted me to teach you. So, let's do it."

"We don't have swords," Miry commented.

"We don't need them. You got broom handles or anything like that?" I set the laptop aside and swiveled in the chair to face her.

Miry wrinkled her nose. "No."

"Well, your first lesson is to go find some."

Miry gave me an eye roll, but flounced out of the room, coming back five minutes later with two brooms. "Here."

I took the first one, balanced it over my leg and broke the brush head off. Miry gave a gasp of surprise at the destruction of property. I didn't care. I could always fix it later. I gave the second broom the same treatment and tossed one to her.

"This didn't work last time," Miry said.

"That's because we weren't doing it right. This time, I'm going to show you how to do the move. Then I'm going to walk you through it step by step verbally and physically at the same time."

"Do you think it will work?"

"Only one way to find out."

I twirled the broom handle in my right hand and planted my feet shoulder width apart. "Okay, I'm going to show you a basic blocking move." I turned my torso to the side, brought the handle up and locked my elbow.

"Seems easy enough," Miry said. Still when she

tried to mimic what I did, she only succeeded in fumbling the handle.

"I said I'd show you step by step." I set my impromptu sword aside and moved to stand behind her. "Here, put your feet shoulder width apart." I nudged her feet farther apart. "You want to hold the sword in your dominant hand."

She passed the handle to her left hand. "Maybe that was the problem?"

"Focus." I wrapped my hands around her waist, trying not to take note of her curves and the feel of her body beneath my fingertips. "Now, you pivot in the opposite direction." Then I wrapped a hand around her left wrist and brought it up to block. "Next you move to block the incoming blow."

"I think I get it, now," she said.

I stepped back, heat winding its way through me in a very uncomfortable manner. I pushed back any thoughts that involved me and Miry touching. I watched her go through the motions a few times.

"Good, now we're going to see if you can put it into practice." I crossed to stand opposite her.

"Are you going to give me some warning this time?" She asked with a hopeful grin.

I swung and she gave a little squeal as she pivoted and brought her arm up to block me. The broom handles collided with a 'thwack.' We both stared at each other. "Guess we figured out your learning style, princess."

MIRY INSISTED we do one self-defense move a day until the weekend. So she had something to show off to her friends at the party. I didn't want to admit it, but it was a welcome distraction from the possibility that I could be dead any day now. How Michael and the other Archangels didn't catch wind of Miry's little party in the woods is beyond me. Considering everyone in school was talking about it in stage whispers that anyone could overhear.

"I'm so glad Damien is coming," Miry said as we hefted a keg of beer out into the woods.

"I still can't believe you stole my phone and got his number," I grumbled as my grip on the barrel slipped, sending both of us staggering sideways.

"Well, you wouldn't have invited him if I didn't take the first step," she said in a sing-song voice.

I still wasn't convinced she understood what

being gay meant. I got the distinct impression she was trying to orchestrate some sort of party hook-up. "Also, why are we carrying all the heavy shit and the boys aren't doing anything?"

Miry's boyfriend and Glasses were sitting around the beginnings of a campfire. "Yeah, guys, you could like help," Miry muttered.

Glasses for his part got to his feet and helped settle the keg by a nearby tree. My phone buzzed in my pocket. I pulled it out to see a text from Damien. "I'll be back. Got a friend to pick up."

"Tell him I said hi," Miry called as I trudged up the small incline that led to the front gates.

Damien stood there in a hoodie and jeans. Despite the fact it was chilly and a little drizzly, he stood there without a jacket. "You are gonna freeze your ass off," I commented.

"Not if I find me a cute little angel to keep me warm," he said with a smirk.

"You are disgusting," I retorted, but looped an arm around his shoulders and ushered him to the party spot.

"So, your dad's been riding my ass about where you are," he said before we reached Miry and her friends.

"What'd you say?"

"That I hadn't heard from you. Which was basically the truth. Z, you have to come home. Please. This is getting out of hand."

"I just need a little more time. Look, I'm close to getting it back."

"Why is it so important that you get it back? I get you are loyal to your dad and everything, but it's just some old relic from a time everyone would rather forget."

"Because it can start the End of Days. And I'm pretty sure we're already on our way there. It's not just about my family honor, D. it's about protecting the world from a demon's hissy fit."

"Well, shit."

"Look, for now can we just focus on getting through what is sure to be a lame ass party?"

"Point me to the beer."

I didn't know how it was possible, but most of the older students had already descended on the spot by the time we got back. Beer pong was in full swing off to one side of the campfire. Couples had paired off to dance or make out and probably hook up out of view. I searched the group for Miry, figuring she should at least say hello to Damien before he went off in search of his next romantic failure.

"So, this is what a good kid's party looks like.

Somehow, I'm not surprised," Damien commented with a snort.

"Hey, I warned you it was going to be lame," I told him.

"Well, where's your new bestie?"

"She's not my bestie. And the fact that word just passed both of our lips makes me want to hurl. I don't know where she is, but you'll probably see her somewhere. Go forth and get horny, weirdo."

Damien did just that, melting into the crowd by the campfire. I spotted Miry's boyfriend standing by the keg and marched over.

"Hey, have you seen your girlfriend?" I called, tapping him on the shoulder.

He turned around, his gaze already unfocused by alcohol. "Nope. Why?"

"I'm looking for her."

"You know she's not available, right?"

I stared at him, mouth agape. "Dude, I'm not into your girlfriend. Though, if you ask me, you aren't giving her what she really needs."

He staggered forward. "And what's that, new girl?"

"A reality check. She's got issues and all you do is coddle her. She isn't going to learn to survive if she's treated like a precious little princess who can't do things for herself."

"I'm protecting Miry, because she's special."

"Please … I bet you're only boning her, because she's the daughter of the most famous archangel besides Lucifer," I scoffed.

"My ears are like burning. Are you two fighting over me?" Miry appeared at her boyfriend's side.

"I just wanted you to say hey to D before he went off in search of an angel to deflower or whatever. But he's already gone so I guess you missed your shot," I said.

"Oh. I'm sure I'll see him around. Hey, can we talk somewhere a little private? It's about … you know …" She made vague miming motions that made no sense to me.

"Sure, whatever."

She led the way to a path that wove between the trees away from the party. I heard something that sounded like a moan, but kept walking. I didn't need to see someone doing the nasty.

"What do you need to tell me?"

"Oh, nothing, really. I just wanted to get you away from all the party noise," Miry answered.

"Why?"

She didn't answer. Instead she grabbed the

front of my shirt and kissed me hard on the lips. My vision went fuzzy and not from the sudden presence of her body pressed to mine. Something was off. I pushed her away and lost my balance, landing hard on my ass. I gazed up at her as confusion and arousal swirled in my mind.

"What the fuck is wrong with you?" I said. At least those were the words I'd intended to say. They came out a slurred mess as the world darkened around me. Miry peered down at me, her face morphing into that of Beelzebub before the sweet silence of unconsciousness pulled me under.

2 0

MIRYAM

My eyes fluttered open before I closed them again. Something was chittering somewhere off to my left. Some sort of bird or squirrel or something. I'm not sure what, but it was making noise to the timing of the pounding in my head. *Yuck.* I didn't drink any booze. Why did my head feel all fuzzy like someone slipped me Angel Blood? Double yuck. So, help me, if someone spiked the keg, I'd go all sword fighting ninja on their butt. Just like Zuri had taught me.

Zuri. I sat up. I rubbed my head, pulling twigs and leaves out of my hair. I threw them at the noisy critter. Stop it already, little dude. The last thing I remembered before waking up in the dirt was Zuri asking me to go somewhere private. She seemed a little too flouncy though. I mean, that was my thing, not hers. I went anyway though. She, uh, got me to let my guard down and then … boom … knocked out on the ground. Only it wasn't Zuri, was it? Not really. I massaged my temples with two fingers, forcing my hazy memory to crystalize. No, it wasn't Zuri. It was Beelzebub, which meant—

"Zuri!" I reconsidered my decision to jump to my feet when the world tipped and spun around me. I almost threw up, but saved myself the disgrace of vomit breath at the last minute. I grabbed a tree and waited for the ground to stop being the sky. "Zuri, are you out here?"

No answer. What did I expect? For her to go like 'I'm totally over here, M, don't worry.' Even if Beelzebub wasn't causing drama, she'd never do that.

I stumbled back to the base camp. There was still no sign of Zuri, but I did spot her friend Damien. It took a couple tries and lots of tree hugging, but I made it over to where he sat with CeCe in his lap. "Hey, like sorry to interrupt and all that, but have you seen Zuri?"

He removed his lips from CeCe's long enough to say: "Nope. She went off with you, remember?"

I crossed my arms over my chest and tapped

my foot. This party was turning into a major bummer. "No, she didn't. I've been, like, drugged up in the woods."

"Kinky," he smirked.

CeCe giggled at his non-humor. "Just relax and have fun, Miry." She winked at Damien. "I know I am."

"Same." He turned so their backs were facing me. Lame.

"Fine, but if Zuri is like killed by that demon non-gender specific dude, it's not my fault. I warned you."

"Dude is gender specific," Damien mumbled.

"It used to be, but now it's just a catch all." I picked a few more leaves out of my hair. "Did you hear the rest of what I said? Zuri might be in trouble."

"Out of everyone at this angel school lame ass party, princess, my money is on Zuri for being the only one able to take care of herself. Now, if you'll excuse me …" He went back to making out with CeCe.

"Fine, but I warned you," I reminded him. "Don't go all freaking out when something horrible happens to her. Just remember I told you so." I waited for Damien to answer. When he went right on sucking CeCe's face instead of helping me, I wandered off in search of Chris. I found him parked next to the keg, red plastic cups full of beer in both hands.

"Hey." He handed me one of the cups. "Where have you been?"

"I don't know." I gestured back in the direction I came from. "Lost in the woods somewhere. It was like, totally awful, Chris. I think Beelzebub pretended to be Zuri to trick me and—"

"What are you talking about?" Chris took a swig of beer. "You and Zuri left together like fifteen minutes ago. I was about to go look for you." He took another long drink from his cup, tipping it back to get the last dregs from the bottom. "Right after I finished my drink."

"But that's what I'm trying to tell everyone and no one will listen," I said. "Whoever Zuri left with wasn't me. It was Beelzebub. You weren't going off to find me, you were going off to find Beelzebub."

Chris frowned, checking the bottom of his cup. "Well, shit."

I wasn't sure if he was upset about the lack of beer or the fact a totally high-level demon was running around impersonating me and who knows how many other people. "So, can like Ant help or what?"

"Help with what?" Ant asked, totally showing up right when I needed him most.

"Finding Zuri." I bounced on my heels. "Whatdaya need to make that happen?"

"Having something of hers helps focus the incantation, but I can go off of anything really," Ant said. "Do you have a picture so I can vibe with the energy?"

"Forgot what she looks like, huh?" Chris snickered. He took my beer cup away from me and downed it for me.

Ant's cheeks turned almost as red as his hair. "*No.* I just think it will help me focus, that's all."

I pulled my phone out of my bra which is where I always keep it if I don't have my bag or pockets. I unlocked it, opened the picture roll, and scrolled to a sideview of Zuri eating pasta from a can. The fork was half-raised to her mouth. I managed to capture a 'get that frigging camera out of my face before I kill you' look on her face which, come to think of, isn't that hard since that's her standard facial expression. I showed the pic to Ant. "Will this do?"

"Send it to me," he said. "It's good enough."

I texted him the picture. As soon as it popped up, he held his hand over the pic while muttering the Prayer to St. Anthony. His phone glowed slightly as his find lost things ability took hold. He swiveled in a circle before pointing off to the woods. "That way."

Ant took off in the direction he pointed, pulled by the location ability looking for its mark. I grabbed Chris by the arm and drug him along after Ant. "Hey! Get with the program!" I yelled at Damien when we passed him and CeCe still in an impressively long lip lock. "Zuri is in trouble and needs our help! *All* of our help."

"Why didn't you say so in the first place, princess?"

Damien stood, yanking CeCe up with him. I didn't think her Saint Cecelia music abilities would be useful up against a shapeshifting de-mon, but whatever. If it got the hellion on our side, I didn't care. Zuri needed us and that's all that mattered. Zuri needed us, now.

21

ZURI

My head throbbed as the world came back to me. I groaned and the sound made my ears hurt. *What the fuck happened?* I lay still, trying to let my brain make sense of the situation. Miry had kissed me. No, *not* Miry. Beelzebub pretending to be Miry. For a second, I couldn't figure out what purpose the demon would have to lure me away, but then it hit me, and I sat bolt upright.

The Emblem.

My stomach churned, threatening to bring up dinner. I couldn't be sure if it was from the realization or whatever Beelzebub had used to knock me out. I sucked down shallow breaths to contain the nausea, but failed. At least I was quick enough to not vomit all over myself. As I sat back, I felt pressure and restricted movement on my ankles and wrists. I tugged and found thick chains snaking their way to anchor points on the wall behind me.

"You coward. You can't even face me on even footing?" I yelled; my throat still raw from throwing up.

"It isn't personal. You didn't ask to be born of your father's blood," Beelzebub answered, stepping into view in their true form.

"Why are you even doing this? So, you're pissed at Dad for showing up and claiming Hell. Newsflash asshole, they didn't have a choice. They got kicked out and it wasn't like they could exist on the human plane. So, they went where they could."

"For someone who is so intelligent, you truly are ignorant, aren't you?" They said, pacing back and forth.

If I could keep them talking long enough, maybe Damien would realize something was wrong and come looking for me. "So explain it to me, then? If you're going to kill me, what harm can it do?"

Their red eyes glowed like hot coals and they crossed their arms over their chest. "I was the Leader of Hell. It was my domain for eons, long before humanity even existed. They had no right to come in and take it from me."

"You're still the Leader of Demons. You have your own followers. So your domain isn't as big as it used to be. It's called sharing. That still doesn't explain why you are bent on unleashing the End of Days."

"I was the one who should have been granted this realm. God created me before his fallible little pets. I should have been able to reign here, but no, God felt me too malleable and flawed. Ha, imagine, the creator only seeing failure in their creation and not their own skills." They began pacing the length of the room. "But I knew that God's skills were flawed. Look at humanity. They are forever sniping at one another over petty grievances. They've had thousands of years on this planet and what have they done with it? Nothing. They've ruined it. So, now, it's the time for demons to take their rightful place. If we cannot have Hell, we will take this place."

"You're insane," I said, continuing to tug on the restraints. Where was that angelic strength when I needed it?

"I am quite sane, child. I do regret that it must come to this. You more than most were kind to me. You respected me in a way no others did."

"So, you got dealt a shitty hand, so what? That doesn't make you special. It means you're just like the rest of us. We all get mad at our parents, but we're adult enough not to hold grudges. It's time to accept what you've actually got."

"You aren't going to talk me out of this." They turned their back and pulled the Emblem from a spot I couldn't see.

It called to me like it had the day it was stolen. I reached my hands toward it, like reaching out would get me closer. *Was it because it wanted my blood?* Had I always been drawn to it, because I could unleash Hell on Earth? Is that why Dad had kept it under lock and key? Beelzebub took the pole of the standard and smashed it to pieces, pulling the fabric with the family crest off the top. They spread it along the floor. I glanced around me and at my feet, noticing chalk markings for the first time.

"Please, you said it yourself you like me. Why would you want to hurt me then? Besides, Dad has all but said I inherit Hell when he decides to step down. We can work something out, give you more territory, more authority. Whatever you want," I bargained.

Beelzebub bent down until we were nose to nose. "Your father has ruled for eons. I am tired of waiting. The time of demons is now. Don't worry, I'm sure your father will know you did not go willingly."

I opened my mouth to respond or maybe just spit in their face when a tiny squeak passed through my throat. Heat rippled upward from my stomach and my shackled hands shook as I reached down blindly to feel the hilt of a knife protruding from my belly. If the chains hadn't been restricting my movements, and in that moment keeping me somewhat upright, I would have collapsed.

The chalk markings around me seemed to blur as my fingers went numb and I tried to pull the knife free. "Argh." Squelching sounds filled my ears as icy fingers danced over every piece of exposed flesh on my body. The blade was serrated and wickedly shaped. The knife slipped from my blood-stained fingers.

"It will be so much easier if you just let go and give in to the inevitable," Beelzebub said from somewhere off to my right.

I had enough muscle control to flip them off. Around me, the chalk began to glow as my blood oozed over the stone beneath me, slithering like a snake toward the Emblem. It shimmered with a sickly silver haze as my blood touched the fabric.

A thunderous crack echoed in the distance, like a tree splitting down the middle and falling in the forest. For all I knew, a tree had in fact fallen. I had no concept of how far Beelzebub had dragged me from the woods. A dull sensation wrapped itself around my body and begged my mind to just give in.

No. Fuck that.

I refused to just sit back and let this demon asshole with a chip on their shoulder ruin my entire life and world just because of a little blood loss. I dragged myself upright and the cuffs on my wrists slid up to the first joint on my thumbs. Apparently, Beelzebub hadn't counted on blood making my hands slippery. I used it to my advantage, drenching my hands in blood—which given the rate at which it was leaving my body wasn't difficult—and slid the cuffs off. Getting my feet free wouldn't be as simple, but I managed to grab the chain and tug, summon what little angelic strength remained to pull it free of the wall. The ceiling above me shook and dust rained down on me.

Vaulted ceilings.

Beelzebub had taken me back to campus. If only Michael could see me and the horrible shit about to be unleashed. If people found out it came from the supposed seat of angelic power, oh how people would lose their faith in the Archangels. It was honestly quite ingenious.

"Hey, douchebag, you're not going to win that easily," I called, staggering to my feet. I snatched a broken piece of wood as my weapon of choice. Despite my ankles still being shackled together, I moved with a little grace.

"You are so much like your mother. Fighting when there is no hope of success," Beelzebub taunted.

"Don't you *ever* talk about my mother," I howled and lunged.

The circle around me flared with reddish light as one of the sets of chalk markings vanished and reappeared in blood red hues on the Emblem. One of the stars in the family crest disappeared as well and the floor shook. Whatever kept the End of Days in check was slowly being undone the more I bled. If I had to guess, as soon as all the chalk markings were gone, saving humanity would be a lost cause. It also appeared that I was stuck in this damn circle.

"Be a good little girl and do as you are told. Now, *sit down*," Beelzebub boomed.

I sunk to my butt as if I had no control over my limbs. The broken piece of wood clattered against the stone and rolled into the ever-expanding pool of my blood. Making a stand had only made things worse. My vision went dark at the edges and I shivered as the warmth of the blood keeping me alive left me little by little.

"Zuri?" I could swear I heard Miry's voice in the distance, but that wasn't possible. She wouldn't come for me. No one even knew I was missing.

Wherever Beelzebub had stashed me was probably in the last place any of them would look. There was little chance Dad would come to my rescue. If he knew the Emblem was in play, he had to know that his blood would do just as good as mine. Who knew if both of ours would speed things up or make it a thousand-fold worse?

"It's locked," a girl's voice said from over my left shoulder. I didn't recognize it.

Someone shrieked and with a boom a door went flying off its hinges, slamming into the wall opposite it, sending millions of spiderweb cracks through the masonry. I thought I spotted a hooded figure at the very edge of what remained of my peripheral vision. Azrael. At least I'd see a familiar face before I died.

"What is going on here?" Dad's voice echoed in the room.

I thought I heard clamoring footsteps as more people filled the already cramped space.

"Oh my God, Zuri!" Miry squealed.

"Stay back," I rasped, unsuccessfully trying to press the edges of the knife wound closed.

"How dare you harm my child," Dad bellowed, stepping into my field of vision.

"Dad, no." He didn't seem to hear me. Instead, his wings burst forth from his shoulder blades, reaching from one side of the room to the other. He produced a sword from somewhere and charged at the demon.

I should have watched them fight. Dad was always such a formidable fighter, but my attention was focused too much on the markings taking over the Emblem. Only one row of chalk remained. Three more hooded figures had joined the first. I'd been wrong. It wasn't Azrael come to carry me to my mother beyond the veil. The Horsemen were waiting for the final seal to be broken so they could descend on humanity and ravage it.

"How do we stop it?" Damien's voice filled my ears.

"Can't," I rasped. "Too late."

"No. I refuse to believe that. We did not find

you here just to, like, watch you die," Miry re-torted, hands on her hips.

For a brief moment, I almost wished she had kissed me. She could be annoying as fuck, but sometimes, like now, she was endearing and kind of sweet. She'd kept my secret and even though I was the daughter of her father's sworn enemy, she'd been nice to me. "Sorry I was such a bitch," I croaked.

"You can apologize when you aren't bleeding everywhere," she answered.

I laughed as everything went cold and heavy. I could feel my heart slowing as it lacked any blood to keep pumping. Before my eyes, Miry's face went stony and determined as a massive blade with a gold hilt appeared in her hands. She looked momentarily surprised to be holding it before she slammed it down along the chalk line that remained. With a metallic ring, the chalk line broke and the Horsemen began to fade.

Nice to know I'd survived long enough to watch Miryam bat-Michael save the fucking world.

22

MIRYAM

I blinked and everything seemed to come back into focus. Zuri bleeding, Beelzebub and *the* Lucifer locked in some sort of mortal combat fight thingy, the voodoo demon Apocalypse Now chalk circle smeared, and me with Dad's sword in my hands. *How did that happen again?* I remembered focusing like Dad had taught me. I focused with all my might to manifest the sword to me, and somehow it worked. It *finally* worked. Maybe I just needed to want it bad enough. Saving the world was totally a 'wanting it bad enough' moment.

Dad's sword clattered out of my now useless hands. I didn't know how to use it. The second it appeared I felt like I was on autopilot. The sword knew what to do, but I didn't.

"Miry, get away from there. You could get hurt." Chris pulled me back from the drama. He held me against him, his arms wrapped tight around my upper torso.

"Did you see what I did, Chris?" I asked. "I totally manifested Dad's sword. I've been trying for years and I actually did it. I actually did it."

"Uh, the horsemen may be gone, but we have other things to worry about." Damien pointed at a Non-Horseman robed figure that had materialized in the center of the room. "Meet my dad, Azrael. Someone is going to die."

"Your dad is the Angel of Death?" CeCe whispered. "That is so cool."

"Why are you even here, CeCe?" Ant took a hit off his asthma inhaler. "Making out with the demon kid doesn't give you an automatic pass into the group."

"I'm not a demon, douche nozzle," Damien snapped. "I'm Fallen. Get it right."

"*Guys*, more important things are at hand." Chris gestured to all the cray-cray bananas stuff happening around us. "This isn't a kung fu movie where the bad guys wait patiently for us to stop arguing before they try to kill us."

"So, like who are the bad guys?" I asked. "I don't even like know anymore. Dad always said the Fallen, but they're not the ones that tried to end us all. Beelzebub is."

I looked around me again, still in awe of everything going on around us. Angel-Demon fight to the death. Bloody stolen relic that almost brought on the apocalypse. Reaper just about to reap. Zuri looking like she's auditioning for a murder-death-kill mystery escape room. Until now, the most exciting thing to happen at Celestial Academy was the unsolved kidnappings. Now we had like a million other things a ton worse all happening at once and in the basement of all places.

"The emblem," Zuri croaked, blood bubbling up and leaking out of the side of her mouth. "Get the blood off the banner."

"How?" I looked at the sword laying half in and half out of the chalk circle. "I'm not sure I can use that again. It was totally a fluke the first time around."

"Blood off emblem," Zuri insisted right as her eyes rolled back in her head and she passed out. *Oh, that's so not good.*

Azrael totally wasn't one of the guys waiting around for us to stop arguing and make up our minds on our plan of action. While Zuri was telling us what to do, he took slow measured steps toward her. He stopped right on the edge of the chalk circle before extending his cloaked arm, one finger pointing directly at Zuri.

"Zuri bat-Lucifer, I am here to reap your soul."

"Oh, heck, no." I broke free from Chris' grasp and ran to Zuri. I picked up Dad's sword and held it out in front of me, pointy side up, ready to take on the Angel of Death himself in order to save my friend. "I'm Miryam, daughter of Archangel Michael, and I will not let you take her."

"Neither will I." Damien stepped in front of Zuri, too. He stood so close his shoes were touching mine. "Can't you look the other way for once, Dad? This isn't some random reap. It's Zuri. C'mon just … I don't know, cut us some slack, will ya? I'll go to the Reaper Academy. You've been harping on that for years. I'll go, Dad. I'll go if you save her."

Azrael lowered his hood. I sucked in my breath and almost dropped Dad's sword. He was surprisingly handsome for a dude that went around collecting the dead. Not that looks really made a difference in job performance. Still if I was dying and on the fence about going all out and kicking the bucket or not, I'd go if Hot Azrael showed up to collect me.

"I'll give you one chance at reprieve," Azrael said. "You won't be so fortunate the next time I come calling for hers or anyone else's soul."

"Tell us what to do," I said. "I … I mean we'll … do anything."

"As Zuri herself said, clean the emblem." Azrael nodded toward the bloodied, gross cloth laying in the center of the broken chalk circle. "Until it is, shall we say refreshed, your healing magic will not work on her. After, well, after," he shrugged. "After is up to you, now isn't it?"

"But we don't know *how* to clean the emblem," I whined. My lower lip quivered, getting ready for a pout. I bit it instead. I couldn't be a whiny baby when Zuri's life hung in the balance.

"You're smart kids." Azrael took a step back to give us room to work. "Figure it out."

"Outta my way, amateurs," Uncle Uriel yelled as he charged down the basement stairs with some weird glowing rope thingy in his hands. "You act like you've never fought in a Heavenly war before."

"That's because we haven't," Chris grumbled.

"Oh, goodness, that's quite a large amount of blood." Uncle Gabriel paused on the last step. He hugged the railing, puffing his cheeks out in the universal sign for 'I'm gonna throw up' before he blew chunks over the railing. He straightened before wiping his mouth on his sleeve. "Oh, dear. That was unfortunate. I'll … I'll find someone to clean that up and fetch Raphael. This is by far more his level of expertise. Not mine."

"Dipshit," Uncle Uriel muttered. He unrolled his rope thingy. It looked like a cross between a lasso and a whip. I did *not* want to know why he had that. Like, at all. "Combined, angelic relics can take down the emblem's protective powers. Individually, the lariat can cleanse it."

"This is a really weird time for a teaching moment," CeCe observed.

I focused on Chris, Ant, and CeCe standing near the staircase. I don't know how I knew this, but this fight—no, this battle—was no place for saint kids. They needed to get out of here … Like, now. "Chris, take Ant and CeCe someplace safe," I said.

He shook his head. "I'm not leaving you."

"I'll be okay." I managed to smile, though I was feeling far from confident in that assessment of my safety. "I'm Miryam bat-Michael, remember? I got this."

Chris pressed a kiss into his palm and held it out to me. "Promise me you'll be careful, Miry."

I smiled again, repeating "I got this."

"That's not what I asked, but I'll take it for now." Chris rounded up Ant and CeCe, as a group they headed up the stairs. I let out the breath I didn't know I was holding once I heard the door close behind them.

I swiveled to check on Zuri. Uncle Uriel was using his lasso thing like a whip, muttering about "cleansing the wicked" with each strike. Whatever he was doing, it was working. The blood peeled off the emblem like a fruit roll up being pulled from wax paper. The last strike broke it in two pieces. Uncle Uriel stood up straight, breathing heavy.

"Your turn, Miryam," he said. "Show your dad why he shouldn't call the reaper on you."

"I, uh, have like no idea what you mean by that, but okay."

Uncle Uriel bounded away to help Lucifer in what looked like a pretty evenly matched fight with Beelzebub. They'd spent the whole-time circling, striking, and blocking each other that I doubted Lucifer even knew how bad of shape Zuri truly was in.

"Hey, Luci, good to see you again." Uncle Uriel

sent his glowing rope flashing through the air at Beelzebub. It wrapped around the demon's upper body and arms, trapping them on the spot. "If you needed my help to end this shitshow, all you had to do was ask."

"I didn't ask," Lucifer said. "The relic must have called to you." He took the time to look around the room for the first time since I think we, like, busted down the door to get here. Uncle Raphael and Uncle Gabriel stood at the bottom of the staircase, assessing the situation or, maybe, the damage. Everyone was here except Dad.

"It must have called to all of us," Uncle Raphael said. He beat his wings once, gliding to Zuri's side. He examined her, his frown deepening with each new vital check. "My medical equipment will do no good for her now. Our only chance of saving her is angelic healing." He positioned his hands over Zuri's bloody stomach. They glowed as he recited the Prayer for Healing. I watched, waiting for the blood, guts, and everything else to go back where they belonged, but … nothing happened.

Uncle Raphael looked down at his hands as if their healing ability was, like, seriously defective or something. "I can't do it. Whatever demonic magic Beelzebub imbibed into the athame is too strong for just me alone to break through.”

I knelt down next to Uncle Raphael and held my own hands out over Zuri. “Here. Let me help you.”

23

ZURI

I expected the Afterlife to be more than just darkness and cold. I expected my mother, the woman my father had loved so dearly, the woman who'd given me life, to be waiting for me, welcoming me to all eternity. There was none of that though. It was just darkness and chills. My entire body shook with the cold. How I knew it was my whole body still confused me. I was dead, I shouldn't have a physical form that could *have* sensations like shivers.

I'd seen Azrael appear in the chamber as Dad and Beelzebub fought. I'd been ready to accept the reaping of my soul. So, what was with the damn cold? A thought suddenly occurred to me: *do I still have eyes?* Not the most rational of thoughts as one hung between life and death, but it came to me all the same. If I still had a body, then it stands to reason I had eyes that worked. The darkness could have just been a function of them being closed.

Come on, Zuri. Open your damn eyes. You are the daughter of Lucifer, Ruler of Hell. Open them.

I forced the spot I assumed my eyes to be at to obey my command and open. Everything was blurry and hazy, but at least it was a start. Sound slowly trickled back as my other senses started to realize they still functioned, too. The icy blanket that had wrapped itself around me as the blood loss took its toll slowly receded, replaced by something like hot pokers everywhere. Tiny pinpricks of white-hot light flashed all around me. I wanted to scream, but my vocal cords were the last thing to realize they still worked.

"Hold on," a voice said beside me. I knew I should recognize the speaker, but I couldn't place it.

My brain was too busy trying to keep me on this side of the veil to do things like tell me who was talking around me. The heat rippled up and down my body, chasing away the chill of death. It was at the same time both soothing and agonizing. I opened my mouth and this time my vocal cords remembered what they were for.

"Aaah!" It was a strangled sound, one better suited for an animal rather than a half-human, half-angel.

"A little more," a different voice said, not addressing me this time. At least I didn't think so anyways.

I let the warmth fill me up and my vision started to blur again. Giving in to the feeling I let it, suddenly too tired to focus on staying alive. Either I was going to make it or I wasn't. A little nap now wouldn't change that.

***

I FELT something press down on my arm, pulling me out of whatever limbo I'd been stuck in. I opened one eye, letting it adjust to the lighting around me. It wasn't a room I recognized so I opened the other hoping it would help. Still the room wasn't recognizable. The pressure was still on my arm and I turned my head to find Dad sitting beside me.

"You're here," I croaked, trying and failing to sit up.

His firm hand squeezed mine. It was enough

to keep me immobile. I glanced down to find myself in a bed. I must be in a hospital or something. I remembered Beelzebub stabbing me in the gut. There'd been blood, so much blood. Dad looked simultaneously relieved and angry as fuck.

"What were you thinking, Zuri? I nearly lost you!" He boomed.

I was never a fan of being the target of Dad's anger. Not that he ever really showed anger that often. It was even more rare that it was directed at me. "I thought I could handle it. I'm sorry."

"You have no idea how worried I was when you didn't come home. When you called and told me you were with Michael's daughter. The daughter of my sworn enemy. You could have been kidnapped."

"Well, I wasn't. At least not until that asshole demon knocked me out, dragged me to a creepy ass basement, and tried to turn me into some twisted sacrifice."

"You should have come to me as soon as you knew the Emblem was taken."

"How'd you know I knew?" I rubbed at my head.

"Damien admitted you were both in the museum when it was stolen. He told me it was your idea to go after the thief."

I wanted to be mad at Damien for giving in to Dad's questions, but at the same time, it was a relief to have it out in the open. "I'm sorry. But I was trying to protect the family's honor. You always told me how important the Emblem was to you. You said it would be mine someday. I thought if I could get it back for you, I don't know …"

"You never had to prove yourself to me, Zuri. You know I love you and I know you are skilled."

"I just wanted to show everyone that I was capable of protecting what should be mine. I didn't know it was going to end up here." Looking around at the room and anywhere but his eyes. I still struggled trying to figure out where we were now. "Where are we now? The last thing I remember is being in some creepy basement at the Academy."

"We are in their long-term medical wing. You are very lucky your friends were able to talk Azrael out of reaping your soul."

"They did what?"

"They were quite brave. Michael's daughter even challenged him with her father's blade."

"Miry stood up to the Angel of Death?" I shook my head in disbelief, because I couldn't make that image compute in my brain. When Dad nodded that it had in fact occurred, I couldn't help laughing. "Damn, guess that's what I get for passing out from blood loss."

"She risked her own life to save yours."

"Where is she?" A sudden image of Miry laying prone somewhere, forgotten and alone, fluttered into my brain. "I need to at least say thanks."

"You'll have to ask your physician when you are able to move."

My brow furrowed. "Physician?"

"What have I told you about getting into fights with inanimate objects?" Raphael said with a tired smile.

"This one wasn't my fault. Someone else was holding the pointy blade this time. I swear."

He chuckled and probed the tender flesh of my stomach. It still stung, but probably wasn't nearly as bad as it had been before he'd gotten his healing touch on it. "You're going to need to rest for a while longer. Rest assured that Miryam is fine. She's resting herself."

"She's here, too?"

"She is. When you're a bit stronger, you can see her." He looked to Dad. "You raised a very brave young woman, Lucifer. Then again, I'd expect nothing less from you."

"Thank you for risking your own safety to tend to my child. I know it could not have been easy, given Michael's feelings toward me."

"As you may have noticed, Michael was nowhere to be seen," Raphael said.

"No, he wasn't."

Raphael disappeared, leaving Dad and I alone again. "What's going to happen to Beelzebub? Did you kill them?"

"I did not. Uriel and I were able to subdue them for now. I'll transport them back to Hell where they will stand trial for their crimes."

Uriel helped? "Can I ask you a question, Dad?"

"You can ask. It doesn't mean I'll answer though."

"Did Damien tell you about the Archives?"

"You mean the fact that you broke in rather illegally and copied information that wasn't for your consumption?"

"Uh, yes."

"He did."

"Well, we sort of looked at some of what was on there. Like about the Emblem and everything. We had to know what we were facing."

"I get the feeling this isn't about the Emblem's capabilities. Zuri, ask your question."

"Well, before, in class Uriel kind of went nuts,

flinging fireballs at everyone. His eyes glowed red. I'd only ever seen Beelzebub do that. I thought maybe they were impersonating him. I needed to find anything I could to prove whether it was really the Archangel or not and I found …. 'Burning Starlight.'

"Ah. I see."

"He was in love with you, Dad."

"I know."

"Did you ever … feel that way about him?"

He took both of my hands in his and kissed them. "My sweet girl. No, I did not reciprocate Uriel's feelings. Perhaps if I had the war would have gone differently. With his considerable power on our side, we may not have lost. However, I could not and would not fake emotions that weren't there just to change an outcome."

"They all have you so wrong. I wish they could see you like I see you," I sighed.

"We did today," Miry's voice said from the doorway. She leaned against the door frame looking pale, but upright and otherwise unharmed.

"I thought you were supposed to be resting," I commented.

"Yeah, well, I had to make sure you didn't like

die on us or something after all the work we put in to heal you."

"Oh, you healed me, did you?"

"Yep, totally did. Uncle Raphael said he couldn't do it alone, because of whatever weird demon poison was on the knife that Beelzebub stabbed you with. So, I helped out."

"She was actually a little bit badass," Damien added, following Miry into the room.

"I'm going to give you some time to get caught up," Dad said and left the room without a word.

"I still can't believe your Dad actually showed up," Miry flounced, sitting at the foot of my bed.

"I noticed yours was MIA," I replied.

"I manifested his sword, though. Did you see?"

"Yeah. I did. I owe you two a thanks for saving me from dying."

"It was super hard, actually. Like way harder than any other healing I'd ever done," Miry replied.

"I meant about keeping my soul on this side of the veil. I don't know how you managed it," I corrected her.

"We just convinced Dad it was a bad idea to let you die," Damien replied.

Miry opened her mouth to say something else, but Damien nudged her in the arm in a very obvious bid to shut her up. Her mouth clamped shut and she pouted.

"What happened to your other friends?" I asked. "Is everyone else okay? The other students?"

"Chris got Ant and CeCe out of there before things got really bad," Miry said. "Most of the other kids were either confined to their rooms or were still at the party."

Who the fuck is CeCe? "That's good. If you hadn't shown up when you did and broke the seal, the apocalypse would be happening right now," I said.

"I'm just glad it all worked out," Miry said. "I would have hated it if you died."

"You wouldn't have even missed me, Miry."

"Yes, I would. I've kind of gotten used to having a roommate."

"No, you didn't. But thanks for saying it anyway."

"You both should get some rest. Besides, I think your boyfriend is looking for you," Damien said, gesturing to the doorway.

"Dad did descend from on high or whatever to like say that he's holding a hearing or something to decide if you can stay," Miry said before she bounced out of the room.

"What did you do to get your dad to back off?" I gave Damien a pointed look.

"I told him I'd go to Reaper Academy."

"You said you never wanted to be pigeonholed for your abilities," I protested.

"It's fine, Z. If you can find a place at a school that literally hates us for our parentage, I can handle a school full of deadies."

I leaned back against the pillows and looked out at the vacancy Miry had left in the room. "So, Michael knows who I am now. Fan-fucking-tastic."

"You aren't going to stay, are you?" He sounded hopeful.

"I mean, why would I? I don't belong here."

"One thing is true. Miry will miss you if you aren't around."

"No, she won't," I argued.

"Yeah, she will, Zuri. You may not believe it, but there's something there between you two. A spark or whatever and you'd be stupid to ignore it."

"Even if there was something there—which there's not—she's got a boyfriend who she's very much into," I said. "D, she couldn't even wrap her head around the fact that I'm gay."

"I'm just calling it like I see it." He shrugged.

"Maybe you won't have to deal with your drama. Maybe you'll get kicked out of this place and come home. Or maybe you stick around and see where it goes."

I flipped him off, effectively ending the discussion. "What happened to Dad's emblem?"

"I don't know. After Uriel cleansed it, it broke and I think your dad must have grabbed it."

"Oh, yeah. He probably did and just didn't want me to know where it was so I couldn't go chasing after it again."

I closed my eyes and urged myself to rest. I had a pissed off Archangel to face in the morning.

24

MIRYAM

Zuri was alive and it seemed like she was going to stay alive. That made our foray into saving the world totally worth it. I bopped into the hallway outside the medical ward, on the lookout for Chris. I found him two hallways away leaning up against the wall, his eyes closed. He looked … tired … but that's totally normal given what we all went through. What a strange day. We started off at a kegger and ended up averting the apocalypse. I wonder if that's a skill I could put on my resume—Miryam bat-Michael aka. Saver of the world.

"Hey there, handsome." I tip-toed to kiss Chris. That made him smile, though he kept his eyes closed after I pulled back. "Someday, huh? I don't know about you, but I'm still kinda juiced up over all of it."

"That might be the Pixie Stix talking," he joked. He cracked his eyes open, blinking as if the overhead lights hurt his eyes, before opening them wider.

"Oh, ha ha." I bounced on my heels. "You sounded like Zuri with that one."

A shadow of something, I don't know what— Anger? Jealousy? Insecurity?— flashed across his face before it was gone. "I'm nothing like Zuri."

"Well, duh." I wrapped my arms around his neck. "But don't worry. I love you more."

"Why would you even say something like that?" Chris shoved me away.

I shrunk back, confused. "It was a joke. I'm sorry."

"Well, I'm not laughing."

"I didn't think I needed to tell you I was joking." I held the spot on my shoulder where he shoved me, even though it was my feelings and not my body that were hurt. "I came to say hey, because Damien said you were like looking for me. Don't make me regret that, Chris."

Chris heaved a massive sigh, like the kind that involved his whole body. "Miry, wait. I'm sorry. I'm stressed over a million different things, but I should never take that out on you. Forgive me, please?"

"What's in it for me?" I asked.

He frowned. "What's in it for you? Harmony in our relationship is what's in it for you. And for me too." He reached for me, but I took another step back. "Come on, Mir. We fight so little; this is really freaking me out. Forgive me?"

I tilted my head to the side, trying to think in terms of WWZD—what would Zuri do? Zuri wouldn't willingly be anywhere near Chris's personal space, but if she was, she would probably give him a stern, profanity laced talking to or punch him in the face. I wasn't sure which one. Still, as exciting as Zuri's don't-care attitude was, I couldn't pull it off. I wasn't her. I was me. I liked to keep the peace and make sure everyone was happy. I'd probably like break my hand if I tried to punch anyone in the face. I didn't like that Chris flew off the handle for some dumb little thing, but maintaining harmony in our relationship was worth a little forgiveness. I hated drama. I liked hearing about other people's drama, but couldn't stand any of my own.

"I forgive you." I held out my hand to him. "Wanna go back to your room? Dad's already sent down a message from on high or whatever summoning Zuri and I to his office tomorrow. I bet it's going to be bad. I could use a little distraction until then."

Chris took my offered hand and pulled me close for a kiss. "Ant is still decompressing after the mess in the basement. What about your room?"

I perked up at the suggestion. "I'm all yours."

"Attention students," the kidnapper announcement blared across campus. "The total number of missing students is now at fifty-seven. Remember to report any suspicious activity and always use the buddy system. That is all."

"What a buzzkill," I murmured.

Chris slung an arm around my shoulders and led me toward my dorm room. "Don't worry, Mir. You're safe with me."

"OH, HEY, YOU BROUGHT YOUR DAD." I made a little half curtsy-half bow to The Prince of Darkness when I found them waiting outside of Dad's office the next morning. For once, I totally made it on time to a meeting. "Are you out of the hospital wing already?" I asked Zuri.

She gave a noncommittal shrug. "Until your dad expels me."

"That's not going to happen." I grinned. "Besides, I don't think you were ever like officially enrolled or anything. Would you stay if he let you?"

"I'm not staying, so it doesn't matter."

"And I'm not letting you go in there alone," Lucifer said as the doors to Dad's office opened on their own. "I know you were just trying to protect me and the family honor, Zuri. I intend to make sure Michael knows that. There will be no smiting or expelling today. Not on my watch."

"Thanks, Dad," Zuri said as we entered the office.

Dad rose from behind his desk when he saw us. He decided to go full Greco-Roman armor religious painting mode today. I bet he meant to look intimidating. The great Archangel Michael ready to lay down the law. Personally, I thought he just looked stupid.

"You look ridiculous," Lucifer agreed with me. "Can't you wear normal clothes? I know it's been awhile since we've seen one another and you want to remind me of our last meeting, but check your ego at the door, Michael. There are more important matters at hand than your pride."

Dad 'harrumphed' and leaned back in his chair, crossing his arms over his armored chest. "As I recall, Luciferiel, you're the one that the saying 'pride goes before the fall' was written for."

"Then your memory is faulty, old friend, because that saying is for Adam and Eve—not me." Lucifer did his own posturing to match Dad's. "Though keep it in mind. It may apply to you sooner or later. We have an eternity to wait, now, don't we?"

"Why are you even here?" Dad asked. "My instruction specifically stated Zuri and Miryam. I did not invite you."

"After how you reacted to our last meeting, there was—pardon the expression—no way in Hell I'd let her face you alone," Lucifer said.

"But she's not alone." I covered my mouth with both hands when I realized the words came out inside of staying in my head. "Sorry," I mumbled when all eyes turned to me. "All I'm saying is I had her back in the basement with the Beelzebub and Apocalypse stuff, sir, and I'll totally have her back now."

Lucifer pressed his lips into a thin line. "Yes. You were very brave in that situation, child." He glanced at Dad. "Your father would know that if he bothered to show up at the call of the relics."

"I have more important things to worry about then relics and your daughter bleeding to death."

"Watch what you say about my daughter!" Lucifer shouted. He jumped out of his chair. I expected fire and brimstone to rain down on all of us with how totally livid he looked. "Don't try my patience, Michael. I'm still of a mind to smite you."

Dad made a 'come and get me' gesture with both hands. "I'd like to see you try. I reigned victorious then and I'll reign victorious now. Face it, Luciferiel. I'm better than you. I always have been, and I always will be."

"As much fun as this trip down memory lane is, can we just get whatever punishment you have for me out of the way so I can go back to where I belong?" Zuri interrupted.

"No one interrupts Dad," I squeaked. "We're going to be in *so* much trouble."

"Bullshit," Zuri said. "What is he honestly going to do with my dad standing right there?"

"I don't want to find out." I covered my head just in case Dad started throwing things. Stuff always ended up breaking—usually near or on me —when he was extra angry.

Dad fixed Zuri with a glare fierier than one of Uncle Uriel's fireballs. "You will leave these grounds and never come back. If I so much as get a whiff of reports that you are hanging around my daughter or campus ever again, I will show you the true meaning of the phrase 'go to Hell.'"

Zuri shrugged, totally unconcerned with Dad's wrath. "Sure. Sounds good. I don't belong here in your lame ass Academy anyway." She swiveled around toward me, expression changing from defiance to concern when she saw what I'm sure was betrayal written all over my own face. "Oh, don't tell me you're going to cry, Miry. Come on. You know you're better off without me here. I got the emblem and now I can go home. That was my plan the whole time."

My chin quivered as I tried to hold in tears. It was totally pointless. I don't know why I even bothered. I scrubbed at my eyes. "I've … I've never had a girlfriend—I mean a friend that is a girl—before. Is it so bad to want you to stick around, Z?"

Zuri stepped toe to toe with me. She hesitated a sec before using both thumbs to wipe my tears away. "Hey, stop crying. You're strong. You're Miryam bat-Michael, remember? You got this. You'll make new friends. You practically rule the school already. People should be lining up to be your friend."

"But none of them are you," I whispered. "None of them call me out when I'm being a whiny baby pampered princess. You said yourself I needed a reality check. Why can't you, like, be that for me?"

"Because this is your home, not mine," she said. "Besides, Archangels and Fallen working together is never gonna happen. There's too much bad blood there."

"What if it could happen though?" I brightened when an ultra-cool majorly awesome plan popped into my head. "What if you *were* my service project?" I bounced over to Dad's desk before anyone—most of all Zuri—could object. "I haven't picked my service project for the year yet, Dad. This is it. Proving Archangels and Fallen can co-exist and work together for the greater good of … well, like the universe or something. I haven't worked out all the tiny little details yet, but I plan to. This is my service project." I looked over my shoulder at Zuri. "*Zuri* is my service project."

Dad raised one blonde eyebrow. "If the daughter of my sworn enemy has no objections, I will give you one chance. If you fail, there will be consequences."

"Oh, totally, I understand." I turned to Zuri

again. "Whatdaya say? Want to hang a little bit longer? I'll let you hang, like, Satanic posters on your side of the room to feel more at home or whatever."

Zuri laughed. "You are so clueless."

I smiled and bounced on my heels. "Is that a yes?"

Zuri laughed again and shook her head. "I can't believe I'm saying this but … yes. Let's show these bitches what can happen when we combine our powers for good … and maybe a little bit of evil."

"Awesome!" I stuck my hand up for a high five. Zuri ignored me. I turned my attention back to Dad. "If you don't like need us anymore, may we be excused?"

"Don't make me regret my decision, Miryam," Dad warned.

"Oh, I won't." I flashed him my best and brightest grin. "I'm Miryam bat-Michael, remember? I got this."

EPILOGUE

ZURI

Four weeks was both too long and too short a time to have spent at Celestial Academy. I honestly hadn't expected Michael to give me a chance to stay and prove that Fallen and Archangels could co-exist together. Don't get me wrong, most of the kids here were far too wholesome for my taste. Although, I guess it wasn't the end of the world to be exposed to different people.

"You've been quiet like all morning," Miry chirped at me from across the room.

I could hear people in the hallways of the dorm chattering away about their mid-term break plans. Apparently having angels as teachers meant they could only stomach having us around for short bursts of time. We'd be back in a month and then we'd only have another two months before winter break hit. This place wasn't like any school I'd ever been to before.

"Just thinking," I answered.

"I thought we were past the two-word answers. Like, we're friends now, remember?"

"I'm your service project, Miry. If I don't make it here, you get the first failing grade of your life and I get sent back to Hell."

"Not like you'd be all that unhappy to go home. I mean, you're headed there this afternoon."

"I meant more like I don't know if Michael would try to banish me from this plane of existence or something."

Miry's nose wrinkled in disbelief. "He couldn't do that."

"Yeah, well, I guess we both have a lot riding on the next three terms. If you can't prove I can fit in and be better or whatever by the end of the year it's over for both of us."

"I remember what Dad said. Although we aren't going to fail, because we have each other. Besides we have already proven that Fallen and Archangels can work together. We saved the world. Plus, Uncle Uriel and your dad stopped Beelzebub, together."

I rolled over and propped my head up on my arm. "I'm pretty sure Uriel only helped my dad, because he's still carrying a torch for him. He may act like he doesn't give two shits about what Dad does, but he still cares."

"I still can't believe Uncle Uriel was in love with another angel."

I gave her a tiny bit of credit for not re-marking on the fact that said angel was also male. "Are you staying here for the break?"

Miry nodded. "I haven't been home for a break since my first year. The less time I spend with my mother the better."

I started to suggest that she could come with me back to Hell, but stopped myself. Not-withstanding the fact we couldn't be sure she'd survive the trip; I wasn't ready for what kind of message that would send to people. We were friends, at least as much as two people who were vastly different could be, but people talked. People who knew things about me and I wasn't going to let them drag Miry into something she wasn't ready for. I owed her that much. After all, she'd saved my life.

"Let's hope things are less apocalyptic next

term," I muttered. Nothing could be as life-altering as what we'd already been through, right?

GABRIEL'S SCROLL

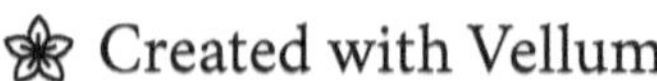 Created with Vellum

1

MIRYAM

I was the only one staying at school during quarter break. It started out fun, but turned B-O-R-I-N-G really quick. I could handle the boredom, usually, if it meant not hanging with Mom. I convinced her six years ago that never coming back to Kansas was part of the deal in being, like, one of the elite students at Celestial Academy. The school campus was my home now and it would totally disrupt my angelic training if I came home for breaks. She bought it hook, line, and sinker. Honestly, I didn't even have to try all that hard to convince her. Voila! One forged letter from Dad later—instant freedom from Mom's special brand of crazy.

I flopped onto my bed before rotating to hang

my head over the side, my hair brushing the floor. It was my thinking position, though there wasn't much left to think about that I hadn't already thunk. I pulled out my phone to text Chris.

Me: Come back early. I'm bored.

I waited for a response, but nothing popped up. Not even those little dots that showed he was typing, just "received." Lame. Well that wasn't very boyfriend-like of him. I scrolled through my contacts until I found Zuri. We weren't BFFs or even BFs, but I was pretty sure I could call her a friend. She might totally regret giving me her phone number once I'm done firing off texts, though. There's only one way to find out!

Me: Come back early. I'm bored.

Z: I'm not here to amuse you, princess.

Me: You're not here at all.

Z: It's been quiet—just how I like it.

Me: Yeah, no one bleeding and almost dying.

Z: Don't remind me.

Me: Or the apocalypse!

Z: Almost apocalypse.

Me: Whatever. You coming back early or what?

Z: Or what.

Me: Lame.

A text popped up from Chris—finally—while I was, like, waiting for an answer from Zuri.

Chris: Can't. Busy.

Me: Be busy with me here.

Chris: Sorry, Mir. Can't.

I tried Zuri again. Maybe if I ask enough, she'll get annoyed and come back just to shut me up. A girl could dream.

Me: You coming back yet?

Z: I'm not your amusement squad, Miry. Go bug someone else.

Me: Haha. Love you too!

I added two kissy face emojis for good measure before hitting send. I waited and waited and waited, but Zuri didn't text back. Lame. I sat up when the most absolutely perfect way to get Chris' attention popped into my head. He'd love it! Oh, and there's totally no way he *wouldn't* text back. I unbuttoned my shirt and made sure my boobs were pushed up as high as I could push 'em in my bra. The more cleavage the better. I turned my phone to selfie mode, held it out at arm's length, and pouted at the camera. Once I snapped the pic, I added it to our less than talkative text chain and captioned it "Like what you see?" Send!

Z: What the hell is wrong with you? Why would you send something like that to me?

Me: OMG! Wrong person. Sorry, Z. That was for Chris. Think he'll like it?

Z: I'm not answering that. Find something better to do with your time, M.

I ignored her. Find something better to do with my time? The only thing better than sexting was real sex and that would have to wait until either I convinced Chris to come back to campus early, or break was over. I hoped he came back early. We wouldn't even have to sneak around if no one else was at school. I re-uploaded the pic to Chris and hit send.

Chris: Damn.

Me: Miss me?

Chris: You know it.

Me: Then come back early.

Chris: Can't. Busy.

I puffed out an annoyed breath. What was everyone so busy with?

I perked up when someone knocked on my door. Finally! Someone to totally save me from my boredom! I didn't care who was behind the door. It could be the janitor and I'd be happy to see them. Seriously. I set my phone down on the nightstand and fixed my shirt buttons before hopping off my bed. I skipped across the room to find out who my save-me-from-boredom savior was.

CeCe grinned when I opened the door revealing her instead of someone more fun to hang with. "Hey, Miry! I got back early. Cool, huh?"

I frowned, but stopped myself before an "ug" escaped. Don't get me wrong, CeCe wasn't bad company, but she spent way too much time trying to impress me. Usually, I wouldn't care since she was useful, like when it came to me not wanting to do my Music Theory homework. Still if I had to pick someone to spend three days alone with before the new quarter started, CeCe wouldn't be it. To be honest, she wouldn't even make the top five.

"Uh, hey, CeCe." I tried to put some pep into my voice. "It's like totally amazing to see you. I can't believe you're back early. How fun is that?"

Her grin widened until I could see all thirty-two of her seriously well taken care of teeth. "I know, right? Wanna grab a coffee or something?"

Or something, but I totally don't say it out loud. That would be rude. Being Archangel Michael's daughter had a lot of advantages. Being nice to everyone because Dad expected me to 'uphold his example' was not one of them, but I was stuck with it anyway. "Sure. Let me get my shoes."

My phone flashed 'one new message from Chris' as I wiggled into my black Mary Janes. I glanced at it longingly. Sexting was totally more fun than hanging with CeCe, but I had already told her I'd caffeinate with her. I sent a quick 'brb' before turning to CeCe with the biggest, brightest smile I could muster. "Ready! Coffee's on me. Dad won't mind."

***

"I HAD THE MOST AMAZE-BALLS BREAK!" CeCe threw her head back as if she was getting off on something the barista slipped into the coffee instead of her memories of whatever amaze-balls thing happened during break. Seriously, amaze-balls? Who even says that anymore? Lame.

"What was so great about it?" I asked.

"Oh, everything," she said. "Damien said—"

Damien? Hold up, now this was interesting. "You're still talking to Damien?" I sat up straighter. Juicy gossip about Zuri's reaper in training BFF would definitely liven things up around here.

CeCe pushed her glasses up the bridge of her nose. "Of course, I'm still talking to Damien. Why would you think I wouldn't be?"

I shrugged. "I dunno. I guess I just thought that saint kids weren't his type."

"Well, I don't know about all saint kids, but I'm his type. At least I think so anyways. I mean, he hasn't ghosted me yet so that's something, right?" CeCe clutched her coffee mug, watching the steam swirl up and disappear into the air before deciding to totally change the subject. Smart girl. "Do you know what I always thought was weird? Why does no one ever get kidnapped during quarter breaks? I mean, think about it. Kids are getting snatched practically every day when school is in session, but when it's off —nothing."

I cocked my head to the side. "I never thought of that. Maybe that means the campus kidnapper is a student."

We stared at each other before CeCe busted out laughing. "A student is the kidnapper? Funny, Miry. Real funny."

I cracked a smile. It did sound kind of silly once the words were out of my mouth. I mean, who totally has time to kidnap kids between classes? Not anyone I know. "Yeah. Hysterical. Haha. Lemme pencil in that kidnapping between angelic history and self-defense class. It will totally work."

CeCe wiped tears from her eyes. "That's the funniest thing I've heard all day."

I laughed right along with her. Even though, a tiny voice in the back of my mind whispered: *"What if I'm right?"*

2

ZURI

I stared at my phone for far longer than I had meant to, trying not to let the image of Miry's cleavage sear into my brain. Like she'd said, it was a mistake to send it to me. Still, a part of me wondered if she'd done it subconsciously. Girl was wound tight as fuck.

"Zuri, is something wrong?" Dad loomed in the doorway to my bedroom. He'd been clingy since the whole nearly dying thing.

"No, just Miry being a twit," I muttered.

"You don't have to go back." We'd been having this argument ever since I got home.

"I survived the public education system; I can survive a bunch of doe-eyed do-gooders for three more terms."

"I'm not doubting your ability to adapt to new situations. I'm concerned with the fact my daughter nearly bled to death while in their custody. I know you think that the Fallen and Archangels can coexist, but a month is hardly a good sample size."

I rolled my eyes and set the phone aside. "That's exactly why I have to stick it out. Besides, if I can make it work with the world's most irritating angel princess, anyone can make it work." I regretted my choice of words immediately. The image of Miry's tits flashed in my mind, sending heat cascading down my neck.

"I'm going back. No one is going to mess with me. They'd all be too terrified I would turn them into dust or some shit. Plus Raphael is okay, Gabriel probably doesn't even remember me, and Uriel has a major angel boner for you," I added.

"Don't be so quick to trust them. Michael may be letting you return, but don't think for a second he won't try to find any excuse to harm you."

I reached out pulling him into a hug. "Relax, Dad. I've got this." *Michael believed I was a completely different person.* "I know this is a big change, but it's a good one. I promise."

He squeezed me tight and I could feel the protectiveness of his love wash over me. I'd done a lot of stupid things in my life, but I'd never run off behind enemy lines before. "Dad, I need to ask you something." I felt his body tense against mine as I asked, "Why didn't you ever tell me what the Emblem did or that I could unleash the End of Days?"

Dad stepped back and looked down at me with heavy lids over his dark eyes. "Come with me."

I followed him to his office. I eyed the panel behind his desk that led to the Archives I'd used to find leverage on Uriel and discover the true power behind my father's Emblem. He sat behind the desk and I couldn't ignore the sense that I'd done something wrong. I sat across from him, one arm slung over the back of the chair. If I looked chill, maybe he wouldn't launch into the world's scariest scolding.

"I never thought the beings I shared this domain with would use it against me," he said, answering the question I'd asked back in my room.

"Demons are kind of douchebags. It's in the job description." I snorted.

"I forget how young you are sometimes, Zuri. Beelzebub and I go back eons. That's a long time for tension to build and fester. If I had shared the truth with you, maybe we would have avoided this whole debacle."

I wouldn't have minded skipping the whole guts spilled on the ground bringing the Horsemen of the Apocalypse. "It's safe now, right? It's somewhere no one who isn't you or me can reach?"

"After what Uriel and your friends did, it broke and lost its power."

My throat went dry. "What does that mean? It was the only thing protecting you from Michael."

"I am not helpless against him, Zuri. Don't worry about your old man." The smile that tugged at his lips didn't reach far though. "I'm not going to talk you out of going back so you ought to get ready."

I tucked a few strands of hair behind my ear and stood up: "I promise I won't be so incommunicado this time round."

"I'm holding you to that promise."

<hr>

I'D JUST FINISHED PACKING when my phone buzzed with an incoming text. For a split second my heart stopped as I imagined yet another mistaken text from Miry. Instead it was a note from

Damien asking me to meet him at the only decent coffee shop. Yes, even Hell has Starbucks.

"So, you're really going back?" He handed me a coffee with a wink.

A sip told me he'd laced it with a hint of Baileys. "Yeah, I am. You aren't going to talk me out of it, D."

He laughed and spilled coffee down the front of his shirt. "Damn it." He blotted at the fabric. "At least this time I don't have to lie to your dad."

"Not about where I am anyway. You might not want to tell your dad that you're banging a saint chick."

"We aren't banging. CeCe isn't like that."

"Whatever." I sipped my coffee. I wanted to share the insanity that was Miry's cluelessness with my best friend. I pulled up the text chain with Miry. "Was this deliberate?"

Damien slammed his coffee down on the table. "Warn a guy, would you? I don't need random tits thrown in my face."

"Answer the question."

He scrunched up his face. "I mean, she said it was a mistake. I only met her for like a hot minute. Most of that time you were dying, but I don't really think she's with it enough to be doing it on purpose."

Despite Damien's assurance that Miry was just clueless and still wasn't used to having a lesbian friend, I couldn't shake feeling that something else was going on. Maybe going back a little early wouldn't be such a bad idea after all. Miry clearly couldn't be trusted to make good decisions on her own. Besides, bartering peace wasn't going to happen in Hell.

3

MIRYAM

I watched from the window seat in my dorm room as students finally started coming back from break. Most hugged and kissed their parents good-bye before coming in through the gates alone. The gates looked all stately and 'gates of heavenly,' but secretly they were the first line of defense in keeping people out who shouldn't be on campus. It was Dad's idea to keep Celestial Academy free of anyone without angel or saint blood. The gates had glitched up a bit last quarter when the demon, Beelzebub was able to get through, but they were impersonating a student so whatever. I'd give the gate-ward a pass for that one.

"Knock, knock."

I turned, expecting Zuri, but saw Chris leaning against the door frame instead. He'd already changed into his school uniform and added a school issued forest green sweater vest for good measure.

"OMG, I missed you *so* much!" I raced across the room and threw myself into his arms. "Did you miss me? Tell me you missed me!"

"You know I did, Miry." Chris laughed when I pulled him into my room, my hands already under his sweater vest trying to pull it over his head and unbutton his shirt at the same time. "Hey, did you delete those pics? We don't need your dad to find them."

"You know Dad doesn't care what I do," I mumbled, landing sloppy kisses near his mouth. "Let's have our own welcome back party, Chris. Just the two of us."

He led me over to the bed. The world always dropped away when we were alone. It could be two minutes or two hours. Time meant nothing as long as I knew he needed and wanted me.

"I'd say get a room, but you're already in one."

Chris reacted first. He sat up, shifting so he was shielding me from whoever was at the door. It was totally noble of him even though there really wasn't much to see. We had all our clothes on still, even if they weren't exactly in the appropriate spots. No big deal.

"Zuri?" I peeked out from behind Chris. "OMG, you're back! I thought for sure your dad would totally talk you out of another quarter!"

"He tried."

"Too bad he didn't succeed," Chris grumbled.

I checked to make sure nothing was showing that shouldn't be showing before I climbed off the bed and bounced my way across the room to give Zuri a hug. She shoved me away.

"What the hell are you doing?"

I rubbed my arm where she had pushed a little too hard. "That's what you said when I sent you the wrong pic too, remember?"

"What pic?" Chris straightened his clothes before joining me where I landed near the closet. He slung an arm around my shoulder and pulled me close. I leaned against him. It felt nice to be wanted.

"Oh, I was bored and sending pics to Zuri," I lied. "No biggie." It was mostly the truth which was better than lying. I smiled to sell the not-the-whole-truth even more. "Tell me about your break. Any time I texted, you said you were busy."

"Tell me about the picture," Chris countered.

"It's just a picture," I sighed. "I said no biggie. Don't you believe me?"

"It is a 'biggie,' because you're my girlfriend. If you're doing anything behind my back, I need to know about it," he said eyeing us both.

I opened my mouth to say something, but Zuri beat me to it. "Back off, Saint Boy," she snapped. Not the tactic I'd use, but what the heck, still like totally worked. Even maybe scared him a little in the process. "Has she ever given you a reason not to trust her?"

"Well, uh … no," Chris glowered.

"Then stop being a jealous douche, and back off," Zuri repeated. "Why don't you tell her why you were always so 'busy' during break, huh? You share, she shares. That's how relationships work, right? You have no business getting on her case when you're keeping secrets of your own."

Chris tightened his arm around my shoulder. "Geez, judgy much? I'm not keeping secrets."

I laid a hand on his chest. "Neither am I."

Chris opened his mouth, shut it, opened it again before sighing and shaking his head. "Look, I'm sorry, Mir. You deserve better." He leaned down to kiss the top of my head. "I'm going to check if Ant is back yet. I'll see you at dinner, okay?"

"Okay," I repeated mostly to keep the peace between Chris and Zuri. I plastered a smile on my face until my cheeks hurt from smiling so big. Once he was gone, I flopped out on my bed. "It was totally boring without everyone here, but at least it wasn't stressful."

"Saint Boy is kind of a prick." Zuri sat next to me on my bed, making sure to be close but not too close.

"You don't know him like I know him." I automatically defended Chris.

"No offense to your taste in guys, but I don't really want to get to know him either."

"He's been sick." More excuses. "It stresses him out."

"He doesn't need to take it out on you ... or me." Zuri stood and started unpacking. She brought suitcases this time instead of just a backpack.

"Is everything you own black?"

"Is everything you own pink?" She countered.

I sat up, smiling a real smile this time instead of a fake one. "Pretty much. It's my signature color."

"We need to change that." Zuri pulled some stuff out of her closet and held them out to me. "Try these on."

I took the offered black leather skirt and lace up the back sleeveless corset top. "Why?"

"Because I just thought of the perfect stress relief." Zuri grinned. "Clubbing."

4

ZURI

Miry had insisted on wearing pink lipstick with the rest of the tight leather outfit I'd loaned her. Sparkling lips notwithstanding, I estimated she wouldn't stand out too much where we were going.

"Where are we going?" She whined at me for the fifth time since we'd snuck off school grounds.

"If you keep asking, I'm going to leave you somewhere and pretend I don't know you," I muttered as the flashing strobe lights and pulsing base of our destination finally came into view.

"How do you wear this thing? I can't breathe," Miry complained, tugging on the corset top, making her cleavage spill over the top of the material.

I let out a frustrated grunt and pulled her into a dead-end alley, where we wouldn't be observed. I loosened the ties along her back, watching her heave a visible sigh of relief as the top loosened. "Better?"

"Totally. Thanks."

"Miry, do me a favor," I said and started back toward the club. "If a word ends in 'ly, forget you know it, okay? Just for tonight."

"Tot … sure." She caught herself and looked up at the sign above the door. "Castoffs? Never heard of it before."

"Considering I was the first Fallen you'd ever met, I'm not surprised." I clasped my hand around her wrist and dragged her toward the bouncer.

"This is a Fallen club?" She rasped.

"Don't act surprised," I said and flashed a card at the bouncer. He waved us through without a second glance. "Some ground rules. Don't take drinks from people you don't know. Don't agree to hold someone's bag while they pee either."

"I'm not clueless," she snapped and reached down to slip the card from my fingers. "Why do you have a playing card?"

I took it back and slid it into my bra strap.

"Forgery powers, remember? That douche out there thinks we're on the owner's private guest list."

"You faked us in? Isn't that illegal?"

I snorted. "Miry, what part of Fallen don't you get? I put up with all the goody-goody shit at school, but we literally aren't saints. Now come on. Time to let off some steam."

I ushered her down the spiral staircase to the dance floor already full of throbbing bodies with glow sticks and iridescent body paint. Please don't let me run into any exes. Being here brought back memories of wild nights and far too many walks of shame. I shoved anonymous faces from my brain and focused on keeping Miry out of trouble.

She stood on the edge of the dance floor, staring at the throng of people when out of nowhere a hand reached out from the mass and snatched her out of view. She gave a high-pitched squeal as she vanished. I barged through people, not giving a fuck if I stepped on toes. I found Miry pressed between two very drunk guys trying to stick their hands up her skirt and down her top simultaneously.

"Hey, dude bros. Get your hands off her. She's with me," I growled.

They glared at me. "Who are you?"

I didn't like to flaunt my status as Lucifer's daughter, but with assholes like these, I knew the fear factor would be in full effect. My wings unfurled and people scrambled aside to give me space. "Zuri bat-Lucifer, jackass. Who the fuck are you?"

Dude bro Number One withdrew his hand from Miry's shirt and grabbed his buddy, stumbling over each other to flee my presence. Miry clung to me. "Thanks."

"You really need to learn to defend yourself," I scolded and ushered her over to the bar, plunking her onto a stool.

"I didn't even know what was happening. Besides … Chris …" She trailed off at the mention of her boyfriend.

"Not that I care or whatever, but he treats you like you're stupid," I said.

"He does not," she pouted.

"He about lost his shit earlier, because you wouldn't tell him about a picture you sent someone else. Hello, that's called emotional abuse, Miry."

"I didn't mean to send it though," she said, her eyes going wide.

Looking at her with those pitiful puppy dog

eyes, I realized Miry was just clueless. The photo text had definitely been a mistake. "He doesn't get to dictate who you send shit to."

"He loves me."

I bit back a laugh. "You know what? Fuck men, okay? We are here to forget about all that drama. This is about the ladies, tonight."

Miry's face perked up and a mischievous grin spread across her lips. "I just had the best idea."

Why did I get the feeling I was going to hate her idea? "Do I even want to know?"

She scooted closer on the stool, forcing me to lean in to hear her. "So, I heard that girls do this thing to make guys leave them alone at clubs. They act like they're lesbians."

I blinked. "Miry, you remember that I am a lesbian, right?"

"Well, yeah … but like I can pretend. Won't it be fun?"

No. "I'm pretty sure my little display earlier is going to keep the creepers away from you."

She gave me her signature pout. "Will you at least dance with me? Just one dance? Pretty please?" She tugged on my hand for emphasis.

I wasn't going to win this battle. "Fine."

The tempo changed. I wouldn't call it a slow dance, but the DJ was obviously trying to encourage couples to hit the floor. In the back of my head, I repeated that Miry had a boyfriend and wasn't interested in me as she slung her arms around my neck. We swayed in rhythm to the music. For just a minute the rest of the world and all the shit that came with it dropped away. It was just her and me with only the music filling the space between us. Her tits pressed against me as she leaned in and my panic set in. I stepped back and her brow furrowed.

"What's wrong?" She called as the song changed and the volume swelled.

"Nothing," I lied.

She shrugged, accepting my answer. "I'm thirsty. Come on, let's get drinks."

I trailed after her, not intending to get any drinks. I knew the kind of illegal shit that went on here and I wasn't going to let Miry go tripping on drugs if I could avoid it. "One drink," I told her and passed over the playing card. Beneath my fingers it morphed into a credit card. The bartender accepted it and passed Miry a frothy neon pink drink. Of course, it was pink.

With Miry beside me I scanned the crowd, checking to be sure our handsy friends from earlier hadn't decided on a rematch. As I turned my head, I caught sight of a flash of a red dress and dark hair. She turned and for a split second I could swear her eyes flashed a kaleidoscope of colors.

"Stay here," I told Miry without taking my eyes off the mystery woman across the dance floor.

"Okay," she replied, slurping from a straw.

I zeroed in on the woman with the strange eyes and the red dress. The air around me grew thick and I realized I was having trouble breathing. Why can't I breathe? My heart hammered in my chest, making my ribs ache one by one until I finally caught her.

"Do I know you?" I asked.

She turned to me and her face was a million people all at once. "You would remember me."

"Why do I feel like we've met?" The words slurred on my lips.

"Shh. It's okay," she pressed a manicured finger to my lips, but my brain interpreted it as a sharp point. Like a claw, I felt it prick against my cheek and she sucked the tiny droplet of blood off her finger.

I blinked as the odd feeling disappeared along with the girl. Oxygen hit me like a truck and I staggered sideways, pressing a hand to my stomach to keep its contents inside my body. What the fuck just happened?

I scrunched my eyes shut against the world and waited for my senses to re-orient themselves. Miry? I'd just gone and left her inside, completely defenseless. I shoved through the crowd outside and made it back to the bar to find her drink abandoned.

"Where'd she go? The girl who was just sitting here. Where is she?" I demanded of the bartender.

"I think your girlfriend may be a little more into dicks than she let you believe."

I slammed my fist down on the bar, anger turning my angelic strength up to an eleven. The bar cracked beneath the weight of my power.

"She went that way," he answered.

I spun on my heel and spotted Miry's blond hair bobbing along under a decidedly male arm. I closed the distance between us in three strides and pulled Miry back to face me. "I thought I told you stay put."

"Look who showed up," Miry said dreamily.

My attention pivoted to the guy she'd been leaving with—Saint Boy. "What are you doing here?"

"I could ask you the same question. Dragging

Miry to a place like this. Real mature," he quipped.

"Let's be real, here. You are butt hurt that she wanted to spend time with someone other than you." I looped an arm around Miry's waist. "We're going back to school."

"Do you hear all the colors? I never knew purple was so loud," Miry said. Damn it. Someone had slipped her angel blood.

"Yeah, it's real loud. We're going to get you somewhere nice and quiet, okay?"

"I'm taking her back," he argued.

"Dude, you're the whole reason we're here. As much as it pains me, like physically makes me want to vomit, you're right. I brought her here and I'm taking her home."

"Fine. But I'm coming too. I've been practicing my safe passage skills. It will be faster than walking."

Spoken just like someone without wings. "Fine. Whatever."

His mystical path brought us back to the front gate of the school after only a couple turns on city streets. We stepped up three across only to find the entrance barred.

"What now?" I groaned.

Miry let out a high-pitched giggle. "The gate's singing at us."

"You are so high, right now," I muttered.

She shook her head. "It says we can't go in, because we're not, like, singing the right notes."

I couldn't decide if she was being serious or if this was some weird side effect of the drugs in her system. Either way, I wasn't in the mood to find out. I offloaded Miry's weight to Saint Boy's arms and stepped up to the gate, prying it open with my bare hands. The moment we were back on school grounds, the gates snapped back to attention as if I'd never been there.

Miry flung herself at me and giggled the rest of the trip back to the dorms. Saint Boy took off for his own room with only a glare in my direction. Miry shed her top without help, breaking the lacing by forcing her way out of it. Her skirt came off next, leaving her in just a bra and underwear. She tugged at my hand. "I don't want to be alone."

I pointed to the bed on the other side of the room. "I'm right over there."

"Please." There was that pout again. I shed my own club attire. I changed into a tank top with shorts before crawling in above the sheet and let Miry curl up against me.

5

MIRYAM

"No, Mom. I already named the books of the bible and in the correct order too. Please don't make me do it again ... Fine. Genesis. Exodus. Leviticus. Numbers. Deuteronomy. Joshua. Judges. Ruth ... Why do I have to go on? Mom, Mom, Mom, Mom! Don't lock me in the closet! I'll be good! Please I swear I'll be good!"

"Hey. Hey, Miry, wake up."

I sat up in bed—how did I get into bed?—my hand raised to pound on the door of the dark closet Mom had stuck me in. I looked down at my hands, half expecting them to be bloody from banging on the door for, like, way too long and hard. Tiny pale scars crisscrossed my knuckles from all my other attempts at getting out of punishment, but no blood. *Where was I?*

"I don't know where your mind took you, but it wasn't good. You okay?"

I turned at the sound of Zuri's voice. Memories flooded back, pulling me to now instead of holding me in the past. I may not be 100% safe at school, but I was free from Mom. "Where … Where's my mom?"

Zuri shrugged. "I don't know. You tell me."

"Kansas. Outside of Wichita. What was I, like, talking about in my sleep?"

"Mostly books of the bible and a closet." Zuri cracked a smile. "Most go hand in hand, you know. Literally and figuratively."

I flopped back onto the bed. Zuri laid down next to me, our heads practically touching. I don't know how we ended up in the same bed, but it was kind of comforting. I'd woken up next to Chris a zillion times over the years. Every single time I always felt like I needed to hold my breath and apologize for waking him up with my nightmares. Zuri seemed, if not exactly cool with it, at least totally understanding which was … new and kinda nice.

"If Dad catches us like this, he'll smite me all

the way down to Hell." I turned my head to look at her. Funny how I never noticed her eyes had flecks of gold in them before now. "But if everyone in Hell is as nice as you and your dad, I wouldn't mind that so much."

"You wouldn't last five seconds in Hell." Zuri stood and moved to her side of the room. She rummaged around in her dresser until she found one of her school uniforms.

"How would you know that if I've, like, never been there?" I sat up. "Besides, you'd totally be there to protect me, right?"

"You really need to learn to protect yourself, Miry." She pulled her school clothes on over her sleep tank and shorts without bothering to find appropriate underclothes.

"I'd protect you if it was the other direction." I pointed up. "You know. Heaven. Angel kids don't have to die or anything to go there. It's like totally a free pass. Like a bonus for being, you know, us. Cool, huh?"

Zuri shook her head. "I'm not Angelic, remember? Trying to re-enter Heaven after being cast out is the quickest way to kill a Fallen. Or haven't they taught you that yet, in this goody-goody school? That's like Day 1 where I'm from."

"I guess I forgot." I bounced out of bed and found my own clothes. The club clothes still in a pile on the floor. I'd have to wash those and buy new laces for the corset top before giving them back to Zuri, but how do you clean leather? Spot clean? Dry clean? I didn't want to stick it in with a load of my own clothes. It would totally bleed all over my school uniforms and pink regular stuff. "I forget a lot of things, sometimes," I added after pulling on my knee-high socks and shimmying into my shoes.

"No, you don't," Zuri shot me a 'busted' look. "You just like everyone to think you do."

I shrugged. "I can't help it if I'm stupid."

"You're not stupid," Zuri insisted. She chewed on her bottom lip, looking all concerned and cute. "Your dad may be a huge douche canoe, but he's one of the most powerful Archangels ever. There's nothing stupid about that. Or you for that matter."

I bounced on my heels. "Thanks."

"Don't mention it." She crossed her arms over her chest. It didn't strain against her ... assets ... like it used to. I guess finding shirts that fit instead of borrowing my stuff would do that for a person.

"I'm going to check on Chris," I announced after we were both ready for the first day of the new quarter.

"Why?" Zuri asked. "For all we know, Saint Boy was the one who slipped you the angel blood to begin with."

"Is *that* what I was tripping on?" I tilted my head to the side. "Huh. Wickedly weird stuff." I shook away hazy memories of swirly colors telling me to do stuff. "Chris wouldn't hurt me, though. He loves me."

Zuri grabbed her black backpack and slung it over her shoulder. She pushed past me and out into the dorm hallway. "Just keep telling yourself that."

"I will!" I called after her before grabbing my own pink backpack. I headed left toward Chris' room instead of right after Zuri. *He loves me*, I repeated to myself as I walked. *He loves me, he loves me, he loves me ... Doesn't he?*

THE DOOR to Chris and Ant's room was slightly ajar. I pushed it all the way open with my toe. "Knock, knock. You ready for the first day of classes? Let's hope this quarter doesn't end as, uh, dramatically as the last one!"

Chris turned from near his nightstand, one arm raised as he absently finished fastening his watch. "Hey there, gorgeous. Ant went to grab coffee and bagels at the coffee cart. I didn't think you'd show up this morning."

"Why wouldn't I?" I stepped fully into his room. "We always totally walk to class together, Chris. Why would today be any different?"

"I don't know. You seem to like going off with Zuri without telling me."

I frowned. "Is this really about you being mad at me for going to that Fallen club last night? It was just a little bit of fun before school started. How can you be mad about that?"

"It's just a little bit of fun until someone roofies you."

"It wasn't a roofie," I said. "It was angel blood."

Chris forked both hands through his hair. "It doesn't matter what it was, Miry! The point is, you could have gotten raped, or kidnapped, or— God forbid— killed. Did you ever think what that would do to the rest of us?" He stepped closer, reaching out a hand until his fingers brushed gently against my cheek. "Did you even bother to think what that would do to me?"

"Um, I was kinda too busy listening to the color purple talk smack about pink to think about any of that." I leaned into him, burrowing my face into his sweater vest soaking up his smell. "Please, don't be mad at me, Chris. Please?"

"Everything was fine until she showed up."

"Until who showed up?"

"Zuri."

The ice in his voice made me look up. "Zuri is my friend."

"Everything was quiet on campus until she showed up," he insisted. "Shapeshifting demons. Kidnappings. Attempted Murder. The Apocalypse—"

"Wait! There were totally kidnappings on campus before Zuri got here," I reminded him. "You can't blame those on her."

Chris cupped my face in his hands. He looked so deeply into my eyes, I forgot we needed to get to class. I forgot everything, but just him and me. "All I'm saying is I liked things better how they were before," he said. "Is that really so bad?"

I shook my head as best I could with my chin still resting on his chest and his hands on my cheeks. "No. That's not bad at all. How much time do we have before class?"

Chris glanced at his watch. "Half hour." He

grinned when his thinking caught up with my own. "We can do a lot in thirty minutes."

I kicked the door shut before leading him over to his bed. "We totally can."

6

ZURI

Part of me considered skipping classes altogether. What did I need to know about music theory or calculus? As much as ditching would make me feel more in control of the situation, it would only prove that I was a trouble-maker and would ruin the whole experiment. I wasn't going to subject Miry to her father's wrath over something so trivial.

I didn't realize where I was until I found myself surrounded by medical supplies. Unlike the last few times I'd been here, Raphael sat behind a desk, staring with great intensity at some papers. I cleared my throat to get his attention.

"Oh, I'm sorry. I didn't hear you come in. Punch any more walls lately?" His smile was genuine. It felt like he wanted to be my friend or at least a confidante. I could use someone here, even if Dad's words still echoed in the back of my mind: *don't trust them so easily.*

"No, just needed someone to talk to. And you're an okay listener," I replied and sunk into the chair opposite him.

Raphael set aside his papers and fixed me with a look that said 'continue.' "I have a few minutes to spare. Also, I can always write you a note to excuse your tardiness for class," he offered.

"Sure." What did I want to talk to him about? I hadn't even intended to end up here when I left the dorms. Then it hit me. "How much do you know about the kidnappings that happen here?"

He rubbed his chin. "To be frank, not much. We know children seem to go missing throughout the terms, but it's no more than what we assumed were just dropping out of the coursework. Well, at first anyway."

"What is he doing to keep us safe then?"

The Archangel's brow furrowed. "He?"

"Michael. He runs this place. Doesn't seem like he gives two shits about what happens to any of the students. I mean, he didn't even notice he had a shapeshifter in the midst of his school until I uncovered it."

"We've changed the wards so that anyone with demon blood cannot enter the grounds."

"Why do I get the feeling Fallen are included in that, too? I mean, we're just as bad in his opinion."

"Given your presence here, I'd have to say that's not entirely true. While he does not exactly welcome your father in his space, he understands that he deserves access like all other parents do." After a breath he added. "Can I ask why you are so interested in the missing students?"

"I think I almost became one last night," I admitted. Having slept on it all night, mulling over what had happened and decided whoever that was, had to be related to the other kids who went missing.

"What do you mean?"

I bit my tongue. Giving him enough information to act upon would mean admitting to sneaking off campus well after curfew. *Screw it.* "I needed to blow off steam so I snuck out. I almost got grabbed, but I don't know by what. It was like whatever it was decided it didn't want me or something and let me go."

My shoulders tensed as I waited for him to respond. I could very well be facing Michael and expulsion if Raphael decided not to keep this between us. Again, I'd be letting Miry down. When had disappointing her become so important to me? Wasn't I happier back home, in Hell?

"What did this creature look like? How did it act?"

"You're not going to call me out for sneaking out past curfew?"

He gave me a small, sad smile. "What good would that do?"

"It was a woman. She looked almost familiar somehow, but I couldn't place her. She was pretty, really attractive. She said something to me and touched my cheek," my right hand brushed against my skin as I spoke and felt the tiny prick from her nail, "and then she just disappeared. I had the worst feeling of vertigo ever."

"Did you see any other children with this woman?"

I shook my head. "No one. To be honest, the more I think about it right now, it feels almost like a dream. Have they ever found any of the missing kids?"

"I'm afraid not. We haven't been able to find any trace of the missing students. The only thing we know for certain is every one of them have angelic lineage." He rubbed at his chin again—a nervous habit maybe—and glanced at his pile of papers again. "Here, let me write you that note. Which class are you going to?"

I pulled the schedule from my bag. "Something called Archangel Studies, whatever that is."

"Ah. No need to write a note then. I'll just walk with you. I almost forgot I'm teaching that class this term. You may find it somewhat informative. Besides, I at least think you'll enjoy getting to show off to your fellow students. Possibly wanting to prove that Fallen are equally as good as their heavenly counterparts?"

I held in a snort as I followed him out of the office and through the hallways to the classroom.

"So, why doesn't Michael teach anything? I mean you, Gabriel, and Uriel are all Archangels. What makes him so special?" I couldn't keep the disdain from my voice.

Raphael remained silent for a few paces before answering. "Not everyone is suited to shaping young minds. Our talents are better intended for those kinds of things." He turned to bar my path onward. "I know you don't have a high opinion of him, and with good reason. However, as you would ask not to be judged by someone else's past, don't judge the rest of us by your father's. And that includes Michael."

"I'm not making any promises."

He nodded and pointed to the door to our right. "Why don't you go in first? You don't want to give the wrong impression. Being seen as too friendly with a teacher."

Is he ribbing me?

I sauntered in like I owned the place. There were maybe three or four other kids sitting at desks scattered in what had once been a circular shape. I took a seat near the back of the room and waited. This was going to be interesting.

7

MIRYAM

"I'm here, I'm here, I'm here! Don't mark me tardy, Uncle Raphael! I'm here!" I burst through the classroom door, trying to make it look like I totally meant to do a header over the front row of desks. I pulled myself up and off the ground before straightening my clothes. (Not the first time I did *that* today.) "Has class started yet? Have I missed anything? Please don't tell my dad!"

Uncle Raphael motioned at the little cluster of desks near the back of the room. "Welcome to Archangel Studies, Miryam. I'm glad you could join us. Please, take a seat."

"I totally meant to do the flip over the desk thing," I announced to all six of us in the class, including me, Zuri, Remy, Roxy, Arabelle, and Jacob that made up Archangel Studies. "You know me and grand entrances, right? Why enter a room when you can really ENTER a room." I plopped down in a seat next to Zuri. She hid her face behind her schedule, pretending not to know me. Well, joke's on her since everyone totally already knows we're roomies. She's stuck with me.

"Who can name the Seven Archangels?" Uncle Raphael got the class off to a lame snore-fest of a start. "I'll give you a hint ... you're all related to them."

He laughed at his own joke. Remy and Roxy—stupid Archangel Remiel's stupid twins—yakked it up right along with him. Roxy's hand shot up to answer the question. Uncle Raphael nodded toward her giving the go ahead to answer.

"The seven archangels are Michael, Gabriel, Raphael, Uriel, Suruel, Raguel, and Remiel," she recited. I bet she totally wrote all the names on her hand. "While rank is not really an issue in Heaven, the four highest or core Archangels are Michael, Gabriel, Uriel, and you, sir, Raphael."

Uncle Raphael nodded his head again. "Why is that? Why do we four get hierarchical preference over the others?"

"Because you fought in the War In Heaven?" Remy guessed.

Uncle Raphael frowned, like the memories of way back then upset him. "Many of us fought in the War In Heaven. That makes us no more special than they. Try again. Why are we remembered when others are not?"

"Good PR," Zuri said from beside me.

Uncle Raphael's lips twitched, totally trying to hold in a smile. He mostly succeeded. "Do you care to expand on that thought process, Zuri?"

"Sure." Zuri glanced around the class. Everyone was leaning over their desks, waiting for her to go on. "History is always written by the victors, remember? Well, Big Winning General Number One, Michael, has had a millennium to dispatch cherubs or whoever the fuck does his dirty work, to proclaim how amazingly awesome he and his pals are. If humanity is told for thousands of years how great you are, they're going to remember your name, right? It doesn't matter if it's the truth or not."

"You are so fucking high," Arabelle, Uncle Gabriel's daughter that he can't even remember he has, scoffed. "Where do you get this crap? Have you even read the text?"

"I don't need to," Zuri said. "I've lived it." She

flashed Uncle Raphael the closest thing I've seen to a smile yet. "Besides, there are fourteen Archangels, not seven. You forgot the seven Fallen."

"That, Ms. bat-Lucifer, is a lesson for another time," Uncle Raphael said.

At the mention of "Lucifer" everyone lost their ever-loving minds. The twins, Remy and Roxy, picked up their desks and moved them as far away from us as they could get. Arabelle did an "o face" that would be funny if it wasn't meant to be insulting. Jacob wrapped his wings around himself for 'protection,' totally a misuse of wings and not funny either. The room went from calm to chaos in like ten seconds flat. Everyone talked over each other, acting like Zuri had the plague or something when just ten minutes ago she was cool.

"That's enough!" Uncle Raphael bellowed. I'd never heard him yell before. "That. Is. Enough!" He unfurled his own wings, extending them until they filled almost all the space from floor to ceiling and most of the length of the room. That alone shut us all up really quick. Nothing was more impressive or more intimidating than an Archangel with fully extended wings. Once we were quiet, he lowered his wings, tucking them into his back until he looked more human than angel again. "Excellent. Now that I have your attention once more, I would like to say that, while all your answers have merit, the one I was searching for is we are re-membered above others, because we have relics. Relics are specific angelic artifacts, if you will, im-bibed with powers beyond what we can normally do with our angelic abilities. These relics turned the tide of the War In Heaven. They are important and, through them, thus we are important."

I raised my hand. "What can the relics do?"

Uncle Raphael paced the front of the room. It didn't seem like he wanted to talk about this, even though he's the one that had put it on the syl-labus. "Michael's blade, as you're aware, smote the Fallen. Gabriel's scroll records all angelic births and deaths throughout history. Uriel's lariat cleanses, yet also burns the wicked. And mine? Well, mine …" He smiled sadly. "I objected to the war. I'm a healer, not a general. I gave mine to an old friend to help even the odds. It, unfortu-nately, did not work." Uncle Raphael ran his fin-gers across the length of his desk, lost in his memories, before he turned back to us with an-other one of his sad smiles. "It saved his life, though, which I am grateful for. Wouldn't you agree, Ms. bat-Lucifer?"

Zuri swallowed hard, before nodding. I caught just the slightest glimmer of tears in her eyes before she said, "Thank you."

8

ZURI

I couldn't decide if his comment was a low blow or not. It certainly had been news to me. Dad had never mentioned getting the Emblem as a gift during the War. As I stared back at the archangel, I wondered why the relic of a healer would unleash the apocalypse.

"Why would your relic unleash Hell on Earth?" The other kids in the room had calmed down, but were now sharing nervous glances.

"That's totally a good question," Miry added.

Raphael faltered, his jaw working to form words, but nothing came out. He cleared his throat and finally answered, "God imbued the emblem with the ability to bring about the End of Days in the event humanity ever reached a point that a reset was needed. Although he also knew that I, as a healer, would only use such power as a last resort."

"I still can't believe you gave it away. Someone bad could have used it," the one boy in the class said.

"I had faith that the recipient would do the right thing with it and they did."

"It's true, I saw it with my own eyes last term ... Lucifer didn't use the emblem. A demon did," Miry announced.

I didn't need her spilling my family's business to these strangers. "Guess that means all of you claiming he is so terrible and deserved banishment don't know what you're talking about," I added.

If the power to unleash Armageddon had always been possible with the relic, then that must mean when it passed to Dad, the key to unlocking it changed. Which meant at one time, the angel in front of me had been the one whose blood needed to be spilled. *Damn, God really must think everything he creates is expendable.*

If he expected his answer to change whatever opinion I had of God—and let's be real, it wasn't all that high to begin with—he'd be wrong. The fact that God had given Michael the go ahead to cast Dad and the other angels out of Heaven had always pissed me off. Maybe it was because all my siblings were long dead before I was born, but I found it absurd a parent—for lack of a better term—would play favorites with their kids to that extreme.

I looked around the room at the horror-stricken faces of my classmates. They clearly hadn't ever believed God would essentially re-boot humanity like that. Miry shrunk back in her seat and wouldn't meet Raphael's gaze. His cheeks were flushed and he rubbed at the nape of his neck nervously.

"Of course, the other relics were powerful enough to stop such an event from occurring."

"Barely," I muttered under my breath.

As Raphael tried to regain his composure and control of the class, I mentally ran through the list of relics. We knew that the emblem was de-stroyed. No more apocalypse, but it also meant whatever power it had to defend against the sword, scroll and lariat was also gone. Since I had been busy dying, I didn't really remember seeing Uriel in action, but I assumed his relic could do some serious damage as could Michael's blade. The scroll was another matter. If what Raphael said was true and only kids with angelic blood were disappearing, the scroll might give us a hint as to who could be next.

"Those relics sound pretty powerful. How do you make sure that they don't fall into the right hands?" I probed.

"Each archangel takes precautions to ensure they are protected. That includes not disclosing their whereabouts to the others. I assure you, this school is safe from attack."

I wanted to argue and tell him that the gates had pushed back against me and Miry just last night. Instead though I kept my mouth shut. I didn't need these other losers knowing my business. Still I needed to share what I suspected with Miry first.

One of the other kids, I didn't pay attention to names, gestured at me. "She's Fallen. Why is she even here?"

I started to open my mouth, but Miry jumped to my defense. "She's here because she's awesome and way better than the rest of you. I think we had it wrong about Fallen kids. They're not bad. They just had different childhoods. Besides, she's my *friend*."

The girl who'd spoken clamped her mouth shut and slid back in her seat. Miry might be a flake and kind of clingy, but I couldn't deny she had power at this school. Obviously, being Michael's daughter came with some serious perks.

"Right … well, I think we've had enough of a lively discussion for today. Before next class, please review these histories of your angelic parents so that we can discuss your individual abilities and how to use them next time," Raphael said, hastily passing out packets of paper. I took the one he offered me and shoved it in my bag. I knew all I needed to know about my family and our abilities. I didn't need him telling me.

"So, class got kind of heated there. I mean, like I can't believe your dad's relic used to be Uncle Raphael's, wow!" Miry said, falling into step beside me.

I could see the fading evidence of a hickey on her neck. "Yeah, crazy."

"I still can't believe God meant to make a weapon like that."

"I can. Plagues, floods, that shit isn't the sign of a nice deity."

She waved her hand dismissively. "Whatever."

"You heard what he said about the scroll right?" I grabbed her arm and dragged her into a vestibule out of the ebb and flow of students changing classes.

"It's one of the relics. Sounds kind of boring in comparison to the others," she answered.

I resisted the urge to slap Miry. "It records all angelic births and deaths. I told Raphael about my brush with the kidnapper last night. He told me none of the other kids had ever been seen again. They might even be dead and they all have angelic blood."

"Wait, what about you and the kidnapper?" Miry demanded.

"I told you, last night at the club something tried to grab me. You were too busy tripping on drugs to notice. Somehow, if we can get our hands on that scroll, we might be able to figure out how the kidnapper is picking their targets … and who is next." Maybe it would even lead us directly to the kidnapper. Beelzebub had been able to take and use the emblem, even with demon blood. There was no telling who or what could have gotten their hands on the scroll to use as a hit list. Besides, I couldn't lie. I wanted another shot at the bastard who'd nearly grabbed me. They had a date with me first and maybe the business end of a sword.

Light dawned in Miry's eyes as my words sink in. "Like that's brilliant." Her face fell almost instantly though. "But there's a big problem with your idea. We aren't supposed to leave school grounds without dad's permission during the school term. I mean he looks the other way with my parties and stuff, but anything like a long time he has to say it is okay. I'm like pretty sure he wouldn't let us leave campus to go looking for lost relics."

"Your dad's micromanaging isn't our only obstacle. Like Raphael said, only the holder of the relic knows where it is. I'm betting even if Gabriel remembers the location, he wouldn't tell us either. I doubt any of the angels would break that silence willingly."

Miry patted my arm like I was an idiot and gave me a toothy grin. "I'll ask him. He likes me remember? Besides, we have someone on our side whose ability is literally to find lost things."

"As much as you enjoy hanging with your dorky little Saint friend, I'm not down to spend long periods of time with him. Plus, I know your boyfriend would insist on coming along to protect you and in case you haven't noticed he doesn't like me." The feeling was entirely mutual.

"He does have his uses and he doesn't hate you." She subconsciously touched her neck.

"Gross." I wanted to shake Miry by the shoulders until she understood that he was manipulating her. Though she was so blinded by his charms she couldn't see the truth if it walked up to her naked and slapped her. It was a battle I wasn't going to win, at least not now anyway. So, I pushed past her into the hallway and waited for her to follow. "Come on, oh great persuader. You've got an archangel to woo."

9

MIRYAM

"I totally, like, got this covered. Trust me." I took the lead in the hallway, winding our way up and down stairs, through doors most people wouldn't even know existed before stopping in front of a gold embossed double door. Intricate scrollwork ran up and down the outside with statues of little cherub heads instead of door knobs. Their blank, dead eyes had always creeped me out. Dad once told me that's what happened when you disobeyed an archangel—you became a door ornament. I'm pretty sure he had been joking, but I never wanted to find out. I disobeyed in my own small ways. Taking too long to show up when he summoned me. Totally sneaking around with Chris before Dad gave his go ahead. Insisting that Zuri and Fallen were worth our time and effort. Little things might add up, but so far I'd been pretty lucky to avoid Dad's wrath.

"Those are so creepy." Zuri leaned in to examine the cherub head doorknobs. "I didn't think Gabriel had it in him to decapitate cherubs."

"They're fake." I put both hands on the cherub heads. "At least I think they are … then again, who knows." I pushed the door open, trying not to think about poor innocent cherubs in the process. "Remember to let me do the talking. Uncle Gabriel barely remembers who I am most days. He'll totally have no clue who you are."

"And that's a good thing?"

"Based on the reaction of the kids in Angelic Studies ... yes."

The cherub door lead to a room Uncle Gabriel called his "antechamber" Bookcases lined the walls and boxes were stacked up so high, I was surprised he hadn't been buried in his own junk before now.

"Uncle Gabriel?" I called. "It's Miry. Can we talk for a sec?"

"Miryam?" Uncle Gabriel emerged from the main office part of his chambers. He blinked, confused as usual, his eyes looking owl sized behind his black round framed reading glasses. "To what do I owe the pleasure?"

"We learned about the relics today in Angelic Studies." I laced my hands behind my back, hoping I looked innocent and totally not fishing for information. "I've seen the emblem, sword, and lariat in action … but not your scroll. Why is that?"

"Oh, mine isn't all that important in the greater scheme of things," Uncle Gabriel frowned at his stacks of boxes and overflowing bookcases. "It keeps a record, that is all. Nothing more, nothing less."

"I think that sounds totally useful." Flattery usually got me everywhere. Time to test out that theory. "I mean, like, if it was me, I'd be showing everyone how awesome my magical scroll was. It has the power to tell us all the angelic births and deaths. How amazing is that?"

"Totally amazing." Zuri chimed in. She grimaced when the word 'totally' crossed her lips. "I'd love a chance to look at it. If you can just point us in the right direction …"

Uncle Gabriel frowned at her. "I'm sorry. Have we met?"

"You're so funny, Uncle Gabriel." I laughed a hyena-style laugh, happy no one cared how totally fake it sounded. "This is my roommate, Zuri. You met her in the basement while averting the apocalypse last quarter, remember? She's totally cool and one of us. I promise."

The blank nothingness never left Uncle Gabriel's face, but he nodded and played along anyway. "Yes. Of course. Of course. I'm afraid I wasn't paying much attention to who was present at that particular time you reference. It's a pleasure to see you again. Zuri, was it?"

"Yes, sir." Zuri nodded. "So about the scroll …"

Uncle Gabriel motioned at the mess in his antechamber. "I've been looking for ages for it, but can't seem to find it anywhere. I must have left it somewhere during one of my annunciation jaunts. I announce all the births of the archangels' children. You see I couldn't keep up if I had to do everyone. That's where the scroll comes in especially handy. You know what I'm referencing, Miryam." He raised his hand in what I called the 'benediction hand' ever since Mom started quizzing me on all the religious paintings when I was five. "'Hail Miryam, Full Of Grace, The Lord is with you.' I announce to the future mother, and then, well my job is done. It looks ever so much more formal and professional if I carry the scroll with me. Still I must have set it down somewhere while making rounds."

"When was the last time you saw it?" Zuri asked.

Uncle Gabriel sat on the floor. "That's the thing. I don't really *remember*."

I crouched down in front of him. "You not re-membering stuff is totally not new, Uncle Gabriel. Can't you give us any sort of hint? Or even a clue? Anything at all?"

"We'd really like to find the scroll for you," Zuri added. "It could help with the campus kid-nappings if we knew the missing kids were still alive or not. It's more than just a record. Maybe it could help solve the cases. What do you remember?"

Uncle Gabriel raised his hand in benediction mode again. "'Hail Miryam, full of grace, the Lord is with thee.' That's what I remember. Your mother ... so like the teenager from Nazareth that shared her name. Your father was very specific on finding someone with similar qualities. I found her so he could ... so he could have you."

"You've told me this story before, Uncle Gabriel." I kept my smile in place, using words as gentle and coaxing as possible. If I spooked him, the memories would slip further away and we'd never get anywhere with the kidnappings. "I was named after Mom. She was named after Miryam, Mother of Christ. She took that, uh, responsibility totally too serious if you ask me, but … I trailed off, trying to shut out the torrent of childhood memories I'd rather forget. "She meant well. Where's the scroll, Uncle Gabriel?"

He hit himself in the forehead as if he was, like, trying to shake the memories free. "That's all I remember. 'Hail Miryam, full of Grace. The Lord is with thee.' That's all I remember. Ugh … That's all I remember."

I looked over my shoulder at Zuri and mouthed "sorry" before standing up. I plastered on the biggest grin I could manage for Uncle Gabriel's sake. "That's okay. You've told us enough. Thanks, Uncle G. I'm totally looking forward to class tomorrow. Bye-ee!"

"What are you doing?" Zuri hissed after following me out of Uncle Gabriel's office. "He told us squat. We're no closer to finding the scroll or solving the kidnappings than we were when we came up with this shit storm of a plan."

"He told us everything we need," I repeated. "The scroll is with my mom. Oh, and … uh, I might be pregnant."

10

ZURI

I stared at Miry, waiting for the punchline to the joke, but it didn't come. *She can't be serious.* "Miry, come on, did your douche boyfriend convince you that not using protection was a good idea?"

"No. Of course not. Chris is totally responsible."

I rolled my eyes. "Then if you haven't screwed without protection, I'm pretty sure you aren't pregnant."

Her eyes widened and she gestured to the door behind us. "You heard him though. He kept announcing and pointing at me."

I gripped her by the wrists and pulled her down the hallway to an alcove for some privacy.

"You really don't listen when anyone talks, even when it's you." Her brow wrinkled in an obvious sign of confusion. "You said you and your mom have the same name."

"So what?"

I balled my hands into fists and clenched them behind my back so I didn't smack her. "He was talking about your mother, Miry. He meant he last remembered using the scroll when you were born. At least, that's what I got from it."

She nodded slowly, probably trying to work herself down from jumping to ridiculous conclusions. If it turned out her boyfriend had actually gotten her pregnant, I was going to beat the shit out of him.

"I should still check right?" Miry faltered under my grasp as she shifted her weight side to side.

"I get the feeling we would need to do an off campus excursion to a pharmacy."

"Uncle Raphael might have some tests."

I shook my head. "He is nice and all, but I don't trust him to keep something like this quiet from your dad. Maybe I'm wrong, but I doubt you want him knowing about this."

Miry's cheeks went from their usual rosy red to pale pink. "Definitely not!"

"Then we need to go off campus." We needed to leave the school to find the scroll anyway. "Look, we know we can't stay here. The scroll is out there somewhere and I'm not sitting around waiting for some other kid to get attacked. We need that information. So, what does your dad need to give us permission to bail on class for a while?"

Miry regained her composure. "He'd believe it if I got something from Mom saying she needs me back home."

Because it means he doesn't have to deal with her himself. "So a letter then. Has he gotten letters from her before?"

"I don't know. I can't imagine my dad like exchanging love letters or anything like that."

"Has she written to you?" When I got a blank stare back, I let out a long exhale. "The forgery will be more convincing if I can actually copy the handwriting and voice."

"Oh. I might have something back in our room."

I gestured for her to lead onward. I stayed silent as we walked, my thoughts warring with themselves. I had no desire to meet Miry's mom, but it felt like she was the next step in finding the scroll. From what Miry had shared she was the kind of person who would say I belonged in Hell for a whole host of reasons that weren't socially acceptable to most people. We made it back to our room to find Saint Boy loitering by the door.

"What are you doing here?" I put myself between them.

"Not that it's any of your business, but I was looking for Miry. We usually have a study period together now."

"You aren't fooling anyone. Call it what it is. You hook up between classes ..." I glanced over my shoulder at Miry. "He must not have a lot of stamina."

"My stamina is just fine," he spat.

"Just keep telling yourself that. We have some very important roommate things to take care of that don't concern you, so your quickie will have to wait." I pushed past him into the room. I really hoped Miry would follow suit and keep her mouth shut about what we were up to.

"I'll catch up with you later, Chris. Promise," she added and kissed his cheek before she closed the door behind her. "You didn't have to be so mean."

"I'm just calling it like I see it. Now about that letter?"

WE'D GOTTEN lucky and Miry found an old letter from her mother. I'd managed to forge a letter to Michael claiming her mom was sick. She needed Miry to come home and take care of her. I'd even slipped a line in about her wanting to meet Miry's new friend. It wasn't a guarantee he would let me go with her, but frankly I didn't care. I wasn't letting Miry go off and face a dangerous kidnapper alone.

"Here goes nothing," Miry sighed and disappeared into her father's office.

I stood outside keeping watch and waiting. Their voices were low enough I couldn't make out the conversation. I could have done a better job spying, but my phone buzzed in my pocket. Damien's face flashed at me with an incoming call.

"Hey D, what's up?"

"Was wondering what you were up to. Sneaking off to meet up with CeCe. Figured I could chill with my best friend while I'm at it."

"You have terrible timing, dude. I'm about to ditch this place for a road trip with Miry."

"You running away together? I knew you'd find the right girl eventually."

He was lucky he was in Hell or I'd have flipped him off to his face. "Fuck you. We're hunting for angelic relics. Trying to stop a kidnapper and potential murderer."

"Whatever you have to tell yourself," he teased.

I gritted my teeth as the door opened and Miry appeared. I ended the call without saying goodbye and closed the distance between us. "What did he say?"

"I can go, but I can't go alone. He wants Chris and Ant there to protect me. Don't worry, I convinced him you needed to come, too. You're my service project after all."

The idea of spending any extended time with her douche of a boyfriend and Glasses didn't thrill me. Although if it meant finding the bitch who'd nearly grabbed me, I'd put up with it. We had to hope her mother wasn't as absent minded as Gabriel.

MIRYAM

"I think a road trip will totally be fun." I opened every single dresser drawer and my closet to get out most of what I own clothes-wise and road trip ready. I'm so used to wearing my school uniform, packing regular stuff seemed weird. "It should take at least two days to get there, maybe three. You know, to extend our time off campus. I'll have to ask Dad for some hotel money. I bet he'll totally make us bunk up with a boys room and girls room like at school. Lame, right? But if he's not there, he won't know if we bend the rules a little bit, right? Have you ever been to Kansas? It's nothing to write home about or anything, but I bet there are worse places on Earth. Maybe not for me, but for other people, you know?"

Zuri blinked. I'm not sure when her eyes had glazed over, but probably somewhere long before I got to 'Kansas.' "How can you say all that without taking a breath? It's unnatural."

I shrugged. "You once said I must like listening to the sound of my own voice. Maybe that's true. Oh! Mom is kind of conservative. Like, reads all the conspiracy theory websites, even goes to rallies and stuff. She's not going to be a fan of you being black, gay, or Fallen. It might be best if you just stay in the car once we get there. We'll like crack a window or something."

"What the fuck, Miry, I'm not a dog! No wait, I take that back ... even dogs are treated better than what you just suggested."

I cowered, covering my head with my arms. "Don't hit me!"

Zuri softened. Everything from her face to her stance relaxed. "Why do you think I'm going to hit you?"

I peeked out from under the protection of my arms. "Well that's what people do when they're mad at me. They hit me or throw things at me. Mom used to lock me in a closet."

"Literally or figuratively?"

"Oh, haha. You wouldn't be cracking jokes if

you had spent most of your time in a coat closet converted into a shrine to Dad." I lowered my arms completely before turning to pull a pile of t-shirts out of my second dresser drawer. I didn't like looking at Zuri when she was all quiet with her silent-sympathy. I didn't want her to feel sorry for me. I wanted to show I could be strong like her. "I know your mom died, that's like tragic and all, but I mean it when I say I wish mine was dead. She's not a nice person. She tried to hide it behind religion, but the cracks show, you know? At least to me anyway. If you asked anyone else, they'd probably say she's Mother Of The Year or something."

Zuri looked like she wasn't sure what to do or say after my little confession. She finally settled on "I'm not mad at you and, for the record, I'll never hit you. Ever. Got that? Friends don't pull that shit."

I perked up at the mention of the word 'friend.' "Is that what we are? Friends? Does that mean I can ask you like totally personal stuff and you won't look at me like I'm high or something?"

"I'll always look at you like you're high when you chatter on incessantly." Zuri settled on keeping her arms crossed over her chest. "I might answer personal questions, but there's no guarantee, okay?"

I bounced on my heels. "That's better than a no! Okay, here goes. Have you ever slept with guys or have you always been 'not for me, thanks' cause I have some questions about you-know-what that I'm not comfortable bringing up with Uncle Raphael or Dad. Dad would probably smite me just for, like, thinking impure thoughts or whatever. Uncle Raphael is cool and all, but not who I want to ask TMI questions of. He might feel all obligated to tell Dad and then I'm back to the smiting option. So, like, my biggest question is—"

"Miry! Miry, take a breath!" Zuri snapped though, to be fair, I think she was more upset about the subject of the conversation versus the me rambling bit. "I can't think straight when you do that. If you ever are face to face with the kidnapper, just talk like that and you'll paralyze them with your vapidness." She wandered over to my side of the room, surveying what I had laid out to pack for the trip. "Geez, I've never seen so much pink, rainbows, and unicorns in my entire life. You dress like a five-year-old."

"Well, you always dress like you're attending a

funeral," I pouted. "Who died and made you the fashion police?"

Zuri picked up a white shirt with a unicorn jumping over a rainbow. I had even bedazzled it myself to make it sparkle more. "Has your boy seen you in off campus clothes before? If so, is he secretly a pedophile?"

"Ha." I scooped up all the clothes on my bed and dumped them into my hot pink suitcase. "Chris hasn't said anything bad about my style, thank you very much."

"Maybe that's why he's always trying so hard to get you out of your clothes—so he doesn't have to look at them."

"At least I have someone who wants to see me with my clothes off." Two could play this game.

"How do you know I don't have a girlfriend back home?"

"Cause, duh, you'd be texting them all the time if you did." I skipped over to her dresser and pulled open the top drawer. "I bet I'm gonna just find, like a bunch of granny panties in here. That means you haven't had you-know-what since, like, the last time Hell froze over." I looked over my shoulder at Zuri. "When was that? Like the day after never?"

Zuri gestured at her dresser. "Take a look and see if your panty logic holds up."

I stuck my hands in the drawer and pulled out the first thing I came in contact with—a black lace thong. I tossed it back in. "How in the world do you wear something like that? An eternal wedgie should be like one of the punishments in a lower circle of Hell."

"Look, I'll cop to being your friend, but that doesn't mean I want to dissect our love lives ... or lack thereof," Zuri said. "If you must know to sate your endless curiosity or whatever, I'm hella picky when it comes to relationships or even hook ups." She rummaged around in her closet while she spoke, probably so she didn't have to look at me. "But that doesn't mean I want to dress like a nun. I wear what I want, you wear what you want, deal?"

"You've hooked up before?" She didn't say I couldn't live vicariously through her. "With who? Damien?"

"What part of 'I don't like guys' is so hard for you to understand?" Zuri jammed a bunch of dark clothes into her backpack. She sounded tired this time instead of mad. Ooh, progress!

"Fine. No relationship talk. I get it."

"Until the next time you don't."

I ignored that one. "Can you help me introduce more black into my wardrobe?" I asked hopefully, thinking about the black lace thong. Chris would go bananas if he ever saw me in something like that. Maybe Zuri was right and the only reason he wanted to hook up so much was because he hated looking at my clothes for too long. I mean, he's never said anything, but that doesn't mean he doesn't think it. I think a lot of things I don't tell him either.

"If you loan me some stuff, I'll make sure no one freaks out when they find out you're Fallen," I bargained. "Whatdaya say?"

"I say I'm not helping you seduce your boyfriend," Zuri shot down my plan. "You're all on your own there, M."

"I have a cool nickname now? Awesome!" I held up my hand for a high five. Zuri ignored that too. "You are such a buzzkill, Z," I sighed. "Can you at least be nice to Ant on the trip? I think he has like a major crush on you brewing. Sweet, huh?"

1 2

—————

ZURI

I gaped at Miry for a minute. "You understand that I'm not into him, and will never be into him. Right? Please tell me you understand that?"

"Yes, I understand but it's still kind of sweet. I haven't seen him have a crush on anyone in school. Ever."

I shook my head and checked the last items I needed to pack. If Glasses and her boyfriend didn't drive me insane on this little quest, I suspected Miry's interference would. "How are we getting there? We aren't flying right?" I didn't mind using my wings to get around Hell, but it felt too conspicuous in the mortal realm.

"Drive, like obviously. The boys can't fly. Oh, but maybe someone else will have to drive. Mom never let me learn how." Her lips puckered and her gaze cast about anywhere, but on me. "Dad doesn't have a car, either."

I smirked. "Don't worry about it. I have a way."

"Is it legal?" She asked with an arched brow.

"Not strictly. But I know people. We'll be fine."

———

AFTER RENDEZVOUSING WITH THE BOYS, we made our way back to the mainland and human civilization. I kept catching Saint Boy ogling me as we walked down the streets of Atlanta. I'm sure I looked super out of place with three white kids, but I didn't care. This is where we were. If I'd been at home or at school in New York, people around us wouldn't have thought twice about seeing us together. But this was their turf, not mine and people were judgmental assholes and I'd learned to deal with it. I'd play nice while we were here if it meant saving lives.

"Do you even know where you're going?" Saint Boy asked after we'd been walking farther and farther out of the city for almost an hour.

I checked my phone. We were maybe half a mile from the coordinates D had sent me when I asked him to do a little digging for me. "You can always go back to school if it's too much for your delicate constitution," I answered and flipped him off.

He shook his head and wrapped an arm around Miry's shoulders. She leaned into him and grinned. I still didn't get the appeal and not just because of the dick swinging between his legs.

"So, uh, you know I could help us find the car if you're lost," Glasses offered, falling into step beside me.

"I know where we're going. You all need to chill out and trust me."

"No problem," he said, his cheeks blushing.

He really does have a thing for me.

"You can't be serious," Saint Boy scoffed as we reached our destination; an impound lot.

"Very serious. Now wait here and I'll get us a ride," I ordered them and strolled up to the booth, pulling a piece of paper from my bag. I focused on making it look legit before handing it to the clerk.

"You got the fee to cover this, little lady?" The beefy white guy with a comb over asked, staring down at me from his perch.

I pulled out a roll of twenties and peeled off several. "You bet."

He eyed the money warily for a minute before finally stuffing it in a cash drawer and pulling down a set of keys. "Last row on the left."

I plucked them from his hand and marched down to the last row, using the key fob as I passed, trying to find the one it belonged to. I finally got a positive 'beep' at the far end of the row. I'd been expecting something beat up and shitty. Not what looked to be a brand new sportscar in gold tones. It would have to do.

I climbed behind the wheel, navigated my way to the exit. After giving the attendant a wide smile, I pulled onto the street to find Miry and the boys.

"Wow, that's a really nice car," Miry commented and climbed into the back seat, Saint Boy hot on her heels.

"Full tank and everything," I said and turned in the seat to look at Miry. "Give me your mom's address."

I put the car in reverse, sped backwards letting the engine rumble at my touch and pulled a highly illegal U-turn in the middle of the street so we were heading back the way we'd come. It was going to take us three days to get to Miry's mom in Kansas. As I glanced in the rearview mirror to make sure that my little stunt hadn't attracted unwanted attention from the police, I caught sight of a woman in a gorgeous red dress again. *Is she following me now?* She was just walking down the street. I craned my neck to try and follow her, but she was gone.

13

MIRYAM

"Whoa, stop the car!" I wrenched my neck to try to get another look at the blonde lady in the plaid shirt and jeans. "Seriously, Zuri, totally stop the car."

"Stop the car in the middle of Atlanta rush hour traffic?" Zuri scoffed. "Are you high?"

I pointed off in the direction of where the blonde lady disappeared. "But I think I just saw my mom. If she's here, we won't have to go all the way to Kansas. We can ask her to send us the scroll and—ta da!— problem solved."

"Not to mention, I won't have to spend endless days in the car with you losers." Zuri swerved to the right to change lanes and found a nearby parking spot on a side street.

"Did we lose her?" Once we were on the side-walk instead of in the car, Ant put a hand up to shade his eyes, scanning the area for my mom.

"Why would your mom be in Georgia?" Chris asked. "You told her we were coming, right?"

"Um, not exactly." I twirled a lock of hair around my finger. "It's just she never leaves home so I thought it'd be cool to not fill her in on all the deets. It's kind of an impromptu trip anyway. Zuri and I totally made it up to stop the kid-nappings."

Chris stiffened, color draining from his al-ready pale cheeks. "Stop the kidnappings? Just leave it alone, Miry. I don't want you to get hurt."

"But there are kids out there—our classmates —that need our help, Chris," I said. "They could be hurt. They might be dead. Don't you want to get some answers? What if I was one of the kids taken?"

"That's not going to happen." He shook his head so hard his carefully gelled blonde hair fell into his eyes.

I lifted my chin. Dad called it my 'defiance look.' I liked to think of it as my 'determined look.' "Why not? Because I'm like some precious princess cause I'm Archangel Michael's daughter?

If anything, that should put a bigger target on my back, not make the kidnapper ignore me."

"It's not going to happen, because I won't let it happen."

"How?" I pressed. "I get you, like, wanting to protect me, Chris, but no one's been able to stop the kidnapper from snatching all those other kids. Just saying 'you're gonna be safe because I said so' isn't enough. We're not together 24/7."

"Yeah, because of your lesbo roommate."

"Don't bring Zuri into this." I grabbed his arm near the elbow when he turned away. "And don't you dare like walk away from me right now. Or else—"

He shook his arm free so roughly, I stumbled back a couple steps and hit a newspaper vending machine. "Or else what?"

"Or else I grind your pretty boy face into the sidewalk." Zuri stepped between me and Chris. Her hands were already balled into fists, just waiting for him to make the wrong move. "Trust me when I say you don't want to find out what will happen if you shove her again, Saint Boy."

"Um, guys, we are in public, remember?" Ant spoke up. "If you get busted for fighting, good luck trying to explain wings and saint powers to the cops."

"Ant's right." I'm happy for a distraction from the impending boyfriend-roomie showdown. "Hey, Ant, can I just show you a picture of my mom? Maybe you can track her so we're not running around the streets, like, chasing a ghost."

"I can track anything or anyone. Well usually. Pictures aren't great but I'm sure I can do this," Ant puffed out his thin chest. He glanced at Zuri when he did it. Poor guy doesn't realize he has a zero percent chance of getting with her.

I unlocked my phone and scrolled through my picture roll until I found one of Mom. It was old, taken before I even came to Celestial Academy. In it, twelve-year-old me held out my acceptance letter toward the camera and Mom stood beside me grinning, wearing the same clothes I had just saw her in like ten minutes ago. She was a taller, more farm-ready version of me. We looked happy in the pic. Too bad pictures lie.

I handed my phone over to Ant. "Her name is Miryam, like me."

His hand hovered over the phone as he recited the Prayer to St. Anthony, a warm glow filling the space between his hand and my phone. "This way." He took off to the left, dodging parking meters and other people, holding my phone out in front of him like a compass.

"Has his tracking abilities ever been off?" Zuri asked as we did our best to keep up with Ant's weird twisting route.

"Never," Chris said as if everything was all sunshine and puppies between him and Zuri now. "If he's got a lock on the lost thing's location, he'll find it."

"Or them," I said. "Mom's not a thing."

"I didn't mean it like that, Mir," he said. "You know that."

I reached for his hand and gave it a squeeze, ready to forgive if not exactly forget. Everything was so much easier without the drama. Zuri scowled when she noticed Chris and I holding hands.

"What are you doing?" She mouthed.

"Being a good girlfriend," I silently whispered back.

She scowled again and shook her head. I don't know what she wanted to say next, because Ant hopped a low stone wall and ended up ... in a graveyard.

"She's here?" I blinked, looking around at the messy, not taken care of headstones. "Why would she be here?"

"Because all good children end up here eventually." Mom stepped out from behind one of those big stone mausoleum thingies. She smiled, but it wasn't one of her happy smiles or even one of her Why-don't-you-know-all-the-answers-to-this-Bible-quiz smiles. Her teeth seemed pointy, almost like fangs, and she shimmered a little, like it was hard to keep the illusion going. *Illusion.* That's it …

"Guys, what do you see?" I squeezed Chris' hand hard, more scared of this fake-mom in front of us than of my real mom. "Like, describe her. What do you see?"

"Red hair," Ant said. "Freckles. Kind of tall. My Mom? What are you doing here? I was tracking Miry's mom, not you."

"White blonde hair and dark, almost black eyes," Chris went next. "Really pale skin. Is this—"

"Red dress. Dark hair. It's the lady from the club and who I saw on the sidewalk right after we liberated the car." Zuri shook her head. She squinted at fake-mom. "We're all looking at the same person, but seeing something completely different."

"A mom demon?" Ant asked. "Is that even possible?"

"We stopped the apocalypse last term," I said. "Anything is totally possible."

"The only demon that can hold that many

glamours at the same time is ... Lilith." Chris pulled me in front of him and wrapped his arms around my chest, sort of like a reverse human shield, though I think he meant it to be protective.

Lilith bowed. "Charmed ... Or am I the one charming you? It's a secret I'll never tell." She winked with a smirk.

"Stop with the riddles," Zuri snapped. "Why are you following me?"

"Tsk, tsk. So much with the thinking you're special and important." Lilith wagged a finger at Zuri. "Take stock, sweetheart, because you're not. I have no quarrel with your father. Now, his father—" Her pointing finger landed on Chris. "His father has many grievances to resolve. So many grievances indeed."

I felt Chris shift uncomfortably behind me. What was Lilith planning to do to his dad? Why would she just blab to us like that? Was it a trick? Or something even more scary?

"Stop hiding behind the glamours," Zuri ordered. "Show yourself. Your real self."

"With pride." Lilith smiled, bowed, and disappeared in a cloud of black smoke.

14

ZURI

My stomach roiled with bile as the demon disappeared. That bitch had tried to kill me and now I was going to return the favor. I tamped down on the desire to vomit before turning to Miry and the others.

"She thinks she has one up on us, but I bet she's the one behind the kidnappings. If she can glamour herself in a way to gain kids' trust, then of course they would go with her."

"Except you heard her, she's got a beef with Chris' dad. How does kidnapping angel kids lead to that?" Glasses piped up as we left the cemetery and traced our way back to the car.

"No idea, but I'd be more worried about

Miry's mom. If she has the scroll and Lilith is gunning for it, then we need to move fast."

Miry paled. "You don't think she would hurt my mom, do you?"

"She's a demon. I think she would do whatever she needed to get what she wants," I answered and slid behind the wheel.

Saint Boy remained uncharacteristically quiet as we finally got out of Atlanta and headed west on the highway. His description of what he saw stuck out in my mind. I could almost picture her, like I had seen her somewhere before. I made a mental note to check the copy of the Archives I still had stashed in my bag. Dad hadn't asked for it back and I hadn't volunteered to return it either.

"You got quiet," Glasses said as the GPS told us to stay on the highway for another twenty miles.

I glanced sideways at him. "Just trying to figure this whole thing out."

"I think it's great that you are helping find the lost kids."

I snorted. "I'd say that's your department, but you led us to a demon and not Miry's mom. I wouldn't go around advertising your skills just yet."

"Her glamour was stronger than my powers." He pushed his glasses up his nose. "Anyway, I thought you were really brave."

I rolled my eyes even though he couldn't see the gesture and turned back to the road. The skyline grew darker as we drove on and just as the sun slipped below the horizon, I spotted a sign for a motel.

"I'm calling it for the night," I announced and took the off ramp, winding my way to the tiny one floor structure.

"Two rooms," Saint Boy told the guy sitting at the front desk.

"You got some ID?"

None of us looked old enough to be renting rooms apparently. I stepped forward and slid my fake ID across the desk. Being good at forgery, definitely had its uses for a teenager. "Two rooms like he said."

The manager looked from my face to my ID several times before he finally slid two keys to us and gestured for me to hand over money. I caught Miry blanch out of the corner of my eye, but I pulled out a clipped roll of bills and peeled off a few. Satisfied we could at least afford the night, he went back to reading or whatever it was he was doing. Together we traipsed along the outside of the building to two adjacent rooms. Miry and Saint Boy darted into the first room before I could object.

"You better not be having really loud sex tonight!" I called as the door slammed.

Glasses opened the door to the other room and I followed after him. I pulled out my laptop and started to set up for an Archives deep dive.

"So, your mom sounds pretty. I mean from what you said you saw," Glasses said, sitting on the other bed.

"Wouldn't know. She died when I was born."

"How would you know what she looks like then?"

"A picture of her my dad kept."

"Oh. I'm sorry you didn't get to meet her."

"Bad shit happens to good people all the time."

"Not to you know speak ill of the dead, but I think you're prettier."

I set the laptop on the tiny table with a thump. "Okay look. I get you think I'm badass or cool or whatever, but there is zero chance of anything going on here. I'm gay. Like the thought of a dick makes me want to puke. Got it?"

His cheeks burned bright red. "I'm so sorry. I didn't mean to offend you."

"Dude, chill. You aren't the first guy to try. We good?"

He nodded so vigorously it made me think his head was going to come off his neck like a bobble head doll. After a minute he moved from the bed to the other chair around the table.

"What are you looking for?"

"Anything my dad's Archives have on Lilith."

"Doesn't she predate the Fall?"

"So did Beelzebub," I reminded him.

The conversation halted as I heard a squeal from the other room. "You know Saint Boy pretty well. He ever hurt her?"

"No. He loves Miry. Sometimes he just says stuff that comes off as mean. He's just protective of her, that's all."

"She can defend herself, though." *If she tried.*

"I think maybe Chris is a little jealous that Miry has another friend too," Glasses said. "There aren't many Archangel kids at school and that means not many people for Miry to really bond with. I think he just feels like he's losing her interest."

"He just comes off as controlling."

"Different perspectives I guess," Glasses muttered.

I turned back to my laptop and stared at the

image on the screen of Lilith's true form. It was exactly like Saint Boy described. All it said was 'Files Restricted.' We'll see about that.

I tapped at the keys, but the machine started to hiss and smoke, like someone had put a living computer virus on it. The program shut down, the screen turning to the Blue Screen of Death. Someone had made sure we couldn't access any more information from the Archives and I couldn't be sure it wasn't Dad trying to protect me.

"Guess we aren't getting information that way," Glasses said.

Though we did have another way. I was going to grill Saint Boy until he spilled everything he knew about Lilith.

"Stay here," I told Glasses, snagging one of the plastic room keys and shoving it in my back pocket.

I slammed the door shut behind me and pounded on the door next to us until it opened. Saint Boy stuck his head out. "What?"

"Let's chat," I said before pushing the door open wide enough for me to grab his shirt and pull him outside.

"You have some serious issues, you know that?" He snapped.

"Tell me what you know about Lilith," I demanded.

"I'm not the one who came from Demon Central," he retorted.

I shook my head, hands balling into fists. This asshole was going to force me to take a swing at him. "And yet you seemed awfully familiar with her back there. So, *what do you know?*"

"She's a demon and powerful too. If I had to guess, she's trying to build an army. Maybe she's tired of having to live under your dad's rule." He crossed his arms over his chest and glared. "Or is that something you already know?"

"Why is she specifically taking angel kids? If she only wanted an army, anyone with abilities would do."

"I don't know. Ask her yourself. Look, I only agreed to come on this stupid road trip to look out for Miry. So, do us both a favor, and don't put her in danger. We both know you attract it everywhere you go. She was safe until you showed up."

"You just can't handle that she's giving someone else attention." I stepped up close to him until I could feel his breath against my cheek. "I see the way you treat her. Lying to her, convincing her that you're her fucking savior. I know what abuse looks like and you're the damn poster child for an abuser. I'm not going to let you hurt her."

"You keep thinking I'm scared of some Fallen bitch. Get real."

I slammed a fist into his face, sending him staggering back and clutching at his face. "What the … I … you broke my nose!"

I flexed my bruised knuckles. "No, I didn't. You walked into a door. Maybe fell down some stairs. Or whatever bullshit excuse you want to tell yourself. I'll be watching you."

I stormed back into the room I was being forced to share with Glasses and flung myself at the unoccupied bed. He was smart enough not to ask questions.

15

MIRYAM

"Chris? Chris, what happened?" I sat up in bed, watching his back as if that would give me some sort of answer. "I thought I heard yelling …"

Chris locked the deadbolt and put the chain on. He rested his head against the door for a minute, before coming to join me on the bed farthest from the door. His nose was swollen and dripping blood onto his shirt. I gasped, reaching out a hand. He winced when I gingerly probed the injury with my fingers.

"What happened?"

"Your anger management roommate decided to shove me face first into the door." His breath hissed out between his teeth as I angelically healed his nose without being asked. "Thanks. You're a life safer."

"Speaking of life saving ..." I reached for his hand, tracing patterns with my finger across his knuckles. "Are you sick again? I mean like sick-sick and not anything external that I can heal with my powers."

"I'm never not sick," Chris said. "That's what chronic means, Mir."

"I know that. It's just—"

"I've had better days." He kicked off his shoes and laid back so he was sideways across the bed. "The thing with Lilith was wild, wasn't it? How could she look like all our mothers at the exact same time?"

I traced patterns on Chris' pant leg next. It gave me something to focus on and hopefully soothed him a bit. I hated when he had a flair up. I felt so helpless. "I just wish the first time you saw your mom was not when a demon was, like, impersonating her. I'm sorry. That totally sucked."

Chris shrugged. "Don't worry about it. I'm over it already."

I glanced at the wall separating our room from Zuri and Ant's. "I feel bad for Ant. He's totally crushing on Zuri and she could care less. I mean, there's the not liking guys thing, but then there's the not liking Ant thing too. She's not so impressed with my friends."

Chris laid his arm across his eyes. "Including me obviously."

I kept my eyes on the wall, expecting yelling or something from the other room. So far there was only silence. "I think it's more like she thinks you're holding me back or whatever, rather than not actually thinking you're an okay guy. I love you. That counts for something, right?"

"That counts for everything." Chris sat up with effort, having to leverage himself with his free arm. I wrapped an arm low around his waist for some extra support.

"I just wish Zuri could see you the way I see you," I said. "It would be seriously less messy if my two favorite people liked each other. Or at least tolerated each other."

"Why do you even give her any of your time and loyalty?" Chris asked. "She doesn't deserve it. I mean, you've known her for how long? Two months? Three? Anyway, not long enough to warrant such blind loyalty if you ask me."

"I dunno. We just click," I shrugged. "I guess it's one of those opposites attract sort of things, but with friendship instead of, you know, romance or whatever. She believes in me," I confessed. "Like, not many people think I'm good for anything besides screaming and running away when bad things happen. Zuri's different. She thinks I'm a fighter. I wanna totally be the best I can be. If that means training to fight or sticking up for myself, then I wanna do that. Zuri thinks I can and so do I." I tapped my chest near my heart with my free hand. "There's so much inside of me, Chris. I want to be the best me possible. Zuri encourages that."

"And I don't?" He did a poor job of hiding the jealousy in his voice.

"Of course you do." I went straight for the 'agree with everything to keep the peace.' "You're like totally the best boyfriend ever. I just wish you'd let me help you when you're sick like this with a relapse or whatever. You say I can, but then you never tell me *how*."

"What I need is a little more complicated than chicken soup and sleep, Mir."

"Then tell me so I can help you." I leaned my forehead against his. His was hot and sticky with sweat. "Chris, please …"

He sighed. "Fine. I didn't want to involve you, but remember when I said there wasn't a cure for my illness? Well, I found one … Angel blood.

Something about it reacting with my saint blood boosts my immune system and I can fight off the illness. If I don't have it, well, I die."

It took me awhile to process what he said. "You need blood."

"Yes."

"Then take mine."

16

ZURI

I tossed and turned well into the early morning as Lilith haunted my dreams. By three o'clock, I knew sleep wasn't coming and I crept out of the room, leaving Glasses to snore blissfully in the other bed. I paused by Miry's room, listening for any sounds that might mean she was in danger. Even Saint Boy had to sleep though and I hadn't heard anything beyond those initial squeals last night.

I wandered the grounds of the small motel, tugging on the thin cord around my wrist. Seeing Lilith appear as my mother had bothered me more than I had let on. I'd never gotten the chance to meet the woman who gave me life. It wasn't fair that the first time I'd really seen her, it had been a mask worn by a demon. I tried to not be prejudiced. I knew demons were as misunderstood as Fallen angels, but I couldn't help feeling resentment toward Lilith and Beelzebub. They were messing with my life and it pissed me off.

"Damn demons," I grumbled, kicking a piece of trash in my path. It felt childish the moment I did it and I was silently grateful no one was around to see it.

The air was chilly as I put distance between myself and the hotel. The rest of the kids were sleeping soundly, if not safely. I needed to clear my head and figure out everything I could about Lilith. I knew calling Damien this early was a no-go. Boy needed his beauty rest more than I did. The fact that the copy of the Archives went haywire told me someone knew I had it and didn't want me looking. Either Dad was punishing me after all, or there was a leak somewhere.

Dad.

I pulled out my phone and hit his number on my speed dial. It rang only once before the line picked up.

"What's wrong?" Dad sounded more awake than I had expected.

"Oh, you know, road tripping with some

wannabe saints to try and hunt down a demon," I answered.

"That's not funny, Zuri. It's three in the morning. What's wrong?"

I heaved a sigh. "I'm actually being serious. Dad, Lilith is on the loose and we think she's been kidnapping angel kids for years. She looked like Mom."

I let my last sentence hang in the ether between us, really letting it sink into Dad's brain. "I'm coming to get you."

"Dad, I don't need to be rescued. You trained me, remember? I can handle myself. Besides, she had a chance to take me and she didn't." I thought back to the night at the club. It felt like ages ago instead of only a few days. The memory of her luring me was hazy, but I could still feel a finger tracing my cheek. No, not trace, prick. She'd drawn blood and tasted it. She had to know I was angelic, but maybe Fallen kids weren't what she was after. Or maybe … "Dad, do you have some sort of deal with her that she wouldn't go after me?"

"I thought last term would have taught you to stay out of any and all demonic affairs," he answered, not addressing my question.

"I'm a rebel. Wonder where I get that from?

But seriously, Dad, do you have some sort of deal with Lilith? If I've got immunity or whatever I need to know."

"Long before you were born, yes, I made a deal with her. I would leave her be and she wouldn't touch any of my children."

So, I did have some sort of immunity. *Good to know.* "I was trying to find anything else I could about her, but the copy of the Archives sort of fried my computer so …"

"So, you thought you'd call your old man in the middle of the night to be an angelic rolodex?" I could hear the smile in his tone.

"I guess. Look, we both know you can't stop me. Michael thinks we're on our way to see Miry's sick mom. Which isn't totally a lie. She sounds pretty sick too from what I've heard about Miry's childhood and we are going to see her, but … please, I need to know what we're facing with Lilith."

"There's not much to tell, Zuri. She's power-ful, older than most of humanity. She was Adam's first wife, but she was unable to bear children of her own. She longs to be a mother. A sentiment I don't blame her for. Being a parent has been one of the most rewarding parts of my existence."

"Mommy issues. Got it. What does she look like normally? In her true form, I mean."

"I don't believe she's ever shown it to me. She's always appeared as a young woman. She could be anyone really."

"She looked like all of our mothers. I can't tell you how badly I wanted to hug her and punch her in the face all at the same time."

"She is dangerous, Zuri. You need to be careful. Whatever you think you're looking for, find it fast and get back to school grounds. As much as I distrust Michael, I know he wouldn't let demonic powers onto campus. Not after Beelzebub."

Somehow, I suspected the increased wards were Dad's doing. "Thanks for the info. I'm going to try to get some sleep. We have a long day ahead of us." I wasn't going to spend another night in some shitty hotel with Glasses. I didn't care if it meant driving all day to get to Miry's mom.

"I know I'm your father and my warnings don't mean much to you, but be careful. Remember I love you."

"I love you, too, Dad."

I hung up and retreated to the room, hoping for a little rest before we got on the road again.

BY SIX O'CLOCK, I couldn't take it anymore and nudged Glasses hard in the ribs. "Come on, get your ass up. We're leaving in ten minutes."

"Ow," he groaned, but sat up and rubbed at his eyes.

I went next door, pounding loudly on the door. "Miry. Get up. We're leaving in ten."

I heard movement from within and thirty second later, Miry stuck her head out. Her normally perky complexion was pale. I eyed thick gauze strips around her wrists. "Get your pretty ass out here," I hissed.

She stepped out of the room, flipping the lock so she wouldn't need the key. "What's wrong?" she asked.

I pointed to her wrists. "Those are what's wrong. What the fuck did he do?"

"Nothing. I'm fine, really."

"Don't give me that excuse, because you're not fine. He did something to you that required bandages, Miry."

"I wanted him to, okay? Just drop it," she snapped.

Taken aback by her tone, I headed for the car, getting myself ready for the long drive to Kansas. Glasses climbed into the front seat beside me while Miry and Saint Boy got in back. He slung an arm around her shoulders, making me grip the steering wheel tight in annoyance. I was going to find out what he had over her and beat it out of him. First though, we needed to get where we were headed.

17

MIRYAM

I tipped my head to the side, studying the drink cooler. Why was deciding on a drink so hard? It was like literally something I'd been doing since I was five. My mind was fuzzy and it was hard to concentrate. I scratched at the bandages on my wrists, staring at the cooler until my eyes went all blank and unfocused.

"You okay?"

I blinked, everything coming back into focus in a whoosh. I was in the convenience store, because I needed a drink. The boys were in charge of munchies.

"Hey, Earth to Miry," Zuri said. "I asked if you were okay."

I scratched at the inside of my wrists again. "Sure. Never better."

She motioned at the bandages. "You don't look 'never better.'"

"I slipped and broke a glass on my hands last night," I made stuff up as I went just like I usually did. "I was totally lucky Chris found the first aid kit and, like, knew how to use it. I can't angelically heal myself with my hands messed up, can I?"

"But it's not your hands, it's your wrists." Zuri pointed at the bandages again. "Nice try, now tell me the truth. Do you feel safe with Saint Boy? Did he hit you? Shove you? Grab you so hard you have bruises? Falling on glass isn't even a good cover story, Miry. It's like you want me to ask questions."

"I'm fine. Chris loves me. There's nothing to get all worked up about." I repeated like the good little Stepford Wife I was supposed to be.

Zuri crossed her arms over her chest. "Yeah, keep telling yourself that. Maybe someday you'll believe it too."

I yanked open the cooler door and grabbed the first drink my hand came in contact with. "Just leave it alone," I hissed. "I mean it, Z. Stop asking questions. It will only get us all in trouble."

I stood on tiptoes to scan the convenience store, hoping the boys were already in line so I could flounce over there. I wanted to forget Zuri and all her twenty questions, seeing right through me. Luck was totally on my side. I bounced on my heels and waved to Chris. He grinned and mouthed something that looked like "Why you hanging with buzzkill?"

"Grab what you want so we can go," I said to Zuri in my perkiest of perky voices, pretending like her twenty questions and, let's face it, concern for me didn't exist. "We got like eight gazillion miles to go."

"Sit up front," she said. "Swap places with Glasses. Saint Boy can go fuck himself if he has a problem with it."

I flinched in pain when she grabbed my wrist to stop me from walking away. "I can't. The front seat makes me nauseous. I don't want to spew all over the rental car. Or stolen car. Or whatever it is."

"Say that a little louder. I don't think the beer delivery driver outside heard you."

I cracked a smile. I was totally wiped from my impromptu blood donation last night, but it felt good to smile. "Come on, Z. It's a long way to Kansas."

WE DROVE and drove and drove and drove some more. I slept when I could, curled up against Chris for warmth. He kept one arm around my shoulder, his fingers brushing the side of my breast. Zuri openly kept watch on us through the rearview mirror. She never said anything, but I'm sure she was thinking tons.

When it got dark, we found a parking lot that didn't tow people and slept a couple hours in the car. I guess Zuri didn't want a repeat of the hotel from night one. We used the truck stop showers and bathrooms in the morning. Everything else we pretty much did in the car. We ate in the car. We slept in the car. If we could pee in the car, I'm sure Z would have found a way to make that happen too. It wasn't a very fun road trip, but the destination wasn't fun times either. The closer we got to Mom's house, the more anxious I felt. I was practically hyperventilating by the time we pulled into the driveway.

"You okay?" Chris whispered. He shifted so his hand was more directly on my breast.

"We didn't tell Mom that we were coming for a visit," I said. "I don't know if she'll be happy to see me or not."

"If she's not, then she's crazy." Chris dipped his head to kiss my forehead. "Besides, Celestial Academy is your home now, not here."

"Hey, Z, remember what we like talked about before leaving campus?" I untangled myself from Chris and leaned across the console so I was half in the front seat, half in the back.

"About your mom being an anti-gay, anti-black, anti-Fallen racist?" Zuri deadpanned. "Yeah, I remember."

"So, I was thinking the boys and I just go in, get the scroll, and get out," I said. "It will take, like, ten minutes tops. It's not going to be so bad to hang in the car for ten minutes by yourself, right?"

"Don't forget to crack the window," Zuri said in that same deadpan voice. I bet she secretly wanted to murder us all in our sleep for suggesting the 'plan,' but decided it wasn't worth the time and effort.

"We'll be ten minutes. Promise." I touched Zuri's arm lightly, but she jerked away. "Mom's best in small doses anyway." I wiggled into the back seat to find my shoes. "I'm Miryam bat-Michael," I reminded myself to give me courage. "I got this."

1 8

ZURI

Before I realized what was happening, I was watching Miry and the boys climb out of the car and walk up to the front door. Miry knocked, leaning on Saint Boy until a woman who could be Miry's spitting image, but twice her age appeared in the doorway.

"Miryam? What are you doing here?" Her voice carried.

"Hi, Mom. You remember my boyfriend, Chris. This is our friend Anthony. We're on a special assignment from Dad. It's like really important that we talk to you. Can we come in?" Miry's voice was just as loud.

Miry's mom nodded vigorously at the mention of Michael and ushered them inside. The front door closed and I could swear Miry's mom peeked out the front window before drawing the curtains. Miry wasn't kidding when she said the woman was paranoid. After about fifteen seconds, I realized that this so-called plan was stupid as fuck and I climbed out of the car. I wasn't going to just walk up to the front door and knock either. I resented being told to stay in the car. I deserved to be in there just as much as the rest of them. If her mother really was a racist, bigoted bitch, then I could have a little fun.

I slipped around the back and found a window that led into what appeared from the outside to be a bedroom. I pulled a knife—city living had taught me to be prepared—out of my bag and fiddled with the latch until it slid open. I climbed through and stepped right into what had to be Miry's room. If her side of the room at school was any indication, the unicorn that had vomited purples, pinks, and rainbows all over the place was a dead giveaway. I had no doubt Miry would eventually convince her mom to give up the scroll. So, I had time to snoop. I eased open dresser drawers and was disappointed to find a bright array of socks and underwear in the same colors that Miry usually wore.

"Come on, Miry. Grow up already," I muttered

peering into the closet to the same result. Whatever secrets Miry may have, she hid them well in this place. It was just as bubbly an exterior as she put on at school, but I knew better. I'd seen her vulnerable and real. *If only she could be that person all the time.*

Leaving her room behind, I wandered down the hall, past the master bedroom and bath. I stopped at a closed door with a padlock. My stomach turned as I remembered Miry saying her mother had locked her in a closet. Picking the lock was child's play and inside was a torture chamber. Scratch marks marred the inside of the door. It was all bare wood with a single light bulb dangling from the ceiling. Even Harry Potter had better accommodations. A board hung on one wall with Miry's neat handwriting listing the books of the Bible starting with the Old Testament. A shrine to Archangel Michael dominated another wall cluttered with pictures and prayer candles.

"Sadistic bitch," I snarled and slammed the door.

The conversation from down the hall halted. I heard furniture creak and then Miry's mom said, "Who's there?"

"I'm sure it was just the wind, Mom," Miry

said. Panic made her voice jump an octave into squeaky territory.

"No, I heard something."

"Mom, tell us again about how you met Dad." Miry's voice lowered.

What is she doing?

"He appeared to me and said—"

"Miryam, I have chosen you to bear my child. You are worthy," Miry and her mom said in unison.

It must have been some sort of test to make sure this was really her mom and not Lilith in disguise.

I didn't wait for her mother to say anything else. I marched into the living room where my traveling companions sat. Miry's mom stood in the center of the room.

"Who are you? Why are you in my house?" She demanded.

"Oh, didn't Miry tell you? I'm her roommate, Zuri bat-Lucifer."

Her mother's face paled in shock. "Devil!"

"Oh, lady. Believe me, I'm not the one sinning in this house. What you did to my friend, that's some criminal shit right there. Child endangerment, neglect. Did I mention my dad knows some *really* good lawyers? If I wanted, I could have your sorry ass arrested."

Miry's lips trembled and she shook her head vigorously, but I didn't stop. This woman had hurt my friend and I was ready to get even. We could take the damn scroll by force if necessary. "Oh, and I guess she probably didn't mention that I fuck chicks. Yeah, love me some tits."

"I'll get rid of this vagrant," Saint Boy said, stepping up beside Miry's mom.

"Boy, you better shut your mouth before I beat your ass," I said. *Let him try and come at me.*

"I can take you," he replied.

I snorted. "Yeah, okay. What are you good at again? Oh, that's right, running away from situations. Your daddy was the patron saint of turning tail and running like a little bitch. What did you even do when the apocalypse went down?"

"Guys, come on," Glasses said meekly.

"At least my father is a literal saint. I'd hate to be the daughter of a Fallen angel. And the apocalypse was all *your* fault."

He lunged at me, but I side stepped him. I grabbed the collar of his shirt and swung him around, swiping his legs out from under him. "You have been treating Miry like shit and I'm done with it," I hissed in his ear.

"She's not yours to protect," he replied.

"Enough!" Miry's voice boomed, filling the space.

I looked up to see Miry standing behind her mother, her wings unfurled. They almost reached from one side of the room to the other. She was impressive and imposing ... and kind of hot.

"I will not have my best friend and my boyfriend fighting like this. I love you both. Now, we came here for a reason. Let's get what we came for and go back to school." She turned her attention to her mother. "Mom, we need Gabriel's Scroll. He said the last place he remembered leaving it was with you."

"I don't ..." her mother trailed off.

"I can say a prayer and see if I can find it," Glasses offered.

His lost-and-found trick hadn't exactly gotten us very far before. Miry's mother seemed to regain some of her composure as she stared at me. "Will it get this devil child out of my house?"

"Give us the scroll and you'll never have to see me again," I replied.

"Fine." She disappeared down the hall I'd come from.

I shoved Saint Boy, but let him up. He scrambled to his feet and shot daggers at me. "I thought Miry told you to stay in the car?"

"Why would I miss getting to kick your ass? Not a chance, douchebag. Besides, do you really think she would have given up an angelic relic that easily?"

Miry's mom reappeared and handed over a long cylindrical tube normally used to store paintings. "I didn't want it to get damaged," she muttered.

I took it, slung the container over my shoulder and gestured to the front door. "Let's get out of here."

I led the way back to the car, uncapping the tube and unfurling the scroll gently on the hood of the car. Hundreds of names were penned in delicate script upon the parchment along with dates of birth and death dating back at least a millennia. I skimmed, not sure what I was looking for until a single name jumped out at me.

Miryam bat-Michael. Except it couldn't be the same girl standing beside me, because this girl had a date of death from two years earlier.

"What the hell is going on?"

19

———

MIRYAM

"Whatcha find?" I stood on my tiptoes to try to get a look at the scroll.

"Nothing. Nothing at all." Zuri rolled up the scroll and stuck it back in Mom's poster tube. "We can look at it more later."

I stretched my arms over my head, my shirt riding up a little to show my belly button. I instinctively glanced at the house, making sure Mom wasn't watching. Showing skin had always got me thrown in the closet. Having a gay black best friend would probably get me sent to a conversion camp even though there was nothing to convert me from. "Can we go now?" I whined. "This place gives me the heebie-jeebies."

"But you lived here," Chris said.

"That doesn't mean I like it." I grabbed his hand and crawled into the backseat. "School is totally my scene now. Who wants to be stuck in Kansas when there's a whole world of freedom at Celestial Academy? Not me. Now let's go."

"We drove a long way for just a piece of paper," Ant complained, but he got in the car anyway. "Remind me again why it's so important?"

"It records all the angelic births and deaths." Zuri gunned the engine, peeling out of the driveway as if she hated Mom's house as much as I did. "We thought it would help with the kidnappings."

"If we cross reference who has disappeared with the scroll's names, we can find out if they're still alive or not," I added.

"It should also help us figure out who is the next target." Zuri kept her gaze mostly on the road, but I caught her eyes outlined in the rearview mirror more than once.

"Why should we even care about the kidnappings?" Chris grimaced, looking car sick. I opened my pink backpack and held it out to him just in case he needed to puke into it. "Aren't the police handling it? Let them do their job."

"Dad won't let the police on campus," I reminded him. "Dad and Uncle Uriel are handling it all internally. They haven't done a very good job so far and that's where we come in."

"The Scooby Gang to the rescue," Chris muttered. "Just leave it alone, Miry. If your Dad and Uriel are working on it, just let them do their thing. They're Archangels. We're not. End of story."

"Except you are a saint. Zuri and I are Archangels," I argued, something I rarely did with Chris. "Shouldn't we, like, want to do the right thing? Finding the missing kids is the right thing, Chris."

"You're an Archangel, she's a Fallen," Chris argued right back. "There's a big difference."

"No, actually there's not," Zuri and I said at the exact same time. I almost called 'jinx,' but this was serious—not a time for games. I caught Zuri's eyes watching me in the rearview mirror again. I waited for her to explain why her dad and my dad had the same rank, but she didn't. It was up to me this time.

"We learned this in history, remember?" I said. "Zuri's dad is an Archangel just like my dad and all the rest. That doesn't change just cause he lives somewhere else now."

"Did you seriously just call Hell 'somewhere else' like he moved to the suburbs?" Chris raised a pale eyebrow as if to say 'yeah, sure, keep be-lieving that.' "Miry, Lucifer was cast out of Heaven for a reason. He fought in the war and lost. It's not like he moved to Hell, because he wanted a warmer climate. He was literally booted out of Heaven. He doesn't deserve to keep the title of Archangel. He's Fallen … and so is she."

"She's my friend." My voice shook, but I didn't back down. I wouldn't either, because this was too important to me. "And I'd appreciate it if you didn't talk about Zuri or her family like that, thank you very much."

"Yeah, sure. Whatever you say." Chris made an obscene gesture that I wasn't 100% positive was directed at me before he turned and stared out the window. Kansas scenery going East was kind of pretty, but I never imagined Chris to be the kind of guy who liked landscapes. So he must still be super mad.

"If Michael and Uriel are handling the kidnap-pings, they're not doing a very good job," Ant broke the silence after we passed like thirty mile markers. "Fifty plus kids going missing is not a great track record. Maybe their methods don't work. I like the idea of using the scroll. At least it gives us a direction to start looking in."

Zuri nodded. "I hate that I'm about to agree with you, Glasses, but ... What he said."

"It's just a piece of paper," Chris muttered. "Big deal."

"It's an angelic relic," Zuri corrected. "And it *is* a big deal."

Chris drifted off into a moody silence. I scratched at the bandages on my wrist. It was a good thing Mom didn't ask about them, though we didn't stay long enough for her to ask anything really. I peeked under the gauze to check how the cuts across my wrist veins were healing. I wish I could angelically heal them. However, there was protocol to all that and hurting yourself—even for a good cause like saving your boyfriend's life —was not on the list of things healing powers worked on.

"How are you feeling?" Chris asked, sounding like the regular, normal Chris and not the moody jerk who comes out to play whenever Zuri was around.

I waved my bandaged wrist at him. "Just more scars to add to the rest. No biggie."

"I'm sorry you had to do that for me."

I shook my head. "I'm not. You needed my help. That's what I do. I help people."

He sighed and leaned over until his head was

resting on my chest. "I don't deserve your goodness, Mir."

"Sure you do," I insisted. "I love you."

"Maybe I don't deserve your love either."

I caught Zuri watching us again from the rearview mirror. Waiting to hear what I was going to say. I kissed the top of Chris' head and stroked his hair. "I'm here for you," I said. "That's what girlfriends do."

20

ZURI

The urge to keep driving until we made it back to Georgia was strong, but my eyes were heavy by the time the clock read 11:30 at night. I scanned the signs on the highway for the first motel and pulled off onto a single-lane road to a dilapidated motel.

"We aren't staying here," Saint Boy objected as I turned the car off and pulled the key from the ignition.

"Scared?" I taunted in spite of myself. Or maybe it was the exhaustion kicking in.

"It looks kind of creepy," Glasses agreed.

I rolled my eyes. "Grow a pair." I climbed out of the car and marched up to the front door, waiting for the others to follow me. They stayed put though. Fine, they could stay in the car all damn night if they wanted. I was going to sleep in a bed. The clerk behind the front desk faced away from us.

"Two rooms," I said, slapping down a wad of cash.

"Bit late to be out on your own," an eerie voice said as the clerk spun around. She wore my mother's face, but I knew that wasn't possible.

My wings unfurled without me realizing or intending it. "I'm going to kill you."

She gave me a smile, her teeth pointed, but in my mother's mouth. "Now, is that any way to speak to your mother?"

I took a step back to get a running start. I could take her out, I just needed to get a good grip on her. Just as my right foot left the ground, she vanished in a puff of smoke. I staggered into the front of the counter and let out an 'oomph" as the air went out of my lungs. Panic started to creep into my head. If she knew where we were, she could go after Miry.

"I help you with something?" An elderly man in well-worn overalls asked, sauntering up to the desk.

I glanced over my shoulder to check my wings were no longer on display and pushed the money toward him. "I need two rooms."

"That's an awful lot for just one little lady."

"I'm not alone." *And I could kick your scrawny human ass in two seconds flat.* He stared at the money, but didn't touch it. I reached for it. "Fine, if you don't want our money, we'll just go somewhere else."

"Now hold on. I didn't say that," he said and snatched the bills from behind my fingers. He slid over two plastic keycards that had seen better days before stowing the money in a drawer beside him.

"First two down on the left," he said.

"Great."

I retreated to the car and grabbed my bag. "Come on, Miry."

"What?" She sounded half-awake.

"We're rooming together."

"Don't be stupid," Saint Boy said.

I flung the keycard at him and it narrowly missed slicing his neck. "In case you missed it back there, douchebag, I don't care what you think. Michael said no co-ed sleeping arrangements. Besides you wouldn't want to piss him off, would you?"

"It's cool, Chris," Glasses said, bending down to pick up the card that Saint Boy had dodged.

I watched them go, Saint Boy glowering at me the whole way before I lightly wrapped an arm around Miry's shoulders and led her to other room. The fresh air perked her up as she looked around our accommodations and the single large bed in the middle of the room.

"I guess we get cozy," she said and threw herself against the pillows. A cloud of dust rose up around her and she coughed. "Gross."

"It's not the Ritz, but we'll survive for a night," I said and eased myself down onto the other side of the bed.

"So, do you think we'll be able to stop Lilith now that we have the scroll?" She asked, propping herself up on one elbow.

"I don't know. I hope so ... I mean, I get that Gabriel is absent-minded. Still you would have thought if the Archangels gave two shits about the missing kids, they'd have realized where the scroll was, gotten it, and put a stop to all of this themselves."

"They're trying," she said, not meeting my gaze.

"Miry, what has your father done in the entire time I've known you to stop it? He has stupid announcements to scare vulnerable children. He didn't even show up when the fucking apocalypse was going down in his own basement."

Miry blinked and her eyes shone with unshed tears in the dim light of the room. "I know he's not like your dad, but he's not that bad. He's better than Mom."

I bit my lower lip to keep from lashing out at her. She didn't need me to yell at her. It wouldn't change things. She'd been yelled at enough in her life. She needed someone to listen and really hear her. "I saw that room. The closet. That's awful. I'm sorry she did that to you. No parent should ever do that to their kid."

She rubbed at her cheeks, the gauze around her right wrist slipping with the motion. "She was trying to show me how special I was … in her own way. But you're right. What she did isn't normal."

I could tell she wanted to say more, but she just picked at the gauze around her wrists. "Miry, you said something about other scars." I pointed to her wrists. "What did you mean?"

Miry curled into herself, hugging the pillow beneath her head. "I don't want to talk about it."

"I think we need to. I need to know that you

aren't going to try and do something I can't bring you back from. We're friends and friends look out for each other, okay?" I brushed a lock of blond hair out of her eyes and tucked it behind her ear.

"I guess back before I went to Celestial Academy, I kind of had this thing where I'd cut myself. It wasn't a big deal. I stopped too, but … it made me feel like there was something that I could control."

I let her words wash over me and a wave of anger crashed into me. Anger at her parents for treating her like garbage. Anger at the world for not seeing that she had worth beyond whose bloodline she carried. I scooted closer and pulled her into a hug.

"I'm so sorry," I whispered into her ear and held her.

We laid there until the anger started to dull. As she pulled out of my embrace, I caught sight of the bandage on her wrist again and the anger bubbled up. This time at Saint Boy and his manipulative tendencies. "What made you think hurting yourself for him was a good idea?"

"I was helping him," she insisted. "He's sick and angel blood helps him."

"Sick with what exactly?" I probed.

"I don't know. He never wants to talk about it. I think he's ashamed that he's sick at all. Chris is so proud of his saintly heritage. I think it's a guy thing, too. You know not wanting to seem vulnerable."

"You didn't think it was weird that he needs angel blood … when we're hunting a demon who is kidnapping angel kids? A demon, by the way, who seems to know where we are, even now. She was in the lobby when we got here."

She blinked at me. "I … no. I didn't. Are you sure it was here?"

"She had my mother's face."

"You must have been so scared."

"Not at all, I was pissed. Miry, she's got some way of tracking us. We won't be safe until we are back on school grounds." I hated having to admit that.

Miry sat quiet for a moment then said, "But you're wrong. Lilith kidnapping kids and Chris needing angel blood aren't related. I'm sure of it. Chris doesn't have an evil bone in his body. Besides, he loves me."

No, he doesn't. I wish I could make her see that what she saw as love was manipulation and control. Still that's how people had treated her all her life and I wasn't going to break through those barriers in one day or even four months. "Let's get some sleep. We've got a long drive ahead of us." As I settled beneath the blankets, I couldn't get the image of the scroll with Miry's name and death date out of my head.

21

MIRYAM

"Please … Mom, I already told you the books of the Bible today. I'll be good, I promise. Mom? I'll be good. Mom! Mom! Mom!" The closet door morphed into my own coffin. I had on a swimming suit—one piece, Mom said only harlots wore two-piece suits—instead of a black dress. The coffin floated in the school's swimming pool, tea light candles bobbing all around my barge to the afterlife. I don't want to die, though. I don't want to die.

"I don't want to die!" I sat bolt upright in bed, clawing at my throat until I drew blood. Wait what … Bed? When did I get into bed? Where was the pool party or funeral …? I looked around the darkened room. Zuri stood in a crouch near the edge of the bed, like she was about to attack the demons in my mind. I remembered where I was now. We were on a road trip. Mom had given up Gabriel's Scroll a whole heck of a lot easier than I thought she would and now we were on our way back to campus. "Was I ... Was I dreaming?" I asked, looking to Zuri for confirmation. The longer I was awake, the dimmer the dream seemed.

"If that's what you call a dream, I'd hate to see one of your nightmares." Zuri sat down on the little pallet of blankets and couch cushions she'd made for herself on the floor. "What do you re-member from it?"

I shrugged. "Not much. Just Mom being Mom and something about a scary pool party."

"You screamed out in your sleep," Zuri said. "You said you didn't want to die."

I shrugged again. "I told you it was a scary pool party."

"What else do you remember about it?"

I hugged one of the nasty hotel pillows against my chest. "Last I checked, psychology was not on our curriculum."

Zuri made one of her 'deal with it' noises. "Last I checked, I didn't know you could make it through an entire sentence without saying 'like' or 'totally.'"

"Oh, I like totally can." I felt like being difficult. "But I have a reputation to uphold, you know? Bubbly people stay bubbly. It's what gets you friends."

"Being kind and willing to help others no matter what gets you friends, Miry," Zuri said. "In other words ... being you."

"However, if being me is so great, why don't I want to ..." I shook my head. "Forget it. Forget I said anything."

Zuri leaned over and tapped my wrists. "Cutting is not the only way to feel or be in control, you know. You've been through some scary shit. That's clear. The sooner you face it, the sooner you can move past it and heal. Dropping the douche nozzle boyfriend might help a little too."

I cracked a smile. "Oh, haha. It's kind of funny how you two can't stand each other. I mean, I know I shouldn't be laughing over it or anything, but I've never had anyone fight over me before. Even if it is just my best friend versus my boyfriend. It's kind of ... exciting." I grabbed her hand in both of mine when a sudden thought struck me. "Promise me you won't fight him for real, okay? Words are one thing. Fist fight or whatever is not cool."

Zuri pulled her hand free. She wiped it on her pants like I had cooties or something. "You do realize he's getting to Mom level manipulation, right? I can't be the only one who sees that."

"You see what you want to see," I said. "Chris loves me. Chris saved me at—" My eyes went wide and a rush of memories flooded my mind. I bounced excitedly on the bed once more of the missing pieces fell into place. "I remember! I remember what happened at that scary pool party! It was the student mixer right before term ended for the summer. Dad even showed up which never—and I mean never—happens. Chris and me, Ant and CeCe, and even Uncle Uriel and Dad were playing volleyball in the shallow end. I thought it was the perfect end to the term. I missed the ball and it had floated out into the deep end. I didn't want to go get it, cause I can't swim. Dad said 'it's time, Miryam' which was kind of weird, but I don't know ... Dad says weird stuff sometimes. He's older than dirt. Anyway, Dad said 'it's time, Miryam' and—before I knew what was happening—Uncle Uriel picked me up and threw me into the deep end."

"He threw you into the deep end when he

knew you couldn't swim?" Zuri clenched her hands into tight fists.

I shrugged, the memory starting to retreat now that I was at the most frightening part of the scary pool party. "It was a fun party up until then."

Zuri stood up and paced the length of the room, muttering to herself and trying to get her emotions under control. Once her anger wasn't fully raging, she looked over at me. "I hate that I need to ask 'how did you survive' when adults are supposed to protect us, not attempt to murder us, but how did you survive?"

I grinned. "Chris saved me, of course. He was totally heroic. He jumped in the deep end, pulled me to safety, and even did CPR. Cool, right?"

"Did he tell you that version of events or did someone else with less, um, stake in what you thought about them?"

I chewed my bottom lip. The more I tried to remember things, the further and further they slipped away. "What do you mean?"

"He wants you to hero worship him," Zuri said. "It actually makes a lot of sense now. Why he's been such a pissant since I showed up. He's afraid your hero worship will transfer from him to me."

I touched the fading remnants of a hickey on my neck. "Chris loves me though."

"You keep saying that, but do you really believe it?"

"Of course I do," I insisted. "Why would you even question me about that? That's not what friends do, Zuri."

"Fine." Zuri sat back down on her blanket and cushion pallet. "When was this pool party, by the way?"

"May," I said without hesitation. "Two years ago."

"Well, fuck." Zuri pulled the scroll from its tube and unrolled it. She pointed at a spot near the bottom. "Things just got a whole lot weirder."

I looked at the name right above her finger. It was my name, but it couldn't be me. My death date was recorded on the same day of the scary pool party.

22

ZURI

"That can't be right," Miry said in a strained tone.

"Well, unless you've got a twin walking around out there who also drowned two years ago … no, that's you."

"I didn't drown," Miry said with a pout.

"We don't know that. You could have died for a minute or two. Maybe just long enough for it to record on the scroll, before you were resuscitated," I replied, snapping the scroll out of her reach and stowing it back in the carrying tube.

"But if that did happen, wouldn't the date have gone away?" She asked.

"It's a relic, a mystical angelic scroll, Miry. I don't fucking know how it works." *But I know someone who might.* "Look, I think we need to make a detour before we go back to school."

"Where?" She was on her feet in seconds.

"Hell."

"Oh, very funny, Z."

"I'm not joking. Azrael knows all things death. It's literally his job and his title. So if something happened to you, he'll know the details. Besides, you've been saying you want to see Hell, right?"

"Well, I mean, yeah but like ... not to find out why I'm supposed to be dead."

"Think of it this way, I've gotten to see how you live in your comfort zone. Now you can see me in mine. Plus, it will give us a chance to check the Archives for anything else on Lilith that my dad left out."

"What do you mean 'left out?'" Miry crossed her arms over her chest and pouted.

"I tried to access the copy of the Archives I made last term the other day and it fried my computer. I called my dad to see what he knew about Lilith, but there's got to be a lot more on the Archives. He wasn't thrilled I was off chasing the mother of demons."

"What if he tells my dad what we're doing?" She whined.

"Miry, think about that question for a minute.

Your father despises mine. There's no chance he'd ever rat us out," I assured her.

"If we are going to Hell, we need to tell the boys."

"No. I can navigate the gates with one person, but I'm not bringing along any extra baggage. They'll just slow us down. I'll be honest, I don't trust Saint Boy."

"When do we leave?" She sat back down on the bed, kicking her legs against the side.

I knew we should get some sleep, but now that the plan was forming I didn't want to wait. We had all the names of the angelic kids in our possession. I didn't want to sit on that information any longer than necessary. "Get them up now. We're leaving in ten."

"But Zuri, it's the middle of the night."

"And it's a long drive to Georgia. Get them up."

PEOPLE WROTE songs about the Devil going down to Georgia for a reason. There'd always been access to Hell there. Dad had popped up in the Georgia portals more than once back in the day, inspiring way too many horrible country songs. It was our closest connection, though.

"You are absolutely not going to Hell alone!" Saint Boy yelled from the back seat.

"I'm *not* going alone, Chris. I'll be with Zuri the whole time," Miry protested.

"Besides, no one is stupid enough to lay a hand on her. Miry may be the golden girl of Celestial Academy, but unless someone has a death wish, they won't mess with Lucifer's daughter," I snapped, pressing down on the gas, the car zoomed forward down the highway.

By the time we reached the portal, it was almost lunchtime. I sent Damien a text, letting him know we were on our way. I'd sent a string of emojis that most people would find incomprehensible. To my best friend, it meant simply 'bring food.'

"Take the car back to campus, we'll meet you there," I said and tossed the keys to Glasses.

"Um, what about the scroll? We went all that way to find it, shouldn't we return it to where it belongs?" Saint Boy asked.

"We will, but we're not done with it just yet," I answered, slinging the tube over my shoulder.

"I still think we should be going with you," he

muttered and wrapped an arm around Miry's shoulders.

"Don't worry about me. I'll be like totally fine," Miry said, laying on the bubbly persona even thicker than normal.

Before he could protest more, I motioned for Miry to follow me down an alleyway that dead-ended at a brick wall. She skipped after me, stopping beside me and leaning in close.

"Are we about to go through it like in Harry Potter?"

"You're such a child," I muttered before grabbing her hand in mine, giving it a squeeze and felt the edges of the portal snap to attention around me. "Don't forget to breathe," I warned her before we slipped into the passageway.

Coming from this side of the divide always seemed easier to me. I never could explain why. Maybe because I was coming home. I'd been born and raised in Hell. It was a part of me as much as my skin color or sexuality. I wouldn't be *me* without it.

The tall buildings with all the hustle and bustle of Hell appeared before us and I grinned. Not only was I happy to be home, but because Damien stood there waiting. He was staring at his phone with a bag of burritos tucked in the crook of his arm.

"Oh my God," Miry gasped before staggering sideways and far enough away from me that I wasn't in danger of getting hit with vomit.

"You get tired of all the pretty people up there?" Damien asked, giving us his full attention now.

"You know me," I said. "Can't stay in one place too long."

We both eyed Miry as she wiped her mouth. "She going to be okay?" Damien asked.

"I'm fine," Miry said, still pale and sweaty.

"It will pass. It's always like that the first time through the portal," I said, gesturing to a bench. "Why don't you sit down a minute until you acclimate?"

Miry nodded and wordlessly settled on the bench. Damien stepped up beside me and hissed, "You are going to catch so much shit for her being here. You know that, right?"

"D, like I care? They can take it up with Dad. We both know I've got his full support."

"I'm not so sure of that."

"Look, I didn't just need you for your burrito game, D. We need to talk to your dad."

"That doesn't sound good," he whispered.

"I'll explain everything, I promise. We just need to see him. I figured it was safer to see him here." I had a feeling if Lilith was going to come after Miry, she wouldn't be dumb enough to do it here.

"When you feel safer here, I know it's bad." He pointed to Miry. "You really think she's going to be okay down here?"

"Yeah. Miry's tougher and stronger than she looks. Besides, she's under my protection."

We strolled to the bench where Miry sat, taking in everything. "It looks so ... normal," she commented as she stood up, letting Damien lead us away from the heart of Hell.

"That's because it is," he answered. "Now, keep up, Archangel. Time for you to see the Angel of Death."

23

MIRYAM

"These burritos are totally awesome." I munched happily on my food as we walked single file down a cobblestone road. Damien and Zuri had stuck me between them. I think it was to keep me safe just in case someone tried to snatch Archangel Michael's daughter, but it felt almost like I was a prisoner being marched off to execution—especially since the guy at the end of this road was the Angel of Death.

"Do they like make these burritos down here or do you have to, like, go topside to order them?" I asked. "Can we get some more for the boys before we go? Chris and Ant would love these!"

"Miry!" Zuri pinched the bridge of her nose

between her thumb and pointer finger. "Stop. Talking."

"Sorry." I took a big bite of food to keep me occupied for a sec. "I talk when I get nervous. Like, a lot."

"So, you're nervous all the time?" Damien asked, but not in a nice way. Seriously, what did CeCe see in him besides the tattoos and danger element? Sure, he had our backs when the apocalypse was going down, but he was not the kind of guy the patron saint of music could bring home to mom and dad. On second thought, maybe that's the appeal right there. Maybe Saint Cecelia was going all rebellious.

"So, what's our cover story?" I ignored Damien's dig at my over-talking. "Do we have one? Do we need one? Are we going to tell people we're together-together or just together and do we—"

"Miry!" Zuri snapped again. "I'm sure I can find some random demon to literally zip your lips if you don't shut up. I mean it."

"Fine." I jammed more food into my mouth. Now that I paid attention to it a bit more, Hell was actually kinda pretty. It had a bit of an old-world charm with all red and brown brick buildings and roads. Dad modeled Celestial Academy in golds, silvers, and whites after Heaven—the better for everything to shine in the light. Hell reflected firelight, but in a cozy, at home way, not flashy at all. The thing with Heaven was that it never looked the same way twice. It shifted depending on the viewer. It was always your own personal Heaven. Though I bet Hell looked the same no matter who was looking at it. No wonder Zuri liked it here so much. It was constant when so many things weren't.

"Can I talk now?" I asked after an unusually long silence for me. For everyone else it was probably only two minutes.

"No," Zuri said. "You listen. Azrael is pretty chill as far as Fallen go, but he doesn't like to be trifled with. Something happened to you at that party. We need to figure out what and who—if anyone—ordered a hit."

"Hit, really? That sounds so mafia or mob boss," I complained. "It was an accident. It could have happened to anyone."

"Your death date should have been erased if that was true," Zuri said. "Just let D and I do all the talking, okay? If you open your mouth, I'm afraid Az will change his mind on reaping us both."

"I made an arrangement to save your soul, remember?" Damien flashed something that looked like a student ID. "You're looking at the latest reaper in training ... Me."

"Oh, cool!" I bounced on my heels. "Do you get to wear a cloak and carry a scythe and-and-and—"

"I know where Frank is if you wanna do the lip zipping thing," Damien told Zuri. "Either that or she can be the first soul I reap. It would save all our sanity. Trust me."

"Last chance, Miry," Zuri warned.

I mimed zipping my own lips. "No talking. Got it."

We stopped in front of a wide mahogany door. It looked big enough for Fallen to walk through with their wings fully extended. I opened my mouth to comment on it before re-membering the zipped lip thing. I clamped my mouth shut with a click. I wanted to prove to Zuri and, by extension Damien, that I could be trusted. It was a big act of trust already to take me down here in the first place. I didn't want to ruin it by being overly chatty, or as I liked to think of it, as myself.

Damien knocked and the door swung open by itself. The inside of Azrael's office was just as im-pressive as the door. The furniture looked like it should be in a miniature dollhouse based on the proportions of the room.

Azrael looked up from whatever paperwork he was working on. Signing death warrants? Making a list of souls to reap? I was dying to ask (no pun intended), but I promised Zuri I'd shut my yap and I would.

"Damien, I already told you, Reaper Academy rules apply to you too," Azrael said. "You have to attend the freshman mixer just like the rest of the class."

"That's not why I'm here, Dad." Damien motioned at Zuri. "Z has a question for you."

Zuri stepped forward and unfurled the scroll across Azrael's desk. "How much do you know about Gabriel's Scroll? We were hoping it would help us solve the Celestial Academy kidnappings." She pointed at several names on the scroll. "We've found all the missing kids' names and there's no death date after them. Does that mean they're still alive?"

Azrael inclined his head slightly. "No death date means their souls still reside in their bodies."

"What about if there's a death date, but the person is still very much alive?" Zuri pointed at another spot on the scroll. "Has that ever happened before?"

"Miryam bat-Michael," Azrael read slowly. He looked up, directly at me. "You were very brave during our brush with the end of days, young lady."

"Um, thank you?" It came out as a question, because—even though I promised not to talk—if the Angel of Death was talking right to me, I figured it would be rude not to respond.

"I remember that death date," he said. "I remember all the death dates from here to eternity. The bat and ben Michaels are special, though. By focusing on one, you missed the bigger picture."

I stepped forward and scanned the scroll. Names jumped out at me as if they were literally rising from the scroll. Hundreds of half siblings I didn't even know I had.

"They're all dead," I whispered. "And I'm supposed to be too."

Azrael shrugged like it was no big deal. "Michael wields incredible influence in Heaven and even, to some extent, here in Hell. If a child displeased him—" He gestured at the scroll. "This was the result."

"Damn." Damien said with a low whistle. "So, the douchiest of douchey angels has been offing his kids for thousands of years. What did you do to get on his shit list two years ago, Angel?"

"Date Saint Boy?" Zuri suggested, almost hopefully.

I shook my head. "Dad loves Chris. He practically threw us a party when we announced we were official."

"A pool party?" Zuri asked.

My eyes went wide as many more puzzle pieces clicked into place all at once. Chris and I had always been friends. I even had a massive crush on him since day one, but we didn't get romantic until I was fifteen. We told Dad right before summer term a year later. I was never exactly the most obedient daughter, but, before then, I at least tried to be more eager to please. Dad and his whims were my focus ... until he wasn't as important to me anymore. Chris was my focus then. My nightmares about being chased by a cloaked figure didn't start until after the pool party.

"Dad really tried to kill me, didn't he?"

Azrael frowned, his face softening. For the first time since we walked into his office, he looked like a dad instead of the Angel of Death to me. "For your sake, child, I wish the answer was 'no.' I'm sorry."

"If Saint Boy saved her from drowning, why does the death date still stand?" Zuri asked.

"I learned long ago to put in a safeguard for Michael's children," Azrael said. "Miryam is just the first to manage accessing it."

"A loophole," Damien nodded. "Way to stick it to The Man, Dad."

"What sort of safeguard?" I stared at my name on the scroll. It was still all a little too freaky to think about.

"If one of Michael's children dies—even for just a second—and is brought back to life, the death contract is invalid. Yes, you died child, but you also lived and still do. Your father cannot try to hurt you ever again. Take heart in that."

"Chris saved me." I looked to Zuri for confirmation. "Chris is the reason my death contract was canceled."

"One nice thing two years ago doesn't make him less of a douche today," she protested.

I shook my head. "No ... No, not just nice. *Saintly*. Don't you see? I owe him my life."

24

ZURI

Miry's words made my brain hurt. The douchebag had brainwashed her well. I was beginning to doubt that I could do anything to get him out of her head. He may have saved her that day, but it didn't excuse the way he treated her now. I watched Azrael as he gave Miry his 'poor lost lamb' look. I couldn't deny that I was grateful for the loophole. At least it meant there was one less person who could harm my friend.

"We really appreciate the help," I said and scooped up the scroll, stowing it away in the carrying tube.

"Might I suggest a visit to your father before

you leave? I'm sure he would appreciate seeing his daughter," he replied with a small smile.

"Yeah, I'll do that," I answered and nudged Miry's shoulder. "Come on. Time for you to see where I really grew up."

I left Damien behind with his dad and led Miry back to the heart of Hell. Until we stood outside the museum that had started us on this collision course of a friendship. Before that day, I'd never considered or even cared about Archangels and their kids. Now I was bound and determined to keep one breathing, and just maybe along the way find a kidnapper too. "Come on."

We walked through the halls, stopping at the suits of armor and paintings. "It all looks so normal," Miry whispered. "Like, it could even be from the Archangel perspective."

"Don't let people around here catch you saying that. They are very proud of their history. They may have lost, but that doesn't mean they aren't still proud of what they were fighting for," I reminded her.

"What's down there?" She bounced toward the wing that used to house the Emblem.

"Nothing," I said. "Not anymore."

She paused mid-step and looked at me, sadness washing over her. "Oh."

"We have one more stop to make before we go back topside," I announced and guided her back the way we'd come.

"Right, seeing your dad." After a pause she added, "What's it like to have a parent who doesn't want to kill you?" She batted her eyes at me with a wistful expression, but I could tell the words terrified her. She'd spent a lot of her life idolizing her father. Believing she had to live up to his legacy and his name thanks to her mom's twisted views.

"I don't know how to answer that, Miry. I know I didn't have a very high opinion of your dad to begin with, but I'm truly sorry that he's a homicidal jackass who can't see your value. Everyone writes you off as a flighty, vapid chick and you're not. You've got feelings and opinions … they matter, you matter."

"Thanks," she mumbled as we approached my dad's office.

Please let him be at some long board meeting. The door swung open and Dad appeared, filling the space. "So glad you could stop home for a visit, Zuri. Good morning, Miryam."

"Azrael called you," I said and shouldered by him.

"Your generation isn't the only one connected by the internet and cell phones," he quipped.

"Damn, you say shit like that and it makes you sound ancient," I teased.

"You just insulted the Lord of Hell," Miry murmured, cowering behind me.

"He started it," I told her and wrapped an arm loosely around her shoulders. "It's okay. I promise, things aren't going to fly and hit you."

Dad's face softened. "So the rumors about the way Michael treats his children are true? A pity he never learned that our children are the better part of us."

"I wish you were my dad," Miry blurted before she could stop herself.

"Thank you," Dad replied. "Now, I know why you've come, Zuri. I've taken the liberty of gathering all the information on Lilith from the Archives."

"Thanks … I think."

"I don't want you going off on your own trying to chase her down. She is powerful. I also have my own hunches about what she's done to the children she's stolen away. I leave her alone and so far, it appears Michael and his ilk have done the same. However, she is no fool. If the kidnapped children aren't dead, I suspect she's somehow turned them into an army."

"Wonderful," I groaned. "Dad, I'm not alone. Miry and I have each other."

"Remember we have the boys, too," Miry chimed in.

I didn't trust Saint Boy and the jury was still out on Glasses. "We just want to find the missing kids and stop her from taking any more kids. Didn't you say she's made an agreement to not touch your kids?"

"If she is pushed, I don't believe even her oath would stop her. She may have restrained herself during your encounters with her, but don't bet on her being so lenient next time," Dad warned.

"We should get back to school. We can double check the names of the students who went missing against the scroll," Miry said.

"Perhaps it is better for you to leave it behind," Dad said, a tightness to his tone I hadn't heard before.

"Why? It doesn't belong down here," Miry challenged.

"Frankly, I don't trust your father and his intentions towards my daughter. Relics are powerful objects and, in the hands that God intended them for, they can be deadly weapons. If you care for my daughter, as I suspect you do," he touched my cheek, "you would not want harm to come to her."

"Of course, I wouldn't! Zuri's my best friend. She believes in me." Miry squared her shoulders. "I don't trust my dad either. He tried to kill me. Maybe it is safer here. For now."

We still needed to verify the information and I had an idea of who I could trust to help. "How about a compromise? We see if we can get a list to crosscheck while we are down here and then we leave the scroll in the museum for safe keeping. At least until the Lilith threat is dealt with," I said.

"But how are we going to get the list?" Miry's lower lip started to quiver into a pout.

"I know an Angel," I replied. "In the meantime, look through the information on Lilith. We need to gather everything we can about her abilities and how to defeat her. Start with how she can look like so many people at once."

GETTING in touch with Raphael turned out to be harder than I had expected. I didn't have a cell phone number for him. I refused to risk the chance that Michael would intercept the call or Gabriel who would inevitably forget to pass on the message. After I'd spent a solid ten minutes trying to figure it out, Dad passed me a phone with a single number programmed in.

"For emergencies," he'd explained before leaving me alone in his office.

"Lucifer?" Raphael answered on the fifth ring.

"Uh, no. It's Zuri," I said, my mouth suddenly dry.

"Only one individual has this number and I know for a fact the phone does not enter this plane of existence. So am I to assume you are off campus?"

"If it makes you feel better, Michael knows about it."

He laughed. "Somehow, I doubt he knows the full extent of your escapades. I'm also assuming you are calling for a reason other than idle conversation Ms. bat-Lucifer."

"Does Michael keep a record of all the kidnapped students?"

A long pause followed by a cough. "A list exists."

"Great. I need it. Now."

"I am capable of a great many things. However, entering your current location is not one of them."

Not entirely true. "I'm assuming your phone has a camera on it? Take a picture and text it to me … please."

"Ah, yes. Modern technology at its finest. I'll see what I can do."

Miry's voice interrupted the call. "Zuri! Come here!"

"Was that Miryam I just heard? Is she with you … in Hell?"

I didn't have time to answer his question. "Send me that picture as soon as you can," I told Raphael before hanging up and going in search of Miry. She was leaning over the information Dad had given us on Lilith in the conference room.

"What's wrong?" I slid into the chair next to her at the table.

"So, you know how at the cemetery we all saw Lilith as our moms?"

"Yeah. Kind of hard to forget."

"All of us even described what we saw?"

"Get to the point, Miry." I had a sinking suspicion I knew where she was going and it did not fill me with much confidence.

"This is what Lilith looks like in her demon form." She passed over a piece of paper with a full color image of a woman with pale skin and dark eyes. Exactly as Saint Boy had described what he had seen, his mother.

"I told you he couldn't be trusted. He's been using you, Miry."

"Wait … There has to be an explanation," she protested. "I'm going back. Take me back to Georgia now. I have to know what's going on."

MIRYAM

"Next time you say let's travel by portal to Hell, remind me to say no." I leaned over and dry heaved into a bush. At least the going was a little better than the coming back.

Zuri looked around, trying to orientate herself. "How close are we to campus? Two blocks? Three?"

I wiped my mouth. "Three. We can totally walk. No more portals."

Zuri pivoted toward campus, taking off at a clip that forced me to jog in order to catch up. "So, what are we going to tell Dad about our little detour?" I asked. "I mean, I don't think he's really going to care, but he might, like, forbid me to go anywhere alone with you or whatever. I mean, I—"

"You're talking too much again," Zuri warned. "I don't really care what your dad thinks. That shouldn't be news to you either."

"I wish my dad treated me as nice as yours did." It's not the first time I had said that and I really meant it. "I know I should expect Dad to treat me with the same kindness and respect yours does with you, but what if I don't deserve it?" I asked. "What if everyone treats me like crap, because that's all I deserve? I'm not good enough or smart enough or—"

Zuri stopped and pulled me into a hug so fast, it took me a sec to orientate myself. I stiffened before relaxing against her. She was the only one in my life who never demanded anything and just accepted me for me. I didn't have to pretend to be someone I was not. Being the perfect, bubbly daughter, all the time was exhausting. I knew I could drop the act around Z. She saw me for me and didn't care about any of the rest.

"You still smell like hellfire and brimstone," I mumbled into her jacket.

"Sorry." She let me go just as fast as she had grabbed me. I was disoriented again, but this time because she *wasn't* hugging me.

"It's okay," I said. "But why'd you, um, do it? Hug me, I mean."

"Because you get stuck in your own head too much. You don't realize how fucked up it is that you still want to make the people who treat you the worst happy," she said. "Just say 'screw it' already and stop thinking about how they feel. I guarantee they don't spare a second thought for your feelings."

"That's not true." I fell back onto old habits. "If you mean Dad and Chris, they love me. They just have a different way of showing it sometimes."

Since I always clung to old habits, I had expected Zuri to say "if you say so" or "keep telling yourself that." Instead, she turned away from me without a word and booked it the rest of the way to campus, forcing me to run after her again for the second time that afternoon.

"IF YOU'RE mad at me, just say you're mad at me!" I yelled once we were back in our dorm room. "Don't do this silent treatment thing. One word from me to Dad, you'd be headed back to Hell *and* banned from campus permanently. How'd you like that, huh? You wouldn't have to deal with any of us ever again. Just how you want it. It would be like we never met."

"Do you even listen to the words that come out of your mouth?" Zuri asked. "How can you jump from me being pissed about you allowing yourself to be walked all over by people who are supposed to love you, to me wanting to bail on you? I'm your friend, Miry. You may be infuriating sometimes, but I still got your back. Okay? I still got your back."

My shoulders drooped. "Really? Thanks, Z. I got your back too. I won't tell Dad about the detour or anything else you don't think he should know. I trust you."

Zuri frowned. "Speaking of trust. You saw what Dad had in the Archives about Lilith. What Saint Boy described—what Saint Boy saw—was Lilith in demon form. There's no way he can just explain that away, Miry. You shouldn't let him either."

I chewed my bottom lip. "I know."

"Then do something for once," she challenged. "Stand up for yourself and demand real answers. Don't let him gaslight you. Not when it could mean life or death for all of the kidnapped kids."

I grabbed Zuri's hand, holding tight when she tried to pull away. "Come with me. I don't want to do this, not without you."

26

ZURI

Part of me couldn't wait to throttle Saint Boy for everything he'd put Miry through. Still another part of me could almost see him as she did—her savior. Although there were still too many pieces to this puzzle that I didn't know, but I was about to find out. I followed Miry to his room where she knocked twice.

"Chris? Let me in." Silence followed her words. "Please don't be mad at me for going ... without you."

At least I didn't have to clamp a hand over her mouth to keep her from uttering the word Hell in these halls. It was dangerous enough if he was in fact tied to Lilith.

"Maybe he's not here," Miry murmured, more to herself than to me.

"If he's not here, where else would he be on campus?" I probed.

"I don't know. He's usually only here or with me. It's not like I keep track of everywhere he goes."

But I bet he knows your every move. "Enough playing nice."

I shoved the door open, slamming it against the opposite wall with a hard thump. Glasses sat on one of the beds nursing a bloody nose and I could make out a cut on his left cheek, probably made by the frame of his glasses.

"Ant!" Miry cried and raced to his side. "What happened?"

"You left and … we planned to just come back to campus. Figure out what to tell Archangel Michael. That's when she showed up and took him."

"Took who?" I assumed the she meant Lilith.

"Chris, obviously," Miry said. I could tell by the unshed tears in her eyes, her resolve to confront her asshole boyfriend was rapidly dwindling.

"Where exactly did she take him?" I paced the

length of the small dorm room, wishing I had the ability to read minds. The way Glasses wouldn't meet my gaze told me whatever words came out of his mouth next were no doubt false.

"I don't know where exactly. She just appeared and attacked us. She hit me, took Chris and then disappeared."

"That doesn't make sense," I said slowly. "If it was Lilith she wouldn't be going after some saint kid. Not when all the other kidnappings were angel born."

"Maybe … maybe because we figured out her plan, she's changing her M.O. Or she's getting payback against us," Glasses rambled.

"Zuri's right. Lilith has only gone after angel kids. And ... we learned something from our trip to Hell," Miry said.

Glasses' cheeks paled and a sheen of sweat glistened on his forehead. "You did?"

"We did and I think you know what's going on. Now tell me, did she take him while the two of you were inside the gates or outside?" I pressed.

"What does it matter? He's gone," he protested, setting aside a wad of bloodied tissues.

I lunged for him, grabbing fistfuls of shirt in

my hands. "It matters, dipshit, because Lilith is demonic. She shouldn't be able to set foot on these grounds. Remember?"

"Z, you're freaking him out," Miry said, tugging on my right arm.

"Good. Then it's working," I replied.

"You're hiding something and you're going to tell me what it is now. Or you're going to really learn what it means to piss off the next ruler of Hell."

A rush of air behind me signaled that my wings had unfurled. I heard Miry gasp beside me and if Glasses could have gone any paler, I'd have said he turned into a ghost.

"Okay, look … don't kill me," he whined.

I let go of my grip on him and he settled back against the wall. "Talk. Now."

His gaze darted around the room, from the other bed to the doorway to the desks. Anywhere, but at Miry and I. Finally, he settled on a point I guessed was somewhere behind my left shoulder. "Um, are you going to keep those out like that?"

"Does it make you uncomfortable?"

"Very," he answered with a vigorous head nod.

"Then yeah, I think they'll stay." I smiled, the kind of smile a predator uses when stalking prey.

"Ant, just tell us what's going on. What really happened to Chris? Did Lilith really take him?"

"No. Well, I mean he went with her, but he went willingly. He was pretty messed up though."

"Because he couldn't hitch a ride to Hell?" I interrupted.

"No. He's sick. Been that way the last few years actually."

"I told you that, Z. He needs blood."

"Right. Angel blood seems to do the trick. Am I getting that part, right?"

"He didn't ask for any of this, you know. He just ... he grew up not knowing anything about his mom. So, a few years ago when he started having these illness episodes, he figured maybe she had some health or medical thing his dad didn't know about. He asked me to find his mother. I did too ... In Hell."

"So, you've been there have you?" I goaded.

"Have you, Ant?" Miry's tone shifted from concern to guarded curiosity. She was beginning to see the cracks in her boyfriend's facade and his bestie—finally.

"Just the one time. Oh and not for long either. It made my skin crawl and it was like every bad thing I'd ever done or thought about doing was all screaming at me in my head."

I'd never heard of Hell having that effect on a mortal, but then again, Glasses was part Saint. So maybe that made him just different enough. "Lilith is his mother, isn't she?"

He turned to Miry. "He hated not telling you the truth, but he knew it wouldn't look good. Seriously if your dad knew, he'd kick Chris out of school."

"So what? His mommy had a place for him at her side," I snapped.

"He doesn't want to be involved with her, not like that. He just wanted to know why he was getting sick. Something to do with his demon blood and saint blood clashing when he hit puberty. Angel blood is the only thing that keeps it in check."

"Which is why they've been stealing angel kids —to take their blood. Are they alive? Do you even care?" My perspective changed, I was now looking down at him and Miry, my feet a few inches off the ground.

"Honestly, it didn't really affect me and Chris swore the kids weren't being hurt. Just a little blood donation."

"If that was all, why haven't any of them ever showed up again?" Miry prompted.

"I don't know."

"Well, you're about to find out." I reached down and hauled Glasses to his feet. "You're going to take us to find Saint Boy and his mommy dearest. If you lead us wrong, I'm going to take you back to Hell and leave you there."

27

MIRYAM

Ant lifted his chin defiantly. "You don't scare me."

Zuri beat her wings giving her a little more lift off the ground. "Oh, really? Try saying that after spending an eternity in Hell." She grabbed Ant by the nape of his neck when he tried to run out of the dorm room, lifting him off the ground.

"I'll help you! I'll help you!" He shrieked. "Let me down! Let me down!"

Zuri tossed him onto his bed. "Start. Now."

"My finding lost things powers don't exactly work like that." Ant dabbed at his bloody lip. "Chris isn't a thing, he's a person. I can't just re-cite the prayer—boom!—and lead you right to him. For it to have any chance of working, I need a focal object. Something meaningful, but not like a math test or pair of socks or whatever. It needs to mean something to him."

"What about this?" I grabbed the framed photo of Chris and me from his dresser. His arm was around me and we were both grinning like crazy for the camera. We were happy then, at least I had thought we were.

Ant hovered his palm over the picture and recited the Prayer to Saint Anthony. His hand glowed dimly before he pulled back and shook his head. "No good. Not strong enough. I ... I don't mean your bond with Chris isn't strong enough, Miry, but this is just a picture. The picture doesn't mean much to him. You do."

"Then use me as your focal object." Now it was my turn to lift my chin. "Do it, Ant, before I change my mind."

"Wait, hold up." Zuri landed, furled her wings, and pulled me aside all in one fluid motion. Next, she ducked to make sure she was looking me dead in the eyes. "There's no way in Hell I'm letting you use yourself as a focal object. You've compromised too much already for Saint Boy."

I swiped at my eyes, hoping she didn't guess or at least didn't say anything about me crying. "You heard Ant. The picture isn't good enough to find him. It doesn't hold enough meaning. We need something with a stronger connection. I mean something to Chris. It's the only way we'll find him and save all the kidnapped kids."

"But what if you don't mean enough?" Zuri voiced my biggest fear. "What if your relationship isn't strong enough to make the incantation work?"

I shook my head. "I can't think like that. If I do, it means the last six years of knowing Chris—of loving Chris—all of it has been a lie."

Zuri rubbed her thumbs under my eyes, catching the tears before they fell. "Do you even know what happens when Glasses' power goes through you? Can you survive that?"

"If I don't, at least the kidnapped kids will be safe. Zuri, I—" I shook my head again, unable to put into words how much her friendship and, well, just her meant to me. "If something does happen to me, give Lilith the self-defense class treatment, okay?"

Zuri pulled me against her just as suddenly as she had done on the walk back to campus after our detour to Hell. Just like then, I stiffened before allowing myself to relax. I rested my cheek against her chest, listening to her solid heartbeat.

"Nothing is going to happen to you," she promised. "Not while I'm around."

I let myself be held—I let myself be appreciated—before I reluctantly stepped away. "Let's hope this works."

"I swear Chris wanted to tell you, Miry." Ant took a hit off his asthma inhaler. "It was killing him to keep this part of himself from you. He needed to suppress the demon blood. If he didn't, your dad would kick him out of school. He wanted to be with you and that's why he kept it a secret. He wanted to be with you."

"Let's test that theory." I held my hand out palm up.

"Don't you try anything like telling your boy and his mommy we're coming," Zuri warned. "If you do, I'll deposit you in the twelfth circle of Hell instead of just the first."

"Got it. No double crossing." Ant held my hand between both of his. A gold glow filled the space between our hands as he whispered the tracking prayer.

"Did it work?" Zuri asked once he finished.

"I don't—" I gasped as a bunch of images flooded my mind: Chris, Lilith, the missing kids standing around with glassy, blank stares. It looked like a warehouse or something. Maybe a basement? Another image flashed in my mind—kids dancing, blaring music, and colored, pulsing lights.

I grabbed Ant for support when a wave of nausea and vertigo hit. "I know where they are! The basement of that Fallen club. If we hurry, we can save everybody before Lilith turns them into a demon minion army."

ZURI

In a way, it made sense. Our first brush with Lilith had started at Castoffs and she probably assumed that Archangels wouldn't set foot in a Fallen club. Of course, she had to know we'd come looking for Saint Boy, though. Well, unless she underestimated our resourcefulness.

"Look, I helped you find him. Now leave me out of this," Glasses said, shrugging away from Miry.

"I don't think so," I snapped.

"Z, he did help us. No offense, Ant, but you're not a fighter," Miry protested.

"She's right. I'm not a fighter. I hate fighting. I'm like the opposite of a fighter. Please, I don't want to go up against my best friend."

"Then maybe you should have thought about that before you kept his dangerous little secret from everyone," I ground out.

"I'm not going to tell anyone where you're going if you're worried about me ratting you out. However, Lilith is scary—like terrifying. She may not need saint blood to keep Chris balanced, but if I got in her way, she'd have no problem killing me. I don't think Chris is strong enough to stop her."

We were wasting time arguing. "Fine. Be a pussy and stay here." I turned to Miry. "You okay doing this? I can face them on my own if it's too much."

Miry squared her shoulders. "I can do this. If there's any part of Chris that is still good in there, I know I can reach him."

"I don't know if that's true. He's got one of the most powerful demons for a mother. He's been lying to you for years like it's second nature. I just hope you're ready to make the tough call if it comes down to it," I said.

"I'm not giving up on him, not yet," she replied.

"Come on, we need to get there before any-thing major goes down. Though we have one stop to make first."

AFTER A QUICK STOP in the armory, I took Miry by the hand to make sure we didn't get separated and we flew off campus. Thankfully the wards keeping demons out didn't keep angel kids in. Maybe Michael thought no one could mount an aerial attack. What a fool.

"What do you think she's doing to all those kids?" Miry asked when she landed at the back entrance of the club. I could hear the pulsing beat of the electronic dance music inside and voices carried around from the front of the building.

"Nothing good," I muttered and studied the lock on the door. Under normal circumstances, I'd forge a lock pick. Now was not the time for tricks. "Stand back."

Miry shuffled backwards half a foot before I slammed the heel of my boot into the door right by the handle. The wood splintered from the impact enough to make the handle and the locking mechanism come loose. I stepped in front of Miry, my left hand resting loosely on the blade strapped around my waist.

"Get ready," I hissed and started down the stairs to the basement.

I expected to hear chanting or … something as

we approached, but it was quiet, save from the music filtering down from the club above us. I stopped at the next door we found, holding my breath as I tried the handle. It was unlocked. I turned the handle and pushed, the door swung inward on silent hinges.

Then, as they say, all Hell broke loose. Glassy-eyed kids of varying ages poured out of the room towards us, swarming around Miry and I like a mosh pit. Bodies pressed against us, trying to weigh us down and keep us from our objective. I nudged one kid aside, realizing too late I should have just let them buoy us into the room. One of them on my left suddenly formed a fist and tried to slam it into my jaw. I dodged and landed a blow to his solar plexus, sending the kid staggering back to be absorbed into the mass of kids.

"What do we do?" Miry yelled as multiple sets of hands latched onto her and carried her into the basement.

"Try not to hurt them. If you fight back, they get violent," I answered even as I elbowed a beefy blond boy in the jaw, feeling bone crack. Given that pain didn't go shooting down my arm, I assumed it was his jaw.

More zombified kids descended on me as something snarled above me. I craned my neck to see something hanging from the support beams within the basement confines. It looked like Saint Boy except he must have not taken a hit of angel blood recently, because this thing was feral, foaming at the mouth. I pushed and shoved my way through the throng of Lilith's minions until I was in the room. Lilith stood at the far end observing everything on a makeshift throne.

"I thought I made it clear, child of Lucifer. I have no quarrel with you."

"Well, see, you kind of do because you're putting my friends in danger. I don't put up with that shit." I hooked a thumb over my shoulder at Saint Boy. "Looks like your kid's gone off his meds."

The angel kid minions fell away from me, forming a loose circle around the room. If a demon as pale as Lilith could blanch, she did. "Oh, that's right, you thought no one knew his little secret. Surprise." I rested my left hand on the hilt of my sword. "I don't know what twisted game you've been playing with him and frankly I don't care either. However, I'm done letting you hurt these innocent kids for fun. So you're going to release them and maybe I don't have to use this."

"Child, how little you truly understand." Lilith

rose from her throne and descended to where the throng had deposited Miry. "I cannot expect you to understand, born of mortal blood. I was made, you see. But there was one fatal flaw in my design." She rested her hands against her stomach. "I could not give the gift of life. So, I was cast aside. Some might say driven mad with the pain of it."

"That's awful," Miry said. I couldn't see her face to tell if she was falling under Lilith's thrall or if she genuinely felt sorry for the demon.

"Yes, I took these children to feed my son. My only child. I did not believe a mortal could sustain my power and so I sought out one of purer blood. Not quite divine, but I did not foresee the pain it would cause his father when he learned the truth about me. To cast me away from my son for so long."

"You so desperately wanted a kid you didn't bother to think about what it would do to him?" I scoffed. I hated to admit it, but I almost felt pity for Saint Boy.

"Perhaps one day you will know the desire that comes with the longing of motherhood. I gave my child what he required to live."

Saint Boy landed on the floor between Miry and I, his eyes still wild. I wasn't sure what Miry was going to do, seeing him in such a state. Would she fall back into old habits, making excuses for him or would she finally see him for the bastard he was?

"Chris, I know you're in there. Part of you is anyway," she said in a tone far stronger than I expected. "I know there's good in you."

"Miry, I don't think you can reason with him," I said, easing the sword out of the hilt.

"Everything was fine until she showed up," Saint Boy said, his voice distorted by too much saliva.

"Zuri isn't our problem, Chris. You should have come to me and told me what was going on. I know you were scared of what Dad would do, but you needed help. You shouldn't have to resort to hurting people just to make the pain stop. I know what it's like to hurt, to want to make it stop and … it doesn't make things better."

"You were an abusive, manipulative jackass before I ever got here," I muttered.

Saint Boy let out a howl and lunged at me. I parried with the blade, making sure I didn't actually cut him. I didn't know what making him bleed would do. "I'm a threat to you, I get that. I come along and now Miry is stronger, she believes in herself. She doesn't need some man to save her, because she's got the strength inside of her. She always has. She stopped the fucking apocalypse. She did that all on her own. She's suffered through more shit than anyone has a right to and she came out of it. Sure, she's got scars. Although they make her tougher not weaker."

"She doesn't need you," he snarled, reaching for the blade.

"Chris, stop!" Miry's voice boomed and filled the small space. We both turned to see her standing there, wings unfurled, hovering off the ground. Not unlike what I'd done back on campus to get Glasses to talk. Hovering there in the dim light, she looked almost regal. "You aren't going to hurt her. I won't let you."

"Your words do not sway my son," Lilith commented, vanishing from one spot to appear in another, wrapping an arm around his shoulders.

"It wasn't supposed to be like this," he said. "It was supposed to be you and me. When you gave me your blood, it was like nothing I'd ever felt before. I need you, Miry."

"No. You need what's inside me. I think ... I think you might even kill me to get it. That's not right, Chris," Miry answered.

With Lilith and Saint Boy distracted, I moved, pressing the blade of my sword to his throat.

"You're going to let all these kids go, release them from your thrall or you're going to lose the one thing that matters most to you in this world," I told Lilith, pressing down just enough to draw a thin river of blood from her kid's neck.

Lilith's gaze darted from Saint Boy to my sword and back again. "We are not done, child of Lucifer. I may have sworn an oath to your father to leave his kin unharmed, but that oath is broken this day. You have not seen the last of me."

Lilith and Saint Boy vanished, leaving the group of kids around us to blink awkwardly, in confusion. Miry lowered to the ground and threw her arms around me. "We did it," she whispered into my shoulder.

"I'm proud of you, Miry. Now, let's get these kids the help they need."

29

—————

MIRYAM

"Uncle Raphael! Uncle Raphael! We need you!" I raced down the hall and into his office. He looked up, startled, when the door banged against the wall.

"Is it self-defense class again?"

I leaned over my hands on my knees, trying to catch my breath. "No. I totally haven't been to class in at least a week. It's ... We found the ... We found the missing kids and I ... I need your help to make sure they're okay. They've been, um, kinda like a zombie horde since they disappeared. We needed to fight our way out before breaking Lilith's hold on them."

Uncle Raphael stood and collected his medical

bag. "By 'we,' I assume you mean Ms. bat-Lucifer?"

"Aren't you going to try to act more surprised that we found the kidnapped kids when Dad and Uncle Uriel couldn't?"

"Unlike your father, I believe you can do anything you set your mind to, Miry-am," Uncle Raphael said as we hurried back to the gates of the school. "If you said that you're going to solve the kidnappings, I believe you would."

"Zuri helped."

"I'm sure she did."

"And, like, long story short, we found Uncle Gabriel's scroll, tracked down the missing kids, and Chris didn't tell anyone that Lilith is his mom." I threw open the gates and ran outside to where Zuri waited with the kids. "We wanted to make sure everyone was healthy before bringing them inside."

Uncle Raphael set up a triage station in the grass, handing Zuri and I each a scanner thing. He showed us how to use it to check if any of the formerly missing kids had demon blood, and got to work. Along the way, he patched up minor injuries anyone may have sustained in the fight. I didn't like to think of it as a battle, even though we were totally battling for our lives. Who knew what Lilith would do if she got her claws on two kids with archangel blood?

"You need to rest," Zuri said when I sat down before I could fall down.

I pushed my hair away from my face. "Don't worry about me. I totally got this."

"You just found out your ex-boyfriend is half demon," Zuri said. "It's okay to not be okay, Miry."

"Ex?" I scrunched up my face, her words taking a while to register in my foggy brain. "Oh, no, Chris and I aren't broken up. Don't you see? He needs me now more than ever."

"Take a break, Miryam," Uncle Raphael interrupted before Zuri could say something I'm sure I wouldn't like, but still needed to hear. She was like my conscious, telling me things that were for the best. Even if I wanted to plug my ears and la I'm not listening the truth away.

I pushed myself off the ground and walked through the gates. At first, I wandered sort of aimlessly around campus. I thought about telling Ant what was up, but decided not to. How long had he been keeping Chris' secret? A year? Two? More? I remembered Chris first talking about a chronic illness a little over a year ago. That's all he would ever say about it. He was sick and there was nothing I could do to help him either. Then kids started disappearing and his flair ups were less and less. I should have put two and two together then, but—even now—I didn't want to admit that 2+2 = 4. It's just ... How could everything I've known be built on lies?

The gate to the pool area was hanging open. Good. It would save me the trouble of climbing over the fence. Once in, I took off my shoes and socks before dangling my feet in the water. I watched my reflection shimmering on the surface. Since when had I started looking so pale? There was, like, zero color in my cheeks. My eyes looked like they'd seen a million sorrows. My perfect facade was cracking. So much for the perky little Celestial Academy princess I tried so hard to be. I might as well give the title to someone else.

I leaned forward, dipping my hand into the water. How easy would it be to just disappear under the surface and never have to worry about anything ever again? I could give Dad what he had always wanted. He could say I lost my balance when no one was around. No one would know the difference and I wouldn't be around to tell.

"I wouldn't do that if I were you."

I startled, almost falling into the pool, before a hand pulled me back. I half expected to see Chris or even Dad with their hand protectively on my shoulder, but it was Zuri. This time Zuri had saved me.

"Mind if I sit down?" She sat down anyway, even though I didn't say she could or not. "Look, I'm sorry for what I said back there on the front lawn. I shouldn't have assumed like I knew anything about what was going on with you and Saint Boy's relationship, well, post big maternity reveal. That's your decision to make, not mine."

"Thank you," I said quietly, stuffing my hands on my lap, because I wasn't sure what else to do with them. "I hate giving up on people. I could never forgive myself if I gave up on Chris."

"You know I'm not a fan of his, but I respect you," Zuri said. "If you say there's still good in him, then there's still good in him."

"Thank you." I glanced down at my phone when my text alert beeped. I was hoping it was from Chris saying this was all some weird dream. Nope. It was Dad.

Come to my office now.

"Whelp, duty calls." I clambered to my feet. "We stopped the apocalypse and rescued the kidnapped kids. We're two for two with showing that Angels and Fallen can work together. Wanna come with and make Dad uncomfortable?"

Zuri grinned. "I thought you'd never ask."

"HOW MANY TIMES do I have to tell you, Miryam, your safety is my number one concern?" Dad said, like he actually meant it. He paced back and forth behind his ginormous desk. If he didn't have his hands behind his back, I'd say he was reading notes off his palm. I guess he could have memorized his little 'I'm a good dad' speech. Stranger things have happened. Especially in the last couple months.

"Yes, sir. I know, sir. I'm sorry, sir."

"Don't apologize," Zuri said. "That's bullshit. You're safe, because you can take care of your damn self. You don't need daddy or anyone else to save you. You save yourself."

Dad's pupils dilated, but he managed to keep his voice deceptively calm. Cold, sure, but still surprisingly calm. "In case you have forgotten, Ms. bat-Lucifer, the only reason I haven't sent you straight back to Hell where you came from is my daughter seems to think children of Archangels and Fallen can somehow co-exist and ..." he shuddered "...

work together. I, for one, believe that is only setting her up for failure. My children do not fail. Ever."

"What if they do?" Zuri challenged. "Failure is part of life. We learn from our mistakes."

"My service project isn't a failure, Dad," I piped up. "And neither am I. Zuri and I together, we stopped Beelzebub *and* now Lilith. The school year isn't even half over, yet."

"You couldn't even bother to show up for either crisis," Zuri added. "Some leader."

"You think your father could do better than I?" Dad asked.

Zuri nodded. "He already does."

Dad and Zuri glowered at each other. I stepped between them to break up the hate-fest. "You gave me all year for my service project, Dad. You can't just yank that away. I'm not dead."

"Yet," Dad said. The word wrapped around me. Was it a promise or a threat?

"To learn more about Fallen, Miry should come home with me on quarter break." Zuri said.

I looked over at her, confused, before whispering: "What are you doing?"

"Saving your life," she whispered back. "Just go with it." She turned back to Dad with a big, insincere smile. "I'm not asking for your permission, either. I'm telling you that she's coming. Think of it as research for her service project. What's the worst that could happen?"

"A demon will figure out who I am and kill me?" I guessed.

Dad wasn't fast enough hiding his smile. "You're going."

"Awesome. Thanks, Dad." I'd hug him, but now I wouldn't put it past him to try stabbing me in the back with his giant archangel sword. It was best to just get out of the room while we still could.

"Am I really going with you for quarter break?" I asked once we were back in our dorm room.

"I'm not leaving you here for your dad or crazy Uncle Uriel to stage another so called accident." Zuri sat down next to me on my bed. "Besides, you deserve a real break for the first time in your life."

I smiled. "You know what? It feels weird to say, but there's no place I'd rather be than hanging out with you in Hell. Can we get, like, matching tattoos or something? Like little angel wings on our ankles? You know, all discreet like or something. What do you say?"

"I say you've put way too much thought into that already."

I peeked over at Zuri, trying to gauge her mood based on her facial expression. It was as unreadable as always. "Is that a maybe?"

"That's an if it makes your dad piss himself, I'm in."

"Totally!" I raised my hand for a high five, but Zuri ignored it again. "Hey, Z, if you're teaching me to be a little bad ... does that mean I'm teaching you to be a little good?"

"Maybe."

I'll take what I could get. We had half a school year left to figure out who was good and who was bad, or if—like with everything else in life— nothing was black or white, good or evil. We were all a mix of everything—even Angel, Saint, Fallen, Demon. Nothing was ever simple, but neither was life.

URIEL'S LARIAT

For information contact; www.sarah-biglow.com

Editing by: Under Wraps Publishing Services

Cover Design by: GetCovers

Interior Formatting by: Under Wraps Publishing Services

Print ISBN: 979-8665735214

Published by Sarah Biglow and Molly Zenk: October 2020

10 9 8 7 6 5 4 3 2 1

❋ Created with Vellum

1

———

ZURI

The trip back to Hell with Miry in tow for quarter break was much easier than the last time we'd visited. She didn't even throw up. Unlike last time, Dad waited for us at the portal exit. Given the time of day, I was surprised to see the square so empty though.

"Welcome home," Dad said and swept me into a hug. The embarrassingly paternal kind of behavior that makes me want to hide my face.

"Dad, seriously, let go. You're making this awkward," I said and shrugged out of his grasp.

"Hello, Sir. Thanks for letting me come stay with you," Miry said, lacking her usual bubbly persona. Maybe she was finally ready to act like a normal person.

Dad turned to Miry and opened his arms to her. "You're welcome in my home any time."

Miry gave me a quick glance before stepping forward and allowing Dad to give her a squeeze. I watched the tension melt out of her neck and shoulders as she sunk into his embrace.

"Who knew the ruler of Hell gave such awesome hugs," Miry whispered to me when Dad had released her and we were on our way back home.

"You can have all the hugs you want, Miry. But you haven't seen anything until you've had his cooking," I said with a sly smile.

"He cooks, too? Like, they never should have let him leave Heaven," Miry exclaimed loudly.

The few people who were out and about looked our way with quizzical expressions.

"Shutting up now," Miry murmured and mimed zipping her lips.

"Good idea."

Dad led us around the back of the house and into the kitchen. Tempting scents of chicken and beans filled my nostrils. I gave an involuntary sigh at the feeling of being *home*. "Have a seat," Dad said and his firm tone yanked me free of reveling in the warmth of being somewhere familiar.

I slid onto one of the high-top stools that lined the center island. Miry wiggled her way onto the one beside me. I leaned over and stage whispered, "He's going to go all stern, but concerned Dad on us now."

"The last time I saw the pair of you, you were rushing off to confront an ancient demon."

I arched a brow, gesturing between Miry and I. "We're alive."

"Details Zuri," Dad answered.

"Turns out her boyfriend is Lilith's kid and mommy dearest was taking angel kids to get him blood so he didn't turn into a demonic rage monster. She's not dead and neither is he, but we rescued the kidnapped kids. You've still got the scroll so we're good."

"It wasn't his fault. He didn't ask to have Lilith for a mother," Miry chimed in. "Not everyone gets awesome parents."

Dad turned his attention to the pots on the stove. "You are both lucky you survived. And am I to assume it was just the pair of you up against her?"

"No archangel assists," I replied before Miry could say anything.

"Uncle Raphael helped … a little," Miry piped up.

"After we did all the heavy lifting."

"While you are both staying in this house, I

ask you to do me one small favor. Do not go looking for trouble. You are teenagers and it is not your job to save the world, celestial, or otherwise." He turned back to look at us. "Do I make myself clear?"

"Yes, Sir," Miry flinched back.

"Okay, fine. No heroics. I promise," I added, wrapping an arm around Miry's shoulders. "Come on, let's get settled while he finishes cooking."

I ushered Miry to the front of the house and down a hallway to my room. Dad had already set up a futon for her.

"It feels very you," Miry assessed before tossing herself onto the futon.

"Look, I know things got kind of crazy at the end of term. I've given you a lot of shit about Saint Boy and I'm sorry. I pushed you and you weren't ready. Leaving a situation like that isn't easy and I forgot that. I just wanted you to be safe and happy … and I sort of just took over."

Miry propped her chin in her hands. "You can be like kind of pushy … or a lot pushy, but you are the first person to ever push me to stand up for myself. You shouldn't apologize for that."

I joined her on the futon, resting my back

against the side of my bed. "I'm glad you came with me."

"It's like a cultural exchange program."

"Sure."

"Can I tell you something?" She leaned toward me in a conspiratorial manner. "I kind of thought your dad was going to freak out about us fighting Lilith."

"Believe me. He was keeping it calm, because we have guests. He's capable of yelling and losing his shit just like your dad."

"Well, we're lucky I'm here, then."

"Just don't go ogling the locals, okay? It's rude and while most people here respect Dad's authority, there are bound to be some demons loyal to Beelzebub or Lilith. Besides if they find out what we did, we're easy targets down here."

Miry waved my words away like they were smoke in the air. "I believe in you, Z. You said you wouldn't let anything bad happen to me and it won't."

HALF AN HOUR LATER, we sat around the dining table. I gaped at Miry as she devoured every last scrap of food on her plate, like it had been weeks since she'd had her last meal.

"You weren't kidding. Your dad can cook!" Miry looked at the empty serving dishes and her lower lip started to form into her trademark pout. "Oh no, did I eat it all? I'm so sorry."

Dad chuckled "Don't worry, I made extra." He collected the dishes and disappeared into the kitchen.

I pulled my phone from my pocket. "Dinner is normally a no distraction zone, but I've been texting Damien all afternoon about meeting up. Though he hasn't been answering and that's not like him."

"He went to that Reaper Academy, right? Maybe he's just busy and they have a different schedule than we do," Miry answered.

"Maybe," I muttered and stowed the phone just as Dad reappeared with more food.

He set the dish down within Miry's reach and she piled on another helping. Dad sighed and rested his chin in his hand. "I do wonder what they're feeding you all at this school."

Neither Miry nor I had time to answer, because the front door burst open, slamming hard against the wall. Dad was on his feet when Azrael appeared, carrying a body in his arms—a decidedly male body.

"Help me!"

The figure had burn marks all over his body and, as his head lolled to the side, a scream ripped its way out of my throat.

Damien.

2

MIRYAM

I watched, shoveling food into my mouth, as Z and her dad scrambled to help Azrael with the half-dead guy. Zuri was right. Her dad totally makes a killer meal. He could, like, open his own business or something.

"What's going on?" I finally hopped off my stool to check out the action. "Why are you all up on saving the guy? It's Hell, right? Isn't being burned alive like a thing here?"

"This isn't just some random nobody," Zuri snapped, the harshest she'd been to me since starting at Celestial Academy. "Look closer Miry. It's Damien."

I stepped closer, looking for any sign that this person with the burned, bubbling skin was Zuri's

BFF and my sort-of-friend—CeCe's boyfriend. I spied a tattoo near his wrist of a scythe with a crooked halo resting on top. CeCe had gone on and on about that tattoo until I wanted to gouge my eyes out with a spoon. She said he had got it for her. The halo represented her saint blood and the scythe his reaper-ness. She'd even got a matching one on her inner wrist to freak out her mom ... as if dating the son of the Angel of Death wasn't enough reason for her mom to freak out. I doubted a tattoo would send her over the edge.

"Call Uncle Raphael." I looked over at Lucifer. "You still have that phone, right? The one that goes straight to him? Call Uncle Raphael. He'll know how to fix this."

"He can't come to Hell any more than I can return to Heaven," Lucifer said. "Neither of us would survive the journey."

I pushed up my sleeves, ready to help Damien with my own limited angelic healing abilities. "Then put him on speaker phone so he can talk me through this."

Zuri rested a hand on my shoulder. Her eyes and expression softened. She was concerned—not just for Damien, but for me too. It was kinda ... sweet. "I saw how wiped you were after playing medic to the formerly kidnapped kids, Miry. You give too much of yourself away. I don't want you to risk your own health. I doubt Damien would want that either."

I bit my bottom lip. "Damien would want to not be in excruciating pain. I can fix that. I know I can. Please …" I turned back to Lucifer. "Uncle Raphael will know what to do. He can help. Please. Call him."

"Please, Lucifer, he's my only child," Azrael pleaded. "Wouldn't you do anything to save Zuri? If the Archangel and little Angel can help, let them ... Please."

Lucifer huffed a sigh, but did what they asked him too. He pulled out his special direct line to Uncle Raphael's phone and hit the number '1' on the speed dial. As soon as Uncle Raphael picked up, he put it on speaker. "Raph, I have a situation here. Azrael's son Damien has been attacked, I assume, because no one would do this to themselves."

"Damien would never hurt himself," Zuri muttered.

"I also have Michael's daughter Miryam here," Lucifer continued as if Z had never said a word. "She says you can help Damien."

"Just talk me through what I need to do, Uncle

Raphael," I called in the direction of the phone. "I got this."

"How badly is he burned?" Uncle Raphael asked.

"Burned?" Lucifer's eyes narrowed. "Uh … We never said he was burned."

"Forgive me," Uncle Raphael said. "Haven't you heard? There have been two other attacks this week on Fallen. I only assumed this was related to those incidents."

"Just tell me what to do." I held my hands above a minor burn wound. My palms glowed white as the meager healing abilities I possessed seeped into Damien. The minor burns puckered and turned pink. My healing trick wouldn't work for the more serious burns, but at least it was a start.

"Put me on video call," Uncle Raphael said. "Show me the layout of the room. I need to know what supplies you have readily available."

Lucifer switched the call to video and gave Uncle Raphael a virtual tour. "See anything we can use?"

"Lay him down by the fireplace," Uncle Raphael advised. "Fire begets fire. We can push the fire raging in his system into the fireplace. Now, listen closely, Miryam, you're going to need to pay attention and repeat after me. Hold your hands over the boy and repeat everything I say precisely."

I tried to follow along as Uncle Raphael spoke the weird Enochian angelic language very, very slowly. It was some sort of incantation from the bits and pieces I could translate. I held my hands over Damien just like Uncle Raphael had instructed, but it felt like the air itself—or maybe it was the fire trapped in his body—pushed back.

"It's no good." I lowered my hands. "I'm getting some sort of resistance. Like, whatever did this to Damien doesn't want him helped."

"It could be demon powers fighting back," Uncle Raphael mused. "Or possibly angel."

"Lilith," Zuri muttered. "I bet she's mad we stopped her little angel blood buffet for Saint Boy and retaliated." She threw the first thing she could grab—a steak knife—across the room. It stuck into the wooden door with a solid 'thunk.' "I'm gonna kill that bitch!"

"Our first priority is Damien," Lucifer warned. "No one is going to be killing anyone this school quarter, young lady."

"Unless, what if Damien dies …" I pointed out. "Then someone killed him, right?"

Zuri pushed my hands back into position over

Damien's body. "Try harder, Miry. You can do this." I flipped one hand over and held it out to her. "Help me. Two are stronger than one, right? As long as you have pure intentions, Z, it should work. Only those with pure intentions can use angelic healing. Help me help Damien. Trust me, you *do not* want to see CeCe cry. She wails like a banshee."

Zuri grabbed my hand so tight I had to stop myself from yelping in pain. I couldn't worry about me right now, though. I needed to think about helping Damien.

Zuri and I formed a healing chain next to Damien. I hovered one hand over his limp body. She mirrored my actions. We repeated Uncle Raphael's angel-talk in unison. The normal pale yellowish white glow of angelic healing grew brighter and brighter until I was forced to shut my eyes against the light. When I opened them, Damien was still unconscious next to the fireplace, but he seemed to be breathing easier—almost like he was asleep—instead of his earlier painful jagged breathing. His skin was splattered with puckered pink splotches where the burns had been. Those too would fade eventually. Maybe sooner with more rounds of angelic healing.

"Did we do it?" I asked.

Zuri squeezed my hand, gently this time, almost gratefully. "Yeah. We did."

"Awesome." I smiled before everything around me went dark.

3

ZURI

We moved Damien and Miry into my room to let them rest. I'd never experienced what Miry and I had done before. She'd obviously exerted herself more than me. Despite that I could sense her pulling on my angelic abilities, bending them to her will to save Damien. I knew I needed rest, too, but I wasn't going to let either of them out of my sight. Not until I knew they were both going to be okay.

"Never thought I'd end up in your bed." Damien's voice was weak, but still loud enough to draw my attention.

I crawled over Miry's still unconscious form to sit beside my best friend. "You nearly died, you jackass! I'm going to pretend you didn't just make a hetero joke."

The pink puckers of the burns were starting to fade as the angelic healing did whatever it was meant to. They'd still leave some faint scars, but knowing D, he'd think they were perfect for wooing girls. I had so many questions, but I kept my mouth shut. He didn't need me pestering him as he tried to recover.

"You know, being the kid of the Angel of Death … the whole concept of dying never freaked me out," he said, rolling over on his side and wincing in pain as he landed on a lengthy bit of scar tissue on his upper arm. "I mean, knowing that Dad reaps souls, I kind of assumed when it was my time, he would show up to usher me to whatever's next. That was always comforting."

"Well, you're not dying any time soon. Not on my watch. That demon bitch has a beatdown coming. Her and her fucked up kid."

Damien's brow creased. "Demon? What are you talking about?"

"Lilith and Saint Boy," I replied and glanced at Miry. "We messed up their plans and now they're coming after the people I care about"

"I met her kid at that party. I don't think I saw him today."

If D was offering up information on what had happened to bring him to death's veil, I couldn't ignore the opportunity. "What did happen?"

"I was on my way to buy a couple little gifts for CeCe, to celebrate our four month anniversary. And all of a sudden there was just pain everywhere. Like nothing I'd ever felt before." A sheen of sweat broke out on his forehead as he spoke, like the memory was triggering a fight or flight response. "I couldn't even fly. It was like my wings were bound."

"So you were on the earthly plane?"

"Yeah."

"And you're sure you weren't anywhere near Castoffs?"

"No. I haven't been there in months."

Maybe Raphael was wrong. "Did you see who attacked you?"

"No. All I know is one minute I'm fine, the next everything's on fire. I closed my eyes pretty fast once I realized I couldn't fight back. Every muscle in my body was screaming. And then, it just sort of stopped." His entire body spasmed with a shiver. "I don't know if it overloaded my system or if I was dying or if it was just shock …"

"Your dad brought you here. Do you remember him showing up?"

He nodded slowly. "I remember thinking that if this was it, at least I'd get to see Dad one last time. And maybe I'd get to see my mom, too. Then the next thing I know, he's standing over me crying." Tears stained Damien's face as he spoke. "Z, I've never seen my dad cry. Ever. He picked me up and I blacked out."

"He brought you here. Miry and I saved you. I don't know how we did it exactly, but I'm grateful."

Damien gave a soft laugh. "So, you're telling me the daughter of the celestial world's biggest douchebag saved me?"

"Yup. You owe her your life." I looked over at Miry as she continued to sleep and I couldn't resist the urge to brush a stray piece of hair out of her face

To say she looked angelic would be ridiculous, but she did look at peace for the first time since I'd known her. It made me wonder what dreams danced through her mind. After everything she'd been through, she deserved some good dreams.

"You care about her more than you admit," Damien said.

"She's a friend. One I never expected to find, but a friend anyway. She thinks we're redeemable, that we matter. No one with archangel blood has ever cared about us."

"I'm calling it now, she's going to be in your life for a long time, Z. You've been looking for the right girl to understand your baggage and you've got her right there. She knows what it means to be the child of a powerful angel and everything that comes with that legacy."

I snorted. "One small problem with your logic there, Romeo. Miry is the straightest heterosexual I've ever met."

"I'm just telling you what I see. There's something there and it's more than friendship. If you're willing to see it and take a chance."

He doesn't know what he's talking about. Whatever he thought he saw was just me wanting to protect someone who needed it. Miry was becoming self-sufficient fast and very soon, she wouldn't need the chick from Hell to have her back. Our year-long service project would be done, she'd prove to her father that she was worthy of his admiration—not his disgust—and we'd go our separate ways. Only before that happened, we were going to put this Lilith bullshit to rest for good. We were only going to be home for a couple weeks and then we'd be back on campus. Dad's rules about no demon hunting under his roof would be null and void. I just had to make it two weeks. I never thought I'd actually be looking forward to setting foot on Celestial Academy grounds again.

"You get some rest. I'm going to crash on the couch," I announced and darted from the room before he could object. We were all going to be fine. We had to be. We'd come too far to fail now.

4

___

MIRYAM

Everything was all white and misty. Like walking through fog or maybe, smoke. Where was I? In my head or dead? My mind was a weird place. Leave it to me to have my dreamscape or whatever this was to be blank.

"I was hoping you'd show up. Perfect timing."

I peered through the mist, squinting until it parted a bit to reveal Chris sitting on a red checkered blanket with a picnic basket in front of him. "Chris?"

He patted the empty spot next to him. "Come sit. We have a lot to catch up on."

I sat down, tucking my skirt around my legs. Somehow even in my afterlife or dreams I still imagined myself dressed in the Celestial Academy school uniform. "Are we dead?"

He smiled sadly I thought, and handed me a glass of something fizzy. Usually I'd trust him and drink, but not today. He may still officially be my boyfriend, but he was also a liar. How long had he known his demon and saint blood was at war and the only 'cure' was angel blood? Fifty something kids were kidnapped to keep him healthy. He had still gone to class, did his homework, and acted like the golden boy I'd always thought he was, all while lying to me. I could have handled the truth. I wasn't as fragile as he and everyone else thought I was.

"Are we dead?" I repeated, setting the fizzy drink down.

Chris shook his head, that same sad smile on his face. "No. You know that spot between awake and asleep? That's where I'm able to still reach you. We share a connection, Miry. Stronger than anything else I've ever felt in my life. It's why I'm able to find you here. I ... Honestly, I didn't know if it was going to work, and I have to sort of go into a trance myself to even be here, but—"

"So it's kind of like astral plane stalking?"

"I thought you'd be happy to see me."

I bit my bottom lip, caught between wanting to be a good girlfriend and wanting him to know how messed up it was that he didn't tell me the mother of all demons was his mom. You'd think that was something you'd tell someone you claimed to love.

"Are you?" He pressed.

"Am I what?"

"Are you happy to see me?" Chris reached for my hand, but I pulled back. I couldn't think clearly when he touched me and now was definitely a 'need to think clearly' situation.

"I'm happy you seem healthy," I said. "You really scared me the last time I saw you, Chris. I don't know why you didn't tell me the truth as soon as you found out about your mom and your illness. I could have helped you, Chris. I could have *handled* it."

"I'm sorry. You have a right to be angry." He took a sip from his fizzy drink. Was it angel blood? Was that how we could connect? Because I gave him blood on that road trip, that now seemed like eons ago?

"Angry is kind of an understatement, Chris." I fidgeted, crossing and uncrossing my arms, unsure what to do with my hands. I was used to touching him when we were together. It was weird to sit so close yet feel so far away. "Zuri says—"

"Can't you go two seconds without bringing up your glorious Zuri? This has nothing to do with her. It's between you and me." His placid normal-Chris expression turned dark and stormy. For the first time I realized it was the demon side coming out. How long had he fought this duality and I skipped through life oblivious of it? A year? More?

"I'm sorry." My reflex to apologize reared its ugly head. Even if something totally wasn't my fault, I still apologized. To Chris, to Dad, to anyone who might be remotely mad at me. "I won't bring her up again. Why did you set up this, uh, meeting?"

"Why do you think?" He handed me a plate that was magically filled with all my favorite foods. "I miss you. I hate that I never got the chance to fully explain about my mom."

"You had plenty of chances to explain." I set the food aside, not trusting it either. "Instead you just chose to lie to me."

"I didn't lie," Chris insisted. "I just ... I was coming to terms with everything myself. How was I supposed to explain something that I didn't even understand? I didn't want you to hate me for something I couldn't control. We can't pick our parents. If we could, I bet we'd both have had much happier lives, don't you think?"

I ignored the question. "You told Ant, but not me."

"That's different."

"How?" I asked. "How is it different? Because he's your roommate? Well, I am your girlfriend, Chris. That should have trumped a roommate."

"You are my girlfriend?" He latched on to me using present tense. "Mir, you've gotta believe I never meant to hurt you. If I can change things, I would. I promise. I would have told you the second I found out about my mom. It was her idea to kidnap the angel kids, not mine. She wanted me healthy and I ... I wanted that too. I wanted to be with you even if that meant hiding certain things to keep you happy and unencumbered with my drama, I'd do it. That's not such a bad thing, is it?" He widened his eyes, looking hopeful and more like normal-Chris. "You're special, Miry. You always have been. I knew that the second you walked through the gates of Celestial Academy. I would do anything to have you in my life. Once I got that, I would do anything to keep you in my life. That's not such a bad thing, is it? To want to be with you?"

"I guess not." I felt myself falling back into old habits of agreeing with whatever he said, because what *I* wanted didn't matter. What I wanted never mattered. "You know, when I first got to wherever here is, I thought I might be in Heaven."

He handed my fizzy drink back to me and this time I drank it. "You're here. That's my Heaven."

"Chris?" I took another drink, my mind starting to go fizzy like whatever was in the glass. "You can make up for not telling me about your mom then, by telling me now."

His eyes narrowed, considering it. "Would it make things cool between us?"

"It would be a start. Just talk. I'll listen." I laid down, lights swirling in front of my eyes. Could you be roofied in your own mind? I could hear Zuri calling my name, but it sounded a million miles away. I didn't want to go just yet though. I wanted to stay here.

"Another time." Chris laid down next to me. I curled up against him. He was familiar and I missed the familiar. He tapped my forehead, then my heart. "If you need me, I'm right here always."

"Does that mean you're not real?" I mumbled, feeling sleepy even though I was already asleep.

He wrapped his arms around me and I snuggled closer. "I'm real. Just don't tell Zuri. It will be our little secret. Can you keep a secret, Miry?"

"Keep a secret …"

I opened my eyes and he was gone.

5

ZURI

The rest of the break wasn't what I'd call restful. I spent most of it worrying about Damien and Miry. Damien seemed to be mostly healed from his attack. Although I'd insisted he stay with us until we went back to classes. He cried in his sleep. Miry had gone quiet and contemplative, skittish almost. She thought I didn't notice that she was hiding something, but I only had enough mental energy to worry so much. Plus, despite Dad's explicit orders not to get involved, I'd done a little digging into the other attacks Raphael had mentioned. They seemed to take place at Castoffs or the demon bar named Renegade Reggie's. Dad had kept too close an eye on us while we were home for me to sneak off and investigate. Except we were headed out of Hell which meant he didn't have control over what I did.

"It's going to be weird," Miry said as we stood at the back door to my house, getting ready to head to the portal and back to the earthly plane.

"What is?" I double checked my bag. Damien stood off to one side, tugging on the sleeves of his shirt.

"Being there … without him."

"And here I thought we'd hit a streak. You'd gone nearly two weeks without mentioning him," I muttered.

"Sor … Actually, no, I'm not sorry. Chris has been a big part of my life. Of who I am and who I used to be. I know you don't like him and I know he lied to me, but I wouldn't be me without him."

"You're right. I just hate seeing what he did to you. All the lies and the deceit. He had no right to use you like that." I reached over and patted her shoulder. "It's going to be different, but different isn't bad, Miry. You get to find out who you are on your own. You get to choose your own path."

She leaned into my touch and I caught Damien giving me a pointed look. I flipped him off behind my back so Miry couldn't see. He and I hadn't talked about his unfounded assessment of Miry's and my friendship. I was going to keep it that way. "You ready?"

She turned and stepped away from me just as I heard a door inside the house close. I followed her back into the house to find her giving Dad a firm hug. His dark eyes widened at the gesture, but he patted her back in a soothing manner.

"Thanks for letting me stay," she said, resting her head on his chest.

"You are welcome here anytime you like Miryam. Always."

She looked up at him. "You mean that?"

"Of course, he means it. He doesn't make promises he can't keep," I said.

"Now, you better get going. And don't forget to bring your winter jackets. It's going to be cold up there."

Miry waited until we were halfway to the portal before saying, "You know, I'd forgotten it was winter up there. It's just so nice and comfortable down here." She tugged on her winter jacket and a bright pink hat.

I pulled on a beanie and an overcoat as we reached the portal. I laced my fingers through Miry's own. "Don't forget to breathe."

With that warning, I tugged her into the portal. Somehow, this time, it was less disorienting with Miry along for the trip. It didn't feel like the portal was trying to rip us apart or squeeze the air from my lungs. When we set foot on solid ground, snow crunched beneath my boots.

"That wasn't so bad," Miry said, her cheeks a little pale. She took a few deep gasps, but managed to keep her lunch where it belonged.

"I think you're getting used to portal travel," I commented and started for the gates to the academy.

"I think I am," she agreed and raced to keep up with me.

"So, I was thinking, we should go out tonight," I said as we reached the gates.

"Z, we just got back," she said, brushing her bare fingers against the icy metal. The gate swung inward without protest, letting us both in.

"But I found out where the other Fallen were attacked," I replied.

"Your dad said we couldn't go looking," Her cherubic cheeks were extra rosy in the cold.

"He said we couldn't get involved while we were at home." I gestured to the snow-covered lawn and looming academy buildings before us. "We are most definitely not in Hell anymore."

"You really think Lilith is attacking Fallen now?"

I shrugged. "Our blood is as good as yours and if she really cares about her kid, it's a logical move. Plus, maybe she thinks Fallen are close enough to demons to sway your boy more to her way of thinking."

"If there's a chance we can find Chris and … and stop him, then we have to try."

"We'll check in or whatever we have to do to make your dad not want to smite us, and then we're outta here."

"Where are you going?" A high-pitched voice called from behind us.

I pivoted to find Glasses standing there in a thick scarf covering most of his face and a hat pulled down over his ears. The sight of him made me want to punch him in the face. "None of your fucking business, traitor."

"He made me keep quiet. I had thought I was helping a friend. I swear. I knew what it would mean if other people found out. If your dad found out, Miry. Look, I know I screwed up. Whatever you're doing I want to help."

"He could be helpful," Miry mused.

"Did he ever mention going after Fallen?" I stepped closer so our voices wouldn't carry as far.

"No. But, he did say that one of the first times he met with Lilith, it was at some creepy demon bar. I guess she wasn't worried about making a good impression."

"Did that place happen to be called Renegade Reggie's?" I prompted.

He pushed his fogged over glasses farther up his barely visible nose. "I helped him get there, but he got back on his own. I didn't see the sign, but that might be it. Are we going to a demon bar?" His voice jumped an octave as the question left his lips.

"No. We're not going. Just tell me how to get there."

"I don't know."

I grabbed the front of his jacket and he flinched. "You said you found it for Saint Boy."

"I used my power. I wasn't exactly paying attention. Besides, if you're going to a demon bar, you'll need a lookout. Or back-up. I can be that. Please."

Miry stepped in and put a hand on my arm, urging me to let him go. I gave him an extra shove just to let out some of my irritation. "Fine. We meet by the gate after dark. Don't you dare screw us over, Glasses."

He swallowed loud enough for me to hear and

I could imagine his Adam's apple bobbing in this throat. "I swear."

Now, we just had to wait a few hours and I could kick some demon ass.

6

MIRYAM

I set my backpack down next to my bed and kicked off my snow boots. One thunked against something under my bed. I crawled on my hands and knees to see what it had hit. I ended up staring at the cardboard box of Chris' stuff. I had never given it back to him. Now I don't know if I'd ever get the chance.

"Do you think there's still good in him?" I asked Zuri after I army crawled out from under the bed. I opened my backpack to start unpacking. It was a good distraction. I needed something to focus on other than memories of Chris being here, especially when he wasn't any more.

"Still good in who?" She asked, preoccupied with putting away her own stuff in her dresser.

"I'm trying not to use his name cause you want me to forget him, but Chris. Do you think there is still good in him?"

Zuri looked up, hands freezing in the motion of putting away her underwear in the top drawer. "I never told you to forget about him, Miry. However, I do wish you'd stop seeing him as saintly and realize he's half demon. A lying half demon who may or may not have been using you for your angel blood."

"He wasn't using me, not the whole time," I pouted. "He wouldn't even let me help him no matter how many times I offered."

"Cause mommy and some unsuspecting kids were all the help he needed." Zuri stuffed her underwear into the drawer with a little more umph than necessary. "Look, I get it. Break ups are hard, but I think—"

"We're not broken up," I interrupted, cringing when she gave me a 'why the heck not?' glare. "Not yet at least," I added to get back onto her good side. "I might be totally off base, but I think I can help him. I *want* to help him."

"Okay. It's your funeral."

I flinched again. "Couldn't you, like, pick a different word? Funeral reminds me of Uncle Gabriel's scroll, which in turn reminds me of the scary pool party, and that reminds me of Dad being, well, Dad which reminds me—"

"Of Saint Boy saving you?" She guessed. "Then we're back at square one with 'oh, there's still good in him. I just know it.' Miry, if he really wanted to fight the demon blood, I bet he could."

"You don't know that!" I snapped. "You know nothing about him, because you … because you don't care. You don't care how I feel at all!"

I was crying before I realized all those emotions needed a way to break free. Zuri made it across the room so fast, I wasn't positive she walked. She might have flown. She wrapped me up in her arms like I was some precious, fragile thing. Something worth protecting and not shattering into a thousand pieces. My heart, my head, my whole self, all of it felt so, so fragile. Would she protect me? Would she put me back together if I fell apart?

"Hey. Hey, it's going to be okay. Do you hear me? It's going to be okay." Zuri patted my back semi-awkwardly. "I don't mean to rag on your boy, but you deserve better. More than that, you deserve to *see* that you deserve better. You're much more than I could ever hope to be. You naturally see the good in people. I just want to punch everyone in the face. Or maybe punch the wall."

"You give terrible pep talks." I pulled back, wiping under my eyes. "And your hugs could use some work too."

"Duly noted." Zuri looked a little lost, like she wasn't sure if she should be hugging me or reading me the riot act for being all Pollyanna Sunshine about everything. Life was so much easier if you chose to see the good. It kept the dark at bay.

"Are we really going clubbing tonight at that demon place?" I asked.

"We are if you want to know who is targeting Fallen."

"Apocalypse. Kidnappings. And now potential Fallen hate crimes." On my fingers I ticked off all the things that had happened in the short time Zuri had been a student at Celestial Academy. "You sure know how to liven up this place."

"We stopped all those other things. We can stop this too." She stood and turned away from me to finish putting her clothes in her dresser.

"We," I repeated. "I like the sound of that."

Zuri glanced over her shoulder at me. "So do I," she admitted. "Don't you dare tell anyone—especially Damien—I said this, but we make a pretty good team."

I smiled, starting to feel less anxious about

being on campus without Chris. Would it be different? Totally, but different wasn't always a bad thing. "I've been part of a couple before, but have never been part of a team. Can we make up a secret handshake or something?"

Zuri pressed her lips into a thin line. "No. Just unpack already, Miry. Try to find club clothes that aren't pink and sparkly."

"How about purple and sparkly?"

Zuri shot me one of her patented 'are you high?' looks. "Do I even need to answer that?"

I giggled. "Nope. Joke's on you, because I got black clothes now." I pulled leather pants and a matching corset top out of my bottom drawer. "Ta da! See? I'm not always so goody-goody. I can be a bad girl."

Zuri laughed, the hint of a smile tugging at the corners of her mouth. "I'll believe that when I see it."

"Really?" I pulled my pink unicorn shirt off over my head without thinking or caring about privacy. Next my skirt followed it. I stood mostly naked on my side of the room for a sec before reaching for my leather outfit. "Challenge accepted."

7

ZURI

Trying not to let the image of Miry in her underwear sear into my brain, I pulled on some club appropriate attire—complete with an actual fake ID—and checked my hair in the mirror.

"You look really nice," Miry said, fiddling with the laces on the boots I'd lent her.

"I look like I'm ready to fight someone," I muttered. *Not far off.* If we found the bastard hurting Fallen, I was ready to thrown down.

"That doesn't mean you don't look nice," she replied.

"Come on. We need to grab Glasses and figure out where we're heading."

I didn't want to spend more time with Glasses

than I had to. The fact he thought he had a chance with me might amuse some people. Except to me, it was just sad. Why pine over someone you know is never going to work out? I'd been there and done that. I'd learned my lesson—the hard way. We found him slinking in the shadows by the front gates.

"I take you to the bar and we're good, right? Please … No more threatening to hit me?" His lower lip trembled.

"Deal," I said, offering my hand.

He shook it with more vigor than I expected before he muttered his little tracking prayer and we were off. I couldn't see what he was using to find the bar, but I assumed it was something Saint Boy had taken from the place. Possibly a memento of his first meeting with mommy dearest.We stopped across the street from a dimly lit sign that read 'Renegade Reggie's.' "That's the place. Can I go now? It freaks me out," Glasses said.

"Yeah, get out of here," I muttered and started across the street.

Miry raced after me, grabbing my elbow to stop my forward motion. "You have to promise me … If he's in there, you're not going to kill him."

I blew out a breath. "Miry, he could have

killed you at the end of last term. How about this? I won't lay a hand on him unless he comes at me first."

She moved to stand in front of me, her rosy cheeks flushed. "And you have to swear not to try and push him into hitting you. Please, I don't want you to get hurt." She slid her hand down my arm until she was squeezing my fingers. "You're too important to me."

Words caught in my throat as she stared at me with those wide eyes, begging me not to lose my shit. I could hear Damien's voice in the back of my head goading me that we would be good together. I muzzled that stupid voice. "Fine. I won't start anything."

She started for the door, but I stepped around her. "Even in those clothes, you stand out, Miry. It's safer if I go in first. And for the love of all that is decent, don't accept any drinks from strangers.'

"That was one time," she protested.

"And you got drugged," I reminded her.

We stepped into the bar and I could immediately feel all eyes on us. We weren't old enough to be in here and not demon-blooded either. Two reasons that gave anyone in this place a reason to want to hurt us. Although, I'd been in places like this before. I knew what it took to fit in. So, I pulled up a stool at the bar, giving me a decent view of the interior. Miry hauled herself up onto the seat next to me.

"What can I get you?" My heart skipped a beat and then decided to hammer triple time in my chest. I knew that voice. I hadn't heard it in months.

Swallowing the lump in my throat, I slowly turned around to see Delilah—my ex—tending bar. Our gazes met and I could see the fiery power of her demon heritage bubble over her skin.

"What the fuck are you doing in my bar?" She hissed.

"Didn't know you owned the place. And I'm also pretty sure I can go wherever I want," I replied, our mission forgotten.

She gestured to a little nook by the end of the bar. "Now."

I rolled my eyes and turned to Miry. "Stay here."

I slid off the stool and followed Delilah to the semi-private space. "We both know you're not old enough to be in here," she chided.

I flashed my fake ID. "ID says I'm twenty-two."

"I was with you when you got that."

"And you made sure it would pass as legit even without my particular skill set."

"I'm not serving you," she said with her arms crossed over her chest, pushing her breasts up even more in her already cleavage plunging shirt. The thought of Delilah's bare tits swaying over me in bed sent shivers down my spine.

"I'm not here to drink. I'm looking for someone."

"Try the gay bar down the block."

"I'm not here for a hookup. Fuck, Del. I'm trying to stop a psycho bitch and her creep of a kid from hurting my friends."

Delilah laughed. "Oh right, I thought I had heard something about you running away to join the goodie-goodies." She turned her head and pointed to Miry at the bar. "Decided your own people weren't good enough for you, had to see what the other side had to offer?"

I snorted. "Jealousy looks ugly on you. And for your information, I didn't run away. I stopped the damn apocalypse. You may hate angels. Believe me, I get it. But, the end of the world is bad business, even for you."

"That was always your problem. So full of yourself. Just because you were his daughter, you thought that made you perfect." She shoved me and I staggered back a step, caught off guard.

"Hey! Don't touch my friend," Miry hollered, managing to speed over and flounce simultaneously.

"You even know who your little friend is, sweetheart?"

Miry's chin jutted out defiantly. "Of course I do." She flung her arm around my shoulder and leaned in, kissing my cheek. Delilah stared at us as shouts erupted just beyond the entrance to the bar. I didn't have time to process the fact that Miry had kissed me. I left Delilah standing there and pushed my way through the crowd. The scent of burnt flesh nauseated me and I waved at Miry to stay back. Singed feathers lay around the body. I couldn't call it a person, because that implies something living. The burn patterns were the same as Damien's injuries. We'd just missed them. If I hadn't been tripping down memory lane with Delilah, we could have caught them. I stood and scanned the crowd and the people walking by. I wasn't searching for an eerie demon. I was looking for my mother. If Lilith was one thing, she was consistent when in public. No dark-skinned woman in a red dress stood out to me.

"What do we do now?" Miry's voice pulled me back to the moment.

"We keep looking. We were on the right track this time. We were just too late to the party. Next time, we won't be."

8

MIRYAM

"What is it? What won't you let me see?" I asked Zuri. She waved an arm behind her, not even looking at me.

"Go back inside. Just ... don't come any closer."

"Why?" I stood on tiptoes, trying to see over the crowd, but kept getting jostled around. Someone grabbed my butt. I squealed, spinning around to try to find the culprit, but the crowd was too thick and the air smelled like burnt feathers and BBQ beef.

"Wait for me inside, Miry. Don't argue." Zuri glanced briefly in my direction, but then she was back to focusing on whatever was smoking on the ground. Were those black Fallen wings?

"Fine, but I'm taking the first drink someone offers me!" I pouted.

"Just go!" She yelled.

I cringed, hurt by her tone, before turning to slink back inside.

The bar was empty which was kind of creepy after how many people were dancing right before whatever had happened outside happened. The music was still going, though the DJ station was unmanned. I climbed onto a bar stool, my feet swinging like a little kid sitting in a too-big chair. I was the only one inside. "Lame."

"I've been waiting for you, Miryam."

I swiveled on my stool. The lady sitting beside me looked and sounded like Mom, but I knew it wasn't my mom. It was Lilith. Technically, I guess she was Chris' mom though it was still majorly weird to think the mother of demons gave birth to my boyfriend.

"You can drop the glamour." I sounded braver than I felt. "I know who you are, Lilith."

She nodded and gave a little half bow even though she was sitting down. "With pleasure." Mom's blonde hair, red and white plaid shirt, and jeans shimmered, replaced by Lilith's true form. She had the whitest blonde hair I'd ever seen, skin almost the same pale shade, and her eyes were all black. No white around the irises or any-thing. "We need to discuss what you can give me, child of Michael."

"I'm not giving you a grandkid if that's what you want."

"Why not? You always said we'd make such cute babies."

Chris materialized next to his mom in a cloud of dark smoke. He looked like the normal Chris, but not him all at the same time. Like he was letting his demon side come out to play now that he didn't have to or want to hide be-hind his saint side anymore. He was unshaved and his usually perfectly gelled hair fell into his eyes. He seemed paler too, closer to Lilith's skin tone. His blue eyes were darkening, soon they too would be completely black. I shivered. Hearing that he was half demon was one thing, but it didn't quite seem real. Seeing him use demon powers right in front of my own eyes made it very, very real. And to be honest very, very scary.

"I told you, if you needed blood, you can have mine, and I meant it, Chris." I tilted my chin up, hoping I could keep my voice and hands from shaking just a tiny bit longer. "I don't want any more kids getting hurt—Angel or Fallen."

"Fallen?" Lilith sneered. "Rebel Angels hold no interest for me."

"But angel blood is still angel blood." Chris leaned back against the bar, crossing his arms over his chest. "What game are you playing at, Miry?"

I shook my head. "No game. Just promise me you won't hurt any more people. I can heal you, Chris. I know I can. Let me help you. Please."

"Stand up slowly and move away from the demons, Miryam!"

Uncle Uriel?

Lilith's eyes narrowed to dark slits at the interruption. I slid off the bar stool and walked backwards toward the sound of Uncle Uriel's voice while Lilith was distracted. He stepped in front of me. My brain only half registered that he was wearing full commando gear. I was too busy gaping at his flaming lasso rope thing. Uncle Raphael's lesson on angelic relics floated back to me. What did he call the rope thing again? Ooh, that's right ... A lariat—Uriel's lariat. It cleansed the wicked, but could also burn them.

"Your war is not my war, Archangel," Lilith hissed. "Leave now before I display my true power."

"Bring it," he taunted. "Everyone knows

demons are all talk and no action. You want to see real power?" The whip flashed out in front of him, glowing the same fiery red as his eyes during a particularly violent self-defense class. The tip snaked around the leg of the barstool, pulling it out from under Lilith. Instead of falling though, she levitated in the air.

"Foolish Creature," she sneered. "You do not want to proceed down the path you are walking. Leave now if you wish to live."

"I don't care how ancient you are, you are no match for me," Uncle Uriel said. "'God shall smite the wicked.' I think I'll start with you."

He pushed me farther behind him before raising the lariat again, ready to strike. He paused when Lilith straight up laughed in his face.

"Oh, I don't mean leave if *you* wish to live. I mean the child of Michael. What say you, Archangel? Would you like to see the child raised as your kin rent limb from limb? I promise to start with her fingers. Those hurt ever so much when they shatter. Next each individual toe, followed by her legs. First left, then right. Next, I'll crush each individual rib bone. Such silly things ribs are, don't you agree? One rib from a single man caused my entire destruction. If it wasn't for him …" She trailed off, her litany of crazy and seriously painful things she planned to do to me forgotten. The next second, she shook her head, jumped back into the groove of torture talk. "After her ribs, I'll pull out each and every tooth in that pretty little head of hers. I can see why my son fancied you so, Child … besides the natural draw of your blood line, of course. Now, I will warn you only one last time. Leave now unless you wish to perish by my hand."

"Let me do it, Mother," Chris said. "It will be more agonizing coming from someone she loves." In a poof of smoke, he crossed the room to right beside me using his new demon power. He grabbed me by the shoulders, leaning close, his breath warm against my cheek. The last thing I saw before disappearing in a cloud of demon smoke was Zuri's terrified expression as she burst into the bar looking for me.

9

ZURI

Son of a bitch! I grabbed the first thing I could find—a bar stool—and slammed it against the bar. The wood shattered, leaving me with a jagged leg. I brandished it at Lilith as she stood in the middle of the room.

"What the fuck did you do with my friend?"

Lilith pointed to the space where Miry had just been. "I did nothing to your friend."

I rolled my eyes, trying to keep the fear at bay. "Fine. Where did your demon spawn take her and don't tell me you don't know? The two of you are working together."

"I did warn her that she should leave or else she'd become my next … pet project."

I lunged forward, but a strong hand wrapped

around my left wrist and yanked me backward. My halted momentum made me twist and pain seared up my arm as Uriel thrust me behind him. I didn't need his protection. I was capable of fighting Lilith all on my own. I owed her the same kind of pain she'd caused Damien. "I am not a child. I don't need some Archangel to fight my battles," I snapped, trying to ignore the throbbing in my wrist.

I'd forgotten how strong Archangels could be. He probably hadn't meant to hurt me, but I suspected he'd broken my wrist with that maneuver. Uriel ignored my pain and whipped his lariat at Lilith. She stepped back without so much as a flutter to her long black dress.

"I do hope your little friend returns to you undamaged. Well perhaps not wholly intact. My dear boy does like to play with his toys," Lilith quipped before disappearing in a puff of smoke.

I grabbed Uriel's jacket with my good hand. "They have Miry. We need to find her. Now."

He slung the lariat over his shoulder and looked at me, his eyes flashing red in that same eerie way Lilith's did. "Oh, what are you doing here?"

"Seriously? That's not important. That bitch

has Miry. Help me find her. Please," I tried playing nice this time.

"Oh, Michael won't be happy about that," he muttered, rubbing at his chin. He glanced down at my wrist and prodded it with his index finger. I flinched in spite of myself. "Does that hurt?"

"No, not at all," I deadpanned. After a beat, I added. "Yes, it hurts. I think it's broken."

Before either of us could say anything else, the door to the bar slammed open and Delilah appeared. She looked pissed as her gaze landed on Uriel. "Get out of my bar. You're not welcome here"

"He's with me, Del," I said, trying to intervene.

"I don't care. I want him out of my bar right now. He's bad for business."

"I'd say the dead body on your doorstep is worse," I muttered.

"I didn't ask for this shit to be dropped into my lap. You broke up with me three months ago and I never heard a word from you. Then, you show up here with your new side chick and what … expect me to look the other way while you try to impress her?"

"She's not … forget it. Miry is missing and I need to get her back. I'm sorry for how things ended with us, Del, but we both knew it wasn't going to last." Delilah pointed to my wrist. "You should get that splinted."

"Just give me a rag, I'll turn it into a makeshift sling. I'll be fine."

"You want my help finding your girl? Then you better damn well take care of your ass first."

If I flew, I could get back to campus and Raphael in under half an hour. Except that meant Miry was in Saint Boy's clutches for that long and he didn't need to be a full-on demon to mess with her head. I turned to Uriel, holding out my hand when I noticed he was looking around like he expected something to jump out and attack him at any second. "I need to reach Raphael."

"There's so many of them," he mumbled.

"It's a demon bar," I pointed out.

He nodded mostly to himself and took a few steps toward the door. I could hear voices coming from outside. People were wondering what to do with the charred body on the sidewalk. Dad would need to be told, but it couldn't come from me. If he knew I'd been here, he'd lose his shit.

"Hey, girl asked you to call somebody," Delilah said, her tone dropping an octave as she let a little of her demon side out.

That snapped Uriel out of whatever memory he'd been lost in. "Oh, you're hurt. Right."

"Get Raphael here, please. I need this wrapped up so I can go find Miry."

He tapped the screen of his phone and in a matter of minutes I could hear the voices outside turn hushed and the sound of beating wings. I left Uriel and Delilah behind, figuring she'd be less inclined to snap at me if a second Archangel didn't have to set foot inside her establishment.

"You do realize you're out well after curfew," Raphael chided before ushering me away from the gawking crowd.

"Spare me the scolding. Lilith is still on the hunt and that insane douchebag son of hers has Miry."

"You're lucky you only suffered a broken wrist if you faced off against the mother of demons a second time," Raphael noted.

"Wasn't Lilith." I nodded as Uriel stepped out from the bar onto the street. He resettled the lariat so it hung across his body and took off without a word.

"He forgets his own strength sometimes." Raphael's hands warmed as he laid them against my wrist.

"Yeah, I get that. Any idea why he showed up here?" *Was he finally hunting Lilith, too? Did*

Michael put him on the assignment after we'd embarrassed him for a second time?

"I've stopped questioning Uriel's whereabouts a long time ago." he patted the top of my hand. "Try not to use it for a few hours and you'll be fine. Now what is this about Miryam missing?"

I flexed my hand. The wrist joint was stiff, but I'd live. "I'm on it. I'll get her back, I promise."

I moved down the sidewalk to where Delilah waited. She held out something in her hand. I studied the dark object, what looked like coal. "What is it?"

"It's a demonic lodestone. Focus on the demon you want to find and it will ignite the path to them."

"Why do I get the feeling, because I'm not a demon, it won't work for me alone?"

"Because you were always so damn smart, Zuri. Now, do you want to get your girl back or not?"

I cupped my hand over Delilah's, lacing our fingers together and called up the image of Saint Boy as he'd been when last we'd crossed paths. The stone grew warm beneath my palm and when I opened my eyes again, a fiery gash wound along the sidewalk in front of us. Time to get my friend back.

10

MIRYAM

Traveling by demon smoke was so much worse than the portal to Hell. The same nausea and dizziness were there, but I also felt ... different. I don't know how to describe it, but it was like a little piece of my soul was missing to be replaced with emptiness and sadness. Was this how demons felt all the time? Was this how *Chris* felt the whole time he was sick?

"Where are we?" I squinted into the dimness, but couldn't make out much besides some big empty room with a lot of dust and not much light. "Where did you take me?"

"Does it really matter?" Chris sat down on the floor. Even in the dimness, I could see the dark bags under his eyes and sallowness of his skin.

Maybe it was a good thing he had sat down before he fell down.

"Chris, when was the last time you slept?"

"I don't know. Three days. Maybe four." He ran a hand through his unusually messy hair. "Why do you even care? You have your dike roommate. You don't need me anymore."

"Don't take your issues out on Zuri." I paced the room, trying to figure out where we were. It looked a little like the warehouse where we had found the kidnapped kids, but I doubted he'd be sloppy enough to keep using it as his secret demon lair after we busted it up. It was, like, the first place someone would look for me. Wait, maybe that's the point? Make it easy to find me. Then he could let me escape without making it seem like he let me go. Normal Chris would totally do that. I wasn't so sure about demon Chris, though.

"I'll take whatever I want out on Zuri," he spat. "She's the reason you're pulling away from me. She's the reason you're—"

"I was always strong on my own." I turned to face him again, finding it hard to see the boy I loved in this broken, pathetic creature before me. "Just no one else saw it until Zuri showed up. Including me." I sighed. "Let me help you, Chris.

You didn't trust me with your secret before, but that doesn't mean I can't be trusted now. Please?"

"Why do you care?" He watched me warily. We used to be all over each other when we were alone, always game for a quickie. Thrilled at the excitement of touching and being touched. Now, he felt like a stranger. Would we ever get back to the point where he felt like my Chris again? Did I even want to?

"I care." I had a plan that pretty much consisted of me making sure he still trusted me, so I stayed alive. It wasn't great as far as rescue plans went, but it was all I had right now. *I'm Miryam bat-Michael*, I reminded myself. *I got this.*

"Why?"

"We have history, Chris," I said. "That doesn't stop just because some bad stuff happened."

"Bad stuff happened?" He laughed. "Miryam bat-Michael: Patron Saint of Denial. Everything I thought I knew about my life, my family, and my very identity changed when I learned who my mom was. That's not just some 'bad stuff,' Miry. That's the worst possible thing that could ever happen to me." He shifted to face me, eyes flashing red in the pale light. "Do you know what happens if I don't get enough angel blood? I die. I die, Miry. I've had to live with the weight of that guilt from my secret for years. Do you think I like what I've become? Do you think I like hurting people? Hurting you? I'm at war with myself. Every day is a God damned war and I ... I can't do anything to stop it."

My Chris was so close to the surface. It filled me with hope and pain at the same time. If I offered again, would he accept my help? How could you save someone who might not want to be saved?

"Angel blood gives your saint side a fighting chance, right?" I held out my arm. The scars on my wrist from my last blood donation were fading, but they were still there. They shimmered like magic track marks, a constant reminder of what I was willing to do to save those I loved.

He frowned at my unspoken offer, the normal Chris creeping closer and closer to the surface of the half-demon he'd become. "You shouldn't have to be my personal blood bank, Miry. It's not fair that you ... that you have to give so much and get so little in return."

"Life isn't fair." I twisted my wrist until my veins bulged blue, hoping it was enough to entice him to take me up on my offer. The last time we did the impromptu blood donation, he had fallen asleep. If that was the MO for this sort of deal, it would give me time to figure a way out of here ... wherever here was. I hoped.

"Why, after everything I've done, are you still trying to save me?" He asked.

"Because I want to." I sat down next to him, offering my wrist again. "Please, Chris, let me help you. My Chris, who I love, is still in there. I know you are. I can help. You don't have to do this alone. I'm here for you."

"I'm sorry, Miry. I wish I could be all you needed me to be." His eyes were haunted in his ashen, pallid face.

"It's okay," I soothed. "I understand." I found a broken piece of something—it looked like shattered glass—nearby and sawed at my wrist until I drew blood. I held it out to Chris again. "I understand," I repeated. "I understand."

"I'm sorry." He leaned against me, sucking at my skin like a baby drinking from a bottle until sleep finally claimed him. Now it was time to figure out how to get myself out of here.

"I'm Miryam bat-Michael," I whispered. "I got this."

11

ZURI

The lodestone led us through the city, behind clean-looking high rises and along run-down and long-forgotten businesses. Everything in me said I should let go of Delilah's hand. I didn't want to give anyone the wrong impression. Not just anyone—Miry. Except, why would Miry care if she saw me holding hands with someone else?

My hand grew slick with sweat from the heat of the stone and I finally had to pull away, massaging the tender red flesh of my palm. "Why is it doing that?"

"It means we're getting closer. That's a good thing," she answered, holding the damn stone like it wasn't made of burning lava.

"Oh … well, good." I didn't want to touch it again, but I knew I had no choice. Not if it meant finding Miry faster. I could only imagine what that asshole was doing to her.

"So, why her?" Delilah prompted as we followed the fiery gash in the ground toward a familiar part of town. Castoffs came into view. It was closed. Ever since the whole demonic minion army incident last term, it hasn't been open.

"She's just a friend," I answered. Delilah laughed and shook her head. "Uh huh. You keep telling yourself that. But, whatever. Why is she your friend? She's one of *them*. I thought you'd hate her just on principle."

"She's not her father. He's cruel, heartless, and manipulative. Miry … she's got a good heart and wants to help people. She sees the best in people, even when it gets her in trouble."

"I just can't picture you in their little gilded paradise. It's just not you."

"Maybe not, but they aren't all bad. Sure, they've been teaching revisionist history, but then it's a good thing I'm there to set them straight. Besides, we're only different, because someone gave us a different name. We're really not that different."

The gash in the ground ended at Castoffs

which meant we'd come to the end of the trail. It was pitiful that he would bring her back here. Like it was still his own little secret base of operations. He had to know I'd come for Miry. I let go of Delilah's hand and my wings erupted from between my shoulders.

"I'm going to check the perimeter," I said in a hushed tone before taking flight.

Getting an aerial view of the place only confirmed that the place was vacant. I didn't see any lights on inside the club. Yet, as I circled back toward Delilah, I caught movement from the back. A figure emerged and I'd know that blond head anywhere. She ran straight into Delilah.

"Miry!" I landed half a foot from them.

She turned to look at me. She was a little paler than when that bastard had taken her. I could see that she had been injured with the way she was holding her wrist and it was bleeding. "I'm okay, Z," she said.

"You're bleeding." I turned to Delilah and gestured to her shirt. "I need to borrow that."

"Oh, you are not getting her goodie-goodie blood all over my expensive clothing."

I yanked at the hem, tearing the fabric anyway. "We both know you don't spend more than twenty bucks on any one piece of clothing, Del." I wrapped the fabric around Miry's wrist, my own recently healed one aching at the sharp movements.

"He's still inside," Miry said leaning against me.

"Then we better not be here," I urged, starting to guide her back toward the demon bar.

"I let him do it," she said as I sped up, glancing over my shoulder every few paces to make sure we weren't being followed.

"I told you he'd just keep hurting you," I muttered.

"No … I knew it would make him tired. With my blood he would fall asleep and I could get away."

"That's … actually pretty smart," I commented.

"Why is the bartender here?" The change in conversation told me Miry was starting to feel the blood loss.

"Because I needed her help to find you."

"Who is she?" Miry prodded.

"I'm her ex-girlfriend, angel," Delilah said, falling into step beside us. Her tone dripped of disdain for Miry's Archangel status.

Miry's eyes widened. "You dated a demon?"

"I've dated a lot of people."

Miry's face grew serious and she stopped

walking, turning to face Delilah head on. "Did you break my friend's heart?"

Delilah's face softened. "No. She broke mine." Delilah leaned in close and whispered something in Miry's ear I couldn't hear.

Before I could ask what she'd said, Delilah vanished in a plume of fire. I'd always hated it when she did that. It did terrible things to my hair and she had always done it whenever we fought.

"What did she tell you?" I waited until the bar, Renegade Reggie's was in sight to ask.

"She thinks I'm your girlfriend," Miry said with a giggle. "She said not to get my hopes up, because you have stupid high standards."

"Well, she's not wrong about my standards. But obviously, she's reading into things that aren't there," I said. "Though, you did kiss me at the bar."

Miry giggled again. "It just felt like the thing to do."

"Well it confused a lot of people." Me included.

Her lips puckered into a frown. "It's not like I kissed you on the lips."

"You know what, don't worry about it. We have more important things to worry about. Like the fact Lilith killed a Fallen outside the club tonight."

"Do you think it was, like, weird that Uncle Uriel was there?"

"Yeah. It was. But … What if we could borrow his lariat? It cleanses demonic energy, right? We could use it on Lilith to subdue her, maybe for good."

"He's not going to part with it," Miry said.

"So we don't tell him." A plan began to form in my mind. It was definitely dangerous and had a low probability of working, but it was worth a shot. "We're going to borrow it and he's never going to know."

"How?"

"Because I'm going to forge a duplicate."

12

MIRYAM

There were a million and two questions I wanted to ask Zuri. How do we get close enough to snatch Uncle Uriel's lariat? What do we do with it once we have it? I think there's a learning curve to using an Angelic relic. I was able to use Dad's sword, but that's only because I was like totally purposeful about needing it to save the world. Playing around with the lariat to figure out how to stop the attacks on Fallen might not be enough intent to use it properly ... if at all. My head whirled with all sorts of questions and half answers, but I needed to sleep. Blood loss was no joke. Maybe catching some zzz would perk me up.

"What? Why are you looking at me like that?"

I squinted at Zuri, sitting on her bed across the room from me. There were weird black swirlies and colored lights flashing around her. Maybe the blood transfusion wiped me out more than I had thought.

"You realize you saved yourself today, right?" Zuri asked. "You don't need Saint Boy, me, or anyone else to rescue you."

I smiled, happy at the compliment. "I'm Miryam bat-Michael, remember? I got this." I yawned, not able to keep my eyes open any longer. I fell into a fitful sleep, letting the world and all its worries fall away.

"So what's the plan?" I asked Zuri the next morning as we loitered outside of Uncle Uriel's classroom. This was the first time I'd really been in any class since Chris had joined his mommy dearest's demon horde. It was weird not having him by my side. Logically I knew I shouldn't miss him. I knew that he had been manipulative in a thousand different ways, but that didn't stop me from wondering if I could have done more to help him. What if he had told me—if he had let me in on his secret instead of Ant—would things be different? Would he be the saint I knew he could be instead of the demon he'd become?

"We go to class like normal. You distract him and I snag the lariat," Zuri said, watching the door as if remembering the last fireball death-match class.

I rubbed my upper thigh that had took a direct hit the last time Uncle Uriel went all fire in the hole and lobbed fireballs as fast as softballs at his students during class. Zuri looked away before I even fully realized she was watching me in the first place. The demon bartender's words floated back to me. *Be careful, she has stupid high standards.* I rubbed my leg again. I mean, how high could her standards possibly be if she was still hanging out with me? Granted I wasn't like a nobody—especially on the Celestial Academy totem pole—but I wasn't like her other friends. I looked terrible in black. Pink and sparkly were more my style. Sarcasm and tattoos weren't my thing either. I was, like, Z's polar opposite, yet she still stuck around ... and I don't think it was just cause she was enrolled in the academy and technically my service project, either. No one made Zuri do anything she didn't want to. She stuck around, because she wanted to. That had to be the only explanation since no Fallen had ever voluntarily gone to this school. She wanted to be here ... But why?

"Hey, Z." I stepped to the side to let some classmates through the door. "When we're done, like, stopping Lilith from hurting Fallen, are you going to go home?"

She frowned. "For the term break, yeah. Why? Are you worried about what your dad will do without me around? Just tell him to fuck off and go do your own thing."

"No, I mean, are you going home for good?"

She shrugged. "At some point. Why?"

"I'll miss you when you're gone."

Zuri opened her mouth to say something, but didn't get the chance to get the words out. Uncle Uriel interrupted by yelling, "Anyone who doesn't have their ass in class in two seconds gets to spend after school detention with me! Move It People!" Detention of any kind was not on my to-do list. Especially private detention with Uncle Uriel. He had always creeped me out.

"We're here, Uncle Uriel!" I called as Zuri and I took our usual spots near the outer perimeter of the kids. There were no desks or furniture of any kind in Uncle Uriel's Self-Defense classroom. It was set up like a giant dojo. The padded walls were supposed to help us feel safe, but the scorch marks littering them told a different story. His lariat hung in a place of honor on the back corner wall near his Japanese style bamboo changing curtain. I nudged Z on the shoulder and pointed it out to her.

"Today we're learning hand to hand combat." Uncle Uriel said, stepping to the center of the room. He shrugged out of his kimono, revealing full commando gear. "You can't always rely on swords, guns, and angelic relics to save you. Sometimes, you need to save yourself with your wits and bare hands. Miryam," He swiveled to face me. "Care to demonstrate?"

"Um, not really," I said. "Can you pick someone else? I'll totally participate in the next class. Promise."

"You. Here. Now." He pointed at a spot on the dojo mat in front of him. "Show the class what you're made of. Show them why you should bear the name daughter of Michael."

I shuffled out to the center of the room. "Um, if you like know the answer to that, I'm totally all ears."

Uncle Uriel's eyes flashed red before they went back to being blue. When I was younger, I called the red look his 'evil eyes.' Nothing good ever happened if his eyes glowed red. It looked like I was about to test that theory ... yet again. *Please don't throw fireballs. Please don't throw fireballs. Please, oh please, oh please don't throw fireballs.*

I didn't realize I had said that last part out loud until Uncle Uriel smiled, happy at my growing panic. "Fireballs would be considered a weapon. No, I won't tip the hand today. It's not me you'll be fighting. It's ..." He scanned the classroom. "Where is Christopher? I'm surprised to see you without him."

"Chris is, uh ... on an extended medical leave," I lied. "He might not be back."

"Pity." Uncle Uriel gave a little pout that made his androgynous features look way more feminine than usual. "I love pitting couples against each other. Chaos is ... invigorating ... to a relationship. Instead, you'll face—" He spun around in a circle, finger extended, before stopping on, "Anthony. Welcome to the party. Show us what you got."

Ant flushed as red as his hair. "I don't fight girls, sir."

"That's because you *are* a girl," Zuri muttered before raising her voice. "I volunteer! Let me go up against Miry."

Uncle Uriel smiled, satisfied with the new

pairing. "Excellent. By all means, Miss bat-Lucifer. Step forward."

"What are you doing?" I whispered when Zuri was in front of me, her hands already balled into fists. "How am I supposed to distract him when the both of us are, like, totally out in the open?"

"Relax," Zuri said. "I'll throw a punch. You make sure that you go careening into the wall, knock the lariat down. I'll swoop over and snatch it up. Easy, right?"

"I, uh, guess so." I held up my hands to shield my face, raising my voice so the whole class could hear. "Not in the face! Not in the face!"

"I'll 'not in the face' you, princess!"

Zuri used just a touch of her archangel super strength to send me flying across the room. I made sure to make my body go limp, remembering another one of Uncle Uriel's lessons—you got hurt less if you went limp. Slamming into a wall with a rigid body and muscles was just asking for trouble.

I bounced off the padded wall right below the lariat. It and me both clattered to the floor. I kicked it behind Uncle Uriel's Japanese bamboo curtain before anyone could notice. "My face! You totally jacked up my face!" I even cried for good measure.

Zuri was beside me in an instant. "You okay?" She murmured. "I didn't shove you too hard, did I?"

"I'm cool." I pointed to where just a tiny corner of the lariat showed from under the bamboo curtain. "Your turn. I'll keep everyone distracted while you stash the lariat."

Z nodded. I stood and staggered back to the center of the classroom, still holding my 'perfectly-fine-but-they-don't-know-that' face. If there's one thing I'm totally good at, it's distracting people by talking a bunch. "Uncle Uriel, how could you let that happen? Forget detention, Dad will totally expel her! Look what she did. Go on and look. Ow, ow, ow. No, don't look. Okay, maybe look. No, don't ... Wait. No. I wanna go to the clinic. Ant! CeCe! Take me to the clinic!"

"Cecelia. Anthony. You heard the girl. Take her to Raphael," Uncle Uriel commanded.

CeCe and Ant stepped forward. They looked confused, but relieved to be getting out of class early. Especially self-defense class.

A plan quickly formed in my brain once the three of us were in the hallway, with Zuri still inside. A plan to lure Lilith to campus for a showdown. Angels were stronger here and, being a demon and all, on hallowed ground should make her weaker. We'd be at an advantage when we needed it the most. You don't face the mother of demons without a good solid plan beyond 'use the lariat.' We'd take what was most important to her, lure her to campus, and then stop her once and for all.

"I have something I need you to help me with," I said. "Don't tell anyone, okay?"

CeCe swiped a finger across her heart. "Promise." She wasn't usually part of the crew. Although she could be useful, especially when figuring out what frequency the school gates sang at to let the right people through and keep the wrong people out. If we could get it to think Lilith and Chris were the right kind of people, we'd have the fight on our home turf. I didn't want to hope too much, but maybe being back on good-guy ground would help Chris remember his saint side.

"Ant?" I tapped my foot on the floor. "What about you? Up for another little redemption mission?"

"Depends on what you want me to do," he pouted.

"Just something you've done before," I said. "Bring Chris here. Lilith is bound to follow. When she does, we'll be waiting."

13

ZURI

I watched Miry leave the room with Glasses and Damien's new girlfriend before turning back to the rest of the class. Everyone else took a step back from me and I dropped my hands.

"Guess I don't need the practice," I said with an exaggerated shrug.

"Now, now, you could have just thrown a lucky punch," Uriel said, stepping up to meet me.

I swallowed the lump in my throat. I'd witnessed Uriel in action. I knew what he was capable of and I didn't need him breaking any more of my bones. Despite that I wasn't going to back down. So, I squared my shoulders, met his gaze and said, "Only one way to find out."

Before he could react, I lunged using my momentum and his surprise to tackle him to the ground. I managed to pin his wrists above his head. I gave a triumphant cheer before he bucked and sent me flying over his head, straight into the same wall where Miry had landed. The impact sent shockwaves of pain down my spine, but I gritted my teeth and dragged myself back to my feet. Catching sight of the end of the lariat, I kicked it farther out of view. I still didn't know how I was going to get it out of the room without Uriel noticing.

"That was very good!" Uriel exclaimed with a clap of his hands. "Taking your opponent by surprise."

"I had a good teacher," I commented, taking a few shuffling steps to my left to put myself in front of the bamboo curtain. I'd set my bag not far from it. I just needed a little time and distraction to get it.

"I see he ensured that you knew all the proper fighting techniques. Weaponry and hand-to-hand combat. Yes, I suppose he would do that. An insurance policy I suppose … In a way," he began to ramble.

The other kids in the class started to inch collectively toward the door. I stayed where I was, watching him as his gaze went unfocused and his hands started moving at his sides like he was trying to pull a sword from its sheath.

"The next line of defense. Yes, that is smart. And thinking we wouldn't be the wiser. Oh, but won't he be surprised in the end."

I nudged the edge of the lariat with my toe until it peeked out the far side of the curtain. Uriel still seemed engrossed in whatever bizarre trip down memory lane had captured his attention. So, I knelt down and grabbed the lariat, stuffing it into my bag before following the rest of the students out of the room.

I found Miry and her friends down the hall, sequestered in an alcove. They looked up at my approach and Miry's shoulders dropped when she realized I wasn't some random student about to overhear her secret plan.

"Did you get it?" She asked.

I patted my bag. "I'm going to need some regular rope to make the switch."

Glasses eyed me and sighed. "Please tell me you aren't doing what I think you're doing?"

"What are you doing?" D's girlfriend nosed in.

"None of your business." I pointed to her and looked at Miry. "Why is she even involved?" Miry stepped forward and looped her arm through mine. "Because she's part of my big plan. I'll fill you in on the way." Glancing at the other two she said, "I'll text you when we need you."

"You realize you're crazy right?" I told her as we looted the storage closet near Raphael's office.

She had to know that manipulating the wards keeping demons out was dangerous as fuck and would attract unwanted attention—namely her father. He may have been absent for most of our little adventures. In spite of that if we went messing with his security system, I had no doubt he would be on our asses.

"But it can work! We're stronger here and she might get hurt or maybe weaker from being on hallowed ground."

"Or it could make no difference at all and she decides to kill everyone in sight!" I argued as my hand brushed against something coarse and coiled. I tugged it free to find an old length of rope most likely used to hang life vests or moor a boat. It would work for what we needed. "Besides, don't forget that Saint Boy could get in no problem and use his demon powers."

Miry's gaze went unfocused for a minute. "But we both saw him, he's not embracing his saint side anymore. And don't forget we will have the lariat, too."

If we can figure out how to use it. I coiled the length of rope around my forearm and ushered Miry out of the storage closet. We raced back to our dorm room and I set both the base for the forgery and the real thing side by side on Miry's bed. Being this close to the lariat without it's master made my skin crawl and my stomach churn.

"So, what do you do now?" Miry prodded.

"Give me some space," I replied.

She retreated to my side of the room, leaving me to do my thing. I didn't want to disappoint her. Yet, I'd never done something this big before and never with something as innately powerful as an angelic relic. I could hear Miry's voice in the back of my head cheering me on, saying "You're Zuri bat-Lucifer. You've got this." Then I damn well better not fail. I gripped the plain rope and concentrated. I placed my palm on top of the lariat, letting the feel of it against my skin take hold in my sensory memory. I willed the other rope to take on the same texture and weight, with the finely braided hairs of each strand turning from black to dark shades of gold.

Sweat prickled along my hairline as I let go of

the real deal and massaged my sore hand. I could see the tiny indentations of the braiding on my palm. The lariat hadn't liked what I'd done, but it could have been worse. I'd seen this thing on fire. I could deal with a little discomfort.

"Is it done?" Miry chirped from across the room.

I moved aside to let her see and she bounced off the bed. Bending over, she studied them, poking and prodding the handles and the ends. "This is the real one, right?" She pointed to the forgery.

"Guess I'm as good as I say I am," I said with a tired smile.

"Wow, you really are," She threw her arms around me in an impromptu hug.

"We need to get the fake back to the classroom before he realizes the real one's missing," I reminded her, wiggling free of her embrace. Her innocent hug made me feel too many conflicting emotions.

She scooped up the forgery and stuffed it in her backpack. "Come on. We can do it on our way to Angelic History."

I let her lead the way and she fell into step beside me, trying to loop her arm through mine again. I stopped walking and Miry passed me by a few paces before she realized I wasn't still beside her.

"Come on, we don't have a lot of time." Her lips puckered in that damn pout.

"Why do you do that?" The words escaped my mouth before I could stop them.

She cocked her head to one side. "Do what?"

"Grab my arm, try to hold my hand. Kiss me and pretend we're a couple in public."

"It's just pretend, like a joke you know?" She said, trying to wave it off.

"It's not funny, Miry. I get that you grew up sheltered, but you do things like this and I can't help feel like you're flirting with me. And that's damn confusing, because up until recently, you had a boyfriend."

"I didn't mean to offend you, Z. I swear. I just ... I don't know, I guess I'm just used to having someone around and you're way better than he was anyway."

"Miry, you're rebounding and I am nobody's rebound chick." In that moment, I realized why her touching and pretending bothered me so much. Maybe Damien and Delilah were right. Could I be feeling something for her, more than friendship? No way I was going to act on it, especially if she couldn't figure out what was real and what was fake.

"You're my best friend, Zuri. Okay, like really my only one and I didn't realize it made you mad."

"You need to think before you act, Miry. You can't just do whatever you want since everyone thinks you walk on water all because of your daddy. When you figure out what you want, let me know. Until then, keep your hands to yourself."

I stormed off down the hall, leaving her to return the lariat on her own. I needed some space from her to clear my head. I wasn't going to be any use facing off against that demonic bitch if all I could think about was Miry.

14

MIRYAM

Uncle Uriel was alone when I snuck back into class to drop off the fake lariat before he knew the real one was missing. He sat all cross-legged Zen Yogi Master on the floor in the center of the classroom, eyes closed, breathing deep and even. With how worked up he got during every class, it's no wonder he needed some time to unwind afterwards. If I was super quiet, he wouldn't even know I was here.

I tip-toed across the padded floor over to the changing curtain. I leaned over and pretended to need to adjust the buckle on my Mary Jane shoe. It would give me a good reason to be close to the floor and drop the replacement lariat where I had knocked the original off the wall. Done! Now time to ... well, I don't know what I planned to do next. I guess I could organize the next phase of our Take Down Lilith To Stop Attacks On Fallen plan, but that seemed like a lot of work for just me alone. Zuri could help ... if she was still speaking to me. I sighed. Having real friends and not hanger-ons was hard.

"Does your father know you are trying to steal my lariat?" Uncle Uriel asked.

I jumped, placing my hand over my pounding heart, and swirled to face him all in one fluid motion. He was still sitting, eyes closed, in the center of the room. That was a pretty cool trick that he knew what I was doing without even opening his eyes. "Uncle Uriel! I'm not trying to steal anything. After I got out of the clinic, I totally remembered the lariat fell so I wanted to be nice and check on it for you. You know, like, pick it up and dust it off and all that. I figured it was too important of an artifact to leave laying on the floor, you know?" I spread my arms wide, hoping I looked innocent. If I didn't look innocent, maybe my babbling would make him zone out and forget I was super suspicious in the first place. "So, here I am ready to help!" I picked up the fake lariat, swiped my hands across it a couple times to make sure Zuri's forgery still held, and hung it up on the wall where the real one usually went. "Ta da! Good as new. No harm, no foul, right?"

Uncle Uriel frowned. "You are truly a perplexing child."

"Thanks." I grinned, determined to take that as a compliment. 'Perplexing' from Uncle Uriel was like anyone else in the known world saying 'interesting.' He couldn't figure me out. If he spent a long time deciphering my babble, that meant less time calling me out on shady behavior.

He stood and walked slowly toward me, kimono robe billowing behind him. I held my breath, waiting for his eyes to flash red and a fireball to appear in his hand, but nothing happened. His eyes stayed their usual bright sky blue. In the moment, he reminded me of Chris—beautiful and bright on the surface, but with a darkness underneath. How long had I ignored the darkness rising in Chris, because I was blinded by the surface? Would he have confided in me if I had guessed what caused his pain? Would Uncle Uriel if I guessed what caused his?

"Tell me about Lucifer," I requested, not intending to get that personal until the words fell out of my mouth. Ever since Zuri found that super secret stash of love letters in her Dad's archives called 'Burning Starlight,' I couldn't shake the idea that maybe some of Uncle Uriel's issue stemmed from loving someone who didn't love him back. Unrequited love could really screw with a person's—or angel's—head.

"What about him?" Uncle Uriel gave a humorless half-laugh, half-snort of derision. "He was a rebel angel. His side fought and lost. End of story."

"That's what the winning side and Bible wants everyone to believe," I said. "Tell me the real story."

"About the War In Heaven?" Uncle Uriel scratched the back of his head absently, lost in the past. "Lucifer was fiery. Fierce. A born leader. Much like that daughter of his you're so fond of. He fought for what he believed in. There's nothing more ... inspiring ... in a leader than belief. He had real passion. Seeing that, I almost joined up myself."

"Why didn't you?"

Uncle Uriel shrugged. "My skill set was needed elsewhere. Your father can be pretty persuasive too, you know. How else do you think he can convince so many virgins to sleep with him?"

"Ew ... and gross." I shuddered at the thought. "That's like totally TMI."

Uncle Uriel shrugged again. "I just call it like I see it." He frowned again, but his eyes didn't glaze over for a trip down memory lane this time. He stayed very much in the present. "Can I give you one piece of advice, Miryam? Watch your back. Your father is not as altruistic as he seems."

Dad? Altruistic? Like he needed to warn me about that. I almost laughed in Uncle Uriel's face. Instead, I smiled my biggest, brightest, perkiest smile and said, "Oh, totally, Uncle U. Thanks a bunch. I better go catch up with Zuri before Archangel Studies class. Bye-ee!"

I ran out the door of his classroom before he could stop me. I wasn't lying when I had said I needed to find Zuri. Uncle Uriel's rambling about Lucifer made me realize something. I needed to find Zuri and, when I did, I needed to apologize.

15

ZURI

I didn't really want to go to class, not with how distracted my brain was thanks to Miry's drama. Although, I knew I couldn't give Michael any excuse to kick me out. I found myself in the classroom for Archangel Studies ten minutes early. I didn't expect anyone else to be there, but Raphael sat at his desk staring at something I couldn't see.

I rapped my knuckles against the doorframe, hoping it would announce my presence. "I can come back."

He looked up in surprise, but gestured for me to sit down. "I don't mind the company. How is your wrist?"

I flexed it, the pain now gone, even if the

memory still lingered. "It's fine." I settled into a chair near his desk, slinging my bag across the back. "I found Miry, too."

"I didn't doubt that you would be successful. I trust since you did not immediately rush her to my care that she is unharmed?"

"She got hurt, but she did it to herself to get away. Things are just … confusing."

He set aside his papers and looked me in the eye. "I'm happy to listen if you would like."

It wasn't that I didn't trust him. He'd proven himself to be my ally time and time again. Except, he didn't really care about a teenage girl's love life, did he? "It's fine," I mumbled.

Raphael leaned forward and I reflexively leaned back. "You have never shied away from the brutal truth before, Ms. bat-Lucifer."

"She just does all these things that tell my brain she likes me and wants to be with me. Only she's straight and honestly kind of clueless. So now I don't know what she wants and I told her to just lay off until she figures her shit out." It all came out in one long breath.

"And what do you want?"

"Someone who loves me like I think she could." The words sounded foreign to my ears. Like someone else had said them. Until that very moment, I hadn't realized that was what I wanted or how I felt. I hadn't come here intending to fall for the daughter of my father's greatest enemy.

"And am I to guess she doesn't know this?"

"Considering *I* didn't know it til it just came out of my mouth, yeah." I laid my head on my forearms and groaned. "I don't have time for this shit. People are dying."

"The Fallen continue to be attacked. But you are just one person and you are so very young. This isn't your burden, Zuri."

"Yes, it is. No one else gives a damn or is doing anything about it. And that demon bitch and her spawn came after my friend. I'm not going to sit by and let her leech off my people, because she got caught doing it to yours."

Raphael nodded slowly, extended his hand like he wanted to touch me or something, but then thought better of it. "I simply meant that it is a tremendous amount of responsibility to place on your shoulders alone. Or even yours and Miryam's."

His mouth hung open like he wanted to say something more, but he stayed silent. I didn't have time to ask what else was on his mind, because the door opened and Miry appeared, slightly out of breath. "Oh, I'm early?"

Raphael stood and mumbled something about checking medical supplies before rushing out of the room. *Way to be supportive.* Miry stopped short of sitting down beside me. Her hands twisted into the hem of her skirt and she wouldn't meet my gaze.

"I put the … you know what back," she finally offered.

"Good," I replied.

She raced forward sliding into the seat beside me. "I'm really sorry, Z. I swear I didn't mean to make you all confused. I guess I've never really had a best friend before and I don't think … no, I don't want you to hate me."

"I don't hate you, Miry. I just … need for you to figure out your priorities."

"I am. I swear." She leaned back and stared at the ceiling. "Listening to Uncle Uriel talk about the war, it's not all that unusual for an Archangel and a Fallen to have feelings for each other."

I didn't want to talk about feelings anymore. I wasn't ready to come clean with Miry about how I felt, especially if she still didn't know what was going on in her own head. "Can we please talk about something else?"

"So, I was thinking we need to set the lure for

Lilith to come here. We could go out and find them tonight. Maybe even use the lariat on them."

"I still think it's a crazy ass idea bringing them here. Have you even told your dad what you're planning?"

"Well … no."

"Miry! He doesn't differentiate between Fallen and demons. If the literal mother of demons shows up on his sacred space or whatever unannounced and gets through the wards, he's going to take that as a personal attack. Do you know the first person he's going to lash out at?"

"Lilith?" She hiccupped.

"My dad. We don't need them coming to blows again." I brushed loose strands of hair from my face. "Okay, look we can go out and try to take them out with the lariat, but we aren't bringing them back here."

She pouted for all of thirty seconds before she nodded. "Okay. You're the boss."

Something in her tone made my skin crawl. Like she was gravitating to whatever I said, because she wanted me to protect her or tell her what to do.

NIGHT FELL AGAIN and I stood outside the gates, the lariat stuffed into a black crossbody bag. I didn't know why Miry insisted I be the one to carry the damn thing around. It still made my skin crawl and I did not pull off the crossbody look well—not my style at all.

"Here, you carry it," I said, whipping the strap over my head and shoving it at her.

"But I don't even know how to use it," she whined.

"Like I do?"

She huffed, but slung the bag over her shoulder as we snuck off school grounds. In the back of my mind, I wondered if Michael didn't enforce the curfew, because he secretly hoped someone would happen upon Miry and take her out for him. I may not know exactly how to tell her what I was feeling, but I wasn't going to let anyone hurt her either.

We checked Castoffs first, but it was locked up tight. I felt bad that the owner had to shut the place down, because everyone was too scared to go there anymore. It had been a fun place. I didn't want to go back to the bar. I didn't want to see Delilah, to catch that knowing look in her eye. Still, if that was the last place someone had been attacked, it was our best bet.

"I'm sorry you have to keep seeing your ex," Miry offered as we turned onto the street.

"It's fine. Not like we were super serious or anything."

"Yeah, but you broke her heart."

"She wasn't the right person for me."

"Why not?"

"Because she just wasn't." I'd liked Delilah. In spite of that the whole time we'd been together, I couldn't help wondering if she was only with me, because she wanted a power grab at my dad's throne.

"I know you're going to find the right person," Miry said, bumping my shoulder with her arm.

"Do you children never give up?" Lilith's voice called from behind us.

I looked around, but Saint Boy was nowhere to be seen. That didn't mean he wasn't lurking in the shadows, waiting to pounce and hurt Miry again. "We're stubborn like that. Maybe you should be the one who gives up, because you have to know at this point we're going to stop you."

She made a show of looking around. "And what is it that I have done to offend you, child of Lucifer?"

"You're murdering my people, you psycho bitch."

She smiled at me with those razor sharp pointed teeth. I didn't dare look beside me to see if Miry was doing anything useful. "Use the damn thing," I stage-whispered out of the corner of my mouth.

"You seem to be rather confused. Why would I kill those your father protects? You have become something of an irritant, but I still have no quarrel with him."

"Then why are you attacking them?" I shouted.

Beside me, I caught just enough movement out of the corner of my eye to see Miry fumbling with the clasps on the bag. *Good. Use the relic and shut this lunatic up.*

"What is it mortals are so fond of saying? Assuming makes an ass out of you and me? Well, certainly out of you."

"Stop being so mean to her!" Miry's voice boomed and the energy in the air crackled with electricity. She held the lariat at her side, the handle gripped tight in her fingers. Probably to keep them from trembling.

"My aren't you brave, daughter of Michael. Or very foolish," Lilith taunted.

"I am brave," Miry said, taking a step back to give herself a better supported stance. She shook the lariat out to its full length and raised her arm. "I will not let you hurt innocent people!"

The lariat lashed out, but Lilith vanished in a puff of smoke. I heard footsteps. Miry and I turned in unison to see Delilah approaching.

"What is it with all the damn yelling?"

We couldn't answer. Not before the lariat changed directions of its own accord, wrapping around Delilah's throat and pulling her to the ground.

"Let go!" I shouted at Miry while I raced to Delilah's side.

She clawed at the relic, her fingers coming away burned and blistered. I'd never seen her hurt by fire before.

"I'm trying. I don't know how to stop it," Miry replied, her eyes welling with unshed tears.

I yanked the handle of the relic from her hand, all the while hoping that I could get the thing off Delilah before it suffocated her or gave her burns that we couldn't heal. As if it had sensed my desire, the lariat loosened, going limp in my hand. I threw it aside, cradling Delilah's head in my lap.

"You're going to be okay," I whispered, stroking her hair. To Miry I said, "Get help. Now!"

MIRYAM

"I don't need to get help." I sunk down onto my knees next to Zuri and her ex-girlfriend. "I am help." I closed my eyes and hovered my hands over the demon bartender's neck, where the worst of the burns were. I focused on sending healing energy from me to her. She was innocent, just in the wrong place at the wrong time. She didn't deserve pain and suffering, because of my mistake.

"Is it working?" I cracked an eye open to peek. Her neck and hands were bright red—like a sunburn—versus the bubbly, blistery second and third degree burns the lariat had inflicted, but it wasn't perfect. It was better, sure, but I could do more to help. I caused this accidentally, and I would fix it. I held out one hand to Zuri. "I need a signal boost. Help me out, okay?"

Zuri grudgingly put her right hand in my left. Focusing together, the healing light flared to a bright, almost blinding white. When I opened my eyes again, Delilah looked about as normal as a demon bartender could look, which was pretty normal considering most demons don't have fangs, claws, hoofs, or horns. They just looked like people. That's why it was hard to tell who you could trust or not. Everyone looked so normal.

"Did we do it?" I asked hopefully. Delilah sat up and rubbed her formerly burned neck and hands. "Damn. Maybe there's some perks to hanging out with the goodie-goodies after all, Z."

Zuri dropped my hand as if she was the one that had been burned and stood up, putting distance between us. I felt tired and amped up all at once. Healing took a lot out of me, but the kick of 'I did it' success always gave me an adrenaline boost. It was awesome to help, but exhausting too.

I pushed myself to my feet. I swayed slightly, almost tipping over. Zuri's hand instinctively shot out to keep me on my feet. "Thanks," I murmured. "I appreciate the help."

"And I appreciate not being turned into a crisp by that freakish rope you girls are playing with," Delilah said. "Thanks. I owe you one. But don't call the favor in too soon, k?" She raised her hands and disappeared in a cloud of dark smoke.

I watched Zuri, not able to read her expression. She looked defeated, but I couldn't tell for sure. "I ... I didn't know the lariat would go after your ex. Honest." I swiped a finger across my heart to show how serious I was. "I thought it would just go after the intended target. Not go off and go all rogue or whatever. My bad."

"The relic's whole purpose is to smite the wicked," Zuri snapped, voice cold, but weirdly expressionless at the same time. "What did you think would happen once Lilith disappeared? It went after the closest wicked being."

"Um ... wouldn't that be, like, you?"

Zuri's cheeks paled slightly. "I don't know what you mean."

"Sure you do." I bounced on my heels, not able to hide the grin that spread across my face. "If you were as wicked as you like people to think you are, Uncle Uriel's lariat would have gone after you. It didn't though. That means there's some good in you. It also means my service project is totally working." I held up a hand for a high five, but Zuri ignored it.

"Let's get back to campus before someone realizes we're gone."

My phone beeped. I pulled it out of my bra and checked the screen. *Dad*. "Uh oh. Too late. Dad wants to see us in his office, like, right now. This is it. He's totally going to expel us both."

DAD WAS WAITING for us in his office once we got back to school. He was wearing his red toga and gold armor breastplate, looking every inch a warring Angel and a super disappointed Dad on top of that.

"How many times have I told you, Miryam, that I make rules for a reason? Every rule you so blatantly flaunt is in place to keep you safe. Going off campus with a Fallen while her kind are being persecuted and attacked? What were you thinking? Do you have a death wish?"

"Um … not really." I scooted the black crossbody bag behind me with a toe. The lariat was safe inside and, as long as Dad didn't go digging into my things, it would stay there. "We were totally just going for a walk. There was supposed to be a meteor shower that Uncle Gabriel wanted us to catch for Angelic History. Turns out, it was too cloudy to catch much of anything. Though we had to, like, stay out for a bit to make sure, you know? We didn't want to get a bad grade on the assignment."

Dad frowned and paced back and forth behind his massive desk. "And Gabriel will collaborate with this story?"

I nodded. "Oh, absolutely."

Dad's frown deepened. "Gabriel can't remember to tie his shoes most days. He won't remember if he told you to look at a non-existent meteor shower or not."

"That doesn't mean he didn't give us the assignment," Zuri picked up the story. "It just means he won't remember."

"A likely story," Dad said. "When you evoke Gabriel's name for any transgression, it usually means you're lying."

I glanced over at Zuri, still unable to read her practiced, blank expression. I bet she totally had tons of experience lying to grown-ups. I didn't though. "Um, not always."

Dad sat down and drummed his fingers on his desk. He waited, no doubt trying to make us more uncomfortable with each passing second. I gulped down the lump forming in my throat. His scare tactic totally worked—at least on me.

"One week of detention for the both of you," Dad decided. "If I catch you breaking more rules, I'll make it two. Or I might just smite your so-called friend, Miryam, and be done with it."

"You can't smite people on hallowed ground." Zuri balled her fists at her sides, but didn't throw a punch at Dad which, I think, totally took a lot of self-control. "It's not allowed."

Dad arched one golden eyebrow at Zuri. "Have you forgotten I cast your father and his ilk out of Heaven, the most hallowed of hallowed ground? If I can do that, I can cast you out of my school without breaking a sweat. Don't test me, little girl. You might just get burned."

Burned? Like what was happening to the Fallen? Like what the lariat did to Delilah? How much did Dad know about the attacks? Had he been looking away this whole time?

"So, uh, who is running detention this week?" I asked as I scooted toward the office door, quietly motioning for Zuri to follow me. If we were super lucky, it would be Uncle Raphael. All he'd make us do is file medical reports and let us go early every day. We could handle that.

"Uriel." Dad's smile grew when my eyes

bugged out in distress. "Enjoy your extra time together. Oh and good luck surviving the week."

"What an asshole," Zuri growled once we were back in the safety of the empty hallway. "We should have taken out the lariat and gone after him. If anyone is wicked, it's your dad."

"He just likes to get a rise out of me." I pointed a finger at my face. "Big disappointment, remember? Story of my life." We were silent, neither of us seeming to know what to say. "Hey, Z?" I finally began. "I know I upset you earlier and I mean it when I say I'm sorry."

She waved my apology away. "Don't worry about it."

I shook my head. "No. No, I want to say this. I know that I can be annoying and clingy and totally oblivious to what's right in front of my face. The longer I'm away from Chris, the more I realize he hasn't been living up to his Saint potential in a really long time. He's familiar and I love him, but that doesn't mean he's good for me, you know? I can see that now. That's, like, the first thing you ever saw. You knew right away and it took me, like, forever to see it as clearly as you do." I shrugged. "I'm sorry I didn't listen to you sooner. The thing is, my obliviousness, the wanting to see and believe the best in everyone, is a defense mechanism. I *need* to believe the best or else I'm going to sink down into the darkest places in my mind." I shook my head again. "I've been there before, back in Kansas. It's no fun. Can you forgive me for being such a dumbbell?"

Zuri sighed before pulling me into a hug. "You're not a dumbbell. You're strong, capable, and a lot smarter than you give yourself credit for. Yeah, you've had a run of shitty luck, but that's gonna change. I'll help you."

"You will?" I stepped back, but not out of her arms.

Zuri nodded. "Just try to stop me."

I grinned. "Awesome! You're amazing!" In my excitement, I jumped up and kissed her, half on the mouth-half on the cheek. Zuri let go of me completely, hand flying up to cover her mouth.

"Why'd you do that?"

"You told me to keep my hands to myself," I reminded her. "You didn't say anything about my lips."

17

ZURI

I stared at Miry in disbelief. Of all the things she could have done in that moment, kissing me was nowhere near the top of the list. It wasn't even *on* the list. Yet, she'd done it and then stood there, smiling at me like it was the most casual thing in the world. Her words rang in my ears. "You didn't say anything about my lips."

"Are you kidding me right now?" I snapped and pushed past her down the hall. The stupid classes could suck it. There was no way I was going to focus on learning a skewed version of history from some Archangels who thought they knew it all.

"Zuri, wait!" She called after me, her shoes

click-clacking against the floor as she raced to follow me.

"I really am sorry for before."

"Your actions say differently," I growled.

"No, they don't." She tried to reach for my hand, but I pulled away. I hated this. My brain was screaming at me to cut and run, but my heart was telling me to let her in. Tell her how I felt. However, I couldn't do that. It would ruin our weird little friendship. Besides, she didn't know what she was saying or doing. Miry was clueless. *Wasn't she?*

"I need space, Miry. So, just back off."

I left her standing in the hallway and I retreated, first to our shared dorm room and then, thinking better of it, I wandered outside to the pool. I could envision Uriel tossing Miry in the deep end like it was all fun and games as Michael watched. As he hoped another of his children died. I pulled out my phone and called the one person I knew that I could talk to.

"Hey Z," Damien answered on the second ring.

"I hate you," I said.

"What happened?" He lightly prompted.

"You ... you were right," I ground out. "Maybe she and I aren't so bad together."

"I told you." I could hear the triumphant smile in his tone.

"She kissed me," I shared. "Full on, kiss on the lips."

"What'd you do?" It could have come off as perverted or seeking too much information, but Damien and I understood each other. We just knew when the other needed to vent.

"I pushed her away. What do you think I did?"

"So, you don't like her?" His voice skittered up in pitch at the end of the sentence.

"I don't know. I think I do, but she's been throwing mixed signals. I can't sort it out. And even if she's into me, what if she's only into me, because she thinks I can save her or protect her?"

"So, you find out," he sighed.

"I don't want to be that kind of person, D. I want someone who takes care of themselves."

"From what I've seen, your girl can handle herself when she needs to. But, there's nothing wrong with leaning on each other, too. That's what makes a solid relationship," he offered.

"I've never … been needed like that before. And it scares me," I admitted. "What if I mess it up?"

"You're the next in line to rule an entire realm of existence, Zuri. You're not going to mess it up.

Now, stop doubting yourself. If you want the girl, go grab her by that perky little ass and show her what you want."

I laughed as his words conjured up a visual of Miry standing in our dorm room in her underwear, oblivious as anything. I could see my hand wrapping around her waist, sliding down to cup her ass as I kissed her back

"Z, you still with me?" Damien's voice broke the fantasy.

"Yeah." My voice was huskier than it had been a moment ago.

"Stop visualizing and make that shit a reality," he told me.

"Okay, I will." I took several deep breaths. "We almost stopped Lilith, but she got away. She's back to her old head games."

"I know you're pissed, because I got hurt. But you don't have to throw yourself in the line of fire."

"Yes, I do. That bitch came after my best friend. She's targeting my people and, like you said, it's going to be my job to protect them all one day. What use am I as a leader if I can't show them that I've got their backs?"

There was a long pause on the other end of the line. "I remembered something."

By the way the words came out slow and measured, I knew whatever he'd remembered wasn't pleasant. I hated that my best friend had to be plagued by memories of nearly dying. He might be okay with the idea of dying some day in the very distant future going off into the afterlife or wherever with his dad to see him off, but I wasn't. Not yet. "Tell me."

"I still don't remember the face except whatever it was had creepy glowing red eyes."

"Sounds like a demon to me," I muttered.

"But demons can burn just by touching you if they really want. Whatever this was didn't touch me. Not with their hands anyway."

Dread settled in my stomach like a stone. I'd been so wrapped up in healing Delilah and feeling guilty about her getting caught in the crossfire, I hadn't stopped to notice that her burns looked a lot like Damien's injuries.

"I think it was a—"

"A rope," I interrupted.

"How'd you know?"

"Lucky guess. D, thanks for all of this. I need to go." I ended the call and raced back inside, hoping that Miry would have been in a mood and decided to skip class, too. I found her sitting on her bed, staring aimlessly at her feet.

"Miry," I said, drawing her attention.

She stood, but didn't approach me. "I'll leave."

Time to put up or shut up. I closed the distance between us, pressed my fingers into the small of her back, and kissed her. I felt her body respond to my touch, pressing against me and craving more closeness. I felt my own body playing off of her energy, longing to take it beyond just a kiss. There wasn't time though.

I pulled back from the kiss to find her dazed. "I don't think Lilith is working alone. I think she's had help."

Lilith's name snapped Miry from her daze. "From who?"

"Uriel."

18

MIRYAM

"Uriel?" I blinked as if the name didn't register with me. "You mean Uncle Uriel, Dad's best general, Celestial Academy's Self-Defense teacher, fireball throwing PTSD head case, Archangel with a glowing fiery rope that burns the wicked ... uh yeah, okay, I see where you're going with that one. Uncle Uriel does sound super suspicious."

I bounced on my heels, trying to think of anything and everything but the feel of Zuri's lips on mine and her body pressed close. I pushed those thoughts back to the recesses of my mind. The place that I always shoved thoughts and feelings I didn't want to deal with. Sometimes it was safer to just ignore scary things until they went away. I'd unpack all that later ... maybe. Right now, Zuri and I had a potential Fallen murder spree cover up to bust.

"But if Uncle Uriel is working with Lilith, why hasn't the lariat burned her, like, ever?" I asked. "You saw what it did to your ex-girlfriend. It smites the wicked. It's not going to discriminate based on if you're a demon or Fallen. If Uncle Uriel uses it anywhere near Lilith, it will go after her, right?"

"Who says it hasn't?" Zuri pointed out. "We don't really know. All we know is someone is attacking Fallen, more than likely for their angelic blood, and Damien remembers glowing red eyes. It adds up, Miry. I'm sorry. I know you were raised to treat him like family, but he's dangerous. How many more people is he going to hurt before someone stops him?"

I chewed on my bottom lip. "When you say 'someone' you mean us, right?" Zuri gave me a 'what do you think?' look. I raised my hands, palms out in front of me. "I'm cool with it. I was just asking! And, if you ask me, most demons are way more wicked than Fallen so why doesn't Uncle Uriel just take them out instead of CeCe's boyfriend and whoever else was targeted? It would make more sense, right?"

Zuri pinched the bridge of her nose between her thumb and index finger. "You're talking too much."

"I'm thinking out loud," I protested. "There's a difference."

"Well, can you think inside your head? The chatter is distracting."

"Sure." I smiled a tight-lipped smile and didn't say anything, because I told Z I wouldn't. I did hum and bounce, though. It helped me think too. Maybe even better than thinking out loud.

"Can you not do that either?" Zuri asked, voice strained. "I can't handle all the bouncing and jiggling. Not after what just happened between us."

"What just happened between us?" I rewound my mind, trying to figure out what she meant. *Got it!* "Oh, right. Right after you kissed me. What's the big deal with me bouncing after something like that?"

Zuri sat down on her bed—hard. Like, she totally just dropped. The mattress springs creaked in protest. "Have you looked in a mirror lately? Bouncing with a body like that should be illegal."

I smoothed my hands down my school uniform from the tips of my shirt collar all the way to the edge of my skirt. "Do you really think so? I have, like, a superpower?"

"Just don't let it go to your head." Z cracked a shaky smile. "With great power comes great responsibility and all that."

I tilted my head to the side, my hair falling over one shoulder. "Do you really think Uncle Uriel could be teaming up with Lilith to take down Fallen? Doesn't he have, like, a total man-crush on your dad? Why would he hurt your dad's people if he's got feelings for him?"

"Because jealous people do crazy shit," she said. "Don't you remember some of the manipulative antics Saint Boy pulled when he had thought your hero worship transferred from him to me? Same thing with Uriel, but more extreme."

"Chris isn't—I mean wasn't—used to sharing my time and attention." I touched the thin scars on my wrists from where I'd willingly opened a vein to give him the Angel Blood that he needed to survive. The sustenance he needed to be normal. "It's not the same thing as killing Fallen."

Zuri pushed herself off the bed and stalked toward the door. "I can't believe you're still defending him. What part of 'lied to you for years' don't you get, Miry?"

"It was only a year!" I hurried out the door after her. "And he said he was sorry!"

"Oh, that makes it all better, right? Give me a fucking break, M. Open your eyes and see the truth for once. It's right in front of you. All you have to do is look."

I ignored that. I'm good at ignoring things I don't want to deal with. To be honest, that should be my superpower, not bouncing. "You swear a lot when you're angry." I scurried to keep up with her long strides. "And where are you going?"

Zuri balled her hands into fists. "I'm going to confront that asshat Uriel. I don't care how screwed up the War In Heaven made his mind, no one tries to murder my best friend."

"I have a better suggestion," I squeaked, not sure if I felt scared or a little turned on by her anger management issues.

Zuri stopped and pivoted to face me. "Talk. Quick."

"We go to Dad's office. No, no, hear me out—" I added when she opened her mouth to interrupt me. "Dad has this thing I call a playbook, but I think it's more like a tracking journal or one of those battle plan thingies that generals have for their troops. He tracks all of the Archangels' movements. I don't know how, but it's some sort of magical angelic power thing." I took a deep breath. "Anyway, we can use it to check where Uncle Uriel was the day Damien got hurt. Then we'll know for sure he was helping Lilith and won't go up against an Archangel without any proof, you know?"

Zuri took a deep breath, her fingers slowly uncurling from the fist. "That actually makes a lot of sense. Lead the way."

"Okay, so we have an hour before Dad gets back from dinner," I said pushing his unlocked office door open. "Lucky for us he's totally predictable with his food schedule."

Zuri looked around at the high ceilings, dark wood paneling, and windows everywhere. The more light, the more Dad could shine, which was kind of funny since Lucifer actually meant Light Bringer, not Michael.

"Let's just find this playbook thing and get out of here," she said. "Whenever I step foot in your dad's office—even when he's not here—I feel like he's judging me."

"That's because he probably is." I opened and closed some of the drawers on Dad's desk, pulling out gold embossed notebooks that tracked the whereabouts of Uncle Raphael and Uncle Gabriel. Uncle Raphael only went two places—Heaven and School. Uncle Gabriel's movements looked like a drunk carrier pigeon, zig-zagging all over the globe, no doubt announcing angel births. No wonder he didn't show up to class half the time. Dad kept him busy. There was a book for someone called Samael—whoever that was—and one for me. No surprise there either. Finally, my hands hit on the right book.

"Got it!" I called to Zuri. "Let's see what Uncle Uriel was up to when Damien got hurt." I flipped to two weeks back in the playbook, but only found marks for Lucifer. "Huh. That's new. Maybe I grabbed the wrong book after all." I fanned through the pages, only finding reference after reference to Lucifer's movements. Nothing about Uncle Uriel. That Samael guy showed up a couple of times in Hell, though. Was he Fallen? Why was Dad tracking a Fallen?

"What's wrong?" Zuri asked. "You went quiet and that's never good ... not to mention weird." She held out her hand. "Let me see the playbook."

I handed it over. "Your dad's, like, all over the

place in this one. Um, maybe it's an old one from the War In Heaven or something?"

Zuri turned a couple pages. "No. No, this is recent." She pointed at a date in the upper left hand corner. "He's tracking my dad. But why?"

19

ZURI

I wanted to be surprised that Michael was keeping tabs on Dad, but I'd be lying to myself. Michael had shown himself to be vindictive and controlling. Always wanting everything to go his way, no matter the cost. I flipped through other pages, spotting Uriel's name occasionally, but nothing stood out. Maybe I'd been wrong? As I reached the end of the log, I saw the same name repeated over and over—Samael.

"Fuck."

"I know you were hoping to find out if Uncle Uriel was teaming up with Lilith, but I just can't see it. And it's creepy that my dad is like totally stalking your dad ..." Miry rambled.

"No, he's been tracking the movements of Samael."

"Oh." Miry picked up another journal and passed it to me. "I don't know who he is, but he's got his own book."

I flipped the second book open to find meeting notes in what I assumed was Michael's tiny, cramped writing. Discussions about Dad's whereabouts and what he'd been doing for the denizens of Hell. "Samael is my dad's second-in-command from back during the War. He's been by his side ever since. This doesn't make sense that he would be talking to your dad."

"Maybe he's trying to make sure my dad doesn't go all crazy on yours?" Miry offered, but even the hopeful lilt to her voice was betrayed by the fact her face looked like she was on her way to attend her own funeral.

"Not likely. With everything we know of your father, do you honestly believe he would listen to a Fallen angel so close to my father? If they're meeting, there has to be more to it."

"Maybe, but one problem at a time, okay? We have to stop Fallen from being attacked first."

"But if my dad's in danger, I have to warn him." I pulled out my phone and started writing him a text.

Miry put her hand over mine, her fingers flinching a little on contact. "We don't want to worry him if there's nothing to worry about."

"Miry, your dad is tracking his movements and could very well be using someone my dad trusts to spy on him. I'd say he needs to know."

She let my hand go and I finished typing. 'Dad, watch your back. Samael has been meeting with Michael.'

I could have been more cryptic in case someone else got ahold of his phone, but in the moment I didn't care. He needed to know exactly what he was up against. I didn't expect a response right away, but when he still hadn't responded after two minutes, I hit the speed dial. The call went straight to voicemail, setting the tiny hairs on the backs of my arms on end. *Something was wrong.* "Dad, call me back. I need to know you're okay."

I hung up and looked at Miry as she put the books back in the drawer and ushered me out of the room. I had one more phone call I could make, but she pulled me into a fierce hug before I had the chance. "We're going to make sure your dad is okay. I promise."

"Thanks," I muttered and tried not to shrug out of her embrace too quickly. I wasn't sure what we were becoming, but I needed to be open to it. She wanted to care about me. She understood what it meant to be the daughter of an Archangel and the type of responsibility that entailed, even if she was set to take over this place like I was supposed to take over Hell.

After a long while she stepped back, not meeting my gaze. "Sorry about all the touching."

"I need to check in with Damien. And then we are going to confront Uriel. I don't care what you say, the way his lariat hurt Delilah, it was the same wounds as on him."

"Okay. But, wouldn't it be easier if we got rid of the Lilith problem first?" She suggested, starting to bounce on the balls of her feet.

"Please tell me this isn't just some messed up excuse to see your ex again," I sighed.

"It's not. I swear. If we defeat Lilith, maybe that saves him. Or maybe he goes down with her. But either way it means one less threat, right?"

I rubbed at the base of my skull, a headache coming on that had everything to do with the damn situation we were in. "Fine. I still don't know how you think we're going to get a demon onto the grounds."

She smiled big. "CeCe and Ant are working on

that for me. She can convince the gates to let them in."

"And Glasses?" I prompted.

"He's going to reach out to Chris. But I think I may have a better way of getting him to show up."

"We aren't using you as bait," I snapped.

"Z, it's the only way. We both know, if I put myself out there, he'll show up. Lilith has to come, too because she is like totally obsessed with having a kid, right? And if I was her, it would be like epic to stick it to Michael on his own school grounds."

"Sure, I guess," I said, turning my attention to my phone. Dad still hadn't called back. So, I hit the number 2 and waited for D to pick up.

"Hey, Z." He sounded tired.

"You okay?"

"Yeah. Just a little worn out. What's up?"

"Have you seen my dad?"

"Today? I don't think so. But, I'm sure he's around. He's been kind of busy trying to keep people from freaking out over the attacks. He's probably just paying visits to the families of the others who weren't as lucky as me."

"I need you to do me a favor. I need you to find him and when you do, tell him to call me. It's important. And, don't ask Samael for help."

After a pause, he said, "So, don't ask the one guy who is likely to know his exact location at all times where to find him? That makes so much sense. Oh wait, no it doesn't. That's dumbass logic."

"Trust me on this one, D. Please."

"All right. I'll see if I can find him. You aren't actually going through with this whole Lilith thing are you?'

My heart skipped a beat. "What do you know?"

"Only that CeCe is supposed to mess with some angelic gates to let that bitch in."

Ugh, that girl had a big mouth. "We are. But you need to stay far away from it. You got hurt once. I'm not putting you in danger again. Besides, if I'm gonna be ruling Hell one day, I'm gonna need my own right-hand man."

"Sure it's not a right-hand girl you need?" I could hear the innuendo in his tone.

'Fuck off," I said and ended the call.

"I didn't think CeCe would blab," Miry piped up immediately. Either she had better hearing than I gave her credit for or D had been talking louder than I thought.

"He's not going to show up," I said. "He's too smart to put himself in the line of fire like that.

Plus, I put him on dad duty so he's out of her crosshairs this time. Now, how exactly are you going to lure Mama Demon and her spawn here?"

Miry wouldn't meet my gaze for a long minute and then, "Chris and I can sort of communicate in dreams. It's only happened like twice since the whole kidnapping thing, but I know it works. He'll listen to me. Let me get him here so we can end this and keep your people safe."

20

—————

MIRYAM

I don't know if my dream-meet-up plan had any shot of working. It's not like every time I went to sleep he was there, but I had to try.

I grabbed my phone off my dresser, flipped it open, and sent a quick text to Ant.

Time to work your Lost Things Mojo. Let Chris know I'll be waiting for him. He'll know where.

Ant texted back almost immediately. *I hate this plan.*

I chewed my bottom lip before typing: *I know, and I'm sorry.*

"You need to stop putting yourself in danger for that asshole," Zuri said when I just stared blankly at the phone in my hand, not sure what to do next.

"He's not an asshole." I cracked a half smile. "Well, not all the time anyway. There's a part of him that's still good, Zuri. A part of him I can still save."

"I've dealt with demons and half demons before, Miry." Zuri twisted the red string bracelet around her wrist. I remember her saying once it was all she had left of her mom. She didn't even have memories of her. "They twist what you want to believe until there's no way of knowing where the truth ends and the lie begins. You've seen as well as I have what Saint Boy has let himself become. He's not the guy you think you love. Not even close."

I nodded, keeping my eyes trained on my shoes. "I still need to try. I don't expect you to understand, Z, but this is seriously important to me. Why can't I try?"

Zuri sighed and ruffled a hand through her hair. "When all this is over, I'm going to hate telling you 'I told you so.'"

"Then don't," I said. "Just let me believe a little while longer, okay?"

Z didn't say anything. Her side-eye glance did all the talking for her. She didn't trust Chris and maybe—by extension—didn't trust me anymore either.

"Z?" I hedged. "I know you don't agree with like pretty much any of my life choices. And you think the color pink should be reserved for babies or whatever, but can you do one thing for me?"

"Depends on what the one thing is," she answered.

I bit my lip again, trying to decide if I should be honest and real or just laugh, yell psych, and push everything—all the feelings, confusion, and more—back to that corner of my mind reserved for stuff like that. The same corner reserved for the real me and not the front I project to anyone and everyone. In the end, I decided on the truth ... but only just a little.

"Can you hold me?" I requested. "Just until I fall asleep. I need someone to hold me and tell me it's going to be okay."

"Even if it's not?"

"Especially if it's not." I motioned at her bed. "Mind if I join you?"

Zuri scooted over to make room for me. "I have rules, though. No saying 'like,' 'totally,' or anything about male anatomy. Got it?"

I nodded before skipping across our dorm room. I crawled into her bed and we arranged ourselves so my back was pressed to her front.

Zuri even threw an arm around my waist for good measure.

"Happy?" She mumbled; her breath warm on the back of my neck.

"Yeah." I burrowed closer. "You've really never been with a guy before? Like never ever?"

"You said like," Zuri murmured, sounding drowsy. "Don't make me kick you out of bed."

"Sorry." I squirmed a little more, trying to get comfortable. "You didn't answer my question."

"Once," she admitted. "And it wasn't Damien so don't even ask."

"And once was enough to know you were into girls instead of guys?" I asked. "What if it was just bad s-e-x? What if you built your whole identity around a mistake?"

"Who we're attracted to is something we feel deep within our soul, Miry." Zuri adjusted so her forehead rested against the back of my head. "We can't change it any more than we can change our skin or eye color. It's part of who we are."

"What's it called when someone likes guys and girls?"

"You really didn't get out much growing up, did you?"

"You met my mom. Humor me."

My breath caught when Zuri opened her

palm, fingers splayed across my stomach. I closed my eyes, trying to think of something neutral, safe, and non-sexy like baseball. Except all I kept coming back to was the feel of her fingers so close to my skin.

"Bisexual," Zuri answered the question I forgot I had even asked. "Bi for short. You love who you love."

"You love who you love," I repeated. "Thanks, Z."

"Don't mention it."

Her voice had that dreamy, sleepy quality again. I closed my eyes, trying to rest. If all worked out according to plan, I would lead my boyfriend right into a trap. How was that love?

21

ZURI

I waited, listening to hear if Miry's breathing changed, but it remained uneven. That meant she wasn't off communing with her douchebag ex, yet. After what must have been a good twenty minutes, I nudged her shoulder with my chin. "Miry, are you asleep?"

"I'm trying, but it's just not working," she answered, snuggling deeper into my embrace.

I sighed. "Have you tried, I don't know, counting sheep or something?'

She wriggled on the bed until she was staring me in the face, our bodies precariously close to each other. Those damn perky tits of hers brushed mine, pulling my focus from the task at hand. "Maybe I'm just nervous? I mean, I've only done this a couple times and never on purpose."

"You can do this," I told her, barely resisting the urge to push the hair cascading over her left cheek out of her eyes.

"I know I have to do this, because we need to save lives. Except I'm scared, Z. What if it does go wrong?'

"You won't be alone. I have your back. And come on, you're Miryam bat-Michael, you can do anything you set your mind to," I reminded her.

"You mean that?" Her lower lip quivered.

"I wouldn't have said it if I didn't mean it," I answered.

She was silent for a moment and then she reached over, twining her fingers into my hair. My body tensed, both anticipating and fearing her next move. She kissed my cheek with a quick peck and whispered in my ear, "And what if my mind wants to kiss you right now?"

I wanted to tell her she didn't know what she was talking about, that she was just pretending again. However, she had no reason to pretend here in the privacy of our dorm room. There were no dude bros trying to grab her ass or other people watching. It was just us and damn it if I didn't want to feel her lips on mine again.

"I'd say you better hurry up before I change my mind." My voice came out low and husky, deep in my chest.

She gave a soft giggle that was quintessential Miry before her lips found mine again and her body was flush with mine.

It wasn't the most passionate of kisses. Not the I'm-so-horny-rip-your-clothes-off kind of passion anyway. It was slow, promising more just around the corner if I let her in. I gripped her waist, hating the fabric of her stupid uniform skirt being in the way. I dug my nails into it, sliding my leg over hers, grinding against her as her hands moved along the curve of my spine. Her breasts pressed against me, begging to be let loose. How could I not oblige? Turning my attention there, I unbuttoned her blouse, pushing it off her shoulders. She did an awkward waving motion to free herself of the fabric before sitting up and staring at me.

"You can feel them if you want," she said, her cheeks rosy. "I mean, like bra on still."

Where's the fun in that? "Thanks."

She took my hand, guiding it to cup her left breast. I gave it a gentle squeeze and she squealed. Getting to explore her body, even just a little was turning me on. Even so I knew Miry wasn't ready for the full experience.

I leaned over her, straddling her hips and whispered in her ear. "You have no idea how badly I want to do more."

"You really think I'm that hot?" She asked, her eyes shining with what read as surprise.

I squeezed her breast harder and she let out a soft moan. "You are by far the most frustrating person I have ever met, Miry. But yes, you are hot." I kissed her, rocking my hips against her. It might not get her anywhere, but I'd be damned if I wasn't going to get at least a little something out of this.

I moved faster, the friction between the fabric of my pants and her skirt building as I closed my eyes, picturing her naked and writhing beneath me. *I was almost there. Just a little more …*

"Fuck!"

"What did I do? I'm sorry if I did something wrong," Miry's voice broke the fantasy as I rolled off of her.

"You didn't do anything wrong," I sighed, taking her hand and pressing it to my pants.

"Oh …"

"Don't get too excited. It's been a long time since I did anything remotely sexual." I rolled over and propped myself up on one elbow. "When you're ready, really ready to see what you want, I promise it's going to be even more satisfying. Now, go to sleep so we can lure your demon boyfriend into a trap. Imagining kicking his ass is just as good as an orgasm."

22

MIRYAM

"I'll pretend you didn't say that."

I crawled off of Z's bed and stumbled over to my dresser. I opened the drawers to rummage around until I found my 'Unicorns sparkle' t-shirt and pink shorts. They were comfortable enough to sleep in, but versatile enough to run around campus in and not look like I was wearing pajamas. "Do you think this will work?" I made sure not to look at Zuri as I shimmied out of my school uniform skirt which was pretty much all I had left on other than my bra and panties. I swapped it out for my t-shirt and shorts.

"Define this?"

I waved a hand, trying to find the right words.

"This. Luring Lilith and figuring out if Uncle Uriel is in on the hurting Fallen scheme … well, everything. There's a lot of moving pieces and I don't think Lilith has been all that predictable up until now."

"But Saint Boy has," Zuri said, sounding sleepy. I hoped she could get a nap in too before we sprung the plan into action. I hoped Ant and CeCe were doing the same right now. "All he wants is you. I hate that we have to use you as bait, but if that stops the killing, we need to risk it."

"I'm not scared," I assured her as I climbed onto my own bed. I hung my head over the side. It's my go to thinking pose and I totally had a lot to think about right now. "You'll protect me, right?"

"You don't need anyone to protect you, Miry." Zuri yawned and flipped over onto her back. She laced her hands behind her head and stared up at the ceiling. "You're strong and capable, as soon as you realize that, you'll be unstoppable."

I twirled a piece of hair around my finger. "That doesn't mean I don't like knowing you'll totally have my back when we go marching into danger. We're better together than apart, remember?"

"You make it hard to forget."

I sighed. There was so much I wanted to say, but nothing came out. Instead, I just settled on the obvious. "Get some sleep, Z. I hope we don't die."

"I hope we don't die either."

I listened to her breathing grow deep and even in the quiet darkness of our dorm room before I laid down, closed my eyes, and slowed my own breathing. I hoped Ant found Chris and—better yet—I hoped all the layers of our plan worked. We would need all the luck we could muster if we wanted to survive the night.

MIST SWIRLED AROUND ME, reminding me of what Heaven looks like right after the big pearly gates opened. That split second before the mist parted and everyone saw their own personal Heaven. What would mine look like? Who would be standing there on the other side of the mist? Chris or Zuri? If you asked me last month or even last week, my answer might be different. Now I don't know anymore. Everything and everyone were all jumbled up in my head. *Things were easier before Zuri was around.* That one thing

Chris had said in jealousy was true. Things *were* easier and no doubt would have continued on that way forever if I had let it. I was happy then or at least thought I was. Despite that, being challenged and believed in by Zuri made me a better, stronger version of me. How could I give that up now that I saw what I could become? When I saw my own potential?

"Chris?" I squinted as the mist parted, revealing Chris sitting on a picnic blanket like the last time we had communed in a dream thing. "I wasn't sure this would work."

He motioned at the picnic blanket. I took the hint and sat down next to him. "We share a connection. Of course this works. Did you ever doubt it?"

"Sometimes," I admitted. "I doubt a lot of things."

"You don't have to doubt me." Chris poured a glass of that weird foaming liquid stuff again and passed it to me. I held it, but didn't drink.

"I know you love me." The words sounded robotic and more than a little hollow. I wasn't sure if he bought my less than stellar acting job or not. Although I needed to stick to the script to make sure he and his mom showed up when and where we needed them to. Part of that script was making sure he didn't doubt my love or loyalty.

"That's right." Chris nodded. "No one can ever take away what we have. We're stronger than that, Miry."

"Totally."

I decided to skip to the part where talking was optional. I leaned into him, grabbed him by the shirt collar, and kissed him. Chris stiffened—as if he wasn't expecting that sort of welcome—before he relaxed and wrapped his arms around my waist. He leaned backwards, taking me with him, until I was laying on top of him, our legs tangled up together. He wanted me, that was clear enough. He had always wanted me. I used to want to be wanted and that was enough. It took me way too long to realize that so much of me and my self-worth was tangled up in being desired. Desire wasn't love, not really. It was shallow and superficial—like I used to pretend to be. Now I wanted something deeper, something more.

"Can you do something for me?" I asked as I undid his shirt buttons, trailing kisses where my fingers just were. I needed to sell this part and sell it good if the plan was going to work.

"Anything." Chris rasped, fingers digging into

the sensitive skin of my hips. "Name it and it's yours."

"I want to meet your mother."

He sat up so abruptly that I slid off his lap down to somewhere around his knees.

"Anything, but that."

"But why not?" I flashed my signature pout. "We're solid, right? You've met my parents. I've met your dad. Why can't I meet your mom? It's like totally the thing solid, committed couples do, right? I'm not saying like throw a party or anything. It can be quiet. Just you, me, your mom, and my angel blood." I twisted so the vein on my neck pulsed. "There haven't been any new kidnappings or attacks on Fallen which means you're due for a ... transfusion, right? Let me help you, Chris. That's all I've ever wanted to do."

He shook his head. "It's too dangerous. I'm not allowed on campus anymore, remember? Your dad put demon wards up."

"I totally found a work around for that." I pulled Chris to me and kissed him again. It was pretty much my only idea for how to get him to agree to anything that came out of my mouth. If he wanted me or my angel blood bad enough, he'd show up. He'd totally show up.

"What kind of work around?"

"CeCe can reconfigure the gates." I forced my voice into perky 'this will totally work trust me' mode. "The wards have a special frequency ... like a song ... she can turn off the demon ward by rewriting the song. See? Easy, peasy. I've missed you." My bottom lip jutted out. "We can do a lot in a half hour, remember? But you have to show up first."

"What time?"

Got him. "Nine," I said. "I'll be waiting."

ZURI

I'd feigned sleep to get Miry to move forward with the risky part of the plan, but I couldn't rest while she dreamt of that douchebag. Not after our little make-out session. I could still feel the curve of her body pressed against mine and damn it, I wanted more. In spite of that I knew it would just amount to a rebound and I was not going to be someone's bounce-back chick. So I waited and watched as Miry rolled over in bed and sighed.

Beside me, my phone buzzed with an incoming call from Damien, his face flashing across the screen in time to the sound. "Did you find him?" I whispered so as not to disturb Miry.

"Not yet. But, Z, Hell is a big place and I don't

know his schedule. Besides, I'm worried about you. Taking on Lilith again. That just sounds crazy."

"I don't love the plan, but it's the only way to get all of this insanity to stop."

"I want to be there when you take her down, so I can look her in the eye and show her that I'm okay."

I doubted he was really okay, but I understood the need to face his attacker head on. "Fine You shouldn't have any problem getting on the grounds."

I eyed Miry as she threw a hand over her head in what seemed like a very flirty gesture.

"You sure you're okay?" D's voice pulled me from my ogling.

"We made out," I said in a hushed tone.

"Was she angelic?" He teased.

"I hate you so much, you know that right?"

"Nah, you love me. But seriously, you did?"

I rolled over to stare at the wall. "I mean it wasn't long, but yeah. She let me feel her tits." I could hear the excited inhale of breath over the line. "Bra on. Damn, D … I could just see what it would be like and now it's all I can think about. I don't get stupid over girls like this."

"She means something to you, Z. More than

just a pretty face and hot body to get you off. You care about what happens to her. That's a good thing."

I craned my neck to find Miry curled up into the blankets with her back to me. "That's what has me worried, too. I can't shake the feeling that caring about her is going to come back and bite me in the ass."

"Don't be so pessimistic," he chided.

Before I could tell him to fuck off, Miry sat bolt upright in bed, her hair matted to one side of her face and her eyes wide. She turned to me and said, "They're going to come. We need to get ready."

***

CAMPUS WAS EERILY empty by nine o'clock at night. Everyone else was safely tucked into their beds—or afraid of breaking curfew. Yet here we stood by the gates, waiting for a mad demon and her abusive spawn to waltz onto the grounds so we could … smite them? The weight of the lariat weighed on me as I repositioned the black cross-body bag.

"You don't have to be here," I heard Miry tell Glasses and the other girl.

"We said we would help you, Miry," Glasses said, although his voice cracked.

"And I have to be here to make sure the wards do what you want," D's girlfriend chimed in.

Speaking of, I heard a beating of wings and felt the rush of air before D landed beside me. I hadn't seen him since we'd come back to campus. The scars had healed more. Although I could still see the haunted look in his eyes when he playfully batted me on the shoulder and gave me a 'thumbs-up' while blowing kisses at his girlfriend.

"You're disgusting," I told him and shifted the open bag so the lariat wasn't as close to him.

He eyed my new accessory and took a noticeable step away. "How'd you get your hands on that thing anyway?"

"How do you think?"

Before either of us could say anything else, Miry bounced over to us, her hands clasped in front of her. "I'm glad you're doing better," she said to Damien.

"Yeah, thanks." He eyed us one more time before wandering off to wrap his girlfriend in a tight embrace, leaving Glasses to stand awkwardly between two couples. Wait ... no, we weren't a couple—yet.

"It's after nine, he should be here," I said, starting to grow antsy with the plan. Besides, we didn't need daddy dearest swooping in and ruining things.

She wouldn't meet my gaze as she said, "I know Chris will show up. He needs me, my blood."

"Look, Miry, I don't need to know whatever went down in that dream between you two. I just need to know that if this thing with us goes any further, when you're with me, you're only with me."

She looked up and I caught unshed tears in her eyes. "Of course."

I checked the time, seeing my phone screen tick past 9:06. "They're late. I'm going to take a lap and see if I can spot them," I told her. My wings unfurled and I kicked off the ground, the reminder of the weapon I carried messing with my balance as I found a perch high up in a tree. I felt like I was a bird of prey stalking my next meal *See how they like it.*

The gates below me slammed open with a bone-jarring clang as Lilith appeared out of nowhere, all dark eyes and pale skin. Saint Boy hung back at a few paces behind her. Glasses, Damien, and his girlfriend had all vanished, leaving Miry standing alone. Just like we'd planned. We needed them to think she was alone if we were going to succeed in catching them off guard.

"Are you alone?" Saint Boy called, not advancing beyond the gate.

"I told you I would be," Miry replied.

Lilith took a tentative step onto the campus grounds and I sucked in a breath, waiting to see if the gates really were being fooled. So far, no exploding demons. She gave a thin-lipped smile and beckoned Saint Boy to join her. "Do not be afraid. She has done as she promised and given us access."

I could see Saint Boy's gaze searching the area, no doubt trying to hunt down the trap. Lucky for me I was high enough up and far enough away, he couldn't catch on to me hiding. Besides, I had the advantage of being able to fly.

"It feels wrong to be here," he said, more to Lilith than Miry.

"That's not true. You belong here just like the rest of us," Miry said, laying it on thick. It turned my stomach to see her catering to his every whim just like she had before we knew what he really was.

"We both know I'm not the same person I was

back then. We should go somewhere safer." He tried to take Miry's hand, but she pulled away.

"You are braver than I gave you credit for, child of Michael," Lilith mused. "Inviting such danger into his house with no regard for what might befall those who claim refuge here."

My side grew warm and I looked down to see the lariat burning through the fabric of the bag. It mirrored my own anger at Lilith's words. She wasn't going to lay a hand on the kids here. Most of them didn't know me and I didn't know them either, but they hadn't asked for any of this. Moreover, I wasn't about to let her hurt my friends again.

"Enough small talk," I grumbled and launched out of the tree, tossing the bag aside mid-air as the lariat coiled around my forearm like a snake.

"I knew you weren't alone," Saint Boy shouted, shoving Miry away as he turned to face me, his skin going blotchy and black-veined as his demon-side took over.

"You did always just think about yourself," I quipped, snapping the lariat in my hand. Unlike the last time I'd held it, I could feel it seeking to do my bidding. It wanted to punish, because I wanted to hurt them. It felt *good* to want to inflict pain on this bastard.

"I should have gotten rid of you when I had the chance," he snarled.

"See, that's the thing. You think you can take me, but I'm faster and stronger than you," I taunted.

"Have you learned to use that weapon, child?" Lilith's tone conveyed curiosity.

"Why don't we find out?"

I let the lariat loose, feeling the end bite into flesh as it wrapped around Saint Boy's chest and arms, binding them to his sides. With a solid yank, I brought him to his knees. His lips began to turn bright red with blood.

"What are you doing? Stop!" Miry's voice cut through the haze of my bloodlust and I let the lariat go.

"I had to stop them," I replied as she fell to her knees beside him.

I staggered back as she clawed at the lariat, trying to free him from its tightening embrace.

Lilith swooped down and clasped the lariat with both hands before letting out a howl of anger and pain so guttural, I wasn't sure it actually came from her throat. She ripped the lariat free and threw it away as her hands blistered and burned. She cradled Saint Boy to her chest and I took a step toward her. If she was weakened, even a little, this was my chance to take her out for good.

"Zuri, wait!" Damien's voice wrapped around me just as his hand clasped my wrist and yanked me backward.

I spun to face him, all of the pent-up emotions threatening to bubble over. "It's not her." he gestured to a figure descending from the sky. "It was him."

Uriel landed softly on the ground, the lariat leaping through the air into his waiting hand. His eyes glowed red and ominous, promising pain and death.

24

MIRYAM

Everything seemed to happen in slow motion and yet fast forward at the same time. Uncle Uriel landed on the front lawn, the lariat returning to its master. Ant and CeCe looking way out of place in the mix of angels, demons, and Chris. Chris was still on the ground, blood soaking through his shirt and dribbling out of his mouth any time he tried to speak.

"Save your strength," I whispered, smoothing back his blonde hair from his forehead. How many times had I done that in our years together? How many times had we whispered secrets under the covers, not wanting to go to sleep, because it meant time apart? I was so stupid in love with him then. I was so sure that what I'd been missing my whole life was him and his love. "I'm here now," I assured him. "I'm here now, Chris."

"Miry, I'm …."

"Shhh." I kissed him, tasting his blood on my lips. "Save your strength, remember? Just rest. I'm going to figure out how to fix this. I promise." I looked up to find Ant standing beside us. "Ant! Call an ambulance or something. We need to get Chris to the hospital."

"I don't think 'angelic relic injury' is in any doctor's wheelhouse, Mir." Ant ducked as the lariat whizzed by his head, seeking Lilith who was bouncing around all over the place thanks to her smoky demon magic. "Sorry, but I'm not getting killed for any of you. I'm outta here."

"Coward!" I yelled as Ant booked it inside the school building. Chris' blood covered hand in mine pulled my focus back to him.

"Let him go," he said. "You're the only one I want beside me now. It's getting dark, Miry. I never liked the dark."

I smiled to cover up the scary fact that I knew he was talking about his impending death and not real darkness. "You always protected me from my nightmares, remember? Now it's time for me to return the favor." I squeezed his hand hard. "I'm here, Chris. I won't leave you."

"Heal him, Child of Michael." Lilith poofed next to me and mimed holding her hands over Chris. "You will have my protection, I swear it. Heal my child. He is all I have in this world and the next. Above and below. I will barter you some time. Please. Heal him."

Lilith poofed away again to confront Uncle Uriel. I watched, confused on why she would run into danger when her MO was totally to run away, when her words finally made sense. She was giving me time to save Chris. *Heal him.* Why didn't I think of that sooner? I totally had angelic healing powers! They worked on Zuri's ex-girl-friend and Damien. That meant they could work on Chris too.

"I'm Miry bat-Michael," I whispered mostly to myself. "I got this."

I pulled my hand free and held them both over Chris' body, focusing my healing energy on his arms and chest which seemed to have taken the brunt of the attack. I tried not to think of the blood seeping out with each shallow breath or how his eyes were growing more and more unfocused. I needed to do this. I needed to try. My hands grew warm as the golden healing light gathered and flowed from me to him. I felt it traveling through his veins, chasing out the dregs of demon blood better than his own Saint Blood or my Angel Blood could ever do. Small scrapes and cuts on his hands and face closed under the light, but no matter how hard I focused—no matter how hard I tried—I couldn't get the deep wounds on his chest to close. It was almost like the lariat energy was fighting against me. Archangel relics didn't play nice with angelic healing. The demon half needed to be smited, even if that meant taking out the saint half in the process.

"Lemme try again." My own strength was next to nothing since I poured it all into him, but I couldn't give up. Miryam bat-Michael didn't give up. "I can do this, Chris, I promise." I looked up, hoping to find someone, anyone, to give me a signal boost, but with all the demon powers, angelic relics, and fighting in play, everyone who could help was occupied. I was alone. The only person able to help me was me.

"Miry. You've done all you can." Chris pulled my hands down to rest against his chest, each breath becoming weaker and weaker. His eyes were so brilliantly blue. Not black demon eyes like before. This was my Chris. I'm glad I had him back, even if it was just temporary. I wanted to remember him like this and not what he had become.

"You're going to be alright." I smiled to cover up the hollowness of my words. "Remember that trip we wanted to take? After we were all done with school? Tell me about it. Tell me where you wanted to go."

He frowned. "How do you know if the good you did will outweigh all the bad? How do I know where I'll end up? Up or down? I'm scared, Miry. I don't like the dark."

"You're a good person, Chris," I said firmly, tightening my grip on his hand. "Don't doubt that. There's nowhere to go but up."

"But how do you know?" He whispered, voice urgent and raspy. "How do you know?"

"I don't know," I admitted. "I don't know anything, Chris, but I believe. I gotta believe. If I don't believe all the bad in the world—in my life—would break me. *This* will break me."

Chris lifted a hand and ran his fingers down my cheek, leaving a bloody trail in their wake. "You are the strongest person I know, Miry. Don't let ... don't let anyone tell you any different. And ... And never doubt I loved you. I just wish ..." He grimaced. "I just wish I could have been who you needed me to be. Always. I want you to be happy."

"I loved you too." I made sure to look him directly in his eyes so he could focus on me. Focus on my words. So he knew I saw him and I heard him. "Never doubt that."

I looked up, confused, when I heard CeCe scream. Why was she still here? She should have run off when Ant did. Wait, when did Uncle Gabriel get here? He stood next to Lilith, his scroll wrapped around her like some sort of containment device. She didn't seem to mind the scroll-jail. Still if the choice was between that and being burned alive by Uncle Uriel's lariat, I could see why. I opened my mouth to call Uncle Gabriel over to help, but I wasn't sure what would happen if he left the scroll. Would Lilith break free? We'd been trying for so long to capture her. I didn't want it to be my fault that she escaped. And the same time, she bought me time to try to heal Chris. Why was everything and everyone so complicated?

"Leave me," Chris said. "Help them."

"Don't be silly." I forced a bright smile. "This is where I want to be." Uncle Uriel turned to focus his relic onto the next and nearest wicked person

... which just happened to be Damien—CeCe's boyfriend.

"You're hurting him! Stop it!" Cece whirled on Zuri, who was standing just as dumbstruck as she was. *"Do something!"*

Zuri jumped into action. She grabbed Damien and shoved him behind her, barking over her shoulder to CeCe, "Get him out of here!" She turned around, planted her feet, and faced Uncle Uriel with all the swagger she'd shown since the second she stepped through the gates of Celestial Academy. "Hey, asshole! You fought against my dad in the War In Heaven. Why don't you try to take me on? I dare you."

"What is she doing?" I murmured, not realizing that I had said that out loud until I heard Chris' already rattling breath catch. I turned my focus back on him, flashing the brightest smile I could muster. "Hang on a little while longer, Chris. CeCe will totally call for help as soon as she gets inside. I just know it."

"I want you to be happy," he repeated what he said earlier. "No matter what that looks like, Mir, I want you to be happy."

I nodded. That sounded way too much like a good bye for my liking. "Hang on, Chris. I'm sure help is coming. Hang on. Please."

He shook his head. "Too late. Too late for me. Be happy Mir. I want you to be happy."

"I will," I promised.

"It's so dark, Miry, but I think I see a little glimmer of light ..." Chris squeezed my hand tight before his whole body went slack.

25

ZURI

What the fuck was I thinking? I'd just challenged a damn Archangel and brought a knife to a proverbial gun fight. I was strong, a badass, and pissed off. Despite that I wasn't stupid. At least, I didn't think I was. However, drawing his attention was exactly that—stupid. I could hear Dad's voice in the back of my head warning me not to punch above my weight class. Still, I'd committed to it so there I stood, fists balled, waiting for the crazed angel to take me on.

"I won't waste my time on you, little angel," Uriel said, his fiery gaze going unfocused.

"Why, because I'm a girl? If you're the one who has been going after Fallen, then you can't get much higher up than yours truly. So come on, we all know you've been dying to take me out since I stepped foot in your precious academy."

I watched Miry draped over Saint Boy's body. He wasn't moving which told me the lariat had done its job. *Would she forgive me for killing him?* He'd treated her horribly, but what I'd done could easily be seen as taking out the competition. Hard to be swayed back to an abusive lover when said lover was a corpse.

"You have sown dissension long enough," Uriel bellowed, snapping the lariat against his thigh.

"You're getting lost in your own head, old man," I taunted before biting my lip.

Uriel threw back his head and laughed. It echoed eerily in the gated courtyard as he kicked off the ground, his kimono fluttering in the current his massive wings created. I had no choice now. I had to defend myself.

"Z, catch!" Damien's voice echoed from behind me. I turned to see a sword hurtling toward me and caught it by the hilt, coming up to meet the lariat mid-air. I expected the lariat to at least bend to the blade, but it clanged off like it was made of metal, too. The force sent me staggering backward as Uriel descended, his face a vicious mask of demented glee.

"You will not escape punishment this time!" He howled and whipped the braided rope at me. Parrying as best I could, I tried to stand my ground. Except every lash of his weapon pushed me a few shuffled steps backward. I looked around to see Miry still hadn't moved from her position over Saint Boy. Gabriel stood with Lilith wrapped in his scroll. My mind had little time to wonder how it had come back to him since we hadn't brought it back from Hell. *Could it act the same way as Michael's sword and come when it's owner called?*

Pain exploded in my wrist and hand—the same one Uriel had broken a few days ago. I looked down to see the lariat scalding my skin. It didn't blister and bubble like I'd seen it do to Delilah or Saint Boy, but it still hurt like a bitch. Cutting through the lariat wasn't an option. God wouldn't purposely create an angelic relic to be so delicate. Even Dad's Emblem had to be drenched in my blood to be of any use. So, I took a new approach, slamming the hilt of the sword into Uriel's face.

"Get your fucking murder rope off me!" It came out mostly as an unintelligible growl.

"We were meant to be better than them. We are better than them," Uriel railed, clearly lost in his mind as I struggled to get free.

A rush of flapping wings filled my ears as I strained against his hold on me. The sense of dread that washed over me signaled I wasn't going to like who'd just arrived. With a sharp jerk of the lariat, Uriel sent me tumbling head over heels landing on my ass as I collided with Lilith's bound form. I let out a garbled 'ooph' as I tried to get to my feet. I wasn't giving up that easily, even as Michael stood there in his stupid gleaming armor with his sword resting in the dirt. Raphael stood off to one side looking from me to Saint Boy and Miry, and then back again. He took a tentative step toward me before reversing course to tend to Miry. She'd been uncharacteristically quiet.

"We have them now," Uriel shouted, waving the lariat above his head like a rodeo rider. It came flying my way again, but I dodged just in time to see it wrap tight around Lilith's throat. She gave a loud hiss and struggled against her binds.

I was no fan of the mother of demons, but she wasn't the one who'd hurt my people, after all. Uriel, chasing down ghosts of a long-ago war had gone after innocents, because they had no say in what they'd become. All because they wore a label these assholes had given to them.

I wrapped my hands around the lariat, biting my lip as the pain in my hands intensified. At some point the pain disappeared, replaced by numbness.

"See how she defends the scum of this world, brothers?" Uriel's gaze was wild as he turned to Michael and Gabriel.

"Uriel, it is time to calm yourself," Raphael said, holding his hands up in a placating gesture.

"No, let him complete his task. We must be rid of the evil that plagues our gates and invades our sanctuary," Michael replied, making eye contact with me.

"Child of Lucifer, you have shown bravery. However, I do not believe you to be foolish. You will not win this battle," Lilith's voice was soft in my ear.

"Fuck them, there's been enough death," I answered, tugging harder.

"And if you take them to task on their sacred ground, yours will be yet another life snuffed," she noted coolly.

I hated that she was right. Despite that, I couldn't just stand here and do nothing, letting them get away with murdering people. Still, I released my grip on the lariat as Uriel danced around Lilith, wrapping it tighter around her. Michael stepped forward; blade held at his side. His gaze was as steely as the sword and it sent icy tendrils of dread down my spine. He was hiding something and part of me didn't want to find out what it was.

Uriel pranced from foot to foot tightening his hold on Lilith as Michael hefted the sword onto his shoulder, moving to stand in front of her.

"You have been a scourge to this world for far too long, demon. You will be snuffed out like you were meant to be when you were deemed unworthy."

"See reason, Michael," Raphael said, pushing me aside and placing himself between us. "There has been enough death, enough loss. Can't you see what this vendetta, this blood lust, has cost your own child? Someone she cared for deeply is now dead."

I wanted to be with Miry, to reassure her that everything wasn't lost, but I couldn't in good conscience tell her that. Not when I had no proof it would be. I was a killer now, too—like Uriel, like Lilith. She wouldn't want me now.

"She has disgraced our sacred space. Manipulated others to allow her entry," Michael boomed. "She must be punished."

I knew in my bones he was no longer describing Lilith. I'd talked plenty of shit about Michael to a lot of people, but in that moment, he truly frightened me. I could see the formidable enemy my father had warred with eons ago, could see why some would consider him a strong leader. He instilled obedience when he wanted.

"I am a healer, brother," Raphael said. "I cannot let you finish what you have started. I will not stand by as you take yet more life that our Creator made, imperfect as she may be."

"She's gotten in his head, Michael, twisted his thoughts," Uriel proclaimed.

"Listen to your brother, archangel," a familiar voice called from the open gates.

I turned to see Samael stride onto the grounds and it made every nerve in my body scream with mistrust. He'd been in contact with Michael. Besides, there's no way Dad would have sent his second-in-command to do a job like collecting Lilith. He gave me a small nod. "I am here to collect the demon and her spawn." He glanced at Miry's prone form. "I see I need not collect him though. All the better."

"This traitor? We cannot entrust him with such a valuable task," Uriel scoffed.

Michael held up a hand. "Why should I give her to you, Fallen?"

"Because my leader, Lucifer, commands that Lilith be punished according to our own rules. He seeks no quarrel with you." Samael's tone was hard, like he had known the archangels were behind the attacks.

"And I've come to collect Ms. bat-Lucifer as well. He would prefer his daughter reside in his own domain for the foreseeable future. I trust there is no objection."

"Take the girl out of my sight," Michael said. "It was a mistake to let her enter these halls."

I didn't want to go with him. Although as Damien joined me, squeezing my forearm, I knew I had no choice. I did something I'd never once in my life done. I prayed. *Please let Miry understand why I did what I did. Please keep her safe until I can come back for her. And please, if you're up there and care at all, protect my father.*

Gabriel unbound Lilith from his scroll and Uriel, after some prodding from Michael, relinquished the lariat. She clawed at her blistered throat. How she was still able to breathe was beyond me. Damien and I fell into step behind her.

"We have a problem. No one's seen your dad in days. Lucifer has gone missing," Damien whispered in my ear the moment we were off school grounds.

Everything had gone to shit, but there was no fucking way I was going to let a bunch of entitled old angels take what was mine—not Miry and not my dad. They had no idea what was coming ...

MICHAEL'S BLADE

1

MIRYAM

My phone's text alert beeped for like the zillionth time since, well, since everything went down. How long ago was that? A week? Two? A month? Time was meaningless to me now. Everything just floated around me in one big cloud of 'bad.' What was the point of getting out of bed, dressed, or even eating? Why should I pretend to be happy or okay when I was neither of those things? Chris was dead. How does a 19-year-old just die? No, not die. Be murdered. He was murdered by someone I trusted more than anyone in the whole wide world —*Zuri*. Some friend she turned out to be. I should have listened to Dad from the start. I should have known Angel and Fallen couldn't work together

—couldn't *be* together—and just sent her home to Hell. Maybe if I'd done that when I had the chance, Chris would still be alive.

Memories, regret, and guilt were funny things. They made me remember the good instead of the bad with Chris, especially now that there would never be any new memories. No new moments to label 'good' or 'bad.' I mean, how much bad was in my relationship with Chris, really? Zuri said tons, but she also said lots of things that weren't true. At least I think they weren't true. Nothing really made sense anymore.

"Go away," I mumbled to my phone when the text alert beeped yet again. I was going to have to turn that thing off. If I didn't get the alerts, I didn't need to answer anything. Ever. Never ever again.

"Miry? You okay in there?" Cece called through my closed door from the hallway. Thanks to Zuri's betrayal, CeCe got elevated to one of a handful of people I'd actually talk to now. CeCe, Ant, Dad, Uncle Raphael, and Uncle Gabriel were the only ones included. Uncle Uriel was on the bad list with Zuri. It was his angelic relic that had killed Chris, even if he wasn't the one wielding it. No, that was Zuri who had done the murdering. Zuri who both Dad and Chris had said was trouble. I should have listened to them. Maybe then Chris would still be alive instead of buried six feet in the ground.

"I'm not hungry!" I yelled, even though I totally didn't know or care if it was meal time or not.

"We're worried about you," CeCe didn't give up. "All of us. Even Damien."

"I don't care what your Fallen boyfriend thinks of me," I muttered mostly to myself, but I didn't care if she heard me either. Damien was BFFs with Zuri which meant he was to blame too. I'm not sure exactly how—I hadn't quite worked that out in my head yet—but I would figure it out. I had nothing to do, but think now.

"Please, Miry, if you won't talk to me, talk to someone." *Dang. Cece was awfully persistent.* "What about Raphael? You know he's an amazing listener and never judges."

I sat up, threw the covers off my head. Then I debated for a sec if I actually wanted to leave my bed or not, before standing and walking across the room. Each step was slow, like I'd forgotten how to walk along with forgetting how to feel anything but sadness. Somehow, I made it across my dorm room—Zuri's side empty since she'd gone back to Hell—and opened the door.

"Thanks for opening the door."

CeCe smiled, her dark eyes all wide and hopeful behind her glasses. I used to look like that. I used to look all hopeful and perky before everything went down with our botched plan on the front lawn of campus. We had thought Chris' mom, the mother of demons, Lilith, was attacking Fallen. It turned out to be Uncle Uriel, trapped in some PTSD mind-warp. Dad didn't even punish him. It all got swept under the rug just like always. Campus kidnappings and the attacks on Fallen weren't important. Dad was a master at ignoring anything that didn't concern him directly which was pretty much everything having to do with Celestial Academy, including me.

CeCe held out a brown bag of what smelled like those really amazing chocolate chip cookies from that bakery close to campus. "I brought munchies. I'm glad you opened the door, Mir. Really I am."

"I always open the door for cookies." I stepped aside so she could come in. CeCe stood in the middle of the room, looking confused on where to sit. My bed was an unmade mess. Zuri's bed was just like she had left it, though I doubt she was ever coming back. You don't murder someone and then pop in to Angelic History like nothing had happened. That left the desks as the only options for sitting. CeCe chose my desk after she handed over the bag of cookies.

"How are you feeling?" She asked.

"Better now," I said around a mouthful of chocolate chip goodness. "This should be like, the only way I open the door. Wanna talk to me? Bring me cookies."

"Is there anything else I can do?" She motioned at the bag of goodies. "Besides baked goods, I mean."

"You can have Damien tell Zuri to stop texting me." I ran a hand through my hair. It wasn't all healthy and bouncy anymore thanks to too many days in bed and too few days of actually showering. "I have nothing to say to her."

"I'm sure it's some sort of big misunderstanding," CeCe murmured. "If you just give Zuri a chance to explain—"

"That's Damien talking, not you," I accused. "You're not a Zuri-fan so why are you running interference for him?"

"I don't *not* not like her."

"Just let it drop," I insisted. "I'm not talking to her. The end."

"If you're sure …"

"Very sure." I grabbed my phone, opened a text to Dad, and composed a text out loud to show CeCe just how sure I was. Let her report back to Damien. I don't care.

"Dad—I don't think my Angel and Fallen service project is working. Expel Zuri. xoxo -M."

2

ZURI

I hated not knowing what was happening with Miry. She'd been ignoring all of my texts and calls since shit went down on campus with Lilith and Uriel. In a way, I couldn't blame her. For all the shit he'd done to her, Saint Boy had still been a big part of her life. He'd even played a part in forming who she was as a person. No matter how much that pissed me off.

"Where'd you go?" Delilah's voice called to me as I stared up at the ceiling of her one bedroom apartment above Renegade Reggie's bar.

Damien would give me so much shit for being here, but I couldn't stay in Hell. Not with my dad still missing. I knew that I wasn't safe there. I hadn't figured out what Samael was up to or why he was meeting with Michael. Though I knew it wasn't good. I sighed and looked at Delilah. "Just trying to figure out how my life got turned to shit so fast."

"I wouldn't say it's completely gone to shit," Delilah countered as she tugged up the hem of her top, sliding it over her head.

"My Dad's missing, Miry won't talk to me, and I can't shake this feeling that there's something even worse on the horizon. Something big. Like heavenly bloodbath big."

She spun to face me, her tits bouncing with the motion. I studied my cuticles so I wouldn't be tempted. I'd been staying on her couch the last few nights.

"So, go do something about it. You've always been a take charge kind of girl," she said and when I looked up she was standing directly in front of me, topless.

"Seriously, what the fuck?" I spat. I envisioned myself getting up and leaving this messed up situation behind.

In reality I sat there, unable to move or think as she leaned over, one hand on either side of my thighs. The closeness of her body to mine was intoxicating. Not all demons are the same. It isn't just all fire, ash, and shit. After all, there was a reason people associated sex with demonic activity.

"Oh, come on, Zuri. Be real here. You aren't attached to your little angel. If you were, you'd be fucking her night and day instead of crashing at my place, giving me side eye every time I take a shower." She grabbed my hand and pressed it to her breast.

"She lost someone important to her. I'm trying to give her space to grieve," I mumbled.

"Some abusive piece of shit boyfriend. Not worth crying over," she replied, pushing her weight into my lap until I had no choice, but to fall back against the bed. "Live a little, Zuri. After all, you came to me, remember? I didn't have to let you stay." Her fingers danced over my shirt. "You could let me have a little fun for old times' sake."

"And if I say no?" I rasped.

"If that's really what you want, then it's over."

I nodded before ripping my shirt off, not caring that I'd just ruined it. Her weight against me drew my mind back to that night when Miry had come out as bi and all the things I'd wanted to do to her.

"How do you want it?" Delilah's husky voice whispered in my ear.

I wrapped my legs around her hips and bucked so I was on top. "I'm in charge."

She grinned up at me. "It was always better when you were on top."

I kissed her hard to stop the talking. I didn't want to hear her voice anymore. I just wanted to be touched, to vent the fear and anxiety raging beneath the surface. I rocked my hips against her, much like I had with Miry, gripping her tits tight between my fingers. I heard her squeal before it turned into a deep growl.

I could start to feel myself getting closer, but I wasn't ready for this to be over too quickly. I shimmied out of my jeans and tugged Delilah's to her ankles along with her underwear. She lay before me naked except I didn't see her. All I could see was Miry's damn little pout and doe-like expression. I leaned up and kissed her, biting her lower lip as I slid a finger inside her. And then another, moving with quick jabs. I could feel her body tensing beneath me with every movement, and could smell the arousal seeping from every pore as I pushed her closer and closer to climax.

Then my fucking phone beeped with an incoming call. Damn technology.

"Don't answer it," Delilah begged, moving her

body against my motionless hand. "Fuck, I'm almost there."

I blinked down at my ex and withdrew my hand. All of the need was gone as I realized what I'd been doing. And with who. And who I'd rather be doing it with. Ugh!

"I'm done," I answered, wiping my hand on a discarded towel on the floor before pulling on my pants and taking one of her shirts.

"You never used to be such a tease," she called after me.

"Tough shit," I muttered and slammed the door behind me, checking my phone. Two missed calls from Damien.

I hit 'Call Back' and waited while the line rang. He picked up on the second ring.

"Please tell me there's news about my dad." The words tumbled out of my mouth so fast I wasn't sure they made any sense to him.

"No. But A letter just showed up for you from Celestial Academy."

"They're still on break," I said.

"They kicked you out. You're banned from ever going near any of their campuses again under penalty of death."

"Fuck Michael and his draconian bullshit."

"There's something else," Damien said. "CeCe

just texted me. Miry was the one who got him to expel you."

Miry got me kicked out? She really was pissed at me. "Fuck."

"Look, you need to come home, okay, Z? Things are getting weird around here. Samael keeps acting like he's in charge. You need to take over before everything falls apart."

I wasn't ready for that responsibility. Despite that, if I couldn't show that I could lead Hell in a time of crisis, then how would I ever prove myself to them as a worthy leader? Ruling an entire dimension should be easy, right? Just add it to my to do list along with saving my Dad and fixing shit with Miry.

No problem.

3

MIRYAM

"... And then Damien said 'I got this tat of a lyre for you.' Isn't that the sweetest?"

"Totally," I agreed, but only because CeCe was looking at me with her big, brown puppy dog eyes and would probably start crying if I said I didn't care what new tat her Fallen boyfriend got. I didn't care what any Fallen did with their time or bodies—not anymore. I just wanted to eat my lunch and go huddle under my blankets forever. Eat and mope. That was my plan for, like, as long as I could get away with it.

"I still don't get what you see in him," Ant commented around a mouthful of cold cuts and bread. "He's training to collect souls for a living.

How does that fit in with your art and music abilities?"

CeCe's eyes widened even more behind her black, oversized hipster glasses. "Why do Damien and me have to fit into any mold or box? Opposites attract." She nudged my shoulder to get me to play along. "Tell him, Miry."

"You liked Zuri, Ant," I poked a sore subject just cause I felt like it. "How'd that work out for you?"

His cheeks turned as red as his hair. "I could ask you the same thing."

I glanced at the empty seat to my right. Where Chris should sit and where he'd be if not for Zuri. "I didn't like her-like her. I only liked her," I said. "And now I don't." I shrugged and stuffed a huge bite of sub sandwich in my mouth. "End of story."

"Prove it," Ant challenged.

"Prove what?"

"Prove that you don't like her," Ant said.

I shrugged. "She went back to Hell. None of us want to hang around there—except maybe CeCe."

"Haven't you been listening to anything I said?" CeCe pouted. "Damien says she's not there. Neither is her dad. They're like both MIA."

"I don't care." And I truly didn't. "Stupid Zuri and her stupid dad can stay gone."

Ant and CeCe exchanged pointed looks as if trying to telepathically argue over who was going to be the bad guy and call me out on my shiz. I was honestly surprised they had waited this long to do it. I had been absolutely terrible to be around for weeks and weeks. Ant sighed. Looked like he lost the 'Be The Bad Guy' silent argument.

"Look, Miry, we know you miss Chris. We all do. But that doesn't mean you can go completely off the rails." He forked a hand through his hair, making it stick up like Harry Potter. "Grief doesn't give you an excuse to treat us and everyone else in your life like shit. If you don't at least attempt to make an effort, you're not going to have any friends left."

I blinked, letting his words sink in. Usually it was Zuri who called me out on my nonsense. When did Ant grow a backbone? "How is tracking Z down going to make a bit of difference?" I asked. "Chris will still be dead."

CeCe reached across the table to pat my hand. "We know, honey, but seeing her might give you a way to channel that grief. I'm not saying go all avenging angel on her or anything, but I think hearing her side might help everything … hurt a little less."

"Oh, cause Damien said so?" I mumbled. "Hate

to break it to you, CeCe, but he's not a reliable source. He's on her side. Your little ambush makes me think the both of you are on her side too."

"This isn't about who is on who's side, Mir," Ant said. "It's about getting you past the anger stage of grief and on to one that makes you a little nicer to be around. Just try it our way, okay? Please?"

He was right about one thing—I hadn't given Zuri time to explain herself. She left before Chris' body had even gone cold. I'd been ignoring all texts ever since. Would something as simple as talking it out really make a difference? I doubted it, but stranger things had happened. Until recently I had counted the daughter of my dad's sworn enemy as my best friend, after all.

"Even if I decided to go along with your cray-cray plan, we don't have anything to track Z with," I told Ant. "When Dad expelled her, he tossed all her stuff in the closest portal to Hell."

"We don't need a focal object." Ant's mouth turned up in a half-smirk. "We have something else she cares about way more than some computer or backpack."

"And what's that?" I arched an eyebrow,

dreading and yet anticipating his answer at the same time.

Ant's smile grew. "Not what ... who. We don't need an object, Miry, because we have you."

4

ZURI

amien's description of Hell being "weird"
wasn't what I expected when I stepped
through the portal, landing in the same spot
where I'd first brought Miry. I could almost feel
her standing beside me, gawking at the scenery
like a tourist. Everything still looked the same.

"You can't just be out in the open," Damien's
voice called to me from my left.

I pivoted to see him waving at me frantically
from within some elaborate cloak. The kind I'd
expect in some lame-ass frat boy prank. I rolled
my eyes and marched over to him.

"I'm here. I'm taking back my realm or whatever. What more do you want from me?"

"For you not to die," he answered and dragged me out of view.

"Seriously, D, what the fuck is going on?"

"You've got a target on your back," he answered, shrugging off his cloak and slinging it over my borrowed shirt and jeans.

"Right, because nobody gonna recognize the daughter of Lucifer in this thing," I quipped.

He tugged the hood up over my head. "Just trust me and stop being so bitchy," he said.

I gave him another eye roll, but followed him the long way to his place. I guessed Reaper school wasn't in session, because there was no way his dad would let him out of going to class. Even if the head of Hell was MIA.

"So, I did a little digging while you've been off … doing whatever with Delilah and you were right. Samael is up to something."

"I haven't been doing anything with Delilah," I snapped.

"Right … you're wearing her shirt, because you forgot to pack enough clothes."

"We're the same size," I muttered. "Look, about Samael. You said he was telling people that he's in charge when he knows I'm next in line?"

"It's worse than that. So, it turns out these

Reaper cloaks come in handy for spying on people."

I smoothed the fabric over my right elbow. Maybe I'd knocked it too soon. "Tell me what's going on."

"He met with Michael personally. And not about Lilith."

I really hated that name. "Please tell me that she's not a problem anymore?"

"She's locked up good and tight. Dad decided to take up jailer duties."

"Why? He doesn't still think she came after you, does he?"

He rubbed one of the faint scars that criss-crossed his forearm, ruining the elegant tattoo. "I didn't exactly mention it was Uriel."

I wanted to grab him and shake some sense into his brain. "D, why the fuck not?"

"Look around Z. Things are going to shit, fast. Your girlfriend or whatever she is, got you kicked out of school—"

"Not one I really wanted to be at to begin with," I interrupted.

"Your dad is missing and Archangels are killing us ... because they're bored? This world is not okay, Zuri."

"I get that everything is messed up and I'm

trying to fix it. But I'm just one person, D. I don't have all the answers. I can't even get my own love life sorted out."

I tugged the sleeves of the cloak around me tighter, hoping whatever invisibility mojo they had really worked. I needed a plan. I was good at plans normally. Except now, my mind pulled me in too many directions and I couldn't see a clear path to solving everything. "Okay, look we know that Dad's last defense against Michael is gone. So if someone wanted to get a jump on him, it would be hard but not impossible." Damien coughed and averted his gaze. "What do you know?"

"Not all of the Emblem was destroyed. Dad's been keeping that safe, too."

"I need to get my hands on it."

"The last time you came in contact with that thing, you nearly died!"

"That's because I bled on it, dumbass. I don't have any intention of doing that ever again."

Damien shouldered the back door to his house open and I stepped inside. It had always been one of my favorite places, like a second home. One wouldn't think the Angel of Death would be good at interior decorating, but everyone needs a hobby. Azrael sat at the kitchen table looking nervous as he stared at something on a laptop screen.

"Dad, I found her," Damien announced.

Azrael looked up and his shoulders dropped half an inch. "This is not the Hell you left behind, I'm afraid."

"I can see that." I slid out of the cloak and laid it across the back of an empty chair before settling in at the table. "You need to know something about Lilith," I began. Damien might not want to start a second war with the Archangels, but it felt almost like we were already there. With Uriel attacking Fallen, Michael kicking me out …

"I know she did not attack Damien," Azrael said. "But that does not excuse the horrible acts she inflicted on innocent children."

"How'd you know?" Damien's voice was soft, almost fearful.

"Prisoners are allowed to talk, Damien. I think perhaps Samael put her in my charge assuming that I would be brutal toward her. But for all the pain she has caused, she, too, is suffering the loss of a child. A pain I know well. As does your father." He looked at me. "You shouldn't have to take up this mantle now; not when you are still so young."

"We're going to find Dad. And figure out

whatever else is going on, too."

"You are one person, Zuri. Certainly powerful and driven like your father, but still only one person."

"But I'm not alone. I've got you and Damien and ..." Wait, I didn't have Miry, not any more.

It's funny how fast she'd become a part of my everyday life and even in my expectations for the future. Although, if she was still mad enough at me to kick me out of school, then she definitely wasn't part of any plans I made.

"Your father has been kind to the people here for a long time. That will earn you some sympathy, but Samael has taken hold of things and it appears he is not keen to let go."

Azrael spun the laptop to face me and I watched Samael sitting in my father's chair. It turned my stomach to see him lounging there like he owned the place. Only then, my eyes widened and the bottom dropped out of my stomach as none other than the fucking Archangel Michael appeared on screen with him.

"Is this live?" My voice came out in a rasp.

"It is."

"We knew Archangel kids could make the trip," Damien began.

"So, he's been lying to everyone else, making

them think they can't set foot here," I finished. I pulled the laptop closer, fiddling with the volume controls.

"I am formally delivering this notice to you that Zuri bat-Lucifer is hereby expelled from Celestial Academy effective immediately," Michael said.

"Well, she's gone underground anyway. I don't think she'll be a problem," Samael said coolly.

Michael leaned over him and I could hear the sneer in his tone. "She is a problematic child; one you should not underestimate. And in her father's absence, I would not be surprised to find her trying to claim what is yours."

"I'm going to punch him in his stupid fucking face," I snarled.

"Taking on an Archangel is unwise," Azrael commented.

"I was talking about Samael," I answered through gritted teeth.

"Taking him on is a bad idea, too," Damien added.

"It's not like I have a choice since this is my domain, not his. And yeah, I'll kick his ass if I have to."

It was time to come home for real this time. Enough pretending I wasn't just the warrior Dad trained me to be. My world was on the brink of falling apart and I was going to hold it together even if it killed me.

"I need to make one last trip to the earthly plane and then I'm back for good. We're going after Samael and I'm going to find my dad."

Azrael pointed to the little hutch in the corner of the kitchen. "Use that portal. It's quicker and safer."

I eyed Damien. "Have you always had a private portal in your kitchen?"

"Maybe." He smiled weakly. "A guy's gotta have some secrets."

I pressed my hand to the bottom cabinet and it slid aside with a slick hiss to reveal a portal. It wasn't like any I'd seen around Hell before.

"You need to think about where you want to be and it will take you there, even if the closest regular portal is miles away," Azrael explained.

Death Santa. My best friend's dad was Death Santa, using his own personal portal to pop into people's houses and reap their souls. *Creepy*. As I put my hand into the swirling vortex and thought of Delilah's place, I could almost feel Miry beside me. I shivered and pushed the feeling away. There was very little chance I'd see her where I was going.

5

MIRYAM

"Here? Why would your locating power bring us here?" I cocked my head to the side and studied the surprisingly quiet-for-once exterior of Renegade Reggie's bar. "Zuri wouldn't be here unless …" I let the thought die before it could fully form. Zuri with Delilah created all sorts of images in my head and none of them were good. I had saw how the demon bartender looked at her. You'd have to be blind not to notice. They may be exes, but I seriously doubted it was by choice. At least not Delilah's. I'd bet my wings that any break up was 100% on Zuri and her so-called "ridiculously high standards." I don't know how high her standards were to begin with if she was messing around with a demon, but maybe non-serious relationships equaled lesser standards to her. Maybe long haul stuff came with more strings and an even higher bar.

"I don't know why it led us here." Ant stuffed his hands in his pockets as if the glow from his saint power would bring all sorts of demons down on us for trespassing in their domain or whatever. "We wanted to find Zuri, so we found Zuri."

"*We* didn't want to find Zuri. You both did." I glanced at Ant and CeCe, trying their hardest to look all innocent and, well, saint like. "And what's up with the you-really-need-to-talk-to-Zuri stuff anyway? Are you two, like, conspiring against me or something?"

"Conspiring?" Ant's voice rose an octave. "Who says we're conspiring against anyone?"

"We just think you owe it to yourself to at least talk to her one more time," CeCe added. It did nothing to stop me from thinking that they were totally ganging up against me. "You holding a grudge is weird, M. It's not like you. Damien says—"

"I don't care what Damien says!" I snapped. "Anyone who has been friends with Zuri since they were in little hellfire and brimstone diapers is not someone that I want to take advice from." I crossed my arms over my chest. "But since we're already here, we might as well get this over with."

"That's the spirit." CeCe led the way to the back of the bar where a flight of stairs led to what I assumed was Delilah's apartment. Again, it didn't instill me with confidence that I wasn't about to walk into a trap. They planned this and "Damien says" probably helped. Zuri might be in on it too for all I know. It seemed like a really elaborate set up to get us to talk to each other.

Zuri. The memory of Zuri kissing me popped into my head, her hands so hot that their warmth burned through my purple lacy bra. It had felt like there was nothing at all between us. That particular memory liked doing that. Always showing up when I didn't want it to.

"You okay, Mir?" CeCe's voice sounded a million miles away. "Whatcha thinking about?"

I blinked, hard, struggling to scatter the memory of Zuri's skin against mine, her lips just as warm as her hands. "Nothing. Let's go."

I led the way up the stairs to Delilah's apartment. The closer we got, the music became louder with heavy bass. Like, really really loud. Drown out other sounds and bust out your windows loud. I jumped back when a non-music thump practically cracked the wall right next to door. *Thump. Bang. Thump. Bang.* What was going on in there?

"Maybe they're fighting?" Ant guessed. "Zuri loves a good fist fight."

"When is a fist fight ever good?" I tested the doorknob, but it was locked. *Thump. Bang. Thump. Bang.* "No good. It's locked."

"Lemme try." CeCe stepped in front of me and waved her hand over the keyhole. "Every lock has a frequency," she explained. "If you find it, you can disable it." She hummed softly for a few seconds before grinning. "Got it!"

"I didn't know you could pick locks," Ant said as the dead bolt disengaged with a loud click.

"There's a lot of things you don't know about me." CeCe shrugged and stepped aside. "Miry, you go first."

If we were walking into the middle of a fight, I didn't think just opening the door all 'hi, honey, I'm home' was smart. In spite of that I didn't have any other plan right now. Maybe the element of surprise would break up whatever was going on inside the apartment and we'd be ... well, I don't know what we'd be, but hopefully not in the middle of a fist fight.

I flung the door open and charged inside. Though instead of smacking into the wall like I had expected the door to do, it hit something solid and person shaped with a sickening thud.

"What the fuck, kid!" Delilah yelped, blood dripping from an already swollen, broken nose. "Learn to knock, will ya?"

"Uh, I can ... I can heal you." I tripped over my own feet to get to her, my hands outstretched and already glowing as I sent my angel healing through them to fix her broken nose. "Sorry, I—" I stopped, mouth dropping open when I realized she wasn't wearing any clothes. Well, not much clothing anyways. Her shirt and bra were completely off and I wouldn't exactly call the skimpy underwear she had on 'clothes.' What's worse, was I had found Zuri alright. She was pressed up against the wall with her clothes half off as well.

My eyes widened, tears threatening to spill and make me look as weak and useless as everyone claimed I was. Before that could happen, I swiveled toward the open door and ran before anyone could stop me.

6

ZURI

I shoved Delilah out of the way and grabbed my pants and shirt. If Miry had come here looking for me then it was a good bet Glasses had helped her. No way D would have narked on me to his girlfriend. As I stepped out of the apartment, I spotted Glasses and D's girlfriend standing dumbstruck at the bottom of the stairs.

"Where'd she go?" I demanded.

They pointed around the corner and with a huff, I followed the outside of the building and shouldered the door open. Miry stood behind the bar gaping at the collection of liquor bottles.

"Bit early, isn't it?" I tried to break the tension.

"Not really," she muttered and grabbed a bottle of vodka and a glass.

"Glasses track me here?"

She rolled her eyes at me. "No, CeCe. Duh, yes Ant did."

"Why? You got me kicked out."

"They think we should talk," she answered waving the bottle of booze toward the door.

I crossed my arms over my chest. "Fine, let's talk."

She slammed the glass down on the bar. "You're the one who's a murderer. How do you explain that?"

"Miry, I didn't mean to kill him." I slid onto the bar stool opposite her and studied my nails. "I know he mattered to you, but all I could see is how he hurt and used you. That just pisses me off so much and I don't know, the lariat just wrapped around him."

"So you say sorry by screwing your ex-girl-friend?" She snapped.

"I can screw whoever I fucking want. We messed around once, Miry. I told you to get your shit together. Clearly you haven't done that and you decided it was better to just cut me out of your life. Fine, I've got enough to deal with. Hell is a shit show and my dad is missing." My gaze narrowed at her as she fiddled with the top of the bottle. "You wouldn't happen to know anything about that?"

"I don't know anything about your stupid dad," she snapped, finally freeing the top and pouring the clear liquid into the glass.

"Look, I don't know what you came here expecting to find, but I don't know what else you want from me. Why don't you just go back to pretending you're perfect and shit doesn't touch you if that's gonna make you feel better."

"Because it won't. Nothing is going to make this feel better," she blurted, slamming the glass down hard enough against the bar to shatter.

Shards of glass tinkled to the floor on either side of the bar. How she managed to avoid hitting me with any of it was a miracle. I rolled my eyes and slid off the stool, traipsing to the back corner of the bar for the broom and dustpan. I nudged Miry aside as I bent to scoop it up so she didn't hurt herself. Even with how she'd been ghosting me and treating me like a criminal, I still didn't want her to get hurt.

"Do you like her better than me?" Her question came out soft, fearful. She sounded like the old Miry.

"Who? Delilah? She gave me a place to crash up here and I guess some old feelings resurfaced, or at least an attraction did," I admitted, brushing the glass into the trash bin underneath the bar.

"She's a demon," Miry continued.

I whirled to face her. "Careful about where you throw stones, Miry. At least I knew my lover was playing with fire."

Tears welled in her eyes and for a moment, I wanted to pull her to me and tell her it was all going to be fine. Despite that, she'd made this about fucking Saint Boy first. I didn't have to stand here and be treated like shit just because she was grieving. It wasn't a license to be a bitch.

"It wasn't his fault and you know it. Deep down he was a good person."

"Maybe he was, but I never saw it. And I'm not going to debate this with you. I said my truth. I didn't mean to kill him. I'm sorry you feel like your life is falling apart, but you're not the only one struggling."

"You should have aimed for Lilith."

"It wasn't my damn relic in the first place!" I shouted. "You ever think of that? I wasn't meant to wield it any more than you were. So, take some of the blame yourself. Because you were in on the whole plan. You brought them to campus remember."

"I was trying to save him."

I stepped closer until we were toe to toe. "Not everyone can be saved. That's just how the world works, Miry."

Those tears in her eyes still refused to fall and I had to give her some credit for keeping the waterworks under control. Though being this close to her, I couldn't avoid the curve of her lips or the way her breasts strained against the fabric of her uniform top.

If she wanted to cut ties, fine. I had more important things to do. Only the proximity was making it really hard not to want to kiss her. Before I could even think about doing anything, she grabbed my face and kissed me. I blinked and pinched my arm to make sure this wasn't some fantasy playing out in my head.

Nope. definitely real.

I pushed her against the back edge of the bar and tugged the hem of her shirt from out of her skirt. Her kisses came faster and more fevered as I cupped her breast over her bra. She bucked her hips against mine, but I wasn't going to give her the satisfaction of getting me off. Not this time. I squeezed her breast hard, making her squeal and stepped back.

"Guess now you know what you're missing. Whatever game you're playing Miry, I'm out. I'm either in your life or I'm not. And like I said, I've got too much other shit I have to deal with, because my world is literally falling down around me. Go back to school with your friends. Try not to get murdered by your psycho dad. But I don't have the time or the energy to worry about whether or not what I do is going to upset you."

She tucked her shirt back in and glared at me. "What could you possibly have to do that's so important?"

"My home is falling apart without my Dad. And that means I have to put it back together, because that's what's expected of me. It sucks, and I hate it, but I accepted that responsibility and now I have to own it."

I strode out of the bar and back to Delilah's apartment. She'd already tossed my stuff out on the ground. At least she had the decency to pack it up. Or maybe the blush on Glasses' cheeks revealed he'd done it.

"Did you talk?" He asked.

"Yeah. I think we've said everything we had to say. I don't know what she's up to or how long she's going to be acting this way, but do me a favor. Keep her away from me."

7

MIRYAM

I checked my phone for like the thousandth time in two days. Sure, Zuri seemed pretty solid about for-real not wanting to talk to me, but that might have just been for show. At least that's what I keep telling myself. I'd been telling myself a lot of stuff the last couple of days. Mostly about how much of a moron I was. I drove away the first real friend I ever had by being ... difficult. Zuri was the first friend to see deep down into the real me and not even flinch at the broken, messed up core hiding behind the peppy outer wall. She accepted me. She *liked* me. Maybe even liked me-liked me. In spite of all that I threw it away.

"Checking your phone will not make it ring,

Miryam," Uncle Raphael said without looking up from his paperwork. Instead of homework (boring) or moping (trying to do less of that), I started helping Uncle Raphael in the clinic after class. If I wanted to be a healer, I needed to learn from the best. Besides, he was the best healer around.

I stuffed my phone into my backpack. "I, like, totally don't know what you're talking about. I was just checking the time, not if anyone called."

"The connection runs both ways, you know," he said, eyes still trained on the work spread out across his desk. "You could always call her."

"I never talk to Mom during school term," I played dumb. "Why would I start now?"

Uncle Raphael looked up, his blue eyes seeing more than I ever thought possible with one glance. Why did I decide to hang out with the perceptive Uncle? I should have helped Uncle Gabriel organize his library or helped Uncle Uriel with whatever he did when there wasn't self-defense class. "You know very well who I meant, Miryam, and it is most definitely not your mother. Call her."

"I, uh, lost her number," I lied. "Besides, she's going through some family stuff and doesn't want to be bothered." I tilted my head to the side, studying him the same way he studied me. "How much do you know about Lucifer's disappearance? You have his cell phone number, right? Have you tried calling? Has he picked up?"

"My line to Lucifer is purely for emergencies only," Uncle Raphael said.

"Since when is Hell falling apart not an emergency?" I asked. "Or a missing former Archangel turned Fallen?"

"Your father says the rumors of discord in Hell are completely unfounded."

I almost laughed, but stopped myself at the last minute. "And you believe him?"

"Your father is my general and the closest thing to a brother I have," Uncle Raphael said firmly. "It is my duty to believe him."

"The War in Heaven has been over for eons, Uncle Raphael," I reminded him, doing my best not to roll my eyes since he was older than me and totally sincere about the whole following Dad's orders thing. "You don't have to listen to Dad like that anymore."

"Yes. I do." His hand resting on top of the desk balled into a fist. "Going against Michael would mean ..." He shook his head, looking like how Uncle Uriel did when he came out of a PTSD haze. "Never mind that. I do not need to burden you with any of my problems. As you said, the war is long in the past. It shall stay there."

"If you say so." I expected that flashback stuff from Uncle Uriel, but not Uncle Raphael. "I think I'm going to hang with my dad for a bit." *Maybe see what he knows about Lucifer's disappearance since you're acting all weird about it*, I added in my head. I jumped up from the desk and forced my biggest, brightest smile. "Byee!"

<hr>

"Dad? Dad, you here?" I pushed his office door open and poked my head inside. Empty. Awesome. That meant I had some quality snooping time before he probably smited me for looking around his stuff in the first place.

Try not to get yourself murdered by your psycho dad popped in my head.

"Sorry, Z, can't guarantee that," I murmured before opening all of Dad's desk drawers at once. I wasn't quite sure what I was looking for to prove Dad knew more about Lucifer's disappearance than he let on, but I'd know it when I found it.

"Bingo." My hands brushed against Dad's

movement tracking ledger books. I ignored the one with my name on it, tossed Uncle Raphael and Uncle Gabriel's ones on top of mine, and opened Uncle Uriel's book. I wanted to make sure he wasn't still making hunting trips to Fallen hang outs. I scanned the ledger, tracking his movements. He stuck pretty close to campus. The only time he left his classroom was to go to some place called "the chapel." We had a chapel on campus?

"Lame."

I tossed Uncle Uriel's book on top of the pile and pulled out Dad's ledger. He could make this way easier on me if he just had one that said "Lucifer" on it.

Dad's book showed the same sort of movements as Uncle Uriel. Not leaving his office much and spending way too much time in the chapel. Though that alone appeared suspicious. For being an archangel and all, Dad wasn't all that religious. I mean, he served God, but never had the need to go to church. He always told me church was an institution, not a requirement. He was spiritual, not religious ... So why was he suddenly spending so much time in the chapel on campus that I didn't know existed until now? I know every inch of this campus and Dad's never shown me a chapel in the five years I've been here. What was up with that?

Next, I found the ledger book marked 'Samael'—that weird Fallen general guy that gave off child molester vibes. (Although to be fair, so did Uncle Uriel.) Samael hung around Hell except when ... wait a second. I squinted at the tiny, scrawling magical handwriting on the ledger in case I was reading it wrong. Michael was written in spidery writing next to Samael's name in Lucifer's throne room—in Hell. Dad had been making secret visits to Hell. I mean, I always hoped he would go to Hell, but I meant it figuratively, not literally.

What game was he playing? Hanging with Samael in Hell? Spending way too much time in some place called the chapel? Something was up here. Something bigger than Lucifer going missing. I just needed to figure out what that something was.

I dug deeper in Dad's desk drawers until I finally found a ledger labeled 'Lucifer.' I grinned. "Bingo." My excitement died after I flipped through a few pages. Oh, no. Oh, no, no, no, no. This was way worse than I thought. Zuri's dad wasn't just missing. He was stuck in limbo.

8

ZURI

I paced the kitchen at Damien's place. At least he and his dad had the courtesy not to ask me how my trip to Earth had gone. I was just so damn confused by everything Miry did. She pushed me away and then acted like she wanted me. I hated games like that. You either want something or you don't.

"Not that I don't love having my best friend crash with me and everything, but are you actually going to do something or just wear a rut in the floor?" Damien commented from the table.

"I'm thinking," I muttered.

"Z, you've been thinking for the last hour. Which isn't like you. Usually, you're already on it with a plan, kicking ass."

I spun to face him. "I've never had to fight for my fucking home before, D. Maybe I don't want to rush things. Especially if we know Michael and Samael are all buddy-buddy."

He held his hands up in surrender. "Okay, I get it. But, really, do you have any idea what you're going to do?"

I twisted the bracelet around my wrist, wondering what my mother would suggest I do in this situation. I'd never know since we'd never met. Still I'd like to think she'd want her daughter to take charge, even if it meant running head-first into danger. "I'm going to go to Dad's office and just … kick Samael out of the boardroom."

"And if he refuses to leave?" He countered.

"I drag him out by his wings if I have to."

"I wouldn't suggest you face Samael alone," Azrael said, stepping into the room from the front hall. He looked tired, like he'd been claiming more souls than usual.

"I don't exactly have a lot of back-up. And I can't put you two at risk." I replied.

He waved off my concern. "Your father is my oldest friend. In his absence, it is my duty to protect you. Now, come along. The more time we spend going back and forth, the more chance there is that Samael will actually do something we can't undo."

***

I'D NEVER FELT nervous walking into the board-room before. Sure, it was meant to be intimidating to the outside observer. We were in Hell after all. Despite that, I'd always known it was a safe place for me. Now, it sent shivers down my spine and I hated that feeling. It wasn't one I was accustomed to.

"What do we do if Michael's there?" I blurted as we reached the closed set of double doors.

Azrael's answer came with the sharp metallic sound of his scythe dropping into his hand. "We fight."

"I've fought an Archangel before. I nearly died," I reminded him.

"That's why you have me," he said, nudging me forward.

Swallowing the lump in my throat, I flung the doors inward. Samael sat alone in my father's seat at the head of the table. I marched in and stopped when I was less than a foot away from him. Just close enough to get in his personal space, but far enough away I could dodge an attack if it came at me.

"Zuri, there you are. I have been looking for you since we returned from that awful business in Michael's domain."

"Cut the bullshit. I know you've been conspiring with Michael. And you have no right to sit in that chair."

"Conspiring? I'm not sure what you mean."

"I know you were meeting with Michael here in Hell," I snapped, inching forward.

"He was here, yes. To ensure that the Lilith situation had been handled in your father's absence and to communicate the unfortunate news that you were no longer welcome at his school. I trust that last bit of news reached you?"

"Yeah, I got the message."

"Samael, are you absolutely certain you don't know anything about Lucifer's whereabouts?" Azrael spoke up. I glanced his way to see him set his scythe on the table. It wasn't exactly a de-escalation of the situation. More of a promise that things would get very reap-y if Samael didn't play nice.

Samael shook his head, still not getting out of the chair. He put on what I guess he thought was a concerned expression and said, "Believe me, I wish I knew. It isn't like Lucifer to disappear and leave his people leaderless."

"They're not leaderless. They have me," I growled. Without intending it, my wings sprouted from between my shoulder blades. Their tips brushed the chairs beside me, sending them sailing backwards on their wheels. "He made it very clear that I am the next in line. Not you."

"Zuri, you may legally be an adult by mortal standards, but you are barely out of infancy in the grand scheme of things. You can't honestly believe your father wanted you to lead now."

His patronizing tone makes my molars ache. My hands balled into fists and I wanted to punch him in the face. Except violence just to sate my temper wasn't going to prove the point I was trying to make. A good leader didn't jump to rash actions just because her honor was insulted. A smart leader played the long game.

So, I forced a smile and said, "You know, you're right. I must have misunderstood what he wanted me to do. I'm just worried about my dad. I mean, maybe it would help if you told me what you're doing to help locate him?"

"I'm doing everything in my power to locate him," Samael answered.

"Yeah, but what exactly does that mean? You look like you're just sitting here twiddling your thumbs. Wouldn't his second-in-command be out actually searching the earthly plane for him?"

"What makes you believe he's on Earth?"

I gestured around us. "Well, obviously he's not here and he sure as shit isn't in Heaven. Where else could he be?"

"That's not …." Samael stopped himself. Clearly whatever he was about to say was something he didn't want me to know.

"I'm sure that Samael is doing what he can," Azrael said from behind me. "Why don't we let him get back to it then, Zuri?"

My wings retracted and I allowed Azrael to lead me from the room. I managed to keep my mouth shut until we were back to his house. Damien sat where we left him, staring at something on his phone.

"Samael knows something and he's not saying it," I railed.

"I know," Azrael answered.

"Where else could he be?" I whirled on the angel.

"Limbo," he replied.

I stared at him. I'd heard humans talk about

the state between life and death as "limbo," but I didn't know it was an actual place. "Sorry, what?"

"Eons back, not long after the War was over, God created Limbo. A sort of weigh station for souls who couldn't be immediately classified as destined for Heaven or Hell. It's neutral territory for Angels and Fallen. We can all exist there. If your father is trapped there, it isn't a good sign."

"It would mean that Samael is actually conspiring with that fucking prick, Michael."

Before Azrael could say anything, my phone buzzed in my pocket. At the table, Damien looked up. "You should probably answer that."

I pulled out my phone to see Miry's name flash on the screen along with the stupid picture she'd taken of herself. "Not interested."

"For fucks sake, Z, just answer your damn phone."

With a huff, I swiped my finger to accept the call. "I thought I told you to leave me alone."

"Zuri, I need to tell you something. It's about your dad. I know …" The line went garbled.

"What do you think you're doing in here?" I heard Michael's voice demand over the line.

"Nothing. I was just …"

If she finished the sentence I would never know, because the line went dead.

My chest felt tight as anger bubbled up inside me. "I'm borrowing your portal," I announced and pushed the shelving aside.

"Where are you going?" Azrael's voice carried only the barest hint of disapproval.

"To get some answers."

9

MIRYAM

"What are you doing here?" Dad repeated, eyes all squinty and suspicious. "This is my office. My personal sanctum. I thought I told you that you were only allowed in here if you were summoned. There is no other reason for you to darken my door, Miryam. Ever."

I cringed, covering my head on instinct in case his little knick-knacks and awards started flying. The Employee of the Year plaques hurt. I didn't believe he had actually earned them either. There was no way Heaven gave an 'Employee of the Year' award since, like, the beginning of time. Dad totally made that up to make himself feel more important and feed his—what I was coming to realize—very fragile ego.

"Nothing." I peeked out from behind my duck-and-cover arms. "I was just, uh, totally looking for something I left behind the last time I was in your office."

"Which is?"

"Um, my school planner?" It came out as a question. "You know, the calendar thingy where I write all my assignments down? I, uh, need that. Like, right now. For class."

"Go request another from Gabriel." Dad waved a hand in a 'begone peasant' way. "I have no time for your presence today, Miryam."

"You never have time for my presence!" I slammed my hands over my mouth when I realized I'd said that out loud instead of in my head. "Sorry. I'm sorry. I didn't mean to say that. What I meant was—"

"I don't care what you meant; I care that you leave me in peace." Dad sat down behind his massive desk, fixing me with what I always called his death glare even before I knew he had actually tried to kill me at that scary pool party two years ago. I shuddered at the memory. Leave it to Dad to make a murder attempt look like an accident.

"Why are you still here?" Dad demanded. "I told you to leave."

"And I told you to treat me like an actual

human being for once instead of something you've grown bored with and just discard!" I clamped my hands over my mouth again. "Sorry. I didn't mean …" I stopped, lowered my hands, and straightened out of my duck and cover position. I imagined I was Zuri, kicking ass and taking names. She wouldn't let anyone speak to her like this—especially a parent. She would tell them to stick it where the sun don't shine and then punch them in the face for good measure. I don't know about the face punching part, but I could totally stand up to Dad. I could be strong like Zuri. I just needed to believe I could.

"No. No, I take that back," I said. "I'm not sorry. I'm not sorry I snooped around in your stuff. I'm not sorry I asked to be treated with a teeny tiny bit of respect. I'm a person, Dad, not an object. Yeah, maybe I'm not the good little soldier you wanted or expected, but I'm an awesome healer. Even Uncle Raphael says so. I have skills. I'm worth something. You might not think so, but I am. I am, Dad. Really I am."

He crossed his arms over his chest. "Are you quite done?"

I shook my head. "Not even close. You know what? I don't care if you don't love me. I'm tired of chasing after something I can never have.

There are plenty of people who love me and think I'm worthy just because I'm me."

"Such as your dead boyfriend and Lucifer's Fallen spawn?"

I faltered for a minute. That was a low blow using Chris and Zuri in the same sentence. I took a deep breath and raised my chin, trying to be a fighter. Trying to be the sort of girl Zuri *would* love. The kind of girl I wanted to be too.

"Yeah," I said, voice steady. "What's it to you?"

Dad opened one of his desk drawers and pulled out a single sheet of paper. He scribbled something on the bottom and slid it across his desk toward me. "This is what it is to me, Miryam. Enjoy your life ... what is left of it."

I picked up the paper and looked down at it. It was an expulsion letter. Dad was kicking me out of school. Effective immediately.

10

ZURI

I held my breath stepping through the portal back to Earth. I hoped it would actually put me where I needed to be. I could still hear Miry's muffled words ringing in my ears. I knew she could defend herself, but her father was a different level altogether. He'd had no qualms about trying to murder her, because she disappointed him or whatever. I was not going to let him hurt her now just because she was somewhere she wasn't supposed to be.

The gates of the school loomed as I stepped out of the portal. The grass felt hard beneath my feet as I sucked air into my burning lungs. Whatever Azrael's special portal was made from, it made even me woozy. I stood still long enough to regain my equilibrium before I marched toward the gates. *Would they let me in now that I'd been expelled?* I was willing to risk whatever it took to find out. Reaching out my hands I wrapped my fingers around the nearest bars and pulled. Electrical jolts danced up my arms and down my spine, sending me staggering backward.

"Fuck," I spat and rubbed my singed fingers on my pants. It didn't help much, but it did soothe my ego. The direct approach wasn't going to cut it, but maybe an aerial one would.

I jogged back a few more paces and let my wings unfurl to their full length. I gave them a flap and kicked off the ground. Higher and higher I went until my feet were a good six feet above the top spires of the gate. I wasn't going to be fooled twice. I approached slowly and kept my hands out in front of me, like I was trying to navigate blindly in the dark. I wouldn't put it past Michael to have some sort of defense to keep out those with wings too.

I was just about even with the top spire when I felt a tangible force collide with my chest, sending me spiraling down to the ground. I landed with a painful 'oomph' and rolled to a stop. I lay still for a minute, letting my senses assess whether anything was seriously injured or not. Everything still seemed to work after a few gentle probes and I scrambled back on to my feet.

"Hey!" A perky voice called from the other side of the gate.

I straightened to see D's girlfriend standing there, her thick black-framed glasses making her eyes look twice as big. What he saw in her, I couldn't fathom. Yet again, I'm sure people couldn't understand what I saw in Miry, either.

"CeCe, what are you doing here?" It was the first time I had ever spoken her name out loud.

"Damien called. He said you needed back onto the grounds. I thought maybe I could help."

I blinked at her. She didn't know me. I hadn't been nice to her in the time we had inhabited the same space and yet she was willing to risk so much to let me in. Perhaps I'd underestimated Miry's friends, discounted them all as being too goodie-goodie. "Thanks."

She flexed her hands. "Stand back. It could get a little um ... loud."

I took a couple of steps back and watched as she started to hum some tune I'd never heard before. She grasped the bars in the center of the gate and the humming grew louder. I could hear a high-pitched keening as the metal bent to her will and swung open.

"Hurry," she mouthed, still trying to keep the humming going.

I darted in and as soon as my feet touched the ground on the other side, I exhaled a sigh of relief. The pressure and the barrier that had kept me out was gone.

"I need to find Miry," I said, grabbing CeCe by the arm and dragging her along with me.

"I don't know where she is," she replied.

"She was in Michael's office when I was talking to her," I explained and headed in that direction.

CeCe dug her heels in and stopped my forward momentum. "I'm not going into his office. Are you crazy?'

I whirled on her. "Miry may be in trouble. I'm not going to let him hurt her. Not anymore."

Before CeCe could respond I heard a door slam up ahead. I caught sight of the perky tits and rosy cheeks of one Miryam bat-Michael. I didn't think. I just raced forward, pinning her to the nearest wall and kissed her hard on the lips.

She wrapped her arms around my shoulders and held me tight. When I finally came up for air, her cheeks burned a new shade of red and her chest heaved for air.

"Not that that wasn't fun, but we need to go," she rasped.

"CeCe doesn't care," I replied.

"Dad expelled me. And I don't know how long I have to get off the grounds before smiting happens," she explained. She was much calmer than I would have expected given the situation.

I took her hand and led her back the way I'd come, leaving CeCe behind. The wards were meant to keep the wrong sort of people out. I had to assume they were very happy to let them out. I stopped just short of the twisted gates. I could see them slowly bending back into formation. I didn't want to find out what happened when they finally righted themselves.

"My things," Miry whined as I dragged her behind me.

"We'll get you new things," I answered and shoved her past the open gate. I hopped over the threshold of the gate just as the bars unbent. They snapped to attention and a low thrum made my eardrums ache.

We weren't getting back in there any time soon. Something told me that even if CeCe had wanted to let us back in, Michael was aware of what she'd been doing. Which begged the question of why he would let me in. Unless he really just wanted Miry out of his precious sanctum.

"Where are we going now?" Miry's brave face was slipping.

"Hell," I said and squeezed her hand tight. "I've got you."

I didn't give her a chance to speak as I felt Azrael's portal calling to me, guiding me back home.

THE KITCHEN WAS CONSPICUOUSLY empty when we arrived. Miry wobbled on her feet as the cabinet hissed shut behind us. She reached for a chair and slumped over.

"He kicked me out, Zuri. He just took away my home."

I knew I should say something comforting, but the only words that found their way out of my mouth were, "Does that really surprise you? Your dad is a first-class douchebag."

"I know it never felt like home to you, but for all the bad stuff, it made me who I am. It helped me figure out who I wanted to be."

I sat beside her and took her hands in both of mine. "You'll get it back."

She sniffled. "You're not mad at me anymore?"

I smiled. "You're not mad at me either."

Her lower lip quivered. "I missed you. I realized, what was the point of being mad at the world when I could still have my best friend. Besides, no one ever kissed me like that before."

The blush that crept into her cheeks made me smile bigger. I knew I wasn't the best lover, but the fact she was giving me that kind of credit was a nice ego boost. "That means a lot."

"So, um, does that mean you want to do it more? The kissing I mean. I don't think I could handle being mad at you all the time." She leaned closer like she didn't want anyone to overhear. "I don't think I'd be good at angry sex."

"You never know until you try it," I quipped. "But I don't want to be mad at you either." I leaned over and kissed her on the lips again. "And yes, we can definitely do more of that."

"Get a room, horndog," Damien said from the doorway.

I flipped him off and slid an arm around Miry's shoulders. "Come on, we are going back to my place."

As we reached the door, I looked over my shoulder and said, "Thanks for asking CeCe for help. I couldn't have gotten in without her."

Damien pressed his hand to his chest and made a grasping motion for the wall. "Careful, you don't want the walls to fall down around here. Zuri bat-Lucifer complimenting a Saint and actually using their name."

I led Miry back to my place. I almost regretted not borrowing Damien's Reaper cloak as we made the short journey. Samael was still watching me, which meant Michael was, too. We arrived back home and I couldn't shake the feeling that something much older than the demons that lived nearby was keeping a close eye on us.

"Your Dad is in Limbo," Miry said once the door was bolted behind us.

"I know. Azrael explained what it is."

"I don't know how he got there or how we get there either," she sighed.

"I have some idea. Samael, my dad's second-in-command is conspiring with your father. I think he's trying to plot a coup. Why Michael gives two shits about who rules Hell is beyond me?"

"I found some other things in his desk when I was snooping. There's some place on campus called the chapel. I've never seen a chapel and believe me, I've been all over every inch of the grounds. Whatever he's hiding, whatever he's planning, it's going down there."

The thought of Michael plotting in earnest made my skin crawl. "What would happen if the Archangels all had their relics together?"

"I um ... I don't know. Probably nothing good. But they don't have them."

"Gabriel had his scroll when we fought Lilith. He bound her with it. And Uriel has his lariat back and I have no doubt your dad has his sword hidden away somewhere. With the Emblem gone, my dad is defenseless."

"So, what do we do?"

"We go to Limbo and save my father. Somehow, we get Michael's sword away from him. Something tells me if they are planning something big, that's going to be the centerpiece."

"But we can't get back on campus. Not without risking CeCe and Ant."

"Are you absolutely sure he keeps the sword on campus?"

"He keeps it hanging behind his desk, remember?"

"After you manifested it when we fought Beelzebub, is that where you put it back?"

Miry's face scrunched up in thought. "Well,

no. I didn't actually put it back. Dad took it. You think that's a fake in his office?"

I wasn't the only one capable of making a forgery. Michael was just self-centered enough to want to remind people of his power without risking it falling into the wrong hands. "If it is a fake, where would he keep the real one?"

Color drained from Miry's face. "Heaven. He'd keep it in Heaven."

Well, shit.

11

MIRYAM

I tugged at my hair, twirling it around my index finger. What happened to Fallen if they tried to enter Heaven was something Dad definitely made sure to include in the curriculum. God liked to flaunt power. Making sure everyone knew first a Fallen Angel's wings burned to a crisp followed by the rest of them if they even made it through the pearly gates, was definitely flaunting power.

"Um, maybe the whole burning alive thing is more like a warning than an actual thing." I tried to look on the bright side. "You know, like a beware of dog sign or no trespassing."

Zuri toyed with the red string bracelet on her wrist. "Your dad may be an asshole, but he's not stupid. We've spoiled all his narcissistic plans this year. What's stopping us from taking down his army or whatever he's planning in that secret chapel of his?"

I chewed my lower lip. "Dad does love a good battle, but do you really think he's building an army? I mean, *why*? What's the point?"

Zuri blinked, looking at me like I was, well, me—slow to catch on and not all that bright. "He got an army together during the first War in Heaven to face off against my dad. What's stopping him from planning a second round? There's no glory in running a school. There is in commanding an army and winning a war."

I wanted to hang my head over the side of a bed to think. Except there weren't any around and I'd fall if I tried that maneuver on a stool. I kicked my feet instead. I watched my shoes go back and forth, hoping the rhythm would help me concentrate. It didn't, but maybe thinking out loud would. "So say my dad kidnapped your dad—"

"I don't say it, I know it," Zuri interrupted. "Dad would never just disappear like this. He definitely wouldn't leave Samael in charge either." She twisted the bracelet on her wrist again. "If your dad was hoping I would think everything was business as usual down here, he did a terrible job of it."

I gasped, eyes going wide. "What if it wasn't part of his original plan?"

Zuri frowned. "This isn't going to surprise you, but I don't follow where you're going with that."

I hopped off the stool and paced around Zuri's kitchen, waving my hands as I talked. That *definitely* helped me think out loud. "So Dad likes armies. Big deal. Maybe he was into that saber-rattling thing. Like where he wants to look totally powerful to your dad and whoever else, but never plans to do anything about it. What if someone in his army—my bet is on Uncle Uriel—went rogue and kidnapped your dad? They'd have to hide him away somewhere until they figured out what to do with him and all that. I mean, once you get in deep enough, you can't just let someone go and be like 'see ya,' you know?"

"No, I don't know. I've never kidnapped anyone before," Zuri quipped.

I crinkled my nose. "Oh ha ha. Just roll with it, k? So Dad has an unexpected prisoner. What's the worst thing he could do to him? Like, what would prove once and for all who the real winner of the war is? Cause Dad is nothing if not predictable.

He wants to win and doesn't care how as long as the result is the same, you know?" I grinned, bouncing on my heels. "So what's the worst thing he could do to a prisoner? Cause that's what's totally going to happen."

"Cut off Dad's wings," Zuri whispered, her hands shaking and her face going a weird grayish chalky color. "He'll lose his divinity and just be ... normal. It's the worst punishment for anyone—Angel or Fallen. I remember Dad said it's what Michael had wanted to do from the start before God intervened and cast the Fallen out instead." She shivered. "I think I'm going to be sick."

"It's okay." I scurried over and patted Z's back while she took deep gulps of air to calm the urge to spew chunks. "We'll stop him. I won't let anyone—not even my dad—hurt your dad. We'll definitely save him, because that's what we do, Z. Apocalypse? Demon kidnappings? PTSD Archangels? We've made it through all that and we can make it through this too. You got me, but I got you too." I swiped a finger across my heart. "Promise."

Zuri gave a shaky laugh. "How am I supposed to survive Heaven to get to Limbo?"

"I don't know," I admitted. "But we'll figure it out together."

12

ZURI

I had no idea how we were going to get into Heaven, let alone do it without me turning into human barbecue. Despite Miry's affirmation that we would figure it out together, by the next morning, Miry still had not come up with anything.

"I know you're worried," she said from beside me on the bed.

Even though we were kind of together, I'd insisted on sleeping above the covers. I told Miry it was because we should take things slow. In reality I didn't trust myself to not push her to go further than she was ready to just to make myself feel better.

"I'm terrified, Miry," I confided.

She made a disbelieving face and said, "Zuri bat-Lucifer doesn't get terrified."

"Yes … Yes, I do. I almost died once this year and that's bad." I touched my stomach reflexively. "The thought of burning to death is worse."

"I told you I won't let that happen," she answered.

"It's a pretty promise, but you can't be sure it will work."

"Yeah, but we all thought Archangels couldn't go to Hell either and we know that's not true."

I sat up and rested my head in my hands. "There has to be another way to get to Limbo. If there's access from Heaven, then there has to be one here, too."

"Duh, of course there's got to be one here, too," she agreed and sat up to wrap her arms around my shoulders. "You're brilliant. I mean, we know that I can survive coming down here so maybe getting to Limbo from here won't do any-thing bad to you."

"We don't know where to look," I sighed. I couldn't explain why, but I couldn't shake the feeling we'd already been defeated. I was still a fighter, but the longer my dad was missing and the more we dug into whatever Michael was planning, my hope dwindled further.

"You are not giving up on me," Miry said, jolting me out of my mental spiral.

"I didn't say I was." At least I didn't think I did.

"We know someone who would know where to look. He seems pretty cool and willing to help," she said.

"I don't think—" I started, but she cut me off.

"Azrael."

How had I been so stupid? Of course, the Angel of Death would know how to access Limbo from this side of the veil. He probably had to go there often when souls didn't have a direct destination. I rubbed my face and straightened up. No more letting doubt control me. I would rescue my dad and stop the mad Archangel from whatever insanity he had planned.

"Let's go," I said and slid off the bed.

"Um, shouldn't we … eat or something first?"

I heard Miry's stomach rumble. Even though I wanted to seize my newfound focus, I sighed and led her to the kitchen. After rummaging, I shoved a couple of protein bars into her outstretched hands. "You can eat on the move. Let's go."

"So," Miry said as we made the short trip to Damien's place. She laced her fingers through mine. "Are we like a couple now?"

"I don't know, Miry. Maybe?" Putting labels

on whatever this was seemed trivial compared to the fate of the world and our families. "Are you ready for that? Having a girlfriend?"

I heard her crunch one of the protein bars and chew loudly. Probably for effect. "I don't know. I like kissing you and I feel like I know who I am when I'm with you. But I haven't actually said the words before."

"That you like girls?" I prompted.

"Mmhmm," she answered.

I stopped walking and turned to face her; our hands still intertwined. "I'll make you a deal. When you can tell someone you know, someone you really care about that truth, I will be your girlfriend."

She worried her lower lip for a second and then smiled. "Okay."

"You two going to stand out there gawking at each other all morning?" D called from the back door.

"How'd he know we were coming?" Miry whispered as I led her inside.

"I tracked your phone," Azrael answered matter-of-factly from the kitchen table.

In all the years I'd known him, I'd never seen him sitting there drinking a cup of coffee out of a 'Hell's Baddest Dad' mug. It felt *wrong*. I should have been offended that he was keeping tabs on me, but I know my dad would have done the same thing with Damien if our roles were reversed.

"Is that legal?" Miry hiccupped.

"I don't care if it is, it's not important right now," I reminded her.

"Oh, right. Limbo."

"I warned you that Limbo can be dangerous," Azrael said from over his coffee mug.

"We need to get there. Dad is being held as a prisoner by Michael. And trying to get to Limbo from Heaven is a suicide mission."

"You're not going to get there from here, either," he replied.

"Whatever safeguards are in place, I can handle it," I argued.

"The entrance from here is located in your father's office. The one that his second-in-command is currently occupying."

"The same asshole who is in on the whole fucking plan," I spat.

"Maybe we can just sneak in when he's not there," Miry suggested. From the weakness of her tone even she doubted that was a viable option.

"He isn't leaving the office unguarded. He

hasn't since your father went missing," Azrael answered.

"What about a diversion? We could tell him that Michael's forces were advancing on Hell," Damien offered.

"He'd know that wasn't true. They're working together, remember?" Frustration began to bubble beneath the surface.

"Damien has a point, though," Miry said, her voice stronger now. "We all know my dad doesn't care about breaking the rules whenever it suits him. And we also know he doesn't think Fallen are the same as Archangels so he probably won't even think twice about stabbing Samael in the back."

I still didn't like the idea of using my friends as a diversion. Even if it worked and we got to Limbo, that still left Damien to fend off a very powerful Fallen angel.

"He will not go alone," Azrael announced, setting his mug down and standing. "I will make it believable." As if by magic, his scythe and cloak appeared and it sent shivers down my spine.

I HELD Miry close to me under the protection of Damien's reaper cloak. It was just as soft and flowing as the last time I'd worn it. Still I worried that it wouldn't provide the same protection. Not with two of us, no matter how close we moved together. We watched from our spot just beyond the door to Dad's office as Damien and Azrael approached, drawing Samael from the room.

"You can't be serious. He'd never do such a thing," Samael retorted.

"I've been reaping souls all week, and they all say the same thing. They've seen the Archangel readying for battle. He's bringing it here to us. To finish what he started eons ago."

"He thinks I'm weak, does he?" Samael ground out, his hands balling into fists.

"We should prepare to defend ourselves," Azrael said, clapping a hand on Samael's shoulder and forcibly leading him away from the room.

It was our cue.

Making a mad dash for it, I let the cloak flutter away from me, letting it drape over Miry alone. I had plausible deniability for being here if anyone caught me. The daughter of the enemy, not so much.

"What's the entrance supposed to look like?" Miry hissed from beneath the cloak.

"I don't know," I answered.

I could hear low murmurs coming from be-yond the wall directly behind the large oak desk. I'd always assumed it was a solid piece, but as I ran my fingers across it, I found a slight indent in the wooden panel. It clicked and slid inward, re-vealing a room with two very well-armed Fallen standing guard at what I assumed to be the en-trance to Limbo.

"You aren't supposed to be here," one of them said, his hand resting on the hilt of his sword. He clearly knew who I was and hesitated to raise his weapon to me.

"I'm pretty sure my dad isn't cool with random dudes hiding in his office," I answered and stepped closer.

"Lucifer's gone," the other guard replied. He'd drawn his blade.

"Not for long," I replied and reached out to take the first guard's sword out of its scabbard.

I spun, kicking him in the solar plexus, sending him crumpled to the floor. The second guard lunged and I parried. Out of the corner of my eye I caught Miry's hands pop out from be-neath the cloak to wave at the entrance.

"Little busy," I grunted and barely avoided a sword to the upper arm.

Before I could do more than lock blades with the guard, I heard shouts from the office beyond and the sound of hammering footsteps. My gut told me they weren't coming to help us. I gave the guard a kick to the groin and grabbed Miry's outstretched hand, hauling ass out of the room and back into the office proper.

I lobbed the sword at the nearest window, glass shattering on impact. "Move your ass," I told her, and gave her a shove in the right direction for good measure.

I could tell she wanted to argue, but Miry dutifully climbed out the window, stretching a hand back inside to pull me up. My boots slid through the window frame just as Samael reappeared, looking livid.

The path to Limbo from here was shot. That meant if we had any chance of making it to my dad, we had to brave the gates of Heaven. Even if it meant I didn't survive the journey.

13

MIRYAN

"**Y**ou're lucky I'm used to running from angry Archangels. That Samael guy's got nothing on Dad or Uncle Uriel when it comes to needing to duck and cover." I ducked behind a literal dumpster fire—this *was* Hell after all—and waited for my heartbeat to slow to normal. "Do you think he's gonna follow us?"

Zuri peeked out from behind the dumpster. "I don't think so. It will call more attention than he wants to deal with. Samael can't pretend to rule Hell if anyone sees me—the actual rightful ruler in Dad's absence."

"We'll get him back," I promised her. "Just one little trip to Heaven, a stop off in Limbo, and you're totally reunited. Promise."

Zuri ducked back behind the dumpster and slid down the side of the brick building next to our hiding spot until her butt hit the cobblestones. "What's the point? We've failed before we even started. I can't take 'one little trip to Heaven.' Not if I want to stay alive."

I crouched down in front of her and held out my hand. "I know a little work around that whole Fallen burning up thing. But you gotta step through the gates first to see if it works."

Z shot me her 'are you high' glare. "That sounds like something your dad would say. How do I know you're not spying for him? Pretty convenient that you ignore me for over a month and then suddenly show up with intel on where my dad is."

"I'm not a spy."

"How do I know that?"

"Cause I'm not." I grabbed her face and pulled her in for a kiss. "Would a spy do that?"

"Maybe." Zuri frowned, mouth and brow both turning down in confusion. Sure, I wasn't usually the one to make a move, but that didn't mean I *never* did ... or would.

I kissed her again, pressing my lips hard against hers. "How about now?"

"I might need more convincing."

"You're incorrigible." I popped to my feet, then turned to determine the way out of here and back to the mortal plane. "And, yes, I know what incorrigible means. What's the easiest way back to the surface world that would get us as close to campus as possible?"

"Why?" Zuri climbed to her feet, her right arm tangling up in my left until her fingers found mine, lacing tight. "Neither of us can enter campus."

"That doesn't stop people from coming out. Heh. I made a joke and didn't even mean to. I meant coming off campus, not coming out-out." I dug my phone out of my bra where I put it for safekeeping before checking the screen. "I have, like, zero reception here. Ugh, I need sunlight and a decent cell tower."

"Come on." Zuri started walking, pulling me along behind her. "I know a shortcut." She led me through a maze of side streets and back alleys before stopping in front of a legit river of lava. Like the kind you'd expect to see at the entrance to Hell.

"Um, what do we do now?" I asked.

Zuri let go of my hand and motioned at the lava. "We jump in."

"Eeeek!" I scurried back from the edge in case

she decided to test her 'Miry's really a spy' theory and throw me in. "We do what?"

"We jump in," she repeated. "The lava is for show. It's an illusion. Come on. We'll do it together." She swiveled the top half of her body, holding out her hand to me.

I took a step back in protest. "How do I know you're not just going to throw me in?"

Zuri sighed, hand still waiting for mine. "You're going to have to trust me."

"If I do, will you trust me with the whole survive Heaven thing?"

"We can figure that one out when we get there," she said.

I shook my head. "No. No, that's not good enough. You either trust me or you don't,

Z. There's no 'maybe.'"

I crossed my arms over my chest and waited. Zuri looked down at her own outstretched hand as if it belonged to someone else. She curled her fingers into a fist, deciding. I held my breath and waited. No matter what label we put on this thing between us—friendship? relationship?—trust was still important to me. Except I needed it to be important to Z too. "I'm waiting."

Zuri sighed again and uncurled her fingers. "I trust you, Miry."

I put my hand in hers. "I trust you too, Zuri." I stepped up beside her, looking down into the boiling lava. "On three?"

She nodded. "On three. One ... two ... three!"

I closed my eyes, held my breath, and jumped.

***

"Ugh. Next time you say 'let's jump into a raging river of fake lava,' remind me that the trip to the Earthly plane is way worse than regular portals." I sat down before I could fall down. "Does my hair look bad? It doesn't have, like, puke in it or anything, does it?"

"You look fine," Zuri said, distracted.

"You didn't even look!" I whined.

Z made a big show out of inspecting my hair. "It's fine. Now do whatever you need to do to get us to Limbo so I can rescue my dad."

I pulled my phone out of my bra again, punched some buttons, and shot Uncle Raphael a quick text. *Need help. Don't tell Dad.*

His answer came almost immediately. *Where are you?*

I looked around. I wasn't even sure where we were. Telling him 'by the bush that smells like puke' wouldn't cut it. I needed something more useful. "Ummm … Hey, Z, where are we?"

"By the post office near campus. Why?"

I typed that into the text chain and hit send. "You'll see. Help is on the way!"

It didn't take long to hear the beat of angel wings. Zuri looked up, shading her eyes to scan the sky. "Miry, what have you done?"

"Nothing," I protested. "I just called—"

"How much trouble are you two in this time?" Uncle Raphael asked as soon as his feet hit the sidewalk in front of us. "Talk quickly. I am not sure how long I can be gone before Michael grows suspicious."

"We think my dad kidnapped her dad and is holding him captive in Limbo," I blabbed, the words running together. No one is better than me at talking fast. "We tried to get in from a portal in her dad's office, but got cut off. That leaves—"

"Heaven," Uncle Raphael said, voice soft. "Oh, Miryam, do you even know what you're asking?" He shook his head. "That is not a trip you or anyone else for that matter should take lightly. Especially Zuri."

"I know the danger and I'm willing to risk it."

Zuri stood and pulled me to my feet. "Can you help us or not?"

"Can I, yes," Uncle Raphael said. "But what you should ask is will I."

"Come on, Uncle Raphael, that's totally unfair!" I grumbled. "If there was any other way, we'd have already found it. This is it. Will you help me or not?"

He opened his mouth to say what I'm pretty sure was "not" when Zuri interrupted. "My dad is in danger. Please. If you don't want to help us, do it to help him. He was your friend once, wasn't he? Before the war?"

Uncle Raphael got that haunted look that cropped up whenever anyone brought up the War in Heaven. "He is still my friend."

"Then help us," Zuri pleaded. "We can't do this, not without you."

Uncle Raphael sighed and motioned for us to follow him behind the post office and away from any potential eavesdroppers. "Do not repeat anything I am about to say, understood?"

"Understood," we chorused. I crossed my heart for good measure.

He sighed again before raising his arm. He made a couple of quick swipes in the air that I recognized as Enochian runes before a glowing portal opened in mid-air. "Go before I change my mind."

I climbed in first before reaching a hand back to Zuri. She didn't look all that enthused to take my hand, but she did anyway. This was the only way to save her dad. "And try to find out what Dad is doing in some place called 'the chapel!'" I called to Uncle Raphael as he closed the portal behind us.

It felt like I only blinked and suddenly we were standing in the misty cloud-like area right outside the Gates to Heaven. They were as pearly and shimmery as you would expect from something called 'the Gates to Heaven.' I turned to Zuri. "Are you scared?"

She shook her head, swallowing hard. "I don't scare easily." I grabbed her hand and pulled her toward the gates. "It's okay. What they told you about the whole Fallen burning and dying thing is true, but I know a work around it." The gates opened on their own when I got close enough. I stepped through them without even thinking about it. Zuri on the other hand was still an arm's length away on the non-burning and dying side. "Dad gave me a tour once right after I got my Celestial Academy acceptance letter," I explained. "He said everyone sees something a little bit different. It's your own personal Heaven. Mine is different from yours, his, or anyone else that steps through the gates. The people that are most important to us will always be waiting too. Since their heaven isn't complete until we are here." I tilted my head to the side, watching Z. "Come on and try it. You won't die."

"How do you know?" Zuri asked, voice hoarse.

"Because I already know my version of Heaven includes you," I said. "And there's someone else who has been waiting for you to make her Heaven complete too." I stepped aside to let Zuri get a view of the person walking toward us through the mist. She had long black hair, dusky skin, and wore an ankle length bright red dress.

She stopped on the Heaven side of the gates and smiled. "Hello, sweetheart."

Zuri's eyes widened in disbelief. "Mom?"

14

ZURI

I stared at the woman who had only ever been a dream or whose face had been worn by a demon. The last few months told my brain not to trust what I was seeing. However, the fact I was literally standing in Heaven without burning to death proved there was some merit to what Miry said about those being in our personal heaven being here.

"Is it really you?" The words sounded lame as they left my mouth.

"It is. I am so proud of the woman you have become," she said and reached out her hand to me.

I rushed her, wrapping my arms around her, and buried my face in her chest like a child. I'd never really known what it meant to have a mother's love. Dad gave me all of his heart and then some to make up for it, but there was no way he could replace the feeling of being held in her arms.

"I wish I'd gotten to know you," I whispered.

"One day, a long time from now, you will. Because where I'm going, you will be, too and we will have all the time in the world."

"That's a nice thought, but I won't be here. I'm Fallen, remember?"

She laughed and tilted my head back so our eyes met. "Sweet girl, that is only a label and labels have no meaning here. And as your friend pointed out, you are here now, because you are part of her heavenly peace."

I let that sink in. The woman who had literally slept with what many people called the Devil had made it to Heaven. Maybe that meant I could get there, too. *Would Dad be here in mine?*

"What about my dad? He's important to me. Would he be able to be here, too? Could my family be together again?" I addressed the question to Miry who had been standing off to one side by the gates.

"I don't know. If my dad had any say then no

he wouldn't. But God created Heaven, not an archangel, so there's hope."

I turned back to my mother and drank in her features, committing every little detail to memory. I could see so much of myself in the shape of her nose and the cut of her cheekbones. There was so much she'd given me that I didn't even realize. "Do you know how we can stop Michael?" It was a long shot, but I had to ask.

"I'm not God, sweetheart. I'm not all knowing or all present. But I do have faith in you, sweet girl."

I'd take the ego boost, but it didn't give us a practical solution to a very dangerous problem.

"Please, whatever you choose to do, be safe," Mom said, wrapping her arms around me one more time.

"I'll try," I replied. As much as I really wanted to get to know her, I wasn't in a hurry to die.

"We couldn't go up against Uriel with his fucking lariat or Michael with his … The sword," I blurted.

"Huh?" Miry stepped away from the gates to stand beside me. "What sword?"

I spun to face her. "Your Dad's sword. It's powerful and I bet for whatever he's planning he needs it."

"Probably," she agreed, clearly not following my train of thought.

"You can manifest it, Miry. If we have it, then he can't use it."

"I've only done that like once. Maybe twice. And I'm always super freaked out and scared when I'm able to do that."

"Does your father starting another war for no reason terrify you?"

She swallowed and nodded. "Like, a lot."

"Then use that fear to motivate you. You're Miryam bat-Michael. You are strong enough to stand up to him."

She squared her shoulders and looked me in the eye. "I can do this."

I waited for her to do whatever it was she did to make the sword appear, starting to feel hopeful again. She closed her eyes and held out her hands. Her lips puckered together in concentration and I couldn't help but picture kissing them. I never would have imagined the girl for me would be Miryam freaking bat-Michael. She was the total opposite of every girl I'd ever been with. Although maybe that was what drew me to her. Sure, she had a great body. Despite that there was just something about her, that belief in the goodness of others that made me smile.

A clatter made Miry open her eyes and we both turned to see the sword appear on the ground. I hadn't exactly been conscious the last time she'd manifested the damn thing, but I assumed it would have appeared in her hands.

"Is that normal?" I asked.

"Uh, I have no idea."

We approached the sword laying there in its scabbard. It looked like someone had just left it there, but that couldn't be right. Michael wouldn't just keep it here. Not when I'd seen it hanging in his office.

"How sure are you that the sword in his office is real?" I prodded.

"Well, I mean, I've never actually held it in his office. He doesn't, like, take it out and let people mess with it. I guess it could be fake."

"And he assumed no one else would bother looking here for the real thing."

"Guess not." She bent down and scooped it up, securing the scabbard around her waist.

Miry looked like a warrior goddess as the mists of Heaven billowed against her skin. She definitely had the part down. Now we had to hope we could make our way to Limbo and rescue Dad.

"Any idea how we get to Limbo from here?" I let the question hang in the air around us.

It could have been a trick of the light or the fact I wasn't supposed to be able to exist here under normal circumstances, but I could swear I saw a portal swirling in the distance. Its opalescence stood out against the calm mistiness of the rest of Heaven.

"Well, that's interesting."

The farther I stepped from the gates, the more the pit of my stomach lurched. I may be part of Miry's heaven, but this place still wasn't thrilled about me being in it. The sooner we left, the better. Miry came up shoulder to shoulder with me and grabbed my hand.

"I know I've been weird lately with, you know, us. And I know you thought I was just pretending or playing a part. I guess, in a way, I was."

"Now is really not the time to do soul searching, Miry. When we've stopped your Dad from starting another war, we'll have plenty of time to figure out what we are," I replied.

"It's just, I don't know if I'm bi. Like, it's hard to explain. I think I like a person for who they are, not if they have boobs or balls."

I turned to Miry and took her other hand in mine. "It's great that you're coming to terms with who you are and how you love, but can we please just focus on the mission?"

"Right, sorry. I just needed to get that off my chest."

I didn't have time to respond, because the portal swirled, sucking us in.

BETWEEN ONE BREATH and the next, we left Heaven and landed in Limbo. I don't know what I expected to see when we got there, but it wasn't just the drab greyness of an ever-expanding void. It didn't seem logical or physically possible that we could be standing there and not plummet into the abyss. Instead, I released Miry's hands and bent down, pressing my fingers to the blandness around us and found it solid.

"Okay, this place creeps me out way more than Hell," Miry said. Her voice echoed strangely around us.

"Miry?" A voice called from nowhere and everywhere all at once.

I knew that voice. I held fast to Miry's hand as a figure emerged out of the greyness.

Saint Boy looked … normal. No demonic pallor. No rabid frothing at the mouth. He looked just like a teenage boy you'd see anywhere on the street and not think twice about. The fact he was here made me nervous though.

"Chris? What are you doing here?" Miry's hand slid out of mine, like she was afraid of him seeing.

"Guess when you're part demon and part saint, reality isn't sure what to do with you after you die," he answered.

"You can't go to Hell," she said before her cheeks flushed a bright pink. "Not that Hell is a bad place to be just um … "

"I don't really want you in my space," I interjected.

"Believe me, I don't want to end up there either." He turned to look at me. "You met me when I was at my worst. And you judged me based on what you saw. I can't blame or fault you for that."

"You can't blame it all on mommy either."

"I know." he averted his gaze. "But she's powerful and her blood runs in my veins, it was overwhelming. Everything I say to you is going to be an excuse and you both deserve better than that."

"Where's my dad?" I was done wasting time.

"He was here," he began.

I closed the distance, hauling him off his feet. "What do you mean was?"

"Some guards showed up from a portal from Hell and grabbed him."

"Maybe Samael just moved him back to Hell, because he figures you already looked there?" Miry offered.

Saint Boy shook his head. "I saw the portal they opened; it wasn't back to Hell. They took him to Celestial Academy. I saw Michael and a bunch of students in armor, with weapons."

"You better not be bullshitting me," I snapped.

"I swear, I'm telling you the truth. Your dad's been here with me since I died. We've had some good talks about my life choices and how I ended up here. And we talked about you. A lot actually."

I lowered him to his feet. "Why would you talk about me?"

"Because, even though I did all this terrible shit, I still care about Miry. A part of me loved her once and I want her to be happy. I needed to know that she would be happy."

"With me?" I filled in the blank.

"Yeah." He smirked. "I mean, I was making all those terrible comments about you, because I was jealous. I thought that was obvious."

"To anyone with eyes," I answered, not bringing myself to look at Miry.

"So, you'd be okay if Zuri and I were together?" She piped up.

"It was my dying wish that you find happiness, Mir. Whatever that looked like. So yes, if she makes you happy. If she makes you a better person, then I absolutely want you to be together."

I blinked at him, not believing my ears. The douchebag who'd gaslit Miry was actually being sincere. I wasn't sure how to handle that information. I filed it under the "deal with it later" category. "That's all nice and everything, but it doesn't help us get to my dad. If they've taken him to campus, whatever they're planning is going down soon. We aren't allowed on campus anymore."

"I can get you past the wards. They're tuned to let people from Limbo in. Please, let me help you get there and save him. Let me do something good for once."

I took Miry's hand in mine and squeezed it tight. "Do it. Please."

He began to whisper the prayer of Saint Christopher and another portal rippled into existence in front of us. I could hear vague voices from within it. Not knowing what we were about to face, I stepped up to it, turned to face him and said "Uh … Thank you, Chris."

Miry dropped my hand and took a step toward him. I didn't want to leave her alone with him, no matter how much he appeared to be helping us. Still she deserved closure. "If you aren't out of this portal in five minutes, I will force my way back in here," I called before falling into oblivion.

15

MIRYAM

I gazed into the swirling vortex that Zuri had just stepped through. "You didn't, like, send her somewhere weird like the boys' bathroom, did you, Chris?"

Chris laughed. "Hey, safe passage is safe passage. I can't guarantee where you end up, just that you'll be safe."

I looked over at him, not sure how to say goodbye. I mean, what do you even say when you're given an unexpected do over like this? "I could stay if you want," I offered. "I mean, if you're lonely or whatever. I could stay."

"I want you to live your life, Miry, and stop worrying about what I want." He glanced behind him, in the direction of the portal to Heaven. "I'm going to be okay. And so will you."

"You were my first love," I whispered, blinking back tears.

Chris smiled sadly and stepped up to kiss the middle of my forehead like he used to do when I woke up from one of my scary pool party nightmares. "But I hope I'm not your last love. You'll be fine, Miry. Trust me. Now, go. I can't hold the portal open forever."

"Can I just say goodnight instead of goodbye?" I asked. "I don't want to say goodbye."

Chris nodded and opened his arms. I flew into them, squeezing him as tight as I could. "Good night, Mir. I hope to see you in Heaven, someday long in the future. Don't be in a rush to get there, okay?"

"I'll try." I squeezed him one last time before letting go and stepping to the portal again. "Good night, Chris. And thank you." I blew him a kiss and stepped through the portal back to campus.

I LANDED with a clatter on the floor of ... somewhere. I sat up and pushed my hair away from my face. It was a dorm room, but whose? Zuri stood near the half open door, monitoring the hallway for whatever threat she thought waited for us on campus. She looked way more poised and ready for a fight than I felt. I stood up, my legs a little wobbly from one too many jumps through a portal. "Ugh. Next time anyone suggests portal travel remind me to just say no."

"At least you didn't throw up," Zuri said, not turning to look at me.

"There's still time for that."

"If you blow chunks all over my room, I'm making you clean it up yourself," CeCe said from somewhere behind me. She was so not the person I expected to see right now or whose room I thought Chris' safe passage power would bring us to.

I swiveled toward the sound of her voice, making sure to plaster a bright smile on my face. "Hey, CeCe! Uh, any idea why the portal thought us ending up in your room equaled safe passage back to campus?"

"Because, duh, no one would think to look for you here." She flipped her brown ponytail over her shoulder. "Plus, I totally have Damien on speed dial." She held out her phone with a video chat sized Damien on screen. "Say hey to Miry, D."

"Hey," he said almost on reflex. "Will you tell Zuri we need a better plan than just running off and punching your dad in the face?"

"Element of surprise!" Zuri barked from the doorway. "It works every time."

"Not when you have an army of brainwashed angel kids and who knows how many archangels to deal with," Damien said. "It's less element of surprise and more suicide mission."

"I don't care," Zuri said. "If it means getting Dad back, I will do it."

I crossed the room to stand next to Z. I touched her arm briefly to get her attention before pulling my hand back. "We need a better plan, Z. We got the sword. That's a bonus, right? What else do we have?"

"To fight a potential army of angels to get to my dad?" Zuri asked. "Not much." Her face brightened as some idea struck. "No, wait, scratch that …" She felt around in all her pockets before pulling out a scrap of the emblem. "We have what's left of Dad's relic. That's two out of the four. We're even with what your dad has on hand."

"Assuming Uncle Gabriel and Uncle Uriel are in on Dad's plan," I reminded her.

Zuri looked down at me. "Head case Uriel not up for a war?"

I chewed my bottom lip. "Yeah, you're right. He'd totally be down for any kind of fight." I turned to CeCe. "Have you heard anything about someplace called 'The Chapel?' It's somewhere super-secret on campus. That's where they're holding Lucifer, but I don't know where to start looking."

"You could always ask the doors," CeCe said as simply as most people said 'turn left at the gas station.'

"Um ... Ask the doors?" I wrinkled my face up. "Are you on something?"

CeCe joined us at the doorway before passing off video chat Damien to Zuri. "Everything has a musical vibration, remember? I can tap into it and learn stuff." She held her hand next to the keyhole below the knob, closed her eyes, and hummed. "Sometimes it's more like pictures in my head than actual words," she explained. "And ... Got it. I think I can get us there safely."

"There is no us in this plan," Zuri told her. "You're not coming."

CeCe opened her eyes. "I am if you want to find the chapel."

"Let her help, Z," Damien said. "It might be the only way to save your dad."

Zuri frowned, not looking happy with this new part of our less-than-fully-formed plan. "Fine. But the second we get to the chapel you turn around and come back here, got it? Lock the door and don't come out unless Miry or I tell you to. No heroics. It's already going to be hard enough to rescue my dad. I don't need to rescue you too. Is that clear?"

CeCe nodded. "Crystal."

Zuri held out her hand to me. I took it. It reminded me that we made a good team. We were stronger together than apart. "Okay then. Let's do this."

16

ZURI

Creeping through the school like trespassers brought back memories of sneaking around only a few short months ago looking for the Emblem. Now, what remained of that relic sat tucked in my back pocket with a new mission. D's girlfriend stopped us at another locked door. We'd gone up two flights of stairs I didn't know existed and then through what felt like the bowels of the building before taking us back up again.

"Are we getting closer?" I hissed. The longer we wandered around trying to find the right door, the longer Michael had my father in his clutches. While he'd been locked away in Limbo, at least I knew Michael wasn't torturing him.

"Yes," she answered in a whisper, pressing her ear to the lock. "It's just beyond this door."

"Now, what do we have here?" Uriel's voice came from above us.

I pivoted to find him hovering several feet off the ground, his head nearly even with the rafters. He carried a lethal-looking broadsword in one hand and his lariat looped around his other forearm. It burned bright against his skin, no doubt looking for a target.

Miry moved to block our door whisperer, her hand on her father's relic. "What you're doing is wrong," she said, her tone firm, assured. Uriel may be downright terrifying when he wanted to be, but she was proving just how strong she was.

"You could have had potential, or so I thought and yet, your father was right. Quite the disappointment," he carried on as if she hadn't spoken.

I moved to stand shoulder to shoulder with her, giving our tour guide enough cover to duck and run. I muttered out of the corner of my mouth, "Now is when you haul ass and don't come back out until it's safe."

I heard her gulp and then the sound of her shoes slapping against the stone floor as she took off the way we'd come. I waited for her movement to draw the archangel's attention, but he stayed laser-focused on us. He lowered to the floor and leveled the sword at my chest.

"You should never have come here."

"Dude, I never planned on crashing your little secret war machine. Shit just happened. And maybe if your boss wasn't such a huge douchebag with a hero complex, it wouldn't have mattered."

"You dare speak that way about—"

"I'll talk about your precious fucking Michael however I want if it will get you to shut up and take me to see him. I'm sure we're prime targets."

Uriel threw back his head and laughed. It shook his whole form and Miry turned to look at me in terror. "What did you just do?"

"We can't rescue my dad and stop a war from out here."

"Yeah, but that was when we had the element of surprise. Remember the plan."

"The plan got fucked way back there, Miry. Like you said, we got this."

Uriel made a show of kicking the door down behind us and shoving us through into a sea of glassy-eyed faces. Some were students I vaguely recognized, but quite a few were older than us. They were most likely graduates who Michael had somehow convinced to join his ridiculous cause.

Between milling soldiers, I spotted my father bound to what looked like some sort of font in the center of the room. His gaze lifted until it met mine.

I've never seen my father afraid, but the look in his eyes just then told me he was terrified.

"Where is Michael?" Uriel boomed to no one in particular.

Several of the students shuffled around to make room for us, but didn't answer. In fact, no one replied as we continued to wade through the sea of faces. I couldn't shake how eerily similar it appeared to Lilith's little army of living donors for Chris. How little distinction there was between the way she used these children and Michael's own methods.

"You, bind their hands," Uriel ordered a slender girl with a pixie cut.

"What is going on?" Raphael's voice cut through the white noise of the milling crowd and I couldn't help but feel just a little safer. He hadn't taken a side in this fight, but he was reasonable. He didn't want there to be deaths.

"Where is Michael? He needs to know we have captured the enemy and are prepared to execute his will at his command."

"Brother, no. They are only children."

"He's not going to listen to you, Raphael," Dad said from his position to my left.

"Do not become a traitor like them," Uriel warned, leveling his blade at Raphael's chest.

"Cut me down if you must, but I will not allow harm to come to them." Raphael's wings erupted from his shoulders, knocking students aside as they spread out fully.

I knelt at Dad's side and began to pick the knot keeping his hands bound to the font.

"Zuri, what do you think you are doing?" He demanded in a tone so low I could almost feel it vibrate in his chest.

"Saving you. Hell is in disarray. Samael is trying to take over and he's working with Michael."

"You think I don't know that?"

I looked at him and rolled my eyes. "Then why'd you let yourself get captured by that asshole?"

"My sweet girl. You really think I would just let myself be held captive? He threatened to kill you. I had no choice."

"I can take care of myself, Dad. You made sure of that," I argued.

"Until you are a parent, you will not understand the sort of sacrifices one makes for their own children."

"You didn't go that far for your other kids," I noted.

"You're special Zuri. Your mother … I loved her in a way I have never loved before. You remind me of her every day. With your strength, your resilience, and even your stubbornness."

"I really hate to interrupt this super sweet moment, but um, Dad's here," Miry interjected.

I stood to find Michael pushing students out of his way to stand beside Uriel. He took in Raphael's stance, reached forward and grabbed him by the front of his shirt. "Where is it? Where did you hide it?"

"I don't know what you're talking about," Raphael answered.

Michael, clearly unsatisfied by that response, threw him across the room. The other angel landed hard against the wall. The students milling around barely took notice as he slumped over, his wings bent at awkward angles. I didn't have a weapon like a sword to face Michael, but I was damn well going to try.

"Zuri, what are you doing?" Dad yelped as I stepped toward Michael.

I reached down at Miry's hip and drew the blade from the scabbard. "Hey, douchebag, you looking for this?" I waved the sword around, cutting wide arcs in the air. I didn't sense any real power coming from it, but it wasn't my family's relic.

I half-expected Miry to cower as her father advanced on us, but she stood tall by my side and took the sword from my hand. "I'm not going to let you hurt anyone I care about," she declared. As she took a step forward, she looked around the room. There were a lot more people she knew here than I did. She opened her mouth, a wide smile on her lips and proclaimed, "Also, I like girls. I'm bisexual and Zuri is my girlfriend … and if any of you have a problem with that, you're going to have to get in line."

I blinked. Michael blinked. As battle cries went, it was definitely unconventional. And perfectly Miry. The stunned silence of the room disappeared as Michael let out a howl and rushed forward. He ripped the sword from Miry's hand and pushed her aside, advancing on Dad and I. This close, I could see the bloodlust in his eyes as he swung the sword down at me.

I didn't plan it. I just reacted, ripping the shred of emblem from my pocket and catching the blade between my hands. I could feel the sharp edges cutting through my skin where it wasn't protected by the emblem. I gritted my teeth, doing what I could to ignore the pain. It meant nothing if I couldn't protect my father and Miry. The two people living who meant the most to me. I wasn't ready to see my mother in Heaven or wherever it was I ended up when I died.

My vision began to blur around the edges as the pain disappeared, replaced by aching numbness. I could see the emblem turning red with blood, losing its efficacy the more he pressed the blade. Then, out of nowhere, another pair of hands wrapped around mine, holding me up and feeding power into me, through me to the emblem. The emblem flared to life, knitting itself back together before my eyes. At least that's what I assumed happened before I couldn't stay on my feet any longer. The last thing I recalled was a sonic 'boom' filling the air and a woman with a shock of red hair and fierce blue eyes appeared.

"That is enough!"

17

MIRYAM

The girl with the wild red hair and intense blue eyes looked around and smiled at all the shocked faces crowding the room. I dropped my hand from near Zuri's wrist, swaying a bit on my feet from the exertion of giving her an energy boost against Dad's sword.

"Excellent," the being that appeared out of nowhere said. "Now that I have your attention … When I say stop it, you better listen." She smiled again before her form melted away into a small child, then to an old man, then back to a woman, and kept cycling through all the ages, genders, and ethnicities known to man like a flipbook on autopilot. The only thing that stayed the same through all the rapid change transformations were the eyes since they are the window to the soul.

Dad blinked and shook his head like he was coming out of a trance. "What are you doing still on your feet, you heathens?" He shouted at his child army. "Bow down before your creator." He pushed through the crowd and knelt at the feet of the flipbook faced being. "My maker, forgive me my trespasses. I was only finishing what we started all those millennia ago during the first War in Heaven. Lucifer must pay for his transgressions. I can finally finish what was started." Dad looked around at all of us still on our feet instead of on our knees and barked out another order. "I said kneel, Heathens! Don't you know Yahweh-Asher-Yahweh when you see them?"

Oh oh. I quickly dropped into a kneeling position and drug Zuri down with me.

She looked over, confused. "What's going on?"

I pointed at the figure standing before Dad. They looked at him like he always looked at me before things started flying. This wasn't going to end well. I doubted Dad could talk his way out of this one, no matter how much he tried. "Yahweh. The name of God. That's God."

"Oh, shit," Zuri murmured. "Is that good or bad that God interceded?"

"Bad," I said. "Very, very bad. At least for Dad. Yahweh never takes sides. If they decided to show up, we're in for a show of, quite literally, biblical proportion."

"It has taken me many millennia to finish what you started, great Yahweh, but now the end to our endless war is in sight," Dad was saying to Yahweh when I turned my attention back to him. Uncle Uriel and the kid army had dropped to their knees, heads bowed. Uncle Raphael still lay in an unconscious heap on the floor. "I finally have the traitor Lucifer at my mercy," Dad continued. "I shall rid you of his rebellious spirit, Yahweh, and secure your realm below."

"Rebel Angels have never been the true problem, Michael, greatest of my angelic generals," Yahweh's voice was loud and soft, male, female, and child all at once. "Your pride was. Lucifer and his ilk did not go against my wishes by advocating for humanity. You only viewed it as such. Compassion, Michael. Love. Those are the lessons all must learn. You have fallen short of those cardinal rules, Michael. What say ye in defense of your transgressions?"

Dad's face contorted. "But I don't understand. I was only doing what you willed."

Yahweh shook their head, red curls turning to

black dreadlocks with the motion. "I never will the death and destruction of my creations. You only view my word as such. Compassion. Love. Those are all ye need to know to please me."

"Stay here," I whispered to Zuri. "Help your dad. I'll be right back."

I inched my way along the wall until I made it all the way to Uncle Raphael's limp body. I checked his vitals, just like he had taught me. He was alive, but based on the awkward angles of his wings, some of the major or minor converts were broken. "Hang on, Uncle Raphael," I whispered. "I'll do my best to fix you up."

I took a deep breath, closed my eyes, and focused all my healing energy into my hands. I felt the warmth extending into Uncle Raphael, racing through his battered body to fix what was broken. He groaned, his eyes fluttering, before they opened fully. He stared at me blankly for a minute before retracting his wings and struggling up to a sitting position.

"Miryam, what are you doing?" He murmured. "Don't weaken yourself for my sake."

"Already done, Uncle Raphael." I pointed at Dad who still thought it was a good idea to argue with God. "What are we supposed to do about that?"

Uncle Raphael sighed as if it wasn't the first time he'd seen Dad act like an a-hole toward God. Knowing Dad, this was just like a normal Tuesday for him. "Leave it to me. I want you to return to Lucifer and Zuri. They will protect you."

I patted the empty scabbard where Dad's super special magical sword used to be. "I can protect myself, remember?"

"You have proven yourself quite worthy of the name bat-Michael," Uncle Raphael agreed. "If only your father saw it that way as well."

"Dad only sees what he wants to see," I said. "It's the pride thing Yahweh called him out on. He sees me as a screw up and that's all I'll ever be to him."

Uncle Raphael touched my cheek, smiling sadly. "I know the truth, child. You are worthy."

I grinned. "Thanks. Can you, uh, talk Uncle Uriel down from the ledge too? I'd do it, but he gives me the heebie-jeebies."

Uncle Raphael climbed to his feet. He flexed his arms and legs to make sure they all worked. "Leave Uriel to me. I have had more than enough practice reasoning with him when he is in this state. As for your father …" He shrugged, the first time I had ever seen Uncle Raphael give up on anything or anyone. "I am afraid he is on his own. I cannot help him now. None of us can."

I turned to leave, but changed my mind and twirled to face him. "Hey, Uncle Raphael? I wish you were my dad. And maybe I could have had a different mom too."

He smiled, blue eyes shining with the compassion and love Yahweh said we all were supposed to learn in life. "Oh, sweet angel child. No title would make me prouder of you than I am in this moment. Now, return to Lucifer. I will see to Uriel."

I nodded before inching my way back through the sea of angel kids to get to Zuri and her dad. She'd untied his wrists and feet, but both of them were still hanging around watching the shitshow that was my dad thinking he knew better than God.

"What are you doing?" I hissed once I was back within range. "Get out of here. Go reclaim your kingdom from that Samael guy."

"And leave this?" Zuri gestured at Dad who was still arguing that he was so awesomely awesome and anyone who didn't think so was wrong. "Your dad is getting verbally bitch slapped by God. I'm not going anywhere."

I perked up slightly when I remembered

something that I had forgot to ask Lucifer. "Oh, hey, um, Zuri's Dad? Do I have permission to date your daughter?"

Lucifer grinned. "You picked a strange time to ask, child, but by all means. Nothing would make me happier ... except maybe making it out of here alive."

I bounced on my heels, even though I was still in a crouching position, which probably just made it look like I needed to use the bathroom. "Awesome. Thanks."

"But all my actions were in Your Name, Yahweh!" Dad insisted when I focused back on him. "Thy will be done in all things, I swear it."

"No, Michael, *thy* will be done," Yahweh countered. "You gave little thought to my wishes. If you did, you would not have followed this disastrous plan through to fruition. Kidnapping? Murder? Discrimination against Fallen? When has my will been anything but 'love thy neighbor?' You forget yourself, Michael. You have elevated yourself to my level in your mind and that cannot stand."

Finally, that got Dad to shut up. "What do you, uh, recommend, my Lord?"

Yahweh held out their hand and pulled Dad's sword to them without even touching it. "Removal of your wings. Perhaps then you can learn compassion. As for Samael's role in your plot, he shall be remanded back to Hell for Lucifer to decide punishment. Now, on to the matter of your wings …"

"Removing his wings strips him of his divinity," Lucifer whispered to us. "Michael tried to do the same to me in the War, but Yahweh cast me out instead. Yahweh needed something that Michael viewed as a punishment so he would end the fighting."

"But without my wings—" Dad started to argue.

"Your divinity will be lost to you," Yahweh said. "Yes, I am well aware of that. Perhaps I shall give you one last chance to regain what was lost. Make of it what you will."

"I shall do anything you will to return to your grace, my Lord." Dad knelt and bowed his head. Dad may be a lot of things, but a coward wasn't one of them.

"The punishment for your actions shall be as thus," Yahweh ordered. "The loss of your wings, thus stripping you of your divinity, along with the loss of your memories. If you learn compassion and love during your mortality, what was lost to you shall be restored."

Dad kept his head bowed. "Thy will be done."

Before I realized what was happening, Dad's sword flashed through the air, severing his wings. Dad fell to the floor. On instinct, I rushed to his side.

"Dad!"

He pushed himself up, looking at me with blank eyes that held only confusion and not their usual anger or disappointment. "Do I know you, young lady?"

"I'm your, uh …" I looked over at Yahweh. "Am I supposed to tell him?"

Yahweh smiled the same sort of smile Zuri's mom gave us when we had entered Heaven. The kind of smile that's pure love with no room for hate. "He shall remember you in time, child. With each positive act he performs, a piece of memory will return. Do not rush the process. He has quite a lot of learning to do in his time on the mortal plane." Yahweh waved a hand and Dad's sword returned to its empty scabbard at my waist. "I shall leave the relic to your safekeeping, child. Protect it well."

"You have my word," I breathed, stoked that God gave me a task. "But what about the school? Who is going to run Celestial Academy while Dad's off learning his life lessons?"

"Who should have run it from the start." Yahweh waved a hand again, pulling Uncle Raphael forward by an unseen force. "Raphael, gather Gabriel who is another innocent and revise the school rules as you see fit. You are in charge now."

"Open enrollment," Uncle Raphael said without hesitation. "Saints, Angels, Fallen, Demons. Anyone who wishes to learn, may do so."

Yahweh nodded, that same 'I'm proud of you' smile spreading across their ever-changing features. "And what shall you do with your defenseless brother in arms Michael?"

Uncle Raphael thought a moment before making eye contact with me. "We will send him to Kansas into the keeping of Miryam's mother. Perhaps they could both benefit from a second chance. It's not quite granting your wish for new parents, Miryam, but it's the best I could do on short notice."

I bounced on my heels, resisting the urge to high five him. "I love you, Uncle Raphael. Thank you."

"If you need help at all, brother, you have my pledge to assist in any way I can," Lucifer vowed. He extended his hand to Uncle Raphael and they shook on it. "Now, gather the students and take them all to the infirmary. I will help heal the wounded. There's still some angelic healing ability left in this old body of mine. After that, I'll return to my realm to deal with Samael's betrayal."

"Who are you calling old?" Uncle Raphael teased. "Yahweh created me before you."

Lucifer clapped his archangel buddy on the back as they rounded up the angel kid army, who now just looked confused instead of glassy eyed. Uncle Uriel, on the other hand, looked contrite. He stepped forward and knelt in front of Yahweh.

"My Lord, forgive me for what I have done. My mind …"

"Is ill," Yahweh said. "While that is no excuse, in your heart, I see you are truly and genuinely contrite. That has earned you a second chance as well. You shall return with me to Heaven and receive treatment. When you are well, you shall return to your position at Celestial Academy."

Uncle Uriel nodded. "Thank you, my Lord."

"My will be done." Yahweh raised their hands and disappeared just as suddenly as they had shown up, taking Uncle Uriel with them. That left me, Zuri, and Dad alone in the chapel.

"Fun school year, huh?" I joked.

"At least we survived."

"Barely." I held out my hand to Z. She smiled and took it, lacing her warm fingers through mine. "Wanna know our secret? I knew it since, like, the first quarter." I grinned, happy to finally be able to speak my truth and not worry about who heard it. "We're better together than apart."

Zuri pulled me to her and kissed me. I wrapped my free hand around her neck and kissed her back for all I was worth. I couldn't remember a time when I didn't want to be loved and accepted. I had always pushed down my own wants and needs to make sure everyone around me was happy. But now … Now I could be happy too. I could finally be happy.

Zuri broke away first. She looked down at Dad as if trying to decide if she should kick him in the nuts or help him off the floor. "Looks like we're going on another road trip to Kansas."

I perked up. "We? You're coming with?"

"Of course." She slung one arm around my waist and used the other to pull Dad to his feet. "Better together than apart, remember? But let's leave Glasses at home this time."

I scrunched up my face. "CeCe is totally gonna want to be part of the gang now, you know. Maybe you can convince Damien to enroll, to distract her."

"We'll figure all that out later," Zuri promised. "For now, let's dump your douchebag dad off at your mom's place."

"Dad? I have no children," Dad muttered, confused.

"But you do have a wicked cool red convertible." I held out my hand. "Hey, Dad, gimme your keys, k? You owe me big time."

Dad fished around in his pockets and produced his car keys. "Why do you have a sword? And why do you keep calling me dad?"

"You'll find out." I jangled the keys at Zuri. "I call shotgun."

"Hey, M, how do you think your service project went this year?" Zuri asked as we strode through the campus parking lot with Dad in tow.

"Awesome." I pointed the key fob at Dad's shiny red convertible and pushed the button to unlock the doors "Totally a success." I tossed the keys to her. "Why? How do you think it went?"

"Not exactly perfect, but it's been a good learning experience, right? I'm always willing to learn."

"Me too. Together."

"Together," she agreed.

Zuri climbed into the driver's seat, I hopped into the passenger side, and Dad climbed into the back with some prompting. Zuri hit the button to lower the top, gunned the engine, cranked the radio up, and we were off, the wind in our hair and music blaring. For the first time, I wasn't afraid of going to see Mom in Kansas. I knew we could face anything. Together.

The End

In a world where shifters are marginalized, join a misfit band seeking to break free of Captivity.

Join Sarah's Newsletter for all the latest news! Subscribe here!

Join Molly's Newsletter for all the latest news! Subscribe here!

Sarah Biglow is the USA Today Bestselling author of several urban fantasy series. She is a licensed attorney and spends her days combating discrimination as an Investigator with the Massachusetts Commission Against Discrimination. Sarah is a lover of TV and runs a recap blog with her longtime friend, Jen. She lives in Boston with her husband and son.

Read More From Sarah Biglow

www.sarah-biglow.com

Molly Zenk was born in Minnesota, grew up in Florida, lived briefly in Tennessee before settling in Colorado. She writes many genres including Young Adult, Historical Fiction, and Romance. She is married to a Mathematician/Software Engineer who complains about there not being enough "math" or info about him in her author bio. They live in Arvada, CO with their daughters.

Read More From Molly Zenk

https://mollyzenkwrites.wordpress.com/